THE EMPTY NET:

A Philip Sarkis Mystery

PETER R. KOWEY MD

Pavilion Press, Inc.

Philadelphia • New York

The Empty Net: A Philip Sarkis Mystery
by Peter R. Kowey MD

ISBN:

Paperback 9 781414507439
Hard Cover 9 781414507446
Ebook 9 781414507453

Library of Congress
Cataloging-in-Publication Data
1. Fiction 2. Mystery

Pavilion Press, Inc., Philadelphia, PA
www.pavilionpress.com

Dedication

To our children, Olivia, Jaime and Susan, and our sons-in-law, Mark and Sean. Ours is very much a "modern family," but Dorothy and I couldn't love and respect all of you more. Each of you has made a difference in your world, and I think that is all any parent can hope for. Not only are you our kids, but our best friends as well. And our special thanks for the six wonderful souls you have produced and upon whom we dote relentlessly.

Disclaimer

The Empty Net: A Philip Sarkis Mystery was inspired by a case that occurred in Boston many years ago. I have used the names of Boston hospitals and sports teams to enrich the narrative, but those institutions and organizations were not involved in the real story. All of the characters in this novel are fictional. Any resemblance to real people, alive or dead, is entirely coincidental.

Acknowledgments

I thank James Kaufmann, PhD, my best friend from high school, for his terrific help whipping this book into shape. Kauf is now a medical editor in Minnesota and worked tirelessly with me to edit the book and improve the story's consistency. Without him, this book would not have turned out as well as it has.

Over the past few years, I have assembled an incredible team that has worked assiduously to make my novels successful. I am deeply indebted to Steve Crane, my publisher who gave me my first break and has been in my corner the whole way; Samantha Lacey, my talented cover designer; Allison Guarino, a wonderful webmaster; and David Ratner and Jennifer Musico, my hard-working publicists. To Donna Simonds, Roe Wells, and Pattie Basile, my office staff of 24 years, my heartfelt thanks for always being there to keep my mood positive, my schedule straight and my direction forward. And special thanks to Ann Marie Chikowski and Marion Fox for helping me find better ways to say things.

Finally, Dorothy, my wife and my best friend. She has understood my need to exercise my right brain from time to time, and consistently encouraged me to pursue my dream of telling stories.

THE EMPTY NET

Chapter 1

Boston is home to many extraordinarily wealthy people, but if you asked Thaddeus T. Robinson, Esquire, tonight it was he who owned the town. As he sauntered across the bridge over the Charles that would take him from Cambridge to his home in Back Bay, Thad mentally reviewed his recent accomplishments with his usual ample measure of self-adulation.

His recent stretch of good fortune had begun a few years ago when, without warning, and really with little cause, he announced to his wife Effie that he had decided to divorce. It happened one winter evening while they dined in their penthouse apartment in Beacon Hill. They sat at either end of an absurdly long, ornate table while an elderly maid served them. As usual, they were nicely dressed and coiffed for their private dinners, observing the best of manners. Thad delivered his announcement in a flat tone, opening with a "my dear" and closing with "my love."

Effie was not surprised. She had seen it coming. They didn't love each other, that much was clear. If she were going to dissuade Thad from divorcing her, she would have to resort to practical arguments. First, they had been married for over thirty years, and their lives and families were hopelessly intertwined. Thaddeus, with a flick of his hand, dismissed that argument by pointing out that all four of their parents were dead, their siblings were estranged for a myriad of reasons, and their two children were launched and no longer needed their parents to be married. The truth was that their adult children had stopped maturing emotionally at approximately age thirteen. Each still leaned on Dad for money or as much psychological support as he was willing to dole out to them. Thad was right: his sniveling adult children were so wrapped up in their own little worlds that he doubted they would care that their parents were no longer married.

Effie next brought forward the financial arguments. As his wife, she should be entitled to a large chunk of his assets, including his large and thriving law practice. Since Thad was the sole proprietor, all of it was his - or theirs, as she saw it. Thad had hired many young and talented attorneys over the years. Boston was awash in law schools that produced hundreds of fresh-faced, brilliant kids who would do just about anything to stay in town. They gladly signed on as associates with no promise and no hope of partnership. Eventually the smartest would leave, but the supply was endless. Besides, Thad didn't need or want senior attorneys in the way. He had enough experience to move cases along just fine. The closed firm was a money cow. With a large number of high-profile cases coming in every year, Thad had a hard time keeping track of revenues.

"Effie, my dear," Thaddeus offered in his most condescending tone, "Perhaps you don't remember the papers you signed just before we were married?"

Choking on her wine, Effie stammered, "What papers

are you referring to?"

It was Thad's secret weapon, his get-out-of-jail-free card. It was time to play it.

About a year before, when he began to tire of Effie's wrinkled face and lackluster performance in bed, Thad consulted with Maria Hernandez, a criminal from Colombia whose stock in trade was forgery. Thad was referred to her by Sheldon Satterwein, one of his scummy friends at their men's club. Sheldon had used Maria's services to protect his girlfriend from deportation and the documents she produced had done the job. According to Sheldon, Maria, who operated out of her luxury condo in Manhattan, could forge any document for a price. When Thad asked about the possibility of her producing a bogus prenuptial agreement, Sheldon scoffed. "That's nothin' for this broad. She's four-star great. And wait till you get a load of her. I just about guarantee a hard-on."

Sheldon had been right about Maria's appearance. When she walked into the bar at the Pierre in New York, where they had decided to have their first luncheon meeting, every head in the place turned. And it wasn't about flashy. Maria was just natural good looks from top to bottom, her dark features accented by a white business suit that showed off her curves. Thad knew he would have to fight hard to keep from being distracted by her beauty. Business first, he reminded himself.

They were shown to a small table by the window. A waitress offered drinks, they ordered iced tea, and settled in, appraising each other. Maria was pleasantly surprised. Thad was more handsome than she had imagined from their phone conversation. Maybe she assumed that any friend of Sheldon was going to be repulsive. Thad still had a thick head of hair, good skin, and a decent body. He wouldn't be hard to look at while they did their negotiating.

They started with small talk, but each quickly ran out of material and neither saw the point. Maria got the business meeting on track.

"From what you told me on the phone, you need some help with a divorce?"

"No, not yet. But my wife and I are growing apart, and I fear the time will soon come when I want out of the marriage."

"And you are worried that if and when you do, your wife will be entitled to a large share of your assets."

"Ms. Hernandez... may I call you Maria?"

"Certainly, Thad," Maria replied.

"Maria, I have spent a large part of my life building a successful law practice that I own. My wife did nothing except stay at home and hang out and play tennis with her girlfriends. She also did a crappy job of raising our two children, who remain dependent on me, so she shouldn't be entitled to a windfall if we were to part ways."

"And back when you were married, prenuptial agreements weren't in vogue."

"Nor would I have even thought about it. I was madly in love with her, and we didn't have much. It wouldn't have made sense."

"But now it does."

"Yes, Maria, now it does, for many good reasons."

"So you want me to create a legal document that was supposedly prepared and signed by your wife thirty years ago."

"Precisely. And that document has to outline how assets will be apportioned should our relationship ever come to an end. Decidedly in my favor, of course."

Maria pondered a moment. "Well, I must tell you that

I've drawn up phony prenuptials before, but I've never had a request quite like this. I'm going to need specifics from you to include in the agreement, and also several samples of your wife's signature. But the trickiest part is going to be aging the document."

"I don't have to point out to you how much scrutiny this document will get if I ever choose to use it. Every aspect of it."

"No, Thad, you don't. My services are expensive because I take care to produce documents that will survive the closest examination. Your wife will immediately deny that she signed anything, so this agreement will be deemed a forgery until proven otherwise."

"So how much is this likely to cost me?" Thad asked.

"I don't know yet, Thad. It'll depend on how hard it is to get the right materials."

"Can you ballpark it for me?"

"I love Americanisms; they are so simple but helpful," Maria said without a smile. "I would say we are in the million-dollar range here, give or take a few hundred thousand."

Thad tried hard not to react. This was substantially more than he had assumed. Maria sensed his discomfort.

"More than you expected, isn't it, Thad? I'm terribly sorry, but as you said, this is far from an ordinary forgery. It will require an immense amount of preparation. Material acquisition will be very difficult. Creating the document will be the least of it."

"I understand," Thad said.

"Ordinarily, I would encourage a client to comparison shop, but I'm sure you understand that I have very little competition at this level. And if you find a bargain, you might end up regretting it later."

The remainder of the meeting was spent discussing

details of their arrangement, Maria explaining next steps, Thad trying to figure the best way to keep their arrangement secret. As they finished their salads and waited for the check, Thad finally couldn't resist temptation. "I'm staying in this hotel and have a great suite on the top floor. Would you like to come up and see it?"

Maria looked down and smiled. When she lifted her head, the smile was gone and she stared coldly into Thad's eyes. "Listen carefully, Thad. I am not a whore. I don't sleep with men I don't care about, and my business is dangerous enough without complicating it with sexual nonsense. Make a suggestion like that again and our arrangement will be over as fast as you can blink. Are we clear on that?"

Thad could only nod. Maria smiled, picked up her purse, said goodbye, and walked off. But true to her promise, Maria called Thad the following week, to say that her research indicated the project was feasible. She could start work on it, but would require $250,000 installments as she met certain agreed-upon milestones. The forged prenuptial agreement was completed six months later, delivered personally by Maria to Thad at his office. It now resided in his private safe deposit box at the Bank of Boston.

Thad had rehearsed his answer to Effie's inevitable question a hundred times and after months of preparation with Maria, he was more than ready with the answer. "You know, dear, the prenuptial agreement you signed just before we were married."

The rest of the conversation was predictable. Effie insisting forcefully that no such document existed, Thad calmly pointing out that it did and that he would produce it at the correct moment. And he did, just a few days after his filing for divorce had been answered by Effie's attorney, an ineffectual dolt who assumed that taking Thad to the cleaners would be a simple task. He also told Effie it would be easy to expose Thad's document as a forgery, and his obvious duplicity would place Thad in an even worse position with the court. He'd be lucky to escape criminal prosecution.

But in the end, Thad had triumphed. Maria's document, so carefully and ingeniously prepared, had been accepted as authentic despite intense scrutiny by Effie's team, including carbon dating of the paper and ink and handwriting analysis of the signature. Effie and her attorney had been humiliated in court, the judge chastising both of them for making a mockery of the proceedings by trying to deny the validity of the document that Effie had obviously signed. In the end, Effie was granted a small stipend to keep her out of homeless shelters, but not much more. She was also saddled with legal bills that would sap whatever meager assets she could claim as her own.

A newly minted bachelor, Thad was now free to live the high life. As with most of his endeavors, Thad went about creating his new persona with great care and foresight. First, he needed new digs. The penthouse apartment he and Effie had shared for the past several years, after they had downsized from their Newton home, was sold, and according to the terms of Maria's prenuptial masterpiece, Thad got the lion's share of the proceeds. He decided to move from stodgy Beacon Hill to a fashionable Back Bay condo with a spectacular view of Storrow Drive and the Charles River. He contracted with an interior decorator, giving her precise instructions about his taste in furnishings. She produced a spacious bachelor pad that was appropriately understated, but ideal for Thad's new lifestyle and nefarious conquests.

Next came the car. Thad didn't drive to his office,

which was just a fcw blocks from his apartment, and he used the condominium shopping service for groceries and miscellaneous needs. But he liked to foray into the country on the weekends for the sheer fun of it, and what better machine to take him there than a Ferrari. The red convertible was housed in a garage next door to his apartment building, secured for an amount that would pay most mortgages. But Thad didn't care - it was his time to live the life he allowed himself to dream about when he decided that Effie had to go.

Thad was approaching sixty and beginning to look like an old man. He tried to exercise regularly and managed to avoid the man-boobs and spare tires that commonly afflicted men of his age. But he hated the wrinkles that were cropping up almost daily and the drooping eyelids of the man who looked back at him in the mirror every morning. So his next move was a consultation with a plastic surgeon at Mass General. He was careful to pick one he had not sued, of course, and someone who could be discreet. A facelift and blepharoplasty procedure was scheduled in just a matter of days and went smoothly. Thad took a week off so he could be mostly healed before going back to work. It didn't matter. The change in his looks was obvious, especially since the surgical enhancements were complemented by a new hairstyle conceived and delivered by a leading salon. As he intended, the alterations took about ten years off Thad's appearance, and about thirty off his psyche.

To complete his transformation, Thad went on a little shopping spree at Louis, arguably the premier clothier in Boston. Thad gave away his frumpy, conservative suits in favor of some striking designer outfits with all the accessories. Breast pockets were adorned with handkerchiefs, matched to $1000 ties and shirts, and finished off with the best footwear Gucci had to offer.

With such accoutrements, Thad frequented the high-profile bars in Boston and New York, where he met some very desirable women. Most were unattached and, like Thad, looking for adventure. Others were spoken for in some way, but out for an evening of fun on a business trip or while their spouses were otherwise occupied. All of them knew how to look good and play the game. As long as he wasn't too picky, Thad knew he could score almost any night he wished. It usually didn't take long until he was unlocking the door to his apartment or to a suite at a swanky New York hotel, and ushering in his latest conquest for a nightcap followed closely thereon by what he'd call "a little roll in the hay."

Tonight's agenda was a bit different. Thad had gone out strictly to celebrate victory in a well-publicized personal injury case.

A young obstetrician at Brigham and Women's needed to use forceps during a difficult delivery. The child and mother survived, but the baby suffered a spinal cord injury. The boy would never walk or control his bowel and bladder.

The defense argued that the physician had no choice but to use forceps and that the injury was unavoidable. They brought in experts who scoffed at the allegations of malpractice. Forceps deliveries had a known complication rate and the child's parents had been apprised of the risks. But they didn't want a cesarean section unless it was absolutely necessary.

Most plaintiffs' attorneys wouldn't have taken the case, but Thad considered cases alleging obstetrical malpractice to be his forte. His essential strategy was to avoid the facts as much as possible, and play on the emotions of the jury. He knew his opening by heart.

"Consider, ladies and gentlemen, that this helpless infant will not only spend his life in a wheelchair, but he'll be unable to use a toilet and will wear diapers until the day he dies. Where will his parents find the resources to care for him for the rest of his days? This is your chance to help this unfortunate family."

The bonus in this case was the defendant doctor. Her perfect blend of anger, disdain, and condescension would make the jury hate her immediately. When Thad got her on the stand during cross-examination, he was the master, working her up to the point that the defense attorney had to ask for a recess to compose his client, who was practically seething with rage. By then, the damage was done, with poison dart stares issuing from nearly every person in the jury box.

Seeing the jury's reaction, the judge, a fair and likeable person, encouraged the defense attorney to settle. Thad proposed $3 million, the limits of the physician's insurance coverage. The defense attorney brought the offer to the doctor, who flatly refused, insisting that she had done nothing wrong and deserved a defense verdict that would vindicate her. What she received was a $10 million dollar verdict against her, delivered by an angry group of people who wanted to send a message. The judge agreed to consider an immediate defense motion to adjust the verdict amount. If that didn't happen, the doctor's malpractice coverage would be greatly exceeded and the doctor ruined. The judge promised to consider it, but to Thad it didn't matter. He had thumped the defense and would be paid handsomely in any event. That was all that mattered.

When the verdict was announced, Thad hugged the parents, making sure everyone in the courtroom could see how much he loved his clients. Good for future referrals, he figured. He nodded to the attorney at the defense table, declining to venture over for the traditional handshake and murmur of "good work." Thad was still bristling after overhearing the defense attorney tell his client before the trial that Thad was "over the hill and overdue for a good ass-kicking."

"Serves the asshole right," Thad thought as he strolled out of the courtroom. "Maybe the next time he won't underestimate old Thaddeus T. Robinson the Third."

The ensuing celebration was excessive, even by Thad's standards. He reserved a room at his private club and coerced his favorite Boston chef to prepare an elaborate feast. He invited all of his firm's attorneys and their significant others, including the four lawyers and two paralegals who had done his bidding during the trial. Dinner was followed by drinks and a chance to play a little blackjack or poker. Small stakes to be sure, but fun for those who enjoyed risk-taking. Thad usually eschewed penny ante gambling, but joined the fun and played a few hands of twenty-one.

Later, during drinks at the club's bar, Thad spied a Boston socialite who was out for a diversion. By her account, her husband was away on yet another business trip, and she was tired of being cooped up in her Cambridge high-rise. In a transparent way, Thad pretended he was looking for some decorating ideas, and the woman was happy to play along and invite him over to see her "draperies." Thad made excuses to his guests, explaining the need to find a taxi and escort this poor inebriated woman to her home.

Within fifteen minutes, she and Thad were ripping each other's clothes off in her apartment's foyer. They never made it to the bedroom, instead copulating noisily in the middle of the lavishly furnished living room on a rug worth more than the annual budget of a small country. Afterwards, they fell asleep naked where they lay.

Thad was the first to awaken and was surprised to see that a few hours had elapsed. He dressed in a hurry and left the apartment, not bothering to leave a note or even cover his most recent partner.

Thad walked out to the street and realized immediately that getting a cab was going to be difficult. There was no doorman, the streets were deserted, and Boston cabs were notoriously slow to respond in the predawn hours. "This is a perfect opportunity to get a little exercise," he thought. He knew the way home, and it wouldn't take more than twenty minutes to cross the Charles on the Harvard Bridge and return to Back Bay.

Within a few minutes, Thad realized he may have made a mistake. Walking alone anywhere in Boston at this time of day was hazardous. He was too well dressed, and his Rolex alone was a sufficient enticement for a thief to accost him. Thad reached for his cell phone to call a cab but realized that he had taken it off his belt during the disrobing mania and threw it on his sex partner's mantle. Her apartment building was a fortress, so re-entering would be impossible. He didn't even know her last name, so getting his phone back tomorrow would be a challenge. For now, he had no choice but to keep walking.

Moving along the deserted streets, Thad was shaken. He had the distinct impression someone was watching him. He spun around several times, convinced there was a person behind him, but squinting into the light fog, he saw nothing. He continued on, picking up the pace, and praying that a taxi or a policeman would happen by.

Suddenly, Thad felt a searing pain in his back. His first thought was a kidney stone. He had chronically high uric acid levels that manifested as gout and renal stones, both of which produced almost unbearable discomfort. He was supposed to take medication, but like many people who knew a little about medicine, he decided that his doctors were being too cavalier with drugs and that they could be avoided. He had paid the price before and was familiar with renal colic.

But Thad quickly realized this was not a stone. There was a person standing behind him, pushing him to the ground. And this person was plunging a sharp object into his back. Now prone on the sidewalk, Thad tried to turn to identify his attacker but to no avail. His glasses had fallen somewhere, and with the assailant's weight holding him down, all he could manage was a brief glimpse of a ski mask and hood. For what seemed to Thad like hours, but was really no more than a minute, the mugger moved the knife around, probing carefully, methodically. By this time, Thad was in a state of shock, unable to resist or call for help. Finally, the attacker pulled out the knife, grabbed Thad's watch and wallet, and then kicked him for good measure before running off toward Cambridge. Thad lay in a heap on the sidewalk.

No one was sure exactly how long Thad lay there before a cab driver came over the bridge around sunrise, saw him, and called for help. The police and ambulance crew who were summoned to the scene were amazed at how little blood Thad had lost, despite the size of the wound in his back and his time on the ground.

The ambulance crew documented stable vital signs and mental status and prepared to move Thad to a stretcher for his brief ride to Mass General. When they asked him to scoot over to the blanket so they could lift him to the gurney, Thad couldn't cooperate. He appeared to have some kind of injury that rendered his lower extremities powerless. What they didn't know was that, just like the infant he represented in court the day before, Thad would never use his legs again.

Chapter 2

Mass General was the closest hospital to the crime site. Its ER was the usual destination for trauma cases almost anywhere in the Boston area. And there were plenty of those. Boston drivers, long known for their aggressive behavior, crashed into each other with predictable regularity. They couldn't quite figure out that excessive speed on inadequate roads was a recipe for disaster. And then there were the usual gun-and-knife-club cases, usually brought in by ambulances from neighborhoods on the north and south end of town, but occasionally 'coptered in for the special expertise Mass General could provide.

When referring to Massachusetts General Hospital as MGH, it was said only partly in jest that the letters really stood for Man's Greatest Hospital. As the principal teaching institution of Harvard Medical School, it attracted the best and brightest in all specialties and at all levels. That's what distinguished MGH from other places: it had the highest number of smart people per cubic foot than any other healthcare facility in the world, and everybody knew it. Even the people at Johns Hopkins, Mayo Clinic, and dozens of other prestigious institutions that competed with MGH and the other Harvard hospitals for patients, grants, Nobel prizes, *U. S. News & World Report* rankings, and everything else that signaled the superiority of one medical institution over another, even they had to admit that MGH was simply the best hospital on the planet.

MGH's ER did its part to uphold the hospital's sterling reputation. Staffed with experienced doctors and nurses supervising smart residents and students, it was intent on providing the very best care to anyone who rolled in through their doors. And the staff could summon top consultants in any specialty at any time. Each department maintained an in-house on-call staff that was larger than many hospitals' entire doctor pool.

Life in an ER generally follows a diurnal rhythm that reflects the ebb and flow of life that surrounds it. One might guess that patient volumes are greater during the day, but the movement of the sun in the sky is not what matters. ER traffic is greatest when people are likely to be traveling, playing, drinking, and arguing. For example, midnight to 3 A.M. is considered prime time for shootings and stabbings, as inebriated persons leave bars and move out into the streets to confront each other, or drive their cars into telephone poles. This is followed by a lull that lasts until about 6 A.M., when the morning rush hour begins. Which is precisely when Thad hit the MGH ER.

Ambulance crews are encouraged to call the ER if they've got a patient they think will need immediate evaluation by a specialist or a specific procedure. Most frequently, it's patients with chest pain who prompt such calls. For these patients, crews obtain electrocardiograms and transmit them electronically to the ER. If a pattern indicating a true heart attack is observed, the ER will not only contact the interventional cardiologist on call, but will also mobilize the catheterization laboratory staff in anticipation of using catheters to open the blocked artery that's causing damage to the heart muscle, and then placing stents to keep it open.

The paramedic on this particular run was James Butler, a former high school football star. James was just out of his training, and had never seen a potential spinal cord injury case before. But once he and his partner observed that Thad could not use his legs, they knew to protect his spinal cord. They immediately placed Thad on a backboard to prevent movement that might further injure the cord. The board was situated carefully on a stretcher, the stretcher was gingerly loaded into the ambulance, and the crew quickly pulled away. James rode in the back with Thad, making sure he was comfortable and checking his blood pressure and heart rate every few minutes. Not unexpectedly, both readings were high. Thad was so upset, he couldn't speak. James could sense Thad's panic and refrained from small talk while trying to be reassuring. James was just pleased that Thad's injury wasn't higher up on his spine. A high-enough injury could bring neurogenic shock into play, a condition that could be life-threatening.

After James had his first set of vital signs, he called the ER to preview the case. He used as much med-speak as he could remember from his classes and practical experience so the ER would be impressed.

"This is paramedic James Butler, operating Cambridge Ambulance Unit number six. We are transporting Mr. Thaddeus Robinson, a Caucasian man, sixty years old, who has a knife wound to the lower back in the region of T12-L1. The wound is fairly large but there is minimal blood loss. He is unable to move his lower extremities and has no sensation. He is strapped into a backboard and has minimal discomfort. Vital signs are stable and he is awake and alert. ETA ten minutes."

Cindy Trace, the triage nurse who took the call, was nonplussed. The details sounded incongruous. "Thanks, Mr. Butler. Can you please clarify? The patient has a knife wound in his back but he has minimal bleeding and his vitals are stable? Can you give me a blood pressure reading?"

"BP one-seventy over one hundred and heart rate one-ten and regular."

"And you checked a couple of times?"

"Yes, ma'am."

Suspecting damage to the aorta, which carries blood to the lower extremities, Cindy asked, "How about pulses in his legs and feet?"

"They are present bilaterally and four plus."

Trace still wasn't convinced that other abdominal organs had been spared. "Okay. Keep him immobile and get him in here as fast as you can."

Cindy had a few things to do in the next ten minutes. First, she needed to alert the ER doc and staff, but most importantly, she had to summon the neurosurgery team; neurosurgery would be the service responsible for treating the spinal cord injury that Cindy had to assume the patient had. She quickly pulled up the call schedule on her computer and was pleased to see that the chief neurosurgical resident on call was Dr. David Korn. If you were going to work at MGH, Cindy knew you had to be flexible and have a sense of humor. Because with brilliance goes eccentricity, and David Korn was a prime example.

A superior student from the Cleveland suburbs, David sailed through Harvard undergrad and medical school in seven years. For as long as anyone in his family could remember, David had told everyone he was going to be a brain surgeon, and he single-mindedly pursued that goal. He matched at MGH for a surgical internship and residency and worked so hard and did so well that he had been a lock for one of the two neurosurgery training positions that MGH offered every year. As this year's chief resident, David had the privilege of being on call every other night. A confirmed bachelor, and with few outside interests, David was only too happy to camp out in the hospital's on-call room, eating junk food while reading medical journals or working on his latest research project. The other residents referred to him as "Dr. Brainiac," to acknowledge his neurological expertise as well as his astounding smarts. One thing Cindy knew for sure: it wouldn't take long to get David to the ER to see a new patient and when he did, he would make decisions quickly and accurately.

"This sounds like an amazing case, Cindy," David said in his deep, almost guttural voice when he heard the story on the phone. Cindy had to smile—he said that about every case. "Hard to know why he isn't in shock or bleeding to death." And now David couldn't wait to dive into the case to try to understand what had happened. Within a minute, he was leaning against the charting counter, gnawing on a pencil, his trademark clipboard under his arm, as they wheeled Thad Robinson into the ER.

The busy ER resident on duty was only too happy to let the neurosurgeons take the lead on a fresh spinal trauma case. David followed the stretcher into the trauma room and began to call out instructions to the team of nurses and ER personnel who had assembled. "Call the radiology department and tell them we need a stat CAT scan of the back and abdomen. Leave him on the backboard until we have him safely on our stretcher. In fact, why don't we just leave it on until we get him to radiology, just to be safe? Plug him into an IV and run in D5 half normal saline at fifty cc's an hour and let's get routine labs drawn. Once we get a swab of that wound, I want him to get a gram of Ancef to cover him for infection."

After this initial flurry of activity, David went to Thad's side and introduced himself. "Hi, Mr. Robinson. My name is David Korn. I'm the chief neurosurgical resident on call this morning, and I'll be helping with your care. How are you feeling? Are you having any pain?" The ER doc had already instructed Cindy to give two milligrams of morphine, but David wanted to be sure the patient was comfortable. The CAT scan would be ruined if Thad squirmed in the machine.

"You're a resident?" Thad answered sharply. "I don't want a resident taking care of me. I want a real doctor. Someone who can see that I get extraordinary care. Understand? Extraordinary."

David had heard similar statements before. Many patients, especially the rich and faux famous, expect special treatment. They didn't understand that departing from ordinary procedures was dangerous and more likely to lead to mistakes and bad outcomes. David answered in measured tones.

"Mr. Robinson, your initial care here will be routine. I have to gather some preliminary information and get a few other things done before I present your case to my attending physician. I can assure you that he will be supervising every aspect of your case."

Thad was only partially assuaged. "He better. Or I will trash him, you, and this whole hospital if any of you screw up."

"Don't worry; you're in good hands," David replied

as patiently as possible, not overly concerned with Thad's threats. Patients under stress sometimes act like jerks—it was the physician's job not to let it get in the way of good care.

David went about a physical examination, confirming loss of motor strength in both lower extremities, and lack of sensation to touch or pinprick. He tried to elicit knee jerk reflexes and thought there was hyperreflexia bilaterally. All of this would be consistent with a relatively recent denervation caused by spinal cord trauma. He decided to spare Robinson a rectal examination to see if his sphincter was intact. A Foley catheter had already been inserted into Thad's bladder, so there was no way to know if he could urinate on his own.

David didn't spend a lot of time on the rest of the physical examination. The drones in the ER and the surgical resident were responsible for all of that. And all of the bedside findings would become academic in just a few minutes, when the CAT scan results were available. So why waste time on the physical examination?

"We're going to send you off for a CAT scan in a few minutes, Mr. Robinson. We have radiology facilities right here in the ER so it'll be a short trip. You'll be monitored by a nurse who will be with you the whole time."

"How much trouble am I in, doc?" Thad asked. Sure, Korn was a pissant resident, Thad thought, but he wanted info fast.

"Hard to say until I see the scan, but we are concerned about the loss of strength in your legs."

"No shit! So am I! What are the chances I'll recover?"

"We'll know better after we see what happened to your spinal cord. If it's only been grazed, I expect that function could return."

"And if it is totally severed? Look, doc, I've been a

malpractice attorney for nearly thirty years. I understand medicine quite well, and I know this is a bad situation. So you don't have to pull your punches."

David hadn't heard much after "malpractice attorney." He immediately wondered if Thad sued doctors or defended them. He recalled the "trashing" threat, which now seemed more ominous. Also, Thad looked rich, and David knew that defense work didn't yield as much revenue as plaintiff's cases. And Thad didn't volunteer that he played on the doctor's side. David's best assessment: scumbag doctor thrasher. He had been taught by his professors that neurosurgeons are regular targets for these buzzards, and they were to be scorned without exception.

David composed himself and tried to provide reassurance. "We can do some remarkable things for spinal cord injuries these days, Mr. Robinson. So I wouldn't be too pessimistic. We'll get the data and then give you a plan and a prognosis. Fair enough?"

Thad nodded and turned away. He had every reason to fear the worst, and he wasn't going to stop feeling that way until his legs starting moving again. But deep down, he doubted they ever would.

While they waited for the CAT scan, Thad was set upon by various personnel, including a surgical intern, medical student, and sundry nurses and technicians who asked seemingly endless questions about his medical history, prior hospitalizations, medications, and finally the attack itself. When he asked what was being done to catch the assailant, they assured him that the police were at the crime scene and would soon be at the hospital to talk to him. For now, it was all about his welfare, making an accurate diagnosis, and figuring out how to help him get better.

David was sitting at the charting station, scribbling

notes about the cases he would be handling that day. He was the "outworlder" today, assigned to do consults, round on the inpatients with the house staff, and generally keep things in order while his counterpart, Zhou Zhang ("Two-zee," as he was known to almost everyone) scrubbed in on cases. As chief residents, David and Two-zee handled routine cases with little or no supervision, and first-assisted on complex surgeries that required an attending physician. Operating was the fun part; the rest was referred to as "scut work" and was tolerated only grudgingly.

David gathered his team of house staff and medical students in the ER while he awaited the CAT scan results. Might as well start with this case and move directly into rounds. One by one they came, some hurrying, some strolling, each with a cup of coffee or tea, fighting off sleepiness.

They were still in the charting area, doing their "dry rounds," when Cindy walked over to tell David that Thad was back from radiology and the CAT scan images were ready. David had already summarized the case for the underlings. Now, he swung his chair around and pulled the computer keyboard out from under the desk. A few quick keystrokes and he was into the hospital's secure picture-archiving system, which would allow him to view the images. They hadn't yet been reviewed by a neuroradiologist, but David didn't care. He could interpret these studies as well as anyone, and spinal cord images were pretty easy to read, even for a resident. Computerized imaging was practically made for this problem, offering image slices in whatever plane the doctor needed. In this case, the spinal cord would be sliced from top to bottom like a loaf of bread, giving the viewer a detailed look at the level of injury and the amount of collateral damage.

The study was of moderately good quality; Thad had clearly been moving enough to blur some of the images. David saw the problem immediately but didn't let on. He turned to one of the Harvard Medical School students on his rotation. "Mr. Rifle, tell me what you see."

Young Mr. Rifle was caught somewhat off guard, his attention having been consumed for the past few moments by the comely medical student standing next to him. As a show of his engagement in the "interesting" case, he pushed toward to the screen and peered into it. He was a clever lad, having graduated at the top of his class from Columbia College. And given his interest in cardiology, where imaging was key, he had already been on his radiology elective. So he recovered reasonably well. "It looks like there's been a transection of the spinal cord at about L1 or L2. There's a good deal of edema around the trauma site, and a small hematoma."

"Very good, Mr. Rifle. What would you say about surrounding structures?"

"You mean like the aorta?"

"Well, yes, in fact that's pretty close by."

"I don't see any trauma to the aorta. If it had been punctured, there would be evidence of bleeding. The kidneys and other abdominal organs look intact."

"So this looks like pretty limited damage to the spinal cord."

"Yeah, pretty lucky guy."

David spun around on his chair. "Lucky, Mr. Rifle? Do you know something about spinal cord healing that I don't?"

David was interested in this very topic, and had spent considerable time researching it during his residency. Some tissues in the body can regenerate when injured, but nervous system tissue generally does not. Although it was possible to sew pieces of a broken spinal cord together, there was little or no chance that thc fibers would reconnect to re-establish normal function.

Mr. Rifle was embarrassed by David's question, which was obviously meant to belittle and not to instruct. "No, Dr. Korn, I don't."

"So, in medical jargon, we would say that Mr. Robinson's spinal cord is kaput, n'est-ce pas?"

Everyone except Mr. Rifle smiled at the weak attempt at black humor.

"Point taken, Dr. Korn."

David rose from his chair and started to walk to Robinson's cubicle to deliver the news. He knew that the conversation with Robinson would be difficult enough; he didn't need an audience. Turning back to the group, he said, "Wait here while I have a word with the patient. Then we'll go upstairs and start gravity rounds." Gravity rounds started at the top floor and worked down through the hospital units where their patients were housed. "We have to get a move on; our attending will be here in an hour or so."

Thad had just been wheeled back to the ER, and moved onto the stretcher bed, where the nurse was getting him settled in. The backboard had been removed. Once the CAT scan results were viewed, it was no longer necessary to keep Thad perfectly immobile. There was nothing left to stabilize. He had been given another few milligrams of morphine in the CAT scan suite, and was obviously sedated and sleepy, eyes closed. It had been a very long night for him.

David was inclined to let Thad sleep before delivering the bad news. In fact, in an hour, he would be back with his attending and could let the senior guy do the dirty work. That was their job and why they got the big bucks. But as he turned to leave the cubicle, Thad called to him.

"Where are you going, Dr. Korn?"

"I thought you were sleeping, Mr. Robinson, and I didn't want to disturb you. I was going to come back later."

"Because you are reluctant to discuss the results of the CAT scan?"

David stammered. He felt exposed. Bedside manner was one of the few areas of medicine at which he didn't excel. He still hadn't learned how to tell someone they had a serious problem without depriving them of hope. He realized that if he was going to be a successful neurosurgeon, he was going to find a lot of malignant brain tumors that would eventually kill his patients. It was something he couldn't dodge forever. But here he was, exposed, without an attending to protect him. It was down-and-dirty time. Thankfully, Thad took him partially off the hook.

"Look, Dr. Korn. I think I know what you are going to tell me. The CAT scan technicians have to learn how to be more discreet. I could sense by their tone and demeanor they saw something bad. So just tell me how bad, please?"

"Mr. Robinson, do you have any family here with you?"

"No. I'm divorced, my kids don't give a damn about me, and I haven't called them yet. Stop beating around the bush. Tell me what you have to tell me."

David at least had the bedside savvy to pull up a chair and sit down. He put his clipboard on the floor next to him, leaned forward with elbows on knees, and looked Thad straight in the eye. "Your spinal cord has been severed at the L1, L2 region. Do you know what L1, L2 means?"

"That's the lumbar, or lower back, region."

"Right. Nervous system function below that level will be compromised. That's why you can't move your legs."

"And there's nothing that can be done?"

"My attending physician, Dr. Slattery, will be here to make rounds in about an hour, and I have to show him the CAT scan images. The question is whether there is any reason to do surgery to try to put the cord back together and hope that some of the fibers re-establish contact."

"That sounds like fantasy, Dr. Korn. I thought nervous system tissue at that level can't regenerate."

"That's generally true. But I'm sure you also know that this place is on the cutting edge of research in just about every therapeutic area, including neurosurgery. Dr. Slattery will know if we have any pertinent projects. Nerve regrowth is a hot topic."

David wasn't sure he believed what he was spouting, but he had learned that delivering bad news in small doses was better than dropping a load of it on a patient all at once. And many pharmaceutical companies were experimenting with bioengineered nerve and blood vessel growth factors that might be helpful to Thad.

Thad himself remained skeptical. "But we will have to assume that I will never regain full function."

"Not full function. The question is how much."

"And what kind? At this spinal cord level, bowel and bladder function are probably shot."

"Yes," David admitted, eyes now diverted to his feet.

"And sexual function as well," Thad persisted.

"Yes."

And then silence, as both men processed what had just been exchanged. Thad was not dead, but he now had a very good reason to wish it were so. At least a few seconds went by, David once again sensitive enough not to interrupt with any nonsense about a bright side. Thad broke the silence.

"I have no more questions for the time being."

"I understand," David replied, as he collected his ever-present clipboard and stood to leave. "I'll be back in about an hour with Dr. Slattery."

"But there is one thing I want to know, and perhaps we should address this to Dr. Slattery as well."

"Certainly. Anything," said David, anxious to provide something positive after offering so little hope.

"I'm hardly an expert on knife injuries. But I would expect that ordinarily, a knife in the back would cause some pretty serious damage to surrounding organs."

"I haven't seen many, but yes, that has been my experience."

"But this injury seems to have been pretty limited to the cord."

"Yes."

"Happenstance, Dr. Korn?"

"I don't know, Mr. Robinson. Maybe that's something the police will wonder about, too."

"Yes, I hope so, Dr. Korn. I surely do."

Chapter 3

Wilson Lentz heard the ringing clearly but couldn't fathom how. He was underwater, swimming with a beautiful woman who happened to have a tail instead of legs. "A mermaid, douche bag," he told himself. "How could you have not figured that out? But why the ringing? Does she have a bell around her neck to guide me through this murky water?" The ringing didn't let up—it just kept getting louder. "What the fuck," he heard himself say. "How can I be breathing if I'm underwater?" The ringing continued and Will finally awakened. "Jesus, what a dream," he mumbled as he slowly regained his senses.

"Shit, it's the phone," he finally realized. He moved to answer it, but something was holding him down. "Ah," he said, regarding the shaved and shapely leg over his stomach, pinning him to the mattress. Tracing the leg upward to its origin, he noted it was attached to an apparently naked person lying prone and sideways in his bed, arms and head thrown over the side, making identification of anything but female sex quite difficult. "You can remind me of your name later, sweetheart," Will murmured to himself. "Right now I gotta answer the phone."

Easier said than done. Like its owner, the leg in question was substantial, and the attached sleeping beauty was unable to help with the extrication. Will, a long and lean and by no means muscular fellow, had to push hard to lift the leg high enough to finally escape. It wasn't until he rolled onto the floor that he realized he too was naked. His clothes and some female outer- and undergarments were strewn all over his bedroom. "What the fuck," he exclaimed to no one in particular as he circled the bed to the nightstand, where his telephone continued its infernal ringing.

"Lentz," he said, receiver finally in hand.

"Will, it's Harry. Did I wake you up?"

"Of course you woke me up, asshole. What the fuck time is it? The sun's not even up yet."

"It's about five-thirty."

"Okay, so what's so fucking important? Wait, let me guess, the President of the United States was assassinated and they asked us to investigate the case."

"Come on, Will. I don't like getting up early, either."

Will immediately regretted his sarcastic remark. Harry Socks, his partner in homicide investigation, was a decent guy and didn't deserve Will's venom. His New Year's resolution had been to stop dumping on Harry. Another good intention forgotten.

"Sorry, Harry. Let's just say that things here in my bedroom are a little confusing right now. Anyhow, what's going on?"

"Well, it isn't the President, but a prominent attorney named Thaddeus Robinson was knifed in the back about an hour ago in the middle of the Harvard Bridge. I'm calling from the scene."

"Is he dead?"

"Surprisingly, no. The beat guys who got here first said he had a gash in his back and couldn't move his legs, but he was stable when the ambulance loaded him up and took him to MGH."

"Are the crime scene people there yet?'

"Just arriving. The beat guys did a good job of isolating the scene—not many gawkers out this time of day."

"Yeah, and not many witnesses, either."

"The cops are starting the door-to-door now but they don't have much hope. The residences on both sides are pretty far from the middle of the bridge, and there's almost no traffic at 4 A.M."

"So you think it was a random mugging?"

"The ambulance guys said the victim didn't have any ID or a watch or rings or a phone. Unless he was walking around without any of that stuff, I assume they were stolen. We'll find out when we interview him."

"If it wasn't a random mugging, somebody must have planned it. We'll have to find out what this dude was doing on the bridge by himself at that hour."

Will unconsciously scratched his groin as he spoke and realized, with some disgust, that he would need to shower before he could head out to join his partner. "Harry, give me a few minutes to wash up, will ya?"

"Take your time, Will. I have the scene covered. Why don't you meet me at the General's ER and we can talk to Robinson."

"Good idea. That's probably where the money is on this one."

"Right. See you there in about an hour?"

Will did some calculations. Fifteen minutes to shower and dress, fifteen to get the obligatory cup of coffee, a few minutes to get whoever was in his bed out the door and into a cab, and fifteen to hustle down the drive from his apartment to MGH.

"Yeah, that should be fine, give or take," he said.

Ninety-seven minutes later, Will hurried into the ER. Harry stood at the desk in the nursing station, scanning his smart phone. He looked up, obviously annoyed, and greeted Will as civilly as he could manage. "Thanks so much for joining me, Will."

"Sorry, Harry. Took me longer than expected to get out of the house."

Getting the woman out of his house had been a monumental task. It took forever for her to wake up and get dressed, and she seemed in no hurry to leave her latest lover.

As he stood in the shower, Will had been able to partially reconstruct the previous evening. After a few stops, he, and a few of his carousing pals, had finished the evening at Danny's Tavern on Comm Ave, just a few blocks from his two-story duplex. They had met some women and paired up. Will, always laid back, had ended up with Matilda, which he assumed was not her real name but it seemed to fit her, given her body mass. One thing must have led to another because the next thing Will could remember was laughing hysterically as he tried to get his key in the door and Matilda asking him if he had the same trouble with his dick. That must not have been a problem, he thought, as he contemplated the matted-down state of his pubic hair. The rest of the night was a blur until the phone call.

"I bet it did," Harry replied sardonically. He liked Will, but as a devoted family man, he couldn't understand the life Will was leading since his wife had ditched him. One-night stands weren't Harry's cup of tea.

"Anyhow, I thought we should interview the vic together," Harry continued. "He was off for some tests when I got here, and the resident who's taking care of him just came out of the room looking pretty glum."

"Maybe we should get the medical scoop before we talk to Mr. Robinson. That might give us a direction. He may not be in a mood to cooperate."

The detectives spotted David Korn, who was leading his team out of the ER on their way to patient rounds. Will and Harry headed him off. "How can I help you guys?" David asked after they introduced themselves.

"Doc, I understand from the nursing staff that you're looking after Mr. Thaddeus Robinson?"

"Our neurosurgical team was called in consultation and yes, he'll be admitted to our service."

"Can you summarize his condition?"

David reviewed what had happened to Thad, emphasizing the discrete nature of the injury and how lucky Thad had been not to have died from the attack.

"So, it looks to you like someone may have tried to kill Mr. Robinson but only succeeded in severing his spinal cord?" Will surmised.

"Yep, that about sums it up."

"Doc, we might have more questions for you later, if you don't mind, after we've had a chance to gather more facts about the attack."

"Sure. I'm just the resident. Our attending, Dr. Slattery, will be in charge of the case. I'm sure he can help you just as well."

"Fine, doc. And if anything occurs to you, give us a call," said Harry handing him a business card. "Is it okay if we go in to talk to Mr. Robinson?"

"Just check with the nurses to make sure he's ready, but I suspect he'll be anxious to talk to you. He's pretty angry."

After a quick word with Thad's nurse, Will and Harry parted the curtains and entered Thad's cubicle. He was hooked up to an IV and had oxygen prongs in his nose, but appeared to be resting comfortably. His eyes were closed but he wasn't sleeping. "Heard you people outside. I've been waiting for you to show up."

Will and Harry offered their greetings and flashed their detective badges. "I'm Lieutenant Detective Wilson Lentz and this is my partner Sergeant Detective Harry Socks. Are you up to answering a few questions?" Will took a chair next to Thad's bed while Harry stood behind him.

"If it gets the investigation started, I'm nothing but ready."

"The investigation has already started, Mr. Robinson. Our crime scene people have been at the site and we're canvassing the neighborhood to see if we can come up with a witness or anybody who heard or saw something."

"It was pretty lonely out there, Lieutenant. I doubt your canvass will yield much."

"You never know. And that leads to my first question: what were you doing out there at that hour?"

"Sheer stupidity, in retrospect, Lieutenant. I was out with a lady and when I left her place, there weren't any taxis in sight. So I foolishly decided to hoof it back across the bridge to Back Bay. You could practically see my place from hers, so I figured it would be a short walk."

"The name of the lady?" Harry asked, pulling out his note pad.

"Uh, that's going to be a tough one, Sergeant. I don't believe I gathered that information. I had just met her at a social event. I can give you her address."

"Okay, Mr. Robinson. We'll follow-up on that. By the

way, you didn't have a wallet or watch or jewelry when they found you. Did you have them on you when you were attacked?"

"I sure did. I had a Rolex that my ex-wife gave me several years ago and a wallet with a lot of credit cards, but not a lot of cash, thank goodness. I'll have to get my secretary to cancel those cards."

"Don't worry about that, Mr. Robinson. I need to get the credit card information from your office so we can put a trace on the cards. That will automatically cancel them."

"Aren't you helpful, Detective? Maybe you can give me some idea of what you're going to do to find the bastard who did this?"

"We're just getting started Mr. Robinson. As we said, our folks are combing the crime scene to see if we get lucky there. I guess the most important issue is whether this was a random attack or somebody trying to hurt you in particular, and covering their tracks by making it look like a mugging."

"Are you serious? I can't think of anyone who would want to hurt me so bad that they would put a knife in my back. Detective, I think it's pretty obvious that whoever did this wanted my wallet, and my jewelry."

"That reminds me. We'll also need a list of the other jewelry you had on—cuff links and that sort of thing, so we can put out a pawn shop alert. As to the possibility of a personal vendetta, is there anyone in your practice or at home we can talk to who might give us another perspective?"

"I'm estranged from my wife, Detective. She lives by herself out in Hanson. I don't think you'll find her very cooperative, nor my children, who've sided with their mother. The person who knows the most about my life at present is my personal secretary, Michelle Mash.

She's been with me for a long time and keeps my business and personal schedule. And then there are my associates at the firm."

"So it's okay if we talk to some of these people?"

"I don't give a fuck who you talk to, Detective. Just find out who did this and make sure they are prosecuted fully or…"

"Or what, Mr. Robinson?"

"Or I'll make sure they get what they deserve."

"I hardly think that will be necessary, Mr. Robinson. In fact, I would caution you against taking any measures on your own."

"Really, Detective? I've been an attorney in this town for several years, and I have witnessed some incredible injustices, including criminals walking because of a technicality or because they managed to bribe a judge. One thing you can count on is that I'll pay close attention to every step you take in my case, and I won't rest until whoever attacked me is punished severely."

Will looked up at the screen next to Thad's bed and saw several of the brightly colored squiggles go bananas. He had no idea what any of it meant, but he figured it was probably not a good idea to get Robinson too worked up this early in his recovery.

"I understand, Mr. Robinson. We're going to get right on this and we promise to keep you posted."

Will's intent was to reassure, but Thad felt he was being managed, so he kept the pressure on.

"I have many friends in this city who will see that you do, Detective Lentz."

Tired of seeing his partner being pushed around when he had only good intentions, Harry decided it was time to go.

"Mr. Robinson, I suggest we stop here so you can rest up and we can get going on the case. We'll be in touch soon." Harry stepped forward and extended his hand. Robinson turned his head away and grunted a goodbye. Harry and Will exchanged exasperated glances and marched out of the room.

"That was a load of fun," Will hissed as soon as they were out of earshot of the staff.

"The guy's an asshole attorney, and he can't imagine anybody who might want to stick a knife in his back?"

Will shook his head. "Right. People with motives might not be too hard to find once we get some background on Mr. Nice Guy here."

"So how do you want to divvy up the work?"

"You already started with the crime scene. Why don't you follow-up with the canvassers and see if they came up with anything. I'll talk to the secretary, Michelle, and see what she has to say. We also have to find the name of Robinson's lady friend."

"Okay, that should take us the rest of the day. Let's meet up tomorrow morning at the station and do a debrief then."

"Swell."

It took Will only a quick Internet search and a couple of emails to set up a meeting with Michelle Mash. After explaining who he was and why he was contacting her, Will suggested it would be better to meet after hours near the office to avoid raising concerns at the firm. Besides, Will was happy to see Michelle's photo on the firm's website. She was easy on the eyes, so their meeting in a local pub wouldn't be his most unpleasant experience of the day. Will told her to look for a tall guy with dark hair, a goatee, horn-rimmed glasses, wearing a tweed jacket with elbow patches.

Will headed downtown and decided to kill some time at a hot dog joint that had just opened near Faneuil Hall.

He ordered the house special, a double dog smothered in sauerkraut, chili, and onions, chased down with a diet soft drink. He sat at the counter, flicking through the usual assortment of useless messages on his not-so-smart phone. There were a couple of text messages from his brother and sister, the only family he had. As usual, they encouraged him to visit and spend time with his nieces and nephews. Will loved the kids and enjoyed their company but usually declined invitations for week-end dinners or birthday parties. He wasn't sure what made him uncomfortable about the occasions. Was it jealousy? Did he secretly covet the lives his siblings had? Or was it his intrinsic shyness and desire to be alone? He had never figured it out, and so every invitation made him a little more uncomfortable.

He scarfed down his lunch, and headed over to the pub where he planned to meet Michelle. He was technically on duty, so he nursed a club soda at the bar until Michelle arrived. He spotted her immediately, as did a few hounds sitting at the bar. The website photo had not done her justice. She was a knockout, with long blonde hair, pinned up discreetly, intense blue eyes, and a curvaceous figure that she hid ineffectively with a loose fitting blouse. Will smiled, silently glad that he was a bachelor again, free to explore his new opportunities. As a fact witness to a possible attempted murder, Michelle might be off limits now, but…

His musing was interrupted by Michelle's greeting and her fatal flaw: her voice was a whiney screech that set Will's teeth on edge. It was made worse by a marked Boston accent that refused to give proper consideration to any words ending in the letter *r*. He instantly knew he could never put up with the voice, no matter how good she might look naked.

"Hello, Ms. Mash," Will said, trying to hide his disappointment. “I’m Detective Lentz, but just call me Will. Thanks so much for coming here to meet with me.”

“I’m happy to help, Detective, I mean Will. And you can call me Michelle. Everybody in the firm does.”

“Can I offer you a drink, Michelle?”

“Well, let’s see, it’s not five o’clock yet but I guess it’s cocktail hour somewhere in the world. Isn’t Puerto Rico an hour ahead of us?”

“That sounds about right. I hear they have some pretty good Puerto Rican rum in this place. Shall we put it to the test?”

Michelle smiled. Perfect teeth, beautiful smile. Maybe if he used ear plugs.

“Sure, how about a rum and coke to start?”

Will got the bartender’s attention, ordered her drink, took a notebook and pen out of his breast pocket, and began.

“Michelle, I assume you know what happened to Mr. Robinson this morning.”

“I heard some of the details at the office. And that it was pretty bad.”

“It was. Somebody attacked him viciously and maybe even tried to kill him. Amazingly, the knife missed major vessels and organs but it did cut through his spinal cord.”

“Is he going to recover?”

“The docs at MGH seem sure he will, but they’re pessimistic about his chances of recovering function.”

“You mean walking?”

“And controlling his bladder and bowels, or having sex. It could be devastating.”

“Oh my God, I had no idea it could be that bad. We were all told that he was stable and would be okay.”

“Well, he won’t die, but I doubt he’s going to be okay living like that. But we’re getting a little ahead of ourselves. Maybe he’ll do better than we think—it’s just too early to tell. In any case, he gave us permission to talk to you to get some background information."

"What do you need?"

"Essentially, do you know of anyone who might have wanted to hurt Mr. Robinson?"

Michelle looked down, trying to suppress a smile. Will didn't miss it.

"Is there something funny about that?"

Michelle was flustered. "No, it's just that it's a little office joke that Thad attracts enemies like most people gain weight—constantly."

"Is that because of the nature of his work?"

"Yes, but also because he's a prick."

Will almost fell off of his bar stool. "Mr. Robinson told us you've been working with him for years."

"I have. My husband tells me that I have an extremely high tolerance for crap."

No ring—but married. No matter, he was not getting used to the voice.

"And Thad pays me a lot of money. I think he knows I don't like him but doesn't care because I do a great job of organizing his life."

"So you handle things in and out of the office for him?"

"You bet. He's a real delegator once he trusts you. Gives me everything. I even pay his personal bills."

"So what can you tell me about the people who don't like him?"

"Well, first of all, let's be clear. I'm *not* going to give you any privileged information. Thad's life has been pretty public so most of what I'll say is widely known. A lot of it has been in the friggin' *Boston Globe*, for crying out loud."

Will made a note to do a newspaper search after his interview with Michelle. He could start that this evening.

"All right, what's the best dirt you can give me?"

"Well, we can start with people Thad has sued in personal injury cases. There's a ton of them. And they're all in the public record."

"Can you give me the juiciest?"

"Let's see. He's brought down a number of public figures, councilmen, legislators, judges. One of the better recent cases was an appellate judge who was boinking one of his young clerks. The clerk, a boy by the way, went to Thad with the case, alleging that the judge had threatened him with dismissal if he told. The criminal case fell apart pretty quickly, but Thad took the judge to the cleaners in civil court."

"I guess that got the judge pretty pissed off."

"He threatened Thad in the courtroom right after the verdict was read, but everybody knew he was a wimp and Thad just stood there and laughed at him."

"Hmm. Any other good ones?"

"Well, there was the Sebastian Bergstrom case."

Will's eyebrows went up. "Wow, I forgot that Robinson was involved with that."

"Involved? That's an understatement. When everybody else was running away from the case, he nearly single-handedly took down the cardiologist for the Bergstrom family."

Will recalled the famous hockey goalie's untimely death and its fallout. "What a sad story that was. I remember it was in the news for a long time, and I don't think this town has recovered from it yet. A huge loss for your boss, of course. Would you mind if I get back to you with more questions about some of his other cases?"

"Not at all. Like I said, if it's in the public domain, I can talk forever."

"So what can you tell me about his family?"

"I can tell you it's a mess. His kids revile him. They hated him ever since they could talk, and his split with Effie was their excuse to skedaddle."

"So no contact with his kids. For how long?"

"Years, I would say. His son, Jamie, is as big a jerk as his father, or so I've heard. He's a slum lord down in Philly. Owns a bunch of burned-out buildings in North Philadelphia, near Temple, that he calls apartments. He managed to hot-wire City Hall and has collected an amazing amount of public money that was supposed to be helping the poor black families in that area. He even disgusts Thad."

"What about his daughter?"

"I don't know as much about her. She's close with her mother and doesn't talk to Thad at all since the divorce. I'm not even sure where she lives."

"And then there's Effie."

"Yes, poor Effie. I haven't decided if I feel sorry for her or not. She married the guy and I'm sure she wanted the money he'd be making. It couldn't have been love."

"How long have they been divorced?"

"Only a year or so? Thad was out there getting all he wanted for years, and she just put up with it. Then one day, he produces a pre-nup and tells her to hit the road. She got a lawyer and tried like hell to contest the document, saying it was a forgery, but it held up to all kinds of testing. It was eventually enforced, and she was on the street before you could bat an eye."

"Thad told us she lives in Hanson."

"In a pretty small house, from what I heard. She also went back to work part-time. I'm not sure if she did that because she had to or she wanted to."

"Do you ever speak with her?"

"Rarely. I've had to call her about financial issues, like taxes, a few times. She was very pleasant on the phone, especially considering the screw job that Thad laid on her."

Will ordered another round of drinks and temporarily moved the conversation to neutral ground while he greased Michelle's tongue. After about four rum-and-cokes, he took the plunge.

"So, Michelle, there's the public Thad Robinson story, but I bet you have some good insider gossip to share."

"I told you we weren't going there."

"Not officially, of course. And I don't want to know anything about his business."

"Well then, what did you have in mind?"

"Vices, my dear. What bad things does Mr. Robinson do with his time?"

"It's no secret that he chases skirts."

"Anyone's in particular?"

"He's an equal opportunity pursuer. He'll go after anybody, even me."

"I suspect he didn't get far."

"You bet your sweet ass, he didn't. First, I find him repugnant, and second, I detest office affairs. They never play out well."

Will sensed that Michelle wanted to be coaxed. "Any of those office dalliances pertinent to our boy?"

"You could say that."

"Do you want to play twenty questions or are you going to tell me?"

"I'm not going to spread rumors. What kind of girl do you think I am?"

"Guess I'll have to do my own research."

"Well then, maybe you ought to talk to a paralegal at the firm named Laura. She'll be able to fill in the blanks about King Thaddeus and his office conquests. And please don't tell her how you got her name."

"I'll add that to my to-do list."

Michelle crossed her legs seductively, but had to brace herself to keep from falling off of the bar stool. Will was worried that he was going to lose his source before he got everything he wanted to know.

Michelle leaned forward and said, "Before you put your pen and paper away, there's one more thing."

"I'm all ears."

"Thad likes to gamble."

"Michelle, I love you, baby, but that's not a revelation. I would have been surprised if he didn't."

"No, honey, I mean really gamble. Like high-roller gamble. Like Atlantic City and Vegas comp gamble."

"Once again, you fail to impress."

Michelle giggled. A little of her drink dribbled from the corner of her mouth.

"Will, what happens to people who gamble heavily?"

"They lose heavily."

"And then what happens?" Michelle teased.

"They get into money trouble."

"And how do they get out of trouble?"

Will was getting tired of the game but decided not to let his exasperation show. "They don't. They just dig themselves a bigger hole. Has that happened to Thad?"

"It didn't at first," Michelle answered. "But recently, he had to take out some loans to cover his debts."

"Loans from whom?"

"Who do you think?"

"Banks?"

"That worked for a while, but lately I've had to call some pretty unsavory characters."

"Loan sharks?"

"I didn't use that term, did I?"

"You mean the great Thad Robinson gambled his way into that much debt?"

Michelle giggled again. "Look Will, I'm just telling you stuff that a lot of us in the office think is true. You're the detective, Detective. So why don't you find out if all of this crap really is true? And when you do, let me know."

"Michelle, I plan to do just that."

Michelle's eyes glazed over and she began to fall sideways off the bar stool. Will broke her fall and got her back to consciousness, realizing the interview was over. "Time to get you home, Michelle. Why don't I put you in a cab and call your husband so he'll expect you."

"Detective, that would be so nice of you, but I don't live far and can walk home."

"No, Michelle, you can't walk home. We'll get you a ride and make sure you're safe. I can't thank you enough for sharing some information with me. You've been very helpful."

Michelle's final cogent thought was appropriate. "Just remember not to tell anybody where you got your clues, Detective."

Will paid the tab, thanked the bartender, and managed to get Michelle out to the curb, where he hailed a taxi, gave the driver an address and then texted Michelle's husband that his lovely wife would be arriving at their apartment soon. On his walk to the parking lot, Will catalogued the leads Michelle had supplied in just a couple of hours: angry defendants, ruined spouse, hateful children, slimy gambling debtors, and aggrieved mistresses and cuckolds. He tried to remember a case in which so many people had a good reason to stick a knife into a victim's back—and twist.

Chapter 4

The next morning, Will's phone once again awakened him. When he grabbed it off the bedside table and saw Harry Socks' name displayed, he launched into a stream of expletives that would have startled any slumbering creature within earshot—of which on this morning there happened to be none.

Will had kept a cat and a dog for a while, but learned that they didn't diminish his loneliness. They just made it more difficult for him to do his job efficiently. He loved the dog but couldn't bear to leave the hound in a cage all day so he let Rocky roam the house, free to munch on furniture, clothing, or whatever quelled his boredom. Will finally gave up after the pup disabled most of his electronics and gnawed on a few favorite shoes. Patti, the cat, was a little easier but punished Will for leaving her alone by hiding in a closet whenever he came home, providing little solace and companionship to compensate for the expensive food she insisted on, the endless kitty litter cleaning, and the periodic trips to the vet.

Now the only creatures that crossed his doorstep were

his occasional one-night ladies, snatched from one of the "Mass Ave" bars that seemed to exist solely for the purpose of facilitating hook-ups. At least that was Will's perception, since he saw little other reason to frequent them. "Better than self-abuse," he told himself whenever he prepared to troll the establishments where everyone really did seem to know his name.

But Will's wake-up outburst did nothing to stop his vintage cell phone from emitting its shrill ringtone. "What the fuck happened to old fashioned bell tones," Will wondered, ignoring the fact that he could program any ringtone he wanted. He hated technology, barely tolerating his work computer and stubbornly resisting smartphones, tablets, or any gadget with an on/off switch. The cell phone was his one compromise—much better than the high-priced land lines offered at his apartment.

Will finally gave up and jabbed at the receive button. "What the fuck now?"

Harry didn't flinch. "Don't you remember? We were supposed to meet at the station this morning to go over the case and plan our next steps."

"Yeah, yeah, I'll be there. Guess I overslept."

"I wonder if you can see my surprised face," Harry chided.

"I'll be there in half an hour. Get some coffee and keep your pants on."

"Maybe if you'd followed that advice, you'd be here already."

"Nobody's in my bed, wise ass. I just need a five-minute shower and I'll be on my way."

Will wasn't exaggerating. His total prep time was no more than ten minutes, and he was in his car and on his way to the station. Will had accepted a small apartment in exchange for the convenience of living in a desirable part of Boston, which was also a short drive to the station where the detectives were housed. He pulled into the lot, found a space, and was bounding up the stairs when he plowed directly into Captain Pokorney.

"Will, where *you* going in such a hurry?"

"Sorry, cap. Harry's waiting for me to review a case."

"The Robinson stabbing?"

"Yep—you been briefed already?"

"Harry filled me in."

"We have to be careful. I suspect it's going to get a lot of media attention."

"Already has, Will. WSLZ has been talking about it all morning."

"You mean all sleaze, all the time." Boston's all-news-all-the-time station was usually one of the first media outlets to pick up popular stories, especially anything lurid or violent. They knew what their audience liked, and murder and rape were right up there with scandals and natural disasters, leavened occasionally with stories about playoff victories for local sports teams. And since they didn't spend much money on research, anything they dredged up was aired several times an hour.

"Great. That'll make our canvass a real picnic."

"Yeah. Harry said your team hasn't completed the interviews…"

"Which means we'll have to wade through dozens of nuts to get any accurate accounts."

"Well, I just hope somebody saw something. What other angles are you working on?"

"I have to get hold of the woman Robinson was with before he got knifed. She might be helpful. I grilled Robinson's secretary yesterday and came up with a host of people who had a reason to use a blade on his back. I plan to follow-up with some of them over the next few days. Most of them aren't plausible as the actual doer, like the ex-wife…"

"But buying a hit man in Boston ain't that hard or that expensive," Pokorney interrupted.

"Exactly, Captain. Don't worry, we're checking every angle."

"See that you do, Will. Robinson is going to be watching us very carefully, and he'll be only too happy to tell the media we screwed up something or other."

Will nodded, said goodbye to Pokorney, and finished his run up the stairs. Pokorney was a decent guy but he was close to retirement and scared as hell of bad publicity or anything else that could lose him his pension. This case was going to drive him crazy if Will and Harry didn't get it wrapped up soon. He'd keep the pressure on.

The detective room was going full tilt. The cash-strapped department had decided a few years back to establish equality in the workplace by going to a modular office design, so now everybody was equally unhappy. No one had privacy, the noise was deafening, and it was impossible to think. "Pure genius," Will muttered to himself as he maneuvered like a halfback through the maze of desks, chairs, suspects, lawyers, and staff to the corner cubicle he shared with Harry. And there sat Harry himself, feet on his desk, reading the newspaper on his smartphone, sipping coffee, and looking as relaxed as could be.

"Can I assume from your posture that we have cracked the case?"

"Fuck you and the horse you rode in on. I was here early and you were still sleeping. So I decided it was time to put the ol' feet up."

Will plopped into his desk chair across from Harry and cleared away a few stacks of paper so he had room to jot down some notes.

"Okay, let's do this." He went on to summarize what he had learned from Michelle at the bar, or at least what he could remember. He hadn't taken notes because he hadn't wanted to spook her while the large amount of alcohol she consumed was taking effect. He had jotted down a few things on the back of a used envelope before he went to bed; he shared these with his partner.

Harry was as impressed with Michelle's thoughts as Will had been. "Not lacking for suspects in this one, are we?"

"Not at all. How'd your guys do with the canvassing?"

"Didn't find much. The neighborhood was asleep and the attack was far enough out on the bridge so any screaming and yelling didn't register, I guess."

"So… snake eyes?"

"Not completely. One of the uniforms told us that an old lady who lives right at the base of the bridge let her cats out around the time of the attack. She claims she saw some guy in running clothes come back across the bridge in a hurry. The rest of it was garbled in transmission."

"Road trip?"

"Thought you'd never ask."

"By the way, did you get the name of the woman who spent the night with Robinson?"

"I did, and it wasn't difficult. Several people at the club knew her." Harry pulled out his notebook from his breast pocket. "Name is Norcross. Lives about three blocks from the Harvard Bridge in Cambridge."

"Great. Let's head over. Maybe we can see them both."

Rush hour was pretty much over when Harry and Will left the station, so their drive in Will's hunk of junk was short—for which Harry was grateful. Will had the perfect downtown Boston ride: an old, dented Ford Fiesta that was small enough to squeeze into insanely small parking places. And not a target for thieves or vandals who seemed to get a kick out of smashing car windows and snatching anything that wasn't tied down. Its interior was disgusting, packed with trash and reeking of lunches long finished and assorted other smells, the origins of which Harry didn't care to ponder. He was satisfied to roll down the window to enjoy the fresh air.

They drove across the Harvard Bridge, admiring the nubile coeds strolling on the sidewalks. It was going to be a glorious spring day, the sun already warming the air, with the sweet smell of blooming foliage all around. "Great golf day," Harry said randomly, as they hunted for a parking spot. They settled for an illegal spot near a fire hydrant. Will put his police sign on the dashboard to deter any ticket maids looking to meet their quota for the day.

"What is this person's name?" Will asked as they approached the house.

"Minnie Stohler."

"What kind of name is Minnie?"

"How do I know?" Harry answered. "The cop who interviewed her said she was a little out there, so be gentle with her, Will."

And the uniform hadn't been exaggerating. Minnie came to the door dressed in a nightgown, looking disheveled and a little bleary eyed. She had a difficult time focusing on Will and Harry, frequently looking past them and over their shoulders.

"Ma'am, my name is Sergeant Detective Harry Socks, and this is my partner, Lieutenant Detective Wilson Lentz." Harry flashed his badge; Will did the same. "Do you have a few minutes to answer some questions?"

"About what?" Minnie said. "What did I do?"

"Nothing, ma'am. This is about the incident yesterday. I believe you told one of our officers that you saw a man running back across the Harvard Bridge, and we were wondering if you could give us some details."

Minnie paused, obviously trying to reset her brain. "Oh, yes, I remember. Come in, Detectives."

Harry and Will walked in behind Minnie. The house was almost completely dark, shades drawn, with a single low-voltage bulb in a lamp next to a rocking chair in the living room providing what light there was. The place was a mess. Minnie was a hoarder. There were stacks of magazines and newspapers on the floor, some in bundles, with random accessories on every table surface. Plus, there were cats galore and fur that covered every square inch of furniture.

"Do you live here alone, Ms. Stohler?"

"Yes, Detective. Except for my kitties. My children live nearby, and I go to their houses once in a while."

No mention of them coming here, Will noted.

"Can I offer you coffee or tea?" Minnie asked.

Harry couldn't imagine the circumstances under which he would drink from one of Minnie's cups. He and Will declined, and Minnie scurried about trying to find a place for the three of them to sit, shooing cats of several breeds and colors off the furniture to make room.

"Now, what is it you wanted to talk to me about?" Minnie asked, once they were settled.

"Ms. Stohler, you told the policemen you saw a man running across the bridge last night when you were putting your cats out," Will began.

"Yes, I did," Minnie said, almost surprised by her own recollection. "Two of my boys always insist on going out before dawn. I wish I could break them of that habit."

"Do you remember what he looked like?"

"My cat?"

"No, Ms. Stohler. The man running across the bridge."

"Oh. It was pretty dark. He had running clothes on and a wool hat."

"Was his face covered?" Harry asked.

"Not that I remember."

"Anything else about how he looked?"

"He wasn't really big or small, but he looked like he was in good shape—running very fast. As he came across the bridge, it looked like he dropped something into the river, but I couldn't tell for sure."

Will leaned forward. "Did he drop the object or throw it?"

"I don't know, Lieutenant."

"So he ran across the bridge, something went into the river, and then he went past your house, and up this street. Did he see you?"

"I don't think so. I was startled when I saw him, so I pulled back into my doorway. But I did notice he went about halfway up the street and then disappeared into one of the houses."

"Do you know which one?"

"I'm not certain. I've lived on this street a long time and I know everybody. He didn't look like any of my neighbors. So maybe he was a boarder."

"A boarder? Is there a rooming house on this street?"

"There's a bed and breakfast. I think it's called Josh's B&B. Just opened last year. One of my best friends lived in that house, Barbara Miller. But then she sold the place and moved in with her kids."

"Is that the only B&B on the street, Ms. Stohler?"

"Yes."

"Is there anything else you can tell us about the person you saw or where he went?"

"No, Detective, it all happened so fast. I have to admit that I was very afraid he was going to run right up to my house, so I didn't watch him as carefully as I could have. But I do remember one thing that was strange."

"Which was," Will interjected impatiently.

"It looked like he had a big grin on his face. Like something good had just happened."

Will and Harry asked a few more background questions, said their goodbyes, and walked back out to the sidewalk. "I guess this would be a good time to visit Josh's place?" Will surmised.

Harry nodded. "Might as well, while we're here." He took a moment to send a text message to the uniforms who were canvassing the area, telling them that a river drag would be necessary. "You need to look for a knife, and you might also find Thad Robinson's watch and wallet."

"A needle in a haystack, Detective," was the immediate reply, and one he had totally expected.

The reply irritated Harry, who didn't like smart-ass text-backs from underlings. "Policy, officer. So get to work."

As they walked past Will's illegally parked car, Harry saw a ticket on the windshield and started laughing. "You are *not* going to like what I just saw."

"What the fuck," was all that Will could manage when he saw the summons. "That's going to cost me hours and a lot of paperwork. Can't these idiots read?"

He was still fuming when they arrived at the B&B. Josh, the proprietor, came to the door wearing an apron. He was a jolly-looking guy, already balding and looking older than his thirties. He greeted Will and Harry with a smile that quickly faded when they produced their detective shields.

"Is there some problem, officers?"

"We're just following up on the attack on the bridge yesterday," Harry said, taking the lead.

"What attack?"

"Didn't a police officer talk to you this morning?"

"Not me. My wife, maybe, but she's asleep. Somebody was attacked?"

"Yes, an attorney named Thaddeus Robinson was stabbed on Harvard Bridge in the early hours of the morning. Your neighbor, Minnie Stohler, said she saw a man running across the bridge. She thinks he went into your place. This would have been about 4 A.M."

"Minnie is a little off her nut. But could have been, I guess. Our guests all have a key so they come and go as they wish."

"So you have no idea if somebody staying at your place came in your front door around that time."

"Nope."

"Can you ask your wife?"

"Sure, she'll be up soon."

"And would you mind if we took a look at your guest list?"

"Uh… is that legal?"

"Do you have something to hide?" Will quickly asked.

"No! Of course not. I just remember something like this happening on *Law and Order*."

Will tried to suppress a grimace. "As good as they are on TV, Josh, they don't always get it right. I don't think there's any law that prohibits us from reviewing your guest list, if we have probable cause. We clearly do."

"If you think it's okay, I'll get it for you."

Josh walked up the hallway to his office and came back in a few minutes with a single piece of paper he handed to Will. "We had five guests last night. Two women, three guys. The women were in a double, everybody else in singles. I wrote all the names down for you."

"Any of them checking out today?" Will asked.

"The two women are, but the men will be here to the end of the week."

"Can you tell us a little about the guys?"

Josh looked down at the book. "I would prefer not to, Detective. I'm really concerned about their privacy. If word got out that we're giving out information about our guests, we wouldn't have a business anymore. And two of the men are regulars here."

Will wasn't happy but he didn't see a reason to push. "Okay, Josh. We'll do a background check on the guys. In the meantime, I'm sure you aren't going to talk to anyone about this… except your wife, of course. When she's up."

"Understood, Detective. But keep me posted. I'm not excited about a murderer maybe staying at our place. It's scary. "

Will and Harry said their goodbyes and walked back to Will's car. "Unless there's something unusual about the women, we can probably ignore them." Harry said. "That leaves three guys to concentrate on."

"Yep. We can run them as soon as we get back to the office. None of them look familiar, and one has a name I never heard before," Will said.

"Is that right? What is it?" Harry asked as he opened the passenger door.

"Sarkis."

"Did you say 'Circus'?" Harry asked.

"No. Sarkis. S-A-R-K-I-S. What kinda name is that?"

Chapter 5

Will and Harry had one more stop before they went back to the station. They drove only a few blocks to pay a brief visit to Maggie Norcross, who was not only already in the bag at lunch time, but had no recollection of meeting or spending an evening with Thad Robinson.

"I have abtholutely no fuckin' idea who you'rl talking 'bout," Maggie mumbled when she came to the door.

"You don't recall a guy named Thad Robinson and having sex with him in your apartment two nights ago?"

Her face reddened. "How dare you 'cuse me of shleepin' 'round!"

"I think we'll come back another time. Is that all right, Ms. Norcross?"

"Thuit yourselv," she said as she closed the door. Will looked at Harry; each shrugged and knew there was little chance of getting any useful information anytime soon from the pickled brain of Ms. Norcross.

"Even if she were sober, I doubt if she has any knowledge of what happened to Robinson," Harry volunteered.

"Back burner, for sure," Will agreed. "But not to be forgotten. She has a husband who could have been pissed off."

"I don't see how he could have returned home fast enough to figure out what happened and then track Robinson down on the bridge."

"Yeah, I suspect you're right. Next time I'm on the computer, I'll see what I can find out about the lovely Norcross couple, and leave it at that."

Neither Will nor Harry said much on the short drive back to the station. They both knew what their next steps would be, and neither was looking forward to it. First, they would have to create a file and begin filling out reports about their investigation. The computers that dominated their tiny work area made this task a little less onerous. Then, they would have to report to Captain Pokorney and let him know where things stood with the investigation. And the part they hated the most was culling through records trying to glean information about the people who were staying in Josh's boarding house before they interviewed any of them.

Harry and Will had worked together for many years; they knew the best way to divide up their tasks. Will, the more introverted of the two, didn't delight in conversations with his superiors or rehashing things he already knew. So he grabbed a cup of well-aged coffee from the common room and immediately set to work at his computer to discover what he could about Mr. Norcross and the three male boarders at Josh's B&B.

Norcross was the easiest. He had in fact been out of town at the time, speaking at some conference where his company was apparently an industry leader. Will also unearthed that Norcross had filed for divorce on the grounds of adultery; even if he had been in town, he was unlikely to care who his "whoring wife" was sleeping with.

Will was always amazed at how quickly people who used to love each other could evolve into bitter enemies. His own divorce had been fairly benign—after his wife had gotten it all out of her system by throwing his belongings out of their bedroom window and telling all their friends what a bastard she had married.

Next came the boarders. He decided to take them in alphabetical order and went directly to the best sources of information money can't buy: Google and Facebook. Joe McGeehin was first, and as it turned out, easy to exclude. He was a middle-aged businessman from Lansing, Michigan, who worked for an insurance company that had its corporate headquarters in Boston. He had no police record, and according to his local constabulary, only a few parking tickets. He was married, had four kids of various school ages, and apparently came to Boston frequently, which probably explained why he was staying at a B&B instead of a hotel. Josh's place was just across the river and an easy walk from his home office building.

Will had started to get interested in Joe until he saw a photo of him on Facebook. Will sat back in his chair and chuckled. No, Joe was not their guy, unless he had found a magical way to lose a lot of weight. Joe was about a 300-pounder, with three chins and flab spilling out of his bathing suit. There was no way Joe could have hauled his carcass across the Harvard Bridge in a dead sprint. "Joe, sometimes it pays to be a fatso," Will said to his computer screen before he moved on to boarder number two.

Robert Price was even easier to exclude. Josh could have saved Will a lot of time if he had told the detectives that Price was eighty years old and needed a cane to get around after a couple of hip operations. He was a retired truck driver who lived in Vermont with his wife. Harry had no idea what the geezer was doing at a Boston B&B but didn't particularly care. They were looking for a runner, and Robert was no gazelle.

That left Sarkis, the guy with the funny name. Philip Sarkis was a doctor—a cardiologist, actually—currently living in the Pocono Mountains of Pennsylvania. He had no Facebook page, but when he Googled Sarkis, Will realized he was in for a long afternoon. There were over ten thousand hits, going back several years, that Will would have to cull through. He was happy to quickly find a recent photo, taken at a promotional event for the medical clinic where Sarkis worked. Will wanted to make sure this boarder was physically capable of running, and he was. In fact, the smiling bearded face was perched atop a lean-looking body that dressed up well in a tuxedo. Sarkis was smiling, his arm casually draped over the shoulders of a stunning woman wearing a black evening gown that showed off an alluring figure. It took a few minutes for Will to take his eyes off her and get on with his search.

Will stood up to stretch and grabbed another cup of coffee before diving into Sarkis' past. He started with the earliest entries he could find and worked forward, slowly piecing together the details of Sarkis' career.

Philip Sarkis was born and raised in the Philly area. Like many physicians, he had professional roots in Boston, having trained in cardiology in the Harvard system before returning to Philadelphia. He had started as a brilliant academic and his meteoric rise brought him to the forefront of his profession in only a few years. He piled up honors and accolades quickly, owing to the ground-breaking research he conducted and the media attention it received in the early years of his career at Gladwyne Memorial Hospital. His cardiology program grew to national prominence, and there was no apparent limit on how far this brilliant doctor might go.

But then Philip was named in a high-profile malpractice case. A prominent Main Line socialite named Moira Hamlin died suddenly and unexpectedly soon after delivering her fourth child, and Philip was sued by the grieving husband, Hugh. The trial captured wide media attention. Philip not only lost the case but punitive damages were added. He and his wife divorced, he left Gladwyne Memorial, and he quickly dropped from public view.

Except for a Philadelphia Inquirer article that appeared several months after the verdict. Philip received a passing mention in a second-pager that reported on the deaths of Hugh Hamlin and a woman named Bonnie Romano. Their bound-and-gagged bodies had been found one morning in the trunk of a limousine submerged in the Schuylkill River. Their deaths occurred two days after a judge dismissed a case in which they were accused of having murdered Hugh's wife, whose death had been the reason for the lawsuit against Philip.

The article contained a quote from a Detective Scotty of the Philadelphia police, who described Philip and his friend Dorothy Deaver as "persons of interest" in the "grisly" murder of Hugh and Bonnie. Aside from the obvious motive, Will couldn't figure out where Scotty's suspicions came from. His Google search for "Dorothy Deaver" found that she was an attorney who had worked in a reputable Philadelphia firm that mainly handled personal injury cases. A photo confirmed that she was the woman on Sarkis' arm. She now worked for a somewhat less prominent firm in Scranton, and had taken up residence with Philip, not far from his clinic.

Nothing about her led Will to believe she was any kind of criminal.

Philip next turned up in a few obscure stories about cardiology care in the Poconos, where Sarkis worked in an outpatient facility owned by Geisinger Medical Center. Despite his obvious expertise, Sarkis received little attention in the medical system advertising, a point not lost on Will.

Will leaned back in his chair and ran his hands through his hair as he tried to integrate the information he had gathered. Sarkis' career path took a major downturn after the malpractice case. The authorities had some reason to indict Hugh and Bonnie for murdering Philip's patient. They got off, but two days later they were drowned to death. Philip and Dorothy headed for the Poconos, where they now live together, and the story ends? Or does it continue when Philip is seen sprinting across a bridge on which a prominent attorney was knifed in the back?

Harry wandered back to their cubicle. "You look deep in thought."

"Deep in shit is more like it."

"I talked to the Captain and filled him in."

"Did he have any brilliant ideas for us?"

"Will, this is Pokorney we're talking about. 'Brilliant' is not an operative word."

"Fair enough."

"What have you come up with?"

Will gave Harry a synopsis of the boarders, focusing mostly on Sarkis, and got back exactly what he expected. "Time to make a few phone calls to Pennsylvania?"

"Yep. I'm going to start with Detective Scotty and see where that leads."

"Okay. I have a couple errands to run. I may stop home for lunch and work from there. I want to start entering information in the case file and keep the captain happy."

"That's what it's all about. God help us if we ever had time to do real police work. We might actually solve some crimes."

"We aren't doing that bad, Will. Anyhow, call or shoot me a text later and let me know if the Pennsylvania people have anything to add."

It only took Will a few minutes to find a phone number for Detective Scotty. He was out of the office, but the person working the phones offered a cell number. Scotty picked up quickly, and Will immediately liked the sound of his voice. Friendly but professional right from the start.

"Detective Scotty, this is Lieutenant Detective Wilson Lentz of the Boston police. I'm working on a stabbing, maybe an attempted murder, in Boston. I have a person from Pennsylvania who was apparently in the area when the attack occurred, and I wanted to get some background information. I saw your name in a newspaper account of a murder that happened in Philadelphia, and hoped you could give us a hand."

"First of all, the name is Lou. Second, I'd be happy to help you if I can. And third, I'm going to have to get confirmation that you are who you say you are before we go on."

"I understand. I'll give you our main switchboard number. You can call there and they'll connect you to me here at the station. Ask for Will Lentz."

"That'll work. I'll call you right back."

Will picked his phone up on the first ring. "Hi, Lou. Is this a good time for you?"

"Sure. Just got in my car, going across town. What would you like to know?"

"The person I'm interested in is named Philip Sarkis. Do you remember him?"

"Quite well. And his partner, Dorothy Deaver."

"Wow. I'm impressed you remembered them both."

"Don't be. They were involved in a couple of incredible cases down here. Makes them hard to forget."

"A *couple* of cases?"

"Well, one here and one up in the Poconos that I wasn't directly involved with."

"Can we start with your case? That's the one I read about."

"I guess you know, then, that Sarkis was sued and lost a big verdict to Hamlin after his wife died. Sarkis took it hard and ended up a derelict. Damn near killed himself, from what I hear. He got involved with Dorothy Deaver and her PI father Dick Deaver, and they pulled together enough evidence to convince a suburban DA to bring an indictment against Hugh and his girlfriend, Bonnie Romano."

"So Sarkis and Deaver got all that going?"

"Yeah, they did. But the case was thrown out of court at an evidentiary hearing. Seems the judge believed that the recording of Hugh and Bonnie's confession had been taped illegally. I don't remember all the details, but they got off. Two days later, they were fish bait."

"Right. The article about their deaths is where I found your name."

"Sarkis and Deaver were conveniently out of town when the murders occurred, and we couldn't find anything to tie them to it. Besides, it looked like a professional job, and they didn't have the money or the juice to arrange anything like that."

"So they walked."

"Clean as a whistle, but the story doesn't end there."

"Whatever happened next is news to me. I couldn't find anything else in the media."

"You do know they moved to the Poconos. He got a job in a clinic, and she's at a new law firm. About two years after they went up there, I got a call from a Lieutenant Steven Detweiler. It seems they got involved in another medical malpractice case that escalated into a murder conspiracy, or so they thought."

"What happened?"

"Detweiler called me again a few months later and told me that some nurses had burned to death in a fire at their agency headquarters. He was pretty agitated. I saw pieces of the story in the news, but I can't tell you how it got resolved. I suggest you call him directly. He's a nice guy and I'm sure he'll help you out."

"I'll look him up. Is it okay to tell him you sent me?"

"Sure. Us cops have to stick together," Scotty laughed. "Good luck with your investigation, Will. I'd appreciate it if you kept me posted on what you learn. Call it idle curiosity."

Will thanked Scotty and wasted no time getting hold of Detweiler, who answered the phone himself at the Scranton police station.

"Detweiler here."

"Lieutenant, my name is Will Lentz. I'm a Boston homicide detective. I just got off the phone with Detective Lou Scotty, from Philly, and he suggested I give you a call."

Detweiler paused. "I'm afraid I don't remember who Scotty is."

"Maybe the name Philip Sarkis will help."

Again silence, but this time not because of recognition problems. "I have to tell you that I've been trying to forget that name for the last couple of years."

"Unpleasant memories, Lieutenant?"

"You could say that. He and that woman he lives with, Dorothy Deaver, did a lot of damage up here and almost cost me my job."

"Can you give me the short version of what happened?" Will wondered if Detweiler would ask for verification of Will's identity, but Scrantonites were apparently a lot less suspicious than Philly folks.

"I guess so. I could also send you some of the police reports. But first you have to tell me why a Boston detective wants to know about Sarkis and Deaver."

"That's fair. Sarkis was one of the boarders at a B&B not far from an attack made on a well-known attorney recently. The other boarders don't look interesting, but Sarkis fits for a few reasons. I'm trying to learn a little more about the guy. Deaver isn't in my case, at least as far as I know."

Detweiler gave Will his version of the Adolphus Nursing Agency case. "They came to me with their suspicion that Adolphus was a front for a neo-Nazi organization that was mercy-killing old men who had served in World War II against the Fatherland."

"Were they ever able to prove anything?"

"They were convinced, but they never had enough to arrest anybody. Next thing you know, a building used by the agency for meetings burned to the ground with a bunch of the nurses in it. We discovered that the windows had been nailed shut and the fire had been started by some pros posing as heating maintenance men who apparently set up the fire the afternoon before."

"I vaguely remember hearing about this. But I don't remember anything about a conspiracy."

"We kept the murder angle under wraps. We didn't have enough evidence to prove anything, we never found the perps, and nobody wanted the negative publicity. So we let it go as an accident, which is what our crime people filed in their official report. The whole thing made the national news. The nurses were all veterans who decided to work in this underserved area. The vice president even came up for their memorial service."

"So you suspect this guy Sarkis and his girlfriend had something to do with the nurses getting roasted?"

"I do, but there was nothing to tie them to the deaths. It was a professional job, and I couldn't figure out how they could have done it, arranged it, or paid for it. And they were out of town when the fire occurred—at some restaurant in Philly with Deaver's father, as I remember. So we didn't pursue it."

Will was silent as he mulled things over. Twice in the past hour, law enforcement professionals had told him about professional-grade killings of people who were themselves guilty of murder, at least in the eyes of Sarkis and Deaver, but in both cases there was insufficient evidence to tie them to the deed. And in both cases, their out-of-town alibis held up quite nicely.

"Will, are you still there?"

"Sorry, Lieutenant. This has been very helpful; thank you. Would you mind sending me any relevant reports?"

"No problem. I'll give you my email address. Just send me a formal request and your mailing address or fax number, and I'll get the stuff to you."

They hung up, and Will immediately opened a Word file on his computer and starting typing, pecking away as fast as his two index fingers would let him. He wanted to get everything he had learned in writing and to share it with Harry before the sun went down.

Chapter 6

Will phoned Harry that evening. Will normally avoided after-hours calls to his partner. Harry was a family man and enjoyed spending time with his kids, and Will wanted to respect that. Just because he was alone didn't mean everybody else had to be available twenty-four hours a day. This call was necessary, however. Will was contemplating an interview with Sarkis, and he had only a few days until this suspect was due to check out and presumably leave town.

Harry answered the phone after several rings, a little short of breath.

"Did I catch you at a bad time, partner? You weren't getting lucky, by any chance?"

Harry laughed. "I'm married, friend. Getting lucky during the week is a thing of the past. I was just outside shooting hoops with the kids. Maribel is out grocery shopping."

Maribel was Harry's wife. She was born in Puerto Rico before coming to the states for an Ivy League med-school education that she parlayed into a top spot in the medicine department at MGH. Harry met her when she was an intern rotating through the ER and he was a uniform cop. After spying her good looks, he started to look for derelicts in the MGH neighborhood he could take in for medical care, hoping for another chance to talk to the pretty intern. It didn't take long for Maribel to notice that this handsome officer was checking her out, and in her typically direct manner, she asked Harry if he wanted to go out for a drink. That was twenty years ago, and they hadn't looked back.

"I don't want to keep you, Harry, but I just wanted to pick your brain. I talked to a couple of cops in Pennsylvania today, and I'm beginning to like Sarkis as our guy. Or at least he's mixed up in this somehow."

"I'm listening. Talk to me."

Will summarized what he had learned from Detweiler and Scotty. "I wrote a pretty long memo and emailed it to you late this afternoon. It has more than what I just told you, but the gist is that this guy has a history of being at the edge of a couple of nasty crimes. I can't imagine what his connection is in this case, but I don't see a downside to talking to him and then doing a deeper background check while he's still in Boston. What d'ya think?"

"Let me read the document after the kids are in bed, and if I agree, we can talk to the guy tomorrow."

"I'd like to surprise him a little, so I was thinking we could stake out the B&B tomorrow afternoon and wait for him to get back from whatever he's doing up here."

"Sounds like a plan. I could spend the morning digging into his background a little more so we have extra ammo."

"Great. I have that worthless court appearance in the morning so I'll meet you at the station after lunch and we'll go from there."

They rang off, Harry back to kid hoops, and Will to the freezer for a frozen dinner and a basketball game on TV. The Celtics were driving him nuts again this year, making a late season April run and flirting with the playoffs. And the Bruins were doing much the same thing, except they were trying to make a season out of it without a quality goaltender, having never replaced the late, great Sebastian Bergstrom. Nevertheless, Will, like every other die-hard Boston sports fanatic, kept rooting for the home teams. For men like Will, when you're Boston-born and Boston-bred, that's what you do.

The Celtics blew an early lead against the hated Sixers, and Will, as he had so many times, fell asleep on the sofa long before the Celtics regrouped and won the game. He awoke as the sun peeked through his yellowing venetian blinds. He had only a few minutes to shower, gulp a cup of instant coffee, and get to the courthouse to meet with the lawyer before the evidentiary hearing.

The subject of the hearing was a loser named Lashawn James, whom Will had collared several months earlier for attempted murder. Seems Lashawn was out partying and screwing another woman and came home to his apartment to find his wife doing the same thing—screwing another woman. This hurt Lashawn's pride so much that he went to the kitchen, grabbed a knife, came back into the bedroom, and started stabbing anything moving in the bed. Their cat was the only thing Lashawn hit directly; his wife and her lover were merely wounded. Neighbors heard the screaming and came charging into the apartment. They tackled Lashawn and sat on him until the uniforms showed up.

Will was called in to investigate. He didn't see much

of a mystery. The arrested and blood-soaked Lashawn was taken into custody. At his arraignment, the judge allowed bail, over the strong objections of the assistant DA, and today was the first time Lashawn was supposed to appear for a legal proceeding. But surprise: Lashawn didn't show up. Will wasted his entire morning sitting in court while the dumb ass barristers argued over what to do next.

On the way to the station, Will stopped to grab a hot dog from a street vendor, and then met up with Harry, who was sitting at his desk, feet up once again, re-reading Will's summary from the day before.

"I'm getting the distinct feeling that Robinson is not a real likeable guy," Harry observed.

"Me too. I'm trying to preserve some objectivity, but even Michelle, the person who knows him best, said he's an asshole."

"But aside from his wife who got screwed with a questionable pre-nup document, I'm not sure we have anybody who got hurt bad enough to want to maim him, or maybe kill him."

"I agree, at least not based on the superficial stuff we have so far. Unless Sarkis turns into an easy collar, we'll have to interview lots of people to see if any of them were pissed off enough to do the deed."

"Speaking of which, what's the plan for this afternoon?"

"I thought we could mosey on over to the B&B in an hour or two and see if he's in his room. If not, we can camp out until he shows up."

"I assume it'll be a low-stress interview?"

"Absolutely. We have no reason to go after him hard. All we have is that nutty lady who saw somebody running across the bridge around the time Robinson was attacked. Ain't much."

They worked a little longer at their desks, left the station, and headed over to Cambridge. It was another splendid spring day in Boston, a city that didn't have a lot of excellent weather, but sparkled when it did. And everybody who could be outside was. The river was alive with rowers tuning up for the crew season, while men and women, young and old, biked and walked and mostly just basked in the sunshine on the lawns along the shores of the Charles.

This time, Will and Harry found a legal parking space and made sure the meter was fed before leaving the car to visit Josh's B&B. They were greeted by Josh's wife, Marie, a portly woman with a friendly face and a big smile, greeting two men whom she hoped were new customers. She was barely able to hide her disappointment when they flashed their identification.

"Oh yeah, Josh told me about you gentlemen. How can I help you?"

"Do you happen to know if Dr. Sarkis is in his room?"

"No, he hasn't come back from his meeting yet?"

"Meeting?"

"Yes, he told us he was attending a cardiology meeting at the convention center."

"Do you know why he was staying up here, and not closer to the convention center?"

"He said he was tired of the crowds at the meeting hotels and wanted to get away from the noise. He lived in Boston when he was younger, and I think he likes this part of Cambridge."

"We need to ask him a few questions. Would you mind if we wait for him?"

"Not at all. He's been getting back around this time most days and then going out for a run, so I suspect you won't have to wait too long. Would you like to use our sitting room?"

Harry answered first. "Beats sitting in the car."

After seeing the "sitting room," neither of them was so sure. It looked like a 'fifties dark living room, with heavy drapes, an old sagging sofa, worn carpets, sparse scratched furniture, and end table lamps that put out the only light in the room. Harry went to get his laptop from the car while Will thumbed through the outdated magazines, finally settling on a year-old *Sports Illustrated*, chronicling the return of the Red Sox. How wrong had they been? The Sox had taken a steep nosedive the previous season that led to the firing of their controversial manager and several of his cronies. But now it was spring and a new baseball season was here, so hope sprang forth once again. That's what Will liked about sports—there was always next year, always a chance for things to change for the better. Unlike homicide, where everything was so damn final.

Will and Harry sat for about an hour, trying hard not to look at the clock. Though they were veterans, they never got used to the endless waiting on stake-outs, or in the courtroom, or wherever else their cases took them. Will got up to stretch a few times while Harry clacked away, trying to finish a report on another case that Captain Pokorney had informed him was long overdue.

Finally, they heard the front door open. Will peeked around the corner and glimpsed the man who had to be Sarkis. This person had a beard and wire-rimmed glasses, not looking exactly like the photo Will had found on the Internet. But he was about the same size, on the short side and in good shape, with brown eyes, a full head of graying black hair, and a dark complexion. He was dressed conservatively in corduroys, vest sweater, and tweed jacket, carrying a computer bag. Yep, this had to be their man.

Before Will had a chance to approach Sarkis, Marie came out of the kitchen to greet her guest. "Hi, Dr. Sarkis. How was your day?"

Will was happy to hear Marie pronounce Sarkis' name: "*Sar-KEECE.*" Hopefully she had it right. Saying people's name correctly was a matter of professional pride for Will. Rhymes with *police*, he thought to himself. Should be able to remember that.

Before Sarkis had a chance to answer Marie, Will and Harry walked into the entryway to introduce themselves.

"Dr. Sarkis, Hi. I'm Lieutenant Detective Wilson Lentz and this is my partner Sergeant Detective Harry Socks." They flashed their badges. "We work at Boston Homicide. I wonder if we could ask you a few questions."

Philip registered what Will thought was genuine surprise. "Homicide? Why on earth do you want to talk to me?"

"I'm sorry, Dr. Sarkis. I should have explained. An attorney named Thaddeus Robinson was attacked on the Harvard Bridge two nights ago…"

"Somebody killed him?"

"No, he survived, but Homicide is sometimes assigned to serious assaults; given Mr. Robinson's high profile, we were assigned to the case, and..."

"So what do you want with me?"

"If I may continue, sir, we have reason to believe you may have been in the area at the time and might be able to help us identify the assailant. Would you mind if we explored that a little with you? It would be very helpful to our investigation, and I promise it won't take long."

Sarkis hesitated but realized he had little choice. "Do I need an attorney?"

"That's up to you, of course, but I can promise you that you're not a suspect, and the questioning will be pretty general. If you're uncomfortable at any time, we'll stop and you can get whatever legal help you desire."

"I guess it'll be all right."

"Why don't we do this in the sitting room? Marie, would you mind if we closed the door?" Harry asked.

"By all means. My other guests rarely use the room and they're out anyway."

Will and Harry sat on the sofa and Sarkis the armchair. Will took a notebook out of his breast pocket. "Do you want some water before we start, Doctor?"

"I'm fine. Let's get on with this," Sarkis said, trying hard not to sound nervous.

"I realize this is intimidating, but as I said, we're just looking for witnesses or anyone who can shed light on what happened to Mr. Robinson."

Harry began. "Dr. Sarkis, are you a runner?"

"I am."

"And do you usually run very early in the morning?"

"I do, except when I'm attending meetings, when I sometimes run in the afternoon. Like today, I hope."

"And were you out running early Wednesday morning?"

"Yes, at about 4 A.M., as I remember."

"Wow. Now that's early."

"It's become a habit. I try to run outside when the weather allows. Otherwise I use a treadmill or elliptical trainer."

"Did you run along the Charles?"

"Of course. Where else in Boston would anyone want to run? It's one of the big reasons I stay out here."

"And did you come back across the Harvard Bridge to finish your run?"

"I did."

"Did you see or hear anything unusual?"

"No. I remember thinking how peaceful it was, actually."

"Think hard, Doctor. Did you see anyone on the bridge?"

Sarkis paused, thinking.

"Well, now that you mention it, I did see a guy standing at the other end of the bridge—on the Boston side."

"What did he look like?"

"Like a guy. Medium build. African American, I think. He had a hoody on, so I couldn't really see much of his face. I think he had a mustache."

"What was he doing?"

Just standing there, leaning on a column, arms folded. Like he was waiting for somebody."

"Do you know about what time you saw this person?"

"It had to be close to 5 A.M. My run was just about over."

Silence while Will scribbled on his notepad. He looked up. "Doctor, do you know Thaddeus Robinson?"

"You mean, know him personally? No, I don't. I've heard of him."

"How so?"

"He's been involved in some pretty high-profile medical malpractice cases and has a reputation."

"A good one?"

"I guess that depends on your perspective. As a physician, I wouldn't describe him as a superhero."

"Would you say he's a villain?"

"I don't know if I'd go that far. Let's just say that he's an aggressive plaintiff malpractice attorney."

"Have you had a lot of experience with people like Mr. Robinson?" Will asked, eager for the answer.

Sarkis stared at Will for a good two or three seconds before replying, "If you're a good detective, you know the answer to that question."

"You got me, Doctor. I confess that I chatted briefly with Detectives Scotty and Detweiler yesterday. They were helpful."

"I'm not going to talk about those cases, Detective. Except to say that I had nothing to do with the deaths of Hamlin and Romano or those Adolphus nurses, as I'm sure you learned in your conversations."

"I understand, Doctor. I'm not accusing you of anything, but you can appreciate our curiosity in light of your previous experiences."

Harry followed up. "Awfully coincidental that an 'aggressive malpractice attorney' was stabbed almost in front of a man who has your background, don't you think?"

Sarkis stood up. "I was afraid our conversation would take this track. I've told you everything I know. Do you have any other questions?"

"No, Doctor," Will said, rising to face Sarkis. "How much longer will you be in Boston—in case we have to talk with you again?"

"I leave Saturday afternoon, after my meeting is over."

"Terrific. I hope you have a good rest of the meeting and a safe trip home. Let me give you my card. Please call or email me if you remember anything else about yesterday morning."

"I will, Detective."

Harry also stood up, intentionally bringing his face close to Sarkis'. "And, Doctor, think very hard about what you saw. It would be helpful if you could remember what that guy on the bridge looked like."

"I'll do my best, Detective Socks."

Harry and Will left the B&B and walked slowly to their car. "Holy shit," Will cried out when his car windshield came into view. "Another fucking parking ticket!

How long were we in that damn place? Can't these ticket maids find something else to do?"

"So what do you think?" Harry asked Will after they got into the car and Will had settled down.

"About Sarkis? I think I need to do some more background research. In fact, I have nothing to do tonight so I might just hammer at the old computer in the office after the place empties out."

"Good idea, Will. We definitely need some intel on this guy. There's something about him—I just can't put my finger on it."

"Neither can I Harry—at least not yet."

Chapter 7

Will dropped Harry off at his car. "Good hunting, Will" Harry said as he exited, wondering if Will caught the movie reference. "I hope you come up with something we can use."

"Yeah, me too."

"Go back as far as you can, and you might get lucky."

"I'll let you know. Say hi to Maribel for me. And I hope you get lucky too."

Harry gave a faint smile, closed the passenger door, got into his Prius, and drove away. Will pulled his heap into the empty space. He wearily climbed the precinct steps, already planning his evening. First there would be a call to the local pizza establishment. That would be easy—Will was such a regular that the proprietor knew his voice and wouldn't even ask what toppings he wanted or what soft drink went with the order. The hard part would be going on Google to check out hundreds of hits for "Philip Sarkis," looking for a clue about the guy. It was all about motive. What would have driven an out-of-town doc to stalk a malpractice attorney and stick a knife in his back?

The office buzz gradually died down. Most of the detective staff were on their way home; only a few stragglers were on phones or staring bleary-eyed into their computer screens. The pizza and Coke arrived promptly, delivered by a disheveled man who looked and smelled like he had been scraped off a sidewalk grate and given a set of car keys. The box was sealed, providing some reassurance that the food inside had not been contaminated. But the seed of doubt had been planted, and Will only ate a couple of slices before offering it around to the remnants of the station's staff.

Will's first task was to get more detail about Sarkis. Seems the guy had been a hotshot academic before his fall from grace in Philly a few years before. He had hundreds of publications in medical journals and he must have traveled like a maniac, giving presentations every which where. But Will wanted to explore the most important fact he had about Sarkis: he had trained in Boston years ago, at the old Peter Bent Brigham Hospital. He had roots in the area.

Will called up several of Sarkis' publications from those early years. Most of them reflected an academic career on the rise: some talks at local meetings and medical societies, and presentations of his early work under the mentorship of Bernard Lowenstein, the distinguished Nobel Laureate, and an international figure who also happened to be a political liberal. Lowenstein had been accused of being a communist early in his own career, and was investigated by Joe McCarthy's Senate subcommittee. He had been judged a small fish, so the case wasn't pursued, but the accusations cast a shadow over Lowenstein's career that was never completely expunged. Will played with the idea for a while, but couldn't find anything linking Sarkis to left-wing groups. Lowenstein's mentoring of Sarkis appeared to be entirely on the medical side of things, and faded after

Sarkis had departed Boston.

Sarkis' four productive years in Boston were followed by his return to Philadelphia, in whose suburbs he had grown up, to start a program at Gladwyne Memorial Hospital. Will stared at Sarkis' face as the young doctor stood in the second row of his fellowship graduation photograph, which appeared in the *Harvardian*. He had a mustache and long hair, but otherwise looked very much as he did now, with that smirk he passed off as a smile. His classmates appeared happy and eager to launch their careers, confident of success after training in what was arguably the most prestigious cardiology program in the world.

Will scanned the photo caption. He recognized none of the names and wondered where these physicians were now and what they were doing. As he chewed on a hunk of crust, Will realized that one of the names was familiar—and so was the face. He quickly went back to Google and typed in "Mario Angelucci" and was not surprised to see that the number of "Angelucci" entries surpassed Sarkis' many times over. And he didn't have to open many of them to unleash a flood of memories about a case that had rocked Boston—the tragic death of Sebastian Bergstrom.

Will was a hockey fan, and he followed the Bruins religiously. But over the past three years, any Bostonian, Bruin fan or not, would have had to be deaf, dumb, and blind not to know about the Bergstrom case. It had been covered fully in the Boston press, occasionally bubbling up to make the national and even the international news, as the bizarre series of events unfolded. Will went back to search mode, typing in "Bergstrom" and "Boston magazine" to find the article he had recently seen, a very long piece, in which the story was told in excruciating detail.

Sebastian Bergstrom was born and raised in a little town near Stockholm. Ice hockey was THE game in his town, played most of the year on the many lakes and ponds that bordered the town where he lived. Known as Sebby to his friends, he took to the game quickly when he was a boy. He wasn't a strong or fast skater, but he was a natural goaltender with quick reflexes and remarkable hand-eye coordination. Success in youth leagues fueled his enthusiasm, and his father's too. Sebby and his father Karl would spend many winter hours on a frozen lake near their home and just as many summer hours at the local indoor rink, Karl firing pucks from point-blank range, challenging his son to stop them with a kick of his leg pad or a flash of his glove. Over time, Karl, himself an excellent amateur right winger, and others who faced Sebby were rarely able to get anything past him. By the time he was sixteen, he was invited to enter the national junior hockey league in Sweden, reserved for elite young players.

Now under the tutelage of Sweden's top coaches, Sebby progressed rapidly. He had an unmatched work ethic, and begged his coaches to spend extra time with him, before and after regular practices and games, honing his technique, sharpening his skills, and building his confidence. The young netminder regarded any goal scored against him as a personal failure, but was self-assured enough to shove any opposing player who came near the crease. He made himself into a good puck handler, and excelled at making crisp up-ice passes to his forwards. An assist, Sebby told his mates, was worth a hundred saves. He even managed to score a few game-clinching empty-net goals.

It didn't take long for professional scouts to discover the Swedish phenom. They came from all over Europe as well as Canada and the US to attend Sebby's games. Karl Bergstrom insisted that his son had to complete two years of junior hockey before he would be allowed to venture into the major leagues, but everyone was convinced that Sebby was going to be a top draft choice whenever he was ready. And Sebby and his dad knew that the destination was the ultimate hockey proving ground, the National Hockey League.

Sebby stayed healthy and matured as he and his father had hoped. At the age of eighteen, he entered the NHL draft. The Bergstroms decided that Sebby didn't need a professional agent; Karl, a businessman of some stature in Stockholm, would represent him and met regularly with the teams likely to draft his son.

At the top of the list were the Boston Bruins. They had just come off a disappointing season, making the playoffs with a two-seed, but then getting eliminated by a scrappy Ranger team. The reason: poor goaltending. They had put up an average of 4.8 goals in the five-game series, but had surrendered more than 6. Tom Timmons, their veteran goaltender, had seemingly run out of gas after a long and exhausting season in which he had played all but ten games. Their backup goalie was a journeyman whom they had decided to use only in emergencies. That had been a mistake. Timmons needed a strong, young backup to lighten his load, and an heir apparent. It was time to go to the draft well. Karl and Sebby studied the Bruins and decided that they had the talent to complement Sebby's skills. It could be an excellent match.

But the young talent was thin that year. There were only a few goalies in the draft who had a chance to make an immediate impact. Sebby was at the top of that short list. The Bruins front office knew he would be gone long before they had a chance to draft him as their own first-

round pick. The general manager called the teams whose woeful records the year before were about to be rewarded with high draft picks. The Islanders, Canucks, and Lightning, fully aware of the Bruins' need, all had the same thing to say: if you want the Swedish kid, we want some real talent and some of your young prospects in return. The Bruins had little choice but to offer a package of promising players that made most of their fans groan in dismay. Nevertheless, the deal was done with the Islanders, who gave the Bruins the top pick in the draft with the Islanders receiving a future of their own in exchange. The Bruins drafted Bergstrom, and immediately began to plan how they would get him ready for the big time.

But first came contract negotiations. Karl Bergstrom was a strong advocate for his son, and he had done his research. He knew what Sebby's value to the team would be, and that his son would be in a Bruins uniform very soon. He rejected a junior league salary, and demanded several million dollars. The team balked but understood that they needed to sign the young man or risk being lynched by the Boston fans, who were already angry about the players given up in the Islanders deal. A contract agreement was finally reached based on one essential compromise by each party: the Bruins agreed to hire Karl as an assistant coach, and Karl agreed that half of the money he sought for his son would be paid only if Sebby hit certain milestones, including making the All-Star team, ending the season with a goals-against average of less than 3.0, and being named Rookie of the Year. Hit all the milestones, and everyone would do just fine.

After many internal discussions, the Bruins' brass decided to assign the Bergstroms to Boston's American Hockey League franchise in Providence. They wanted

Sebby to play regularly, and to be tutored by the Providence coach, himself a retired NHL netminder who knew all the tricks the NHL veterans would unleash on his unwitting protégé. Sebby was reassured that he had a stamped ticket to the big leagues as soon as everyone felt comfortable with his early experience at Providence.

Within a month of the start of the AHL season, all questions about Sebby were answered. Although still a youth, he played like a man among boys. Despite a porous defense in front of him, he was an impenetrable barrier. Playing every game, his goals-against average was a ludicrously stingy 1.1. He stopped nearly everything, allowed few rebound opportunities, and handled the puck adroitly. He was the consummate stand-up goalie, rarely going into a butterfly, covering the crease with unexpected speed, and a cool demeanor had come to characterize his play. His seeming impassivity was reinforced by the unchanging expression on the plain white mask he wore. Providence fans nicknamed him The Ice Berg. He played big, and he played cool. Nothing got past The Ice Berg.

Meanwhile, up in the NHL, Tom Timmons was off to a wretched start with the Bruins. He hadn't fully recovered from last year's late-season injures, hadn't kept himself in good shape in the offseason, and couldn't focus on the task at hand. He started to blame his defensemen, and quickly lost their confidence. The coaching staff knew it would be a tough season with Timmons in goal, and were more than ready to consider alternatives.

The call came in late November. Sebby and Karl were watching a movie at their modest apartment when the phone rang. Sebby answered, listened silently, and thirty seconds later said "Okay" and hung up. He told his father he was to report to the Bruins practice the next morning at eleven. They exchanged nods, and went back to the movie, content that Sebby's destination was now in view. The following day, they drove up to Boston. Sebby was issued a practice uniform and told to work out with the team in preparation for his first NHL start that evening at home against the Philadelphia Flyers.

Sebby played brilliantly that night and for the rest of the season. Timmons was relegated to the bench, seeing action only when the Bruins had back-to-back games. Sebby, however, played relentlessly, the grind of the season having no obvious effect on his enthusiasm or his skills. It seemed that each time he was presented with a new challenge he would elevate his game a notch or two.

Sebby excelled against the elite teams, and played even better in the playoffs. The Bruins made it to the Stanley Cup semi-finals for the first time in several years, losing a low-scoring series to a Penguins team that effectively shut down the Bruins offense. Sebby was named Rookie of the Year in a landslide, won the Vezina trophy as the NHL's top goaltender, and received a respectable number of votes for the league's Most Valuable Player award.

Sebby returned to Sweden, a country quietly proud of its new national hero. Not since Bjorn Borg had anyone represented their country with such cool, measured excellence. Karl and others in Sebby's family protected him as best they could from the US media that followed him home, and the modest goaltender managed to have some well-deserved fun with his friends that summer. He was, after all, still pretty much a kid.

As the next season began, Bruins fans were buzzing with anticipation. Expectations were high as fans assumed that their star goalkeeper would put them in position to get to, and then win the Stanley Cup finals. And it certainly looked that way in the early going. Sebby was again brilliant, registering four shutouts in the Bruins' first twelve games, backing up a defense that grew more confident as the season progressed. He loved shoot-outs and penalty shots because of the unique test of his abilities that they represented. Opposing gunners tried every trick to put one in the back of the net against the young goalie, and invariably he turned their shots away. On these occasions, the Boston fans rhythmically chanted the nickname that had followed Sebby from Providence. "I-I-I-I-C-E berg, I-I-I-I-C-E berg." As defeated opponents skated away, Sebby smiled behind his mask. No one could see it, of course. But his father Karl knew.

Shortly after the Christmas holidays, the Bruins were at the Boston Garden playing the pesky Rangers, one of the few teams that seemed to be able to solve the Bergstrom puzzle. It was the third period. The Rangers were leading, 3 to 2, and were on a power play. A bullet from the right point was tipped by a Bruin defenseman, and Sebby made a reflex glove save. What happened next was clearly shown on the live broadcast, and the replay would be watched millions of times around the world. Sebby extended his open glove to the linesman, then suddenly crumpled to his knees and fell face first onto the ice. His mask and pads prevented injury. The linesman and referee who had been stationed behind the net immediately came to his side but before they could do anything, Sebby came to, rolled onto his back, and sat up on the ice, staying that way for several seconds, dazed and confused, and unable to respond to questions from the players and officials now gathered around him.

Karl, who had been standing behind the Bruins bench, ran onto the ice. He could get Sebby to answer questions, but his son was clearly not himself and unable to carry on. After a brief examination by the team physi-

cian, Sebby was removed from the game in favor of Timmons, taken to the locker room, and eventually transported with the team doctor to New England Presbyterian, the closest hospital, and also the team's "official" hospital.

Over the next twenty-four hours, Sebby was subjected to dozens of tests measuring every aspect of his brain and heart, the two organs most likely to have malfunctioned to cause loss of consciousness. The doctors could find nothing conclusive. All players have a full battery of tests in the preseason, and Sebby had passed all of them. The only abnormality discovered had been thickened walls of the left ventricle, the chamber that pumps blood to the body and major organs. Many athletes have this finding—Sebby's was a little thicker than others'. But with no history of a cardiac problem in Sebby or his family, the Presbyterian physicians discounted its importance.

They watched Sebby for three days at Presbyterian before discharging him. He was instructed to stay home and rest and to stay off the ice for another few days until he recovered his strength. Karl was deeply concerned. He repeatedly asked the doctors to explain what had happened to his boy, and was frustrated when they shrugged their shoulders and said they didn't know for sure. "So how can you tell me he'll be all right if you can't tell me what happened?" Karl asked, in a way that sounded more like a plea.

"Mr. Bergstrom," they would reply, "Most people who pass out have nothing wrong with their heart and do just fine. We just have to make sure he gets enough fluids while he's playing. He was probably just a little dehydrated."

"But he's been playing hockey for years and has never passed out. He knows that he must drink water

during a game. That's why he keeps two bottles on the top of the net. He drinks whenever play is stopped. Dehydration could not be the reason," Karl said.

"People can suddenly develop a low blood pressure and faint at any time. It's a very common problem. We aren't worried."

Well, I'm worried, Karl thought. He was concerned that the team doctors might discount Sebby's problem so they could get their franchise player back on the ice. So, immediately after Sebby's discharge, Karl searched the Internet, spoke to some friends, and eventually came up with the name of a cardiologist who had been on the cover of Boston Magazine, acclaimed as the "best heart doctor in Boston." He called the cardiology office at Mass General.

"I would like to speak with Dr. Mario Angelucci, please."

The polite secretary asked, "Is this in reference to a patient?"

"Yes, I want to arrange for my son to be admitted to your hospital."

"And your son's name?"

"Sebastian Bergstrom."

The secretary couldn't help herself. "The hockey player?"

"Yes."

"Oh my. Well, let me get Dr. Angelucci for you right away."

And she really meant "right away." Angelucci picked up in about ten seconds. "Mr. Bergstrom, this is Dr. Angelucci. How can I help you?"

"You heard what happened to my son?"

"Yes; it's been all over the news. I was very sorry to hear it."

"I would like you to admit my son and check him over

before he rejoins the team."

"I'd be happy to see him. Can you bring him to my office this afternoon?"

"Not the office, doctor. I would like him in the hospital, so you and the other doctors can see him, and do whatever you must to find out why he passed out and what we need to do to prevent it from happening again."

"Wasn't he just in the hospital, Mr. Bergstrom?"

"Yes, and they did a great many tests. I'll make sure you are sent all the results, but please repeat whatever you like."

"Mr. Bergstrom, I have to warn you that your insurance company may not cover any of this."

"I'm not concerned about the money, Doctor. Sebastian is a millionaire, and we'll pay cash if we must. I'm not sure I trust the team doctors. They want my son to play at all costs. I don't think they have his best interests in mind."

"All right, Mr. Bergstrom. We'll make the arrangements. My office will call you back with instructions within an hour. By the way, how did you get to me?"

"Back in Sweden I'm a businessman, Dr. Angelucci. I gather information before taking action. And my information says you're the best heart doctor in this town."

"That's a little bit of an exaggeration. I do run the heart center here, but I will emphasize that we work as a team. There will be a number of doctors and nurses who will see your son with me."

"I understand, Doctor, and the more the better. All I ask is that when you have finished examining my son, you will give me your assurance that he will be fine. I don't care if he never plays hockey again. I just want him not to die."

"You have my word, Mr. Bergstrom, that I'll do my very best."

Chapter 8

Will was getting bleary-eyed from staring into the computer. He looked over at the clock: midnight already. He continued to plow through the "Angelucci" citations, trying to determine what had really happened to Sebby Bergstrom and Mario Angelucci. Everyone in Boston knew how Sebby's story ended: another sudden collapse on the ice (this time during a playoff game in Washington), a poorly performed resuscitation by inexperienced team doctors, severe brain damage, and weeks on a ventilator until his grief-stricken father requested that care be discontinued so Sebby could be allowed to die. And then the public battles over the legality of letting him die with dignity, ended by Sebby's death weeks later from the inevitable complications of brain damage. And finally, an autopsy report that took months to be made public, and again showed thick heart walls but no pathology to explain Sebby's tragic sudden death.

And what about Angelucci? The ignominy of having his most famous patient die of the very thing he was supposed to be treating him for, and with millions of people following the story. The scorn heaped on him by the

Boston fans and entire sports community for his apparent negligence. His fall from the academic heights it had taken him so long to scale. And finally his death in a one-car accident that had all the hallmarks of suicide, after a Pyrrhic victory in one of the bitterest malpractice cases in US history.

Will leaned back in his chair, rubbed his eyes, yawned, and tried to think clearly about the next logical steps. He wondered whether Philip Sarkis felt any lingering allegiance to his long-ago fellow trainee Mario Angelucci. And if he did, might it have been strong enough to have prompted him to exact revenge on Thaddeus Robinson for his role in the malpractice case against Mario?

"There's only one way to find out, and it ain't going to be on Facebook," Will said aloud to no one in particular. He wrote a note to the administrative assistant who helped with logistical support for the detectives. She was usually swamped with requests but if he got this one to her early, he might have a reply by lunchtime. "Need an address and phone number for a Deborah Angelucci, widow of Dr. Mario Angelucci, former member of the cardiology department at Mass General. By 10 A.M. if possible. Thanks." Then he texted Harry who was probably snoring at home in his bed. "Will be in about 10. We may have a lead."

Will drove home, parked his car, glanced at his mail, and collapsed onto his bed fully clothed. He was asleep for about fifteen minutes (or so it seemed) before his cell phone awakened him. It was Harry.

"Harry, why the hell are you calling me again in the middle of the night?"

"Will, it's after 10 A.M. Open your shades and let the sunshine in."

"Crap, I can't believe I slept this long."

"Seems to be turning into a habit, my friend."

"Did you get my text last night?"

"Well, actually it was about 2 A.M., and yes, I got it. Is the lead you've got named Deborah Angelucci?"

"Yeah. How did you know?"

"The admin put your note back on your desk with the address and phone number. I assumed this is what you were referring to in your text message."

"Okay. Well, she's the wife of the doctor who was sued in the Sebby Bergstrom case and then killed himself."

"And we want to talk to her why?"

"Her husband and Sarkis trained together at the Brigham. They were probably friends."

"And…"

"Give me a fucking break, Harry. Robinson was the lawyer for the Bergstrom family. It was their lawsuit that pushed her husband over the edge. Connect the dots."

"Interesting. So you want to find out if Sarkis had a revenge motive."

"Elementary, my dear fuck."

"Okay, Will. How about I call this lady and we go see her this morning?"

"See her where?"

"Looks like she lives and works in Newton."

"Great. I'll get dressed and meet you downstairs in half an hour. Oh, and pick me up a triple espresso at Starbucks on your way, or you'll be sorry."

"Yes, my liege."

"No milk and no sugar. Just pure jet fuel."

"As you please, your royal assness. Just be downstairs in thirty minutes."

Harry arrived on time and waited on the steps for a few minutes until Will emerged. Harry bowed deeply at the waist as he presented Will with his espresso. "If it doesn't meet your expectations, I'll draw and quarter the coffee fool, your highness."

"Okay. Cut the crap, Harry. Did you get hold of Ms. Deb?"

"I did and when I explained what we wanted, she didn't sound surprised at all. Almost like she was expecting the call."

"Did you tell her who the victim was?"

"No, I just said we had some general questions about a case related to her husband's death."

"Did the admin at the precinct give her a heads-up?"

"No. Said she never contacted the woman. Just gave you her address and phone."

"I guess we'll have to explore that one a little. Let's go."

Will used the twenty-minute drive to tell Harry what he had learned about the Bergstrom case. "Now I understand why you're so hot to talk to this woman."

"Let's just hope she can answer our questions and draw a line from her late hubby to Philip Sarkis."

Deb Angelucci's house in Newton was a modest ranch on a nice, but not fancy street. There weren't many neighborhoods like this one in the most fashionable suburbs of Boston. Real estate in this area was expensive and grossly inflated because of its proximity to Boston, and the relatively easy commute. You could buy a lot cheaper outside the 128 beltway, but also quadruple your commute time—and probably take several years off of your life.

Deb answered the door dressed in nice jeans and a purple pullover. She was short, blonde, and cute in a perky kind of way, with a smile that showed off her dimples. The detectives showed her their IDs. She ushered them into her living room and offered them coffee or tea.

"No thanks, Mrs. Angelucci, but nice of you to offer. We don't want to take up a lot of your time."

"Not a problem, Detective. My children are in school and this is my day off."

Will took the lead asking questions. "You have two children, is that correct?"

"Yes, Detective, ages fourteen and ten."

"And you work at Filene's?"

"I do, as a purchasing agent. I had a similar job before I was married, so it was pretty easy to get back into it."

"Mrs. Angelucci, the last thing we want to do is upset you, but we have to ask you a few questions about your husband's case and his relationship with a person named Philip Sarkis."

"Philip! Why are you asking questions about him?"

"He isn't in any trouble. We're just trying to get some information about an incident near a place where he's been staying in Cambridge. Did you know he was in town?"

"No," Deb answered, perhaps a little too quickly.

Harry interrupted, trying to get the background questioning back on track. "How did your husband know Philip Sarkis?"

"They met in college and roomed together in Philly. They went to different medical schools and residencies, but ended up in the same fellowship program at Harvard."

"At the Peter Bent Brigham, as it was known back then?"

"Yes. They remained close all those years. In fact, Philip was best man at our wedding, and Philip is godfather for our daughter. And my husband, rest in peace, was best man at Philip's wedding. The four of us, including Philip's ex-wife, Nancy, were friends. We were very excited when we had a chance to be with Philip for those four years up here."

"And then they took jobs in different places," Harry continued.

"Yes, Philip went back to Philadelphia, to Gladwyne Memorial, and Pudge stayed in Boston, at Mass General."

"Pudge?"

"Mario's nickname. He was a little heavy as a child, so his family called him that. I guess it stuck."

"Did Dr. Sarkis and, uh, Pudge compete with each other?" Will asked.

"No, just the opposite, actually. They collaborated on many projects and saw a lot of each other at scientific meetings. They liked to golf together and played whenever they had the chance."

"So it's fair to say they were pretty close?"

"Ultra-close."

"Hmm. So I guess they communicated about your husband's case."

"Pudge had been a big help to Philip when he was going through his own malpractice ordeal in Philadelphia a few years ago, so Philip went out of his way to talk to Pudge frequently about the Bergstrom case."

"Maybe we can talk a little about that. Your husband was sued for wrongful death, correct?"

Deb paused, choking back a few tears. Harry and Will realized they were getting into a sensitive area. Instinctively, Harry leaned forward and spoke more softly to show respect and concern.

"We know this is hard to talk about."

"Thanks for your understanding, Detective. Yes, he was sued for the death of Sebby Bergstrom, and it changed his life."

Will and Harry waited for Deb to gather herself and continue.

“Pudge was the most compassionate physician I had ever known. He really cared for his patients. So when he was accused of carelessly recommending that Sebby go back to hockey, it simply devastated him.”

“As I recollect, it was a controversial decision, right?” Will asked.

“That’s a huge understatement, Detective. Every two-bit doctor in this town had an opinion about what to do with Sebby, including that crazy ‘dream team’ that the Bruins insisted on assembling.”

Will remembered seeing references to a super-committee of doctors that was asked to advise the Bruins about the best approach to Sebby’s case.

“And many of them thought Sebby needed to have an implantable defibrillator device, one of those shock boxes, and be restricted from playing again, correct?”

“Yes, without ever seeing Sebby or taking a history or examining him. Those bastards went to the press and said Pudge was wrong and Sebby should be pulled. All they succeeded in doing was inflaming the entire city and putting my husband in an impossible position.”

“Why?”

“Sebby was desperate to play, and after Pudge laid things out, so was his father, Karl. They trusted Pudge. And what got lost, in all the screaming that occurred when Sebby died, was that Pudge had expressly recommended that an external defibrillator be available on the bench and that personnel always be present who could take it out and use it.”

“Which didn’t happen in Washington.”

“No, it didn’t. We were home watching the game. I thought Pudge was going to have a stroke—he was screaming at the TV to get the defibrillator charged and shock Sebby. ‘Shock him! Shock him!’ he kept yelling. But by the time they finally did, it didn’t do any good.

His brain was already damaged."

"The trial was hard on your husband?" Harry asked, knowing the answer before it came.

"Well, there were actually three of them. The first was a non-binding panel that ruled that Pudge hadn't been negligent. In Massachusetts, all malpractice cases are reviewed like that, and ninety percent of the time, the family abides by the ruling. Not the Bergstrom family and its lawyer, though. The Bruins had paid off the remainder of Sebby's contract, but they still decided to sue Pudge, and also the hospital. Their big-shot lawyer, a guy named Robinson, Thaddeus Robinson, held a news conference and made himself sound like a crusader for justice."

"Robinson. Yeah, I've heard of him. You say there were three trials? What was the second one?"

"That was the first jury trial. All the other defendants were left out, but they took Pudge to court and tortured him for three weeks, and then the jury came back and said they couldn't reach a verdict. I think a few people dug in and wouldn't exonerate Pudge."

"Your husband must have been devastated."

"Not really, because there was hope the family would drop the case. But the family, I guess they were just grief-stricken and let Robinson run things, and he was on his high horse. He whipped the public into a frenzy, saying the jury was just one vote away from a verdict against Pudge. That had to be a lie, but he got the family to do it all over again."

"So there was a second jury trial."

"Yes. And now the media coverage was at a fever pitch. Hundreds of reporters were all over the place, even in our front yard. Pudge couldn't go to work for weeks without being harassed. I've never seen him more depressed."

"Was he in touch with Dr. Sarkis during this time?"

"Just about every night. They'd talk on the phone and commiserate. Pudge found it very helpful. Anyway, the second trial was longer than the first, and even more contentious. This time the jury was out for three days, but they came back with a verdict in our favor."

"That must have been quite a courtroom scene."

"It was a madhouse. Robinson was a maniac—screaming at the jury and at Pudge, too, about a 'miscarriage of justice.' What a jerk!"

"How did your husband react to all that?"

"He just sat down and cried like a baby. And when I got him home, he sat right in that chair, the one you're sitting in, and wept on and off for days. Philip came up to see him, and Pudge barely talked. When he did, it was only about weather and politics. Anything medical, or about the case, or even sports was very upsetting to him. He'd actually get up and just leave the room."

"Did he get better?"

"It took about a month before he began to pull himself together. And just as he was getting on his feet, the death threats started."

"Death threats? From *whom*?"

"We never found out. We thought it was crackpot fans because they kept saying they were going to get Pudge for ruining the Bruins' chances to win the Stanley Cup."

"What did your husband do?"

"He told the police, and they sent some patrols, but that didn't stop the threats, or the rocks coming through our bedroom window. We had to start sleeping in the guest room. Pudge tried to be calm about it all, for our family's sake, but I could see he was rattled. Maybe he was afraid for us, and that's why he bought a gun."

"When did he do that?"

"About a week before he died."

Deb lowered her head. When she looked back up, her eyes brimmed with tears.

"It was a huge gun. I was petrified when he came home with it. He tried to calm me down, saying it was only for self-defense, and that he'd be real careful. To this day, I don't know if he bought it for self-defense or maybe to shoot himself."

"But he didn't shoot himself, did he?" Will said, remembering the newspaper pieces he had seen during his research the night before.

"No, sir. He died when his car went off a cliff. It was ruled a suicide."

And that opened the floodgates. Deb began to sob, and Harry and Will knew that the interview, or at least this part of it, was over.

Will grabbed a tissue box and handed it to Deb, who clutched it without looking up.

"Detectives, can you find your way out?" Deb said between sobs.

"Mrs. Angelucci, we're so sorry if we upset you."

"Not your fault, Detectives," Deb managed. "If you need more information, perhaps you can come back another time? And maybe you can tell me why you're interested in Philip."

"We'll do that, Mrs. Angelucci. We'll fill you in next time we meet."

Will and Harry made their way out of the house and to Harry's car.

"I told her we'd call again, but that will be never, I hope," Will remarked as Harry started the car for their return trip to Boston.

Chapter 9

On his third hospital day, Thaddeus Robinson awoke with a startle. He blinked several times, hoping, as he had several times since his admission, that he would wake up and the nightmare would be over. But no, he wasn't dreaming. He was in a real hospital room at MGH, shades thoughtfully pulled down for sleep, but with the usual hospital din seeping in from the hallway. The worst of it was the endless cackling and giggling by the young people who thought they were the most important people in the medical universe. After all, they worked at Man's Greatest Hospital, didn't they? Well, Thad thought, if they were so damned smart, how come they couldn't fix his torn spinal cord? To Thad's way of thinking, medicine remained a primitive science, still adhering to senseless practices formulated in the Middle Ages, made only marginally better with the advent of mind-altering drugs intended to distract patients from the fact that their doctors helped little, while curing almost nothing. Wasn't that George C. Scott's famous line in that damn movie, *The Hospital*?

He looked down at his legs—useless trunks under the

covers, unmovable and inert. And his penis, all shriveled up. He thought he had caught one of the nurses smirking at it during his last sponge bath. Maybe the bitch would like to see it in action someday. Wishful thinking, Thad knew. From what he had heard so far, prospects of recovery were dim at best.

At just that moment, David Korn and his entourage parked their cart outside his room and began their rounding discussions. Thad couldn't quite hear what they were saying, but he could see the youngest doctors on the outside edge of the throng staring off into space, obviously bored. There were no revelations or interesting discoveries here. Just some old fart who got knifed in the back and would never walk, pee, or crap normally again.

After a few minutes, Korn walked into the room and stood at the foot of Thad's bed. In Thad's view, Korn didn't even have the decency to sit down so Thad could look him squarely in the eye.

"How are you, Mr. Robinson?" Korn asked.

"Peachy."

"Any pain anywhere?"

"I would kill to have some pain in my legs. They're just dead."

Thad scanned the white-coated nitwits who had followed Korn into his room. None seemed interested in him or his case. A few were punching away on their infernal smartphones. Others were gazing out the window. Korn himself was looking at his clipboard.

"Well, we'll continue to monitor your progress," Korn finally replied.

"There is no fucking progress, Doctor." Thad's obscenity at least shocked a few of the medical students and residents to attention.

"You're supposed to be getting physical therapy," Korn continued, sidestepping Thad's scorn.

"Yeah, and that's going well, too. They come in, move my legs around for a few minutes, put them up on pillows, and stroll out. Is that supposed to help me walk again?"

"We're just trying to avoid contractures and decubiti."

"We certainly don't want that to happen, do we, Doctor?" Thad spat in his most sarcastic tone. "No black marks on the MGH report card, right?"

"Tell me, Dr. Korn," Thad continued, "in your learned opinion, is the treatment of this condition any better than it was a hundred years ago?"

Korn blushed, realizing that Thad was trying to embarrass him in front of his minions. "Actually, Mr. Robinson, there has been some interesting work done with stem cells. In fact, I was going to ask if you were interested in participating in one of our research projects. We're implanting cultured stem cells into the damaged area and seeing if they can stimulate nerve re-growth."

"So you want to know if I'd like to be a guinea pig? How many patients have you boys treated and what are the results so far?"

"Not too many, and the results are preliminary. They're actually changing the cells lines they're using to see if they can optimize their results."

"In other words, their results suck so they're going back to the drawing board. And I assume I have a fifty-fifty chance of getting a sham treatment, not the experimental therapy?"

"I think that's right. Mr. Robinson. Listen, why don't I have the principal investigator on the project come by and speak with you? She'll give you the up-to-date information. That way you can make an informed decision."

"That would be divine. At least it will give me something to do. In the meantime, when do you think I can get out of here?"

"That depends, Mr. Robinson. Usually we recommend transfer to a spinal injury unit. There's a particularly good one over at St. Elizabeth's."

"And what will those Catholic idiots do for me over there? Say a fucking novena? Let's be frank, Dr. Korn. I'm cooked. No research or physical therapy is going to bring my spinal cord back. I'd prefer to be sent home and have my rehabilitation done there—privately."

Korn was working hard to remain composed. In an even tone, he said, "I'm sure our home health people can work with you to set that up. As you might imagine, it's more expensive that way."

"I don't give a fuck about the money. I have plenty of that. I just want out of this hole and back to familiar surroundings. Where I can actually get some rest."

"Okay, Mr. Robinson." Korn asked one of the nurses in the room to have a hospital social worker drop by.

"And Dr. Korn," Robinson added in his most scornful tone, "could we get her here before the end of the decade?"

Korn nodded, trying to save some face in front of his youthful cohort. As he turned to leave, he ran straight into a very large man who had entered the room a few moments before and stood silently behind him. He looked up to see a man in his late fifties or early sixties, with a generous crop of gray hair, a pock-marked but clean-shaven face, and a beak of a nose, looking down at him disdainfully.

"Sorry," David managed as he maneuvered around the hulk.

"No worries," was the amazingly well enunciated reply. "I apologize for sneaking up on you."

This brought a few snickers from the peanut gallery, quickly suppressed by a nasty frown from the chief resident.

Korn hurried from the room, followed by his ducklings. The beast stepped forward and sat in the armchair next to Thad, who wondered if there was a weight limit for furniture in the unit.

"Thanks for coming over, Luke."

"I wanted to update you. I thought this would be better than over the phone."

"Good thinking. The walls have ears in this frigging place. And it's impossible to get any privacy. Thanks for looking over things for me."

"We go back a long time, Thad. It's the least I can do."

It had been a long association. Luke Benjamin and Thad Robinson met when Thad was fresh out of law school, working for the local DA. Luke was a burned-out detective, tired of pushing paper around and being bossed by snot-nosed academy graduates who didn't know a perp from a perv. Thad also hated his superiors, too, put off by their penchant for always making the politically expedient but usually incorrect decision.

Before long, Thad began to look for an office where he could launch his own firm and make money. He had been impressed by Luke's no-nonsense style, and talked to him about doing some part-time work. Since detectives' wages were barely livable, Luke jumped at the chance. In a few years, Thad's book of business was large enough to take Luke on as a full-time employee whose job was to gather intelligence on just about every plaintiff and defendant with whom Thad interacted.

And it paid big dividends. Thad was able to get the upper hand in just about every situation. Sometimes all it took was a subtle hint about a skeleton in the closet that the person on the other side of the table was des-

perate to keep hidden. Luke was Thad's secret weapon, and he used him for all he was worth, and then some.

Thad had another reason for keeping Luke on the payroll: he didn't trust anyone who worked in his firm. First, none of them was a true economic partner. He let a few of his senior people pretend they were important by putting their names on the firm's letterhead, but the reality was that Thad made all the decisions. He rarely took long vacations, and when he did, he made sure that each of his attorneys reported to him daily. Thus his current illness was a major stress for Thad—he couldn't keep as close a watch on things as usual. He needed Luke to be his eyes and ears.

"So what's the situation at the office, Luke my boy?"

"Things look pretty stable, as best I can tell. There's been a lot of whispering in the restrooms about the fate of the firm, for obvious reasons, but the senior people are keeping cool. I sat in on the firm meeting yesterday, and the discussion was businesslike."

"Good. Just your being there will probably keep any revolutionaries from doing something rash."

"Maybe, although a few of them were cracking inappropriate jokes."

"I bet that asshole Slavinsky was one of them."

"Stu doesn't know how to keep his mouth shut."

"I'd can the little fuck if he weren't so valuable to the intellectual property part of the business."

And it doesn't hurt that he has enough dope on you to cook your goose, Luke thought to himself. It was time to change the subject. "I suspect you also want to know the status of the police investigation?"

"Yeah. What have you heard?"

"They put Harry Socks and Will Lentz on the case. They're veterans who know their stuff."

"And what are they up to?"

"I couldn't get much information from my contact in that precinct. She's an admin. She's been my source there for a long time."

"Didn't you have a thing with her years ago?" Thad asked with a smirk.

"Yeah, but her husband started wising up, and we had to call it quits. Nice tits but definitely not worth a battle with a hubby. But we still have a drink now and again. She gave me a name she saw in the detectives' notes. I've been running it the last few days."

"Who?"

"Some doctor named Sarkis. Lives in Pennsylvania but he's here in Boston for a conference."

"Why on earth would they suspect him? I never even heard of the guy."

"The lead came from a witness who saw some guy running across Harvard Bridge around the time you were attacked. The lady swears he ran right past her house at the edge of the bridge, up the street, and into a boarding house. This Sarkis guy was staying there."

"So they questioned him?"

"Apparently, but they didn't bring him in or charge him."

"Is he still in town?"

"I think so."

"What do you know about him?"

Luke spent the next few minutes telling Thad about Sarkis' background, including his involvement with a couple of malpractice cases.

"Sounds like a zealot. The kind you need to worry about."

"I don't know, boss. He has no assault history or anything like that."

"I think you need to put a low-level tail on him until

we figure out what the story is. What else have Socks and Lentz been doing?"

"The admin told me they were going to see Deb Angelucci."

"Angelucci. Any relation to Mario Angelucci?"

"Yeah, the wife. Well, the widow."

"Why would they want to talk to her?"

"Best I can tell is she has a motive to hurt you."

"But she didn't stick a knife in my back. It wasn't a broad who did this to me."

"She could have hired someone."

"And of all the doctors I've screwed, why would they pick her?"

"Not many of the people you tried to nail for big judgments killed themselves. I guess this one stood out."

"You know better than to guess. Find out why they're snooping around Deb Angelucci and if it ties to Sarkis."

"That's my next task. I'll go through their biographies tonight."

"Socks and Lentz aren't stupid. They wouldn't be going randomly to one of the pathetic pieces of shit I beat up in a malpractice case."

Luke nodded in agreement. By everyone's account, Thad was a very big asshole, but he was a brilliant lawyer and strategist. Luke had learned to trust Thad's instincts.

"I guess I'll be doing some computer searching tonight," Luke said as he rose to go. "I hope you get better soon."

"I'm not going to get better, Luke. I'll almost certainly never use my legs again. And from what I've heard, the doctors whispering in the hallways, it's possible that whoever did this didn't want to kill me—but to disable me, to torture me. The attacker is either out of his fucking mind, or I did something that pissed him off royally. Does that perspective help you hone your search?"

"That it does, boss."

"Killing my spinal cord without killing me makes me wonder if the person who did this knew something about anatomy."

"Like maybe Sarkis?"

"The possibility does suggest itself."

"I'll call you later and let you know what I find out."

Luke shook Thad's hand, gave a wisp of a smile, and departed. Thad was left alone to mull over the significance of what he had just heard, and to fantasize about what he would do to the person who ruined his life.

Chapter 10

Will and Harry didn't say much as they drove back to Boston from Deb Angelucci's house. They knew they had a lot to process. Will raised the most obvious question: "Think we have enough to haul Sarkis in and question him further?"

"Let's see. We have him in the area at about the time of the attack, and now we may have a motive, although it isn't the most compelling reason for a knifing I've heard lately. So, the answer to your question is probably no," Harry said.

Will was not surprised. "Can't disagree with you. Next question: should we see if he'll answer some questions voluntarily before he leaves town?"

"Can't hurt to ask."

"I can't see a downside, either. It'll be a hell of a lot harder to get him back here after he's back in Pennsylvania."

"He said he was leaving town on Saturday."

"He also said he was attending the cardiology meeting at the convention center," Will recalled. "Maybe we should take a ride over there tomorrow morning and see if we can catch him off guard."

"Not a bad idea. Having a couple of cops show up on his turf might shake him up enough to let us get something out of him."

Will and Harry grabbed a sandwich and a soft drink at the food truck stationed outside their office, and parked themselves at their desks for the rest of the afternoon, catching up on paperwork and working a few leads on the lukewarm cases they still had on the board. But their minds were only half on their work. The next Sarkis interview would be important. They knew they would catch hell about the Robinson case if they didn't come up with something to show Captain Pokorney soon. And then there was the issue of Thad Robinson himself. As Harry pointed out to Will during an afternoon work break, "Robinson's the kind of guy who likes to throw his weight around, so I can't imagine he's going to lie there in a diaper and not want to make somebody pay for what happened to him."

"I just hope he doesn't try to get revenge on his own."

"I wouldn't put it past him, Will. Hey, remember a private detective named Luke somebody? Big guy with attitude? Comes around here sometimes, chasing skirt?"

"Yeah. Luke Benjamin, I think his name is. Sort of a goon. What about him?"

"Isn't he working for Robinson these days? I gotta believe he's snooping around even as we speak."

"All the more reason to get this guy Sarkis off the street before Robinson jumps to a conclusion."

They finished early and walked out to the parking lot together. Will would head to another local watering hole and Harry home to domestic bliss. Each uttered routine complaints about their respective social situations with the implicit understanding that neither would change a thing.

"See you at nine tomorrow, right here?" Harry asked.

"Yeah. You drive this time. I'm tired of getting parking tickets."

"Seaport Convention Center, right?"

"Yep, that's where the docs are hanging out this week."

"Think I can get some free Viagra while we're over there?" Harry laughed.

"They're cardiologists, Harry; they ain't hard-on docs. Besides, nobody has enough of that stuff to give your sorry dick a lift."

Harry and Will enjoyed the bantering, neither exactly sure why it made them feel more comfortable with each other.

"You're a real prince, Will. See ya tomorrow."

Boston weather reality returned the next day. Spring disappeared, replaced by a nor'easter complete with wind and rain and temperatures struggling to get out of the forties. Harry was parked in the precinct building's lot with the wipers going, hoping Will had remembered to set his alarm and didn't have some bimbo draped all over him. After fifteen minutes, just as Harry was about to pull out his cell phone, Will came wheeling around the corner. He parked next to Harry and hustled over to the passenger side, trying not to get soaked.

"I hate this fucking weather," Will said as he buckled in.

"If you want to live in Boston, you put up with it."

"Doesn't mean I have to like it."

The drive to the Seaport area and the new Convention Center was a start-and-stop hassle, taking them twice as long as usual. Even so, Will was unreasonably annoyed by the snarled traffic and pointed out every bad driver to Harry.

"You obviously got out of the wrong side of bed," Harry chided. "What else do you have to do that's more important?"

Will bit his tongue. He didn't want to get into a fight with his partner just now. It would just distract him from the task at hand. He quickly changed the subject. "Now, when we get to Sarkis, let me do most of the questioning. I'll push him hard and then you can pull me back and be nice."

"Good cop, bad cop. Pretty creative, Will. Never heard of that tactic before."

"Fuck you, Harry."

Harry had to smile at his partner's mood.

"In your dreams, Will. Okay, listen: let's remember that this guy isn't some hayseed from the Pocono Mountains. He's been involved in some complex cases, and I'm sure has been interrogated by skilled people before. Why not just confront him with what you know about Mario Angelucci and see what he has to say?"

"It's precisely because he *is* sophisticated that I want to approach this tactically. Otherwise, he'll just clam up and walk, and we'll be stuck."

Thcy wcnt back and forth, arguing strategy all the way to the Westin Hotel, next door to the Convention Center, where Harry parked the car. They walked through a connector to the convention center, avoiding the inclement weather, and walked up to an information booth where they were greeted by a friendly, elderly lady with fiery red hair and too much make-up, wearing a blue jacket and a name tag that said, "Hi, I'm Elsa."

"Welcome to the Heart Rhythm Society meetings, doctors. How can I help you?"

Will patiently explained. "We're not doctors, ma'am. We're detectives with the Boston Police Department. We need to speak with one of your conference attendees.

How would we go about locating him?"

"Oh my, I hope he isn't in any trouble."

"Not at all," Harry answered. "We just need to ask him a few questions."

"I'm just a temporary. Let me ask my supervisor."

Elsa headed off and came back a few minutes later with a much younger and attractive woman. Her name tag said, "Hi, I'm Elaine."

Now Will's mood improved. "Hello there, I'm Lieutenant Detective Wilson Lentz and this is my partner Sergeant Detective Harry Socks. Can you give us some idea of how we can locate Philip Sarkis, one of the doctors attending this conference?"

"Do you have some identification?" Elaine asked.

"Oh, right," Will replied. He and Harry flashed their IDs.

"Well, Detective, we don't usually track the attendees at our meetings. Do you have a cell phone number for him?"

Will tried to hide his embarrassment that he had neglected to get a cell phone number from Sarkis at their first interview.

"We've talked to him once, but at that point we didn't ask for his number."

"Sometimes our doctors do sign up for specific sessions; I could check on that for you," Elaine offered.

"That would be great," Will replied, smiling in what he hoped was an endearing manner.

"Okay. Wait here and I'll access the registration records. His name is Sarkis, you said?"

"Yes, Philip Sarkis." Will suppressed his desire to add a "sweetheart" at the end.

Will watched as Elaine left, then whispered to Harry. "Looks pretty good walking away, doesn't she?"

Harry just shook his head. No denying it: Will was a

hound. Fortunately, he didn't have a wife to cheat on, at least not any more.

Elaine returned after a few minutes. "We're in luck, Detectives. Dr. Sarkis is signed up for a tutorial that starts in about fifteen minutes."

"Could you take us to the room, Elaine?" Will asked.

Harry interrupted. "Will, I think we can find it if she'll just direct us."

Will shot a nasty glance at Harry, then turned to Elaine with that smile again. "We just don't want to get lost."

Elaine recognized Will's true intent and answered sarcastically. "No, Detective, we wouldn't want you to get lost in this great big place. But your partner's correct; the hall where the tutorial will occur is just a short walk from here. Go straight back across the bridge behind me, and you'll see the C concourse. Turn right and go to room C22.

Will and Harry said their thank you's, and Harry started for room C22. Will grabbed a brochure from the information booth's counter and perused its map of the convention center, hoping to get Elaine to engage him again. There was still a chance to score her phone number, he hoped. But she made small talk with Elsa and left. Will hurried off after Harry.

"Get anywhere with her?" Harry asked.

"Man, check out how many companies are here, pitching themselves to the docs. This must be a pretty important conference."

"So what kind of docs are these people?" Harry asked.

"They take care of people with heart rhythm problems."

"Is that a common problem?"

"Judging from the size of this meeting, I guess so. My

mother had some kind of rhythm problem before she died. I think they called it atrial fibrillation. They gave her a pacemaker."

"I've seen commercials about that on TV. And didn't Wilt Chamberlain have atrial fibrillation?"

"Probably from going up against Bill Russell all those years. But I guess athletes can get heart rhythm problems, too, wouldn't you say? All those demands on the heart?"

Elaine had been correct: concourse C was easy to find. They stood outside C22 and five minutes later, throngs of well-dressed people emerged from the rooms lining the concourse, moving about and looking for their next location.

"Buncha nerds," Will cracked.

"I don't know, Will. They don't look like nerds to me. In fact, a lot of them are pretty good looking. And the younger ones look downright athletic."

"Ah, those people probably work for drug companies or something."

"Well, Sarkis is in pretty good shape. A runner and all."

"Okay. Whatever."

They stood by the door, making aimless observations about everyone who entered C22 until they saw Sarkis in the hallway. He was walking toward them, speaking earnestly to a young woman. As they approached, Will and Harry could hear Sarkis answering a question. "I've seen that in a few patients, but I'm not sure if it's a real association, and I'm not aware of any trials to prove the causality." His companion was listening attentively. She and Sarkis turned to enter C22, but when he saw Harry and Will, Sarkis stopped short. "Can I find you later and finish my explanation?" he asked his companion. As she walked into the room, he turned to the detectives. "Are you guys here to learn about electrophysiology, or is there another purpose?"

"No, Dr. Sarkis, I think you know why we're here," Will answered.

"I know why, but I can't imagine what else I can tell you."

"How about telling us about your friend, Mario Angelucci?"

"If we're going to do this, let's get away from the doorway."

Sarkis led them to a deserted place in the hallway. Will and Harry observed that Sarkis was maintaining his cool.

"Okay, now what about Dr. Angelucci?"

"He must have been a good friend. How did you feel when he killed himself?"

"Terrible, of course."

"Terribly angry, Doctor?"

"I wouldn't say that. I'd describe my emotional state as sad. Maybe even terribly sad?"

"Do you know why Dr. Angelucci would have committed suicide?"

"Look, Detective, I'm busy, so let's not play games. I'm sure you did your homework and don't need me to tell you why Pudge killed himself."

"Pudge?" Will asked, pretending not to know Mario's nickname.

"Nickname from his parents. I gather he was heavy as a baby. It was how I knew him when we were in college, and later at the Brigham."

"So we should believe the newspaper accounts saying he was depressed about the Bergstrom case."

"I believe 'depressed' is a gross understatement. He was devastated by the whole thing: Bergstrom's death, his treatment in the trials, the public's reaction, everything. The verdict in his favor wasn't much consolation, I guess."

"You guess, Doctor? You don't know for sure? Weren't you in touch and seeing Mario, I mean Pudge, through this period?"

"Of course, but he wasn't terribly forthcoming. He tried to keep his emotions to himself."

"How did you feel about Thad Robinson's role in the case?"

"How was I supposed to feel? I guess he was doing his job."

"Come on, Doctor. You said he's an aggressive plaintiff's attorney. Did you believe he was just doing his job, or was he trying to ruin your friend so he could make a lot of money?"

Harry cut in, trying to play his role. "That's not a fair question, Will."

"I wasn't talking to you, Harry," Will snapped. "Tell me, Doctor, how did you like Thad Robinson's performance in the courtroom? A little over the top, was it?"

Sarkis stared at Will and for a second. Harry and Will could sense a mounting anger that Sarkis was trying to contain. Finally through gritted teeth, "It is not my place to judge Robinson's courtroom demeanor, Detective."

"Certainly not, but you could see why any of Pudge's friends who thought Robinson went after him vindictively might be inclined to seek revenge? Hypothetically, of course."

"Come on, Will, that's enough. There's no basis for that kind of question here," Harry said, trying to mean it.

"Fuck if there isn't! Dr. Sarkis here was the closest person to Thad Robinson the night he was attacked, and we have a potential motive. I think there *is* a basis for this line of questioning."

Sarkis was quiet, obviously considering his reply. "I'm finished talking to you, Detective."

"Are you sure, Doctor? This is a good time to clear up some of our concerns so they don't come back to haunt you later."

"I have nothing more to tell you."

"Have you been in touch with Deb Angelucci lately?"

"None of your business, Detective."

"Fine, Doctor. But not answering questions doesn't help your case any."

"Are you charging me with anything, Detective?"

"No, but I need to ask you to remain in Boston while we pursue this investigation a bit further."

"I'm due to drive home tomorrow. If I'm not under arrest, I see no need to cancel my travel plans."

"No, Doctor, we can't compel you to stay in Boston. But if you leave, we'll consider that a possible sign of guilt. If you stay, we'll be able to clear the case faster and get you off of our list of 'persons of interest' so you don't have to come back up here again. The choice is yours."

Sarkis nodded. "I'll think on it."

"Do that, Dr. Sarkis. In the meantime, could you give me your cell phone number in case we need to reach you again?"

Sarkis handed him a card. "Here's all my contact information. If I stay in Boston, it will only be for a few days. I'm due back at work on Tuesday and I have a full day of patients."

"Thanks, Dr. Sarkis. That should be enough time," Harry said. "And we do appreciate your cooperation. We're under a lot of pressure to clear this case as soon as possible."

Harry and Will walked away. They speculated all the way back to the station about Sarkis' next move. "I guess we'll call him tomorrow night to see if he stayed in town," Will finally concluded.

"Why do I have the feeling that I'm the one who will be making that call?"

"Because you know I'll be having a beer at a local watering hole and chatting up some sweet young thing?"

"That sounds familiar," Harry said, rolling his eyes.

Dorothy Deaver sat in her cluttered law office in Scranton, elbows on her desktop, head in her hands, waiting for her father to pick up his line, ruminating about the events of the last several minutes.

Her afternoon had been going well. She had been in the middle of a settlement conference with a new client, one she had worked hard to cultivate, when her secretary Claire interrupted with an urgent call from Philip. Though she was winning multiple concessions from the hapless attorney on the other side, she decided to wrap up quickly. She knew she was short-changing her own client a little, but Philip rarely called her at the office, which meant something was wrong. Returning to her office to take the call, she reviewed a list of potential disasters. He was in Boston at a cardiology conference. What could have happened to him there? She remembered stories he had told her of doctors getting mugged, raped, or shot by criminals preying on distracted and naive out-of-town doctors attending medical conferences. Or had he had a heart attack or a stroke or something? She could not stop imagining horrible scenarios until she had heard his voice, but then his message did anything but reassure her. When she put the phone down, she realized there was only one person who could help: her private detective father in Philadelphia, Dick Deaver.

"Dick Deaver here," came the familiar voice from the speaker phone.

"Hi, Dad. It's Dorothy."

"What a nice surprise. I always like hearing from my little girl."

"I don't think you're going to like this call, Dad."

"Why? What's the latest disaster?"

"It's Philip."

"And why am I not surprised?"

"Dad, don't start," Dorothy said impatiently. Dick didn't have a high opinion of Philip, but she didn't need attitude from Dad right now. "He's in Boston, and he's in trouble."

Silence on the line, which meant her father was turning beet red, ready to explode, but trying to suppress his anger for his daughter's sake.

"Dad, you still there?"

"I'm here. Tell me what your knucklehead boyfriend's done this time."

"I don't think he's done anything, but the police have questioned him about a possible attempted murder."

"Murder? Why on earth…?"

"Long story, Dad." Dorothy recounted what Philip had told her about the attack on a prominent malpractice attorney near the B&B where he was staying, the police interrogation concerning Mario Angelucci's suicide, and finally their "request" that he remain in the Boston area over the weekend while they sorted through the facts of the case.

"What does that guy do to get himself into these jams?" Dick asked.

"Dad, it doesn't sound like he did anything. He was just in the wrong place at the wrong time, as best I can tell."

"If it were that simple, I'd agree with you. But the

Angelucci connection makes me worry. It supplies a motive, and I'm sure the detectives will work that angle."

"I told Philip to sit tight and not leave Boston, at least for the next few days."

"That was good advice."

"I also told him I'd go up there."

"Huh? To do what, exactly?"

"I don't know. Provide moral support?"

"How sweet of you," her father observed sarcastically.

"Do you have a better idea?"

"I can't believe I'm saying this, but I think we both need to go up there to do some looking around."

"You mean investigate the case ourselves?"

"I think 'investigate' is a strong word, darlin'. We don't want to spook the cops. But a few inquiries might provide some clarity, especially if we can come up with some other explanation for what happened."

"Sounds like 'investigation' to me, Dad, but I'll defer to you on this one. Are you really willing to go up there with me?"

"Only for you, my dear, not for that bozo you live with."

Dorothy was so relieved that she chose to ignore the barb. "Thanks, Dad. I'm so grateful. This is scary business and having you along means a lot. How do you think we should travel?"

"We can probably drive faster than we can fly, and we'll need a car up there anyway, so I'll clear my calendar, throw a few things in a bag, and pick you up at your house in about two hours. We'll be in Boston before midnight."

"Thanks, Dad. You just made me feel so much better."

"And you'd make me feel better if you'd just dump

this guy. How many times does he have to pull you into a mess before you wake up?"

"Dad, we can't have that conversation now. Can we just get going and deal with this issue some other time?"

"Of course," Dick relented, hearing the angst in his daughter's voice. Dick loved her to death and the last thing he wanted was to make her uncomfortable.

They rang off, and Dorothy buzzed her secretary. "Claire, I'm leaving now, and I'll be in Boston for the weekend. I'm not sure when I'll be back, so you should reschedule my appointments for Monday and Tuesday."

With that, Dorothy left the office and headed home, her thoughts squarely on Philip's predicament, and what she and her father could do to extricate him from his latest misadventure.

Chapter 11

Dorothy hurried to her car for her drive from her office in Scranton to the Pocono lake house she shared with Philip. Traffic was light; the twenty-mile trip was easy. Good thing, too, because she knew her father was on a mission and would be at the house on time, if not early. Her mind was racing, alternating between trying to imagine how Philip had gotten into another fix, and laying out what she needed to do to get ready for her trip to Boston.

Her first order of business was to contact her neighbor, Dana, to see if she could take care of the dogs for a few days. Mitten and Buffy had been joined by a new "sister" named Meeko, a feisty pup who spent her time harassing her elders or chewing anything left on the floor. Three dogs and two working people meant a constant need for doggie day care, which Dana, a true dog person, supplied happily. Weekends were not included in the deal, but fortunately, Dana had no plans for this particular weekend and was happy for the extra cash.

Dorothy packed carefully. She anticipated needing to meet with people under a variety of circumstances, so conservative business attire as well as some casual clothing would be the best thing. She hoped her stay in Boston would be brief, but knowing Philip, he was probably minimizing the trouble he was in. Extricating him might be more difficult and time consuming than her father was thinking when they talked on the phone.

Dick was right on time. He pulled into the driveway in his 500 series BMW, honked the horn, and waited impatiently for his daughter. When she finally emerged, Dick popped the trunk and helped her load her bags. After a peck on her cheek, he opened the passenger door for her, got himself situated, and then made his usual hasty departure, spewing dust and stones behind him.

"In a hurry, Dad?" Dorothy teased.

"You bet. I want to get up there, extract your bonehead boyfriend, and get home. I have a lot on my plate this coming week."

"As do I, Dad."

Dick was in business mode. "We won't hit much traffic. Should be up there in about four hours. I made reservations at the Ritz for two nights. I figure we can talk to the police up there first thing in the morning, work out a deal to get Philip sprung, and hopefully be home Sunday."

"That might be overly optimistic, Dad. We don't know what kind of case the detectives have or if they'll even be available over the weekend."

"I know the chief of detectives up there. Called him already, in fact. He owes me a favor so he promised the lead detective would meet us at their stationhouse tomorrow morning."

"Does he even know who the lead detective is?"

"No. I just gave him Philip's name and the name of the victim, and he told me he'd get hold of the right detective team."

"How do you know this guy? And what did you do to make him owe you a favor?"

"He was a Philly detective before he moved to Boston. Let's just say there was a little misunderstanding about a racing bet, and I made the problem go away."

They spent the rest of the drive talking about the Bergstrom case. An avid sports fan, Dick had followed the media coverage closely. "It was sensationalism, pure sensationalism. They must have played the tape of him passing out during that game a million times. People went crazy for it."

"The Boston fans in particular, from what I understand."

"And that goalie's death was just the start. Then a doc on the case got sued. Not a team doc. A guy at Mass General. Angelucci, Mario Angelucci. Took a couple of trials to clear him of malpractice, but they sure dragged that poor bastard through the mud along the way. I'm not surprised he killed himself. I don't know what took him so long to get around to it."

"I knew Philip trained with Angelucci, but whenever I asked him about the lawsuits, he'd just grunt and evade my questions."

"So he never went up to visit when Angelucci was in trouble?"

"I remember him saying something about reviewing records in the case for one of the other defendants, an electrophysiologist."

"Yeah, plaintiff's attorneys go after everyone they can, don't they?"

"I just can't recall Philip talking about it very much."

"I find that incredible."

"I know. Before they trained together, they also knew each other in college. But all that stuff happened before I ever met Philip."

Their conversation alternated between planning their approach to the Boston police and wondering about the relationship between Philip and Angelucci, and whether Philip could have had enough of a reason to attack the attorney who basically badgered his friend to death. The time passed quickly and they arrived at their Boston hotel with precious little understanding of what they were really getting into.

After a restless night at the hotel, and a good breakfast, Dorothy and Dick set out for the Boston police station. They parked in a visitor's section and were directed by the desk sergeant to the detective's squad room. The place was empty except for a ragged-looking guy dressed in a golf shirt and jeans, sitting at one of the desks, feet up, reading the sports section of the *Globe*. He briefly glanced at Dick, had a longer look at Dorothy, put down the paper, smiled, and jumped to his feet.

"Hi, you must be the Deavers. Have a seat."

"We are," Dick said, annoyed that this scumbag was checking out his daughter. He and Dorothy sat. Will waited for them to settle into their chairs before he sat himself.

"And who might you be?" Dick asked.

"Wilson Lentz. I'm the lead detective on the Robinson case."

"Nice to meet you, Detective," Dorothy replied, oblivious to Will's lecherous examination, or simply not caring. "Thanks for meeting with us on a Saturday morning."

"No problem, Ms. Deaver. Please call me Will."

"And we're Dorothy and Dick. We don't want to take up a lot of your time, Will. We just want to know where you are with the case, and if there's anything we can do to clear Philip."

"And as I was told, you live with Dr. Sarkis, is that right, Ms. Deaver? I mean Dorothy."

"That's correct."

Will wondered why Sarkis would have ever left his home for a conference in Boston when he had someone this good-looking in his bed every night.

"Okay. Well, it's still early in our investigation, so I don't have a whole lot to tell you. I'm sure you know that there's a woman who placed Dr. Sarkis near the scene right around the time of the attack."

"Is she a reliable source?" Dick asked.

"I think so. She was pretty specific about the house he went into, and Dr. Sarkis admitted he had been out for a run along the Charles early that morning."

"And we assume you're concerned about Philip's relationship with Dr. Angelucci."

"Yes, we know they were friends, so Dr. Sarkis would have been distressed when Dr. Angelucci killed himself."

"Maybe distressed enough to go after the lawyer who went after his friend?"

"Now don't get upset, Dorothy. We're not jumping to any conclusions here. We just want to ask Dr. Sarkis some more questions, so we suggested that he stick around a couple of days."

"And how the hell will a couple of days over a weekend help, Detective?"

"Well, for one thing, I got a judge to issue a search warrant. I'd like to examine Dr. Sarkis' room over on Amherst Street."

"So what's stopping you?"

"I'd prefer to do it without alerting him. Now that you're here, can I assume you're his legal representative?"

"For the time being, anyway."

"Great, then here's the warrant. Have a look."

Will handed Dorothy the warrant and waited until she had a chance to review it. "Everything in order, Dorothy?"

"Yes," Dorothy hissed.

"I'd appreciate it if you could call Dr. Sarkis and meet him some place away from the B&B where he's staying so we can conduct an uninterrupted and thorough search of his room. Can I also ask you not to warn Dr. Sarkis about the search or interfere in any way?"

"Of course, Will. I'm an officer of the court. I won't risk being accused of interfering with the execution of a search warrant."

"Thanks. I'll have a team at Dr. Sarkis' room around 11 A.M., if that's okay with you."

Dick and Dorothy looked at each other and nodded. "We're meeting Philip for lunch somewhere. It might work better if you did your search at noon."

"Sure, we could do that. I'll let you know right away if we find anything troubling."

"I seriously doubt you will, but yes, we'd appreciate that."

"Anything else to tell us, Detective?" Dick asked.

Will rose stiffly from his chair. "No. I don't have any other information but I'll keep you posted."

"Thanks," Dorothy said.

"But this should be a two-way street. I hear you both are good investigators. Can I ask you to do the same and let me know what you learn as well?" Will asked.

As he walked Dick and Dorothy to the door, he handed them each a business card. Reluctantly, they accepted Will's card, and gave theirs to him in exchange.

Will thanked Dick, said goodbye to the Deavers, and returned to his desk to phone Harry.

"I just spoke with the Deavers," Will announced.

"They're going to get Sarkis out of the way so we can search his place. We're going at noon, not eleven. You in?"

"Sure, I'll be there. Are you sure his girlfriend isn't going to warn him?"

"She doesn't want to risk tampering with a search warrant so I don't think that'll happen. But just to be sure, I'm going over there now to make sure he's out for the morning, and to tell the owners not to throw anything away. I'll stake out the place until you get there. If he comes back or leaves with stuff in hand, I'll stop him."

Will needn't have worried: Philip was attending the last few sessions of the cardiology conference at the convention center when Dorothy finally reached him on his cell. After Philip berated her for not calling him on arrival, they made plans to meet for lunch near Copley Square, Dorothy being careful not to mention the impending search. She knew that Will would have the place staked out so Philip could only make himself look bad if he tried to pull any tricks.

Dorothy and Dick decided to walk around the area in Cambridge where the attack had occurred, to locate the B&B, and to assess its proximity to the site of the crime. They walked across the Harvard Bridge to Beacon Street. There were few lights on the bridge itself, and they could easily imagine how spooky the place must be in the dark. They walked back across the bridge, tracing the path of the attacker, and didn't notice Will, parked across the street from the B&B on Amherst Street. But he saw them, smiling at the fantasy of bedding Dorothy, a truly good-looking woman.

Noon finally arrived. Will had been watching for funny business and waiting for Harry and the search team. Harry drove up, spotted Will's car, parked, and walked over to Will's window. "Who else is in on the search?" he asked.

"I coerced Tim and Gail from the crime scene unit into kindly joining us."

"Tim was probably not happy. Today was his first golf outing of the year."

"And Gail works part-time at a car dealership on the weekends. After I told them that our balls are in a vice, they caved. But we're going to owe them."

Will and Harry strolled over to the B&B and waited on the stoop for a few minutes until Gail and Tim arrived. They looked like twin geeks, with short haircuts, horn-rimmed glasses, and wardrobe by Kmart. Each carried a bag with their wares, and neither looked particularly pleased to be there.

Will addressed them. "I don't have much to add to what I told you last night. We're proceeding on the assumption that Sarkis attacked a lawyer a few days ago, so we're looking for anything to tie him in. He's a bright person, so I doubt he left anything for us.

"We'll be the judge of that," Gail replied.

She and Tim smiled at each other, confident of their ability. It wasn't an accident that they had won the Best Boston Crime Scene Team award four years running.

Marie met the team at the B&B's door. She took a cursory look at the warrant and escorted them to Philip's room. "He was supposed to check out this morning but he extended his stay until Monday. I'm not sure why," she offered.

Will and Harry decided not to go into it with Marie, and instead immediately set to work, apportioning parts of the room to each of the searchers. The room was in excellent order. Philip's clothing was either hung in the closet or placed neatly in drawers, with personal effects carefully arranged on the dresser top and bedside table.

Neither the bedroom nor the attached bathroom was large, and so the search went quickly. They found Philip's running clothes and sneakers. Taking them into the darkened bathroom, they sprayed them with luminol and examined them under fluorescent light. No signs of blood. The waste baskets were mostly empty, having been serviced by Marie on her cleaning run. The previous day was also trash day, so anything she had collected had already been taken away by the garbage truck.

Will and the crew concluded that their search found nothing and prepared to leave. On an impulse, Will went back into the bathroom and picked up Philip's shaving kit, which Tim had already poked through. Under the kit, Will found an empty package of rubber surgical gloves. After silently berating his crew for having missed it the first time, he asked aloud, "Why would he need surgical gloves?"

Gail heard Will and joined him in the bathroom. "People use them for a lot of things," she said, assuming that Will wanted an answer.

"Yeah, I guess so," Will answered testily, suppressing the impulse to tell Gail that she had blown it. "Maybe we should take the package with us. It might come in handy, don't you think," not hiding the sarcasm.

Oblivious, Gail placed the package in a plastic bag, labeled it, and threw the bag into her evidence kit. "I'll check it for fragments and blood when I get back to the lab. Do you need us for anything else, Will?"

"Let's not forget his rental car; it's included in the warrant. It's a Toyota Corolla and it's out back. Josh has the keys."

The car search came up empty. Will checked the odometer against the car's mileage as shown on the rental contract. "Looks like he hasn't driven it much," he told Harry. "Maybe sixty miles. But it's only about five from the airport. I wonder where else he's been?"

"I can't figure why he even rented a car. Airport to here, here to the convention center. It's all pretty easy on public transportation, and this guy can afford cabs. Why a rental car?"

"Don't know, but something to keep in our pocket."

Harry looked impatient to leave. "I told my wife I'd be back in time for the middle kid's soccer game. Okay to go?"

"Okay for us to go too?" Tim asked?

"Yeah. I've got some errands to run," Will replied. "Let's bounce."

And so the team split up. Will and Harry agreed to touch base with the lab rats the next day, and then determine what to do next about Philip Sarkis.

Who, at that moment, was standing on a street corner in Copley Square, waiting for Dick and Dorothy. He saw them coming from a block away and felt enormous relief. He crossed the street to meet them, and immediately embraced Dorothy. They hugged for several seconds, Dorothy choking back tears of anger as much as angst, while Dick stood by, embarrassed. When they finally released each other, Philip grabbed Dick's hand in both of his, saying, "Dick, thanks for coming up. I can't tell you how happy I am to see both of you."

"I wish I could say the same, Philip," Dick countered, which drew a dirty look from Dorothy that didn't dissuade him in the least. "You have an amazing ability to get yourself into trouble."

"This one wasn't my fault, Dick."

"It never is, is it, Philip? Trouble always seems to find you."

Dorothy intervened. "Why don't we find a place for lunch, sit down, and then have this conversation?"

And so they did. They chose a crowded delicatessen, promising the best sandwiches in Boston, waited a few awkward minutes for a table while perusing the menu, then sat, ordered, and immediately plunged into the conversation each of them, for different reasons, was very eager to have.

Chapter 12

Their table was in a remote corner of Hymie's Deli, purveyor of all things kosher. Their sandwiches, especially their pastrami and corn beef deluxe specials, were famous not only in Boston, but throughout New England. Looking around, Philip could see that you didn't need to be Jewish to be drawn to the place; he was the most Semitic-looking person in the joint by far. Dorothy with her Irish beauty, and Dick, doing his "most interesting man" impersonation, didn't look out of place at all. Most of the people were out-of-towners, betrayed by the walking-tour maps they spread out on their tables or their shopping bags stuffed with Boston souvenirs they'd haul home on the plane or train but really didn't need.

Philip and Dick ordered the house special: corned beef on rye with just about every condiment known to man. Dorothy ordered a more modest turkey club salad but didn't wait for the food to arrive before starting her interrogation.

"All right, Philip. We heard Lentz's perspective. How about if you tell us just what the hell happened."

"Where do you want me start?"

"Don't get cute, Philip," Dick cut in. "And spare us the bullshit. We want you to start from the beginning, going back to your relationship with Mario Angelucci and how you were involved in his case, and going up to what you were doing the night Robinson was attacked."

"Okay, fine," Philip replied defensively. "I have nothing to hide, especially from either of you."

"Then get on with it," Dorothy said.

"It goes back to college. Pudge…"

Dorothy interrupted. "That's Mario?"

"Yes. Weight problem when he was a kid. His parents called him 'pudgy' and it stuck but got shortened to Pudge."

"Go on," Dick said impatiently.

"Anyhow, Pudge was in my pre-med group, and after our sophomore year, we decided to get an apartment together. There were two other guys, also pre-meds. We all worked hard, scored good grades, and had a solid junior year. We did so well that we all got into medical school by Thanksgiving of our senior year, and pretty much partied our way to graduation."

"Where was Pudge from originally?"

"Just across the bridge in Jersey. Cherry Hill. His dad had been a politician over there—pretty powerful councilman. There were always rumors about Mafia connections, but nothing was ever proven."

"Did you believe it?"

"I didn't, until Uncle Donato showed up at our place one day."

"Uncle Donato? Was he really Pudge's uncle?"

"I still don't know. I only saw him once. Our upstairs neighbors complained to the landlord that our parties were a little loud, which they were. They were young parents with kids who should never have lived in that building. It was stuffed with asshole college students like us who made a lot of noise, especially at night. I remember one night, after way too many beers, we all decided to tunnel through to the physics majors who lived next door, to have better access during our joint orgies. So we got a sledge hammer, and… you can imagine the rest."

"Your neighbors didn't call the police?"

"Oh yeah, that too. Lots of times. But the calls were answered by young patrolmen who would just join the party. But the landlord took it more seriously and threatened to evict us. He even sent us a certified letter notifying us that we'd be out of the place if he got one more complaint. Pudge thought it was funny and, in an altered state, pissed on the letter. Literally. After he sobered up, he said he'd take care of it."

"What did that mean?"

"That's where Uncle Donato came in. The people upstairs *did* make another phone call to the landlord, and he told us to pack up our stuff. That evening, Pudge told me to keep an eye on the street in front of our apartment. Uncle Donato from South Jersey was going to pay a visit and help us out with our neighbor problem. Sure enough, about 8 P.M., a chauffeured black Lincoln Town Car pulled up to the curb. Out of the back stepped a large man, wearing a black suit, black shirt, and white tie. He had a wide-brimmed hat so I didn't get a good look at his face, but his driver didn't look real friendly.

"Uncle Donato strolled up the walk and entered our building. We could hear his slow footsteps as he ascended past our apartment to the third-floor apartment above us. I desperately wanted to hear what was going on up there, but Pudge convinced me to stay put and keep our door closed. And it looked like he really meant it."

"How long was he upstairs?"

"About ten minutes. Then we heard him come back down the stairs, past our landing, and down to the street. He glanced up at our window, and, as he turned away, he gave a little wave. I guess he knew we were watching. He got back in the car and I never saw Uncle Donato again."

"I'm going to predict you didn't lose your apartment," Dick said.

"No, we didn't." Philip sighed. "And surprise, no more complaints to the police or the landlord. Just a lot of dirty looks from our neighbors whenever we'd bump into them. The people with the kids moved out about a month later."

"What happened after graduation?"

"We all went to different medical schools and kinda lost contact with each other for a while. Pudge went back to Jersey and I saw him occasionally. He graduated and took a residency in New York, at Cornell. Independently, we each decided to specialize in cardiology, and by pure chance, we ended up in the same fellowship program here in Boston, at the Brigham."

"So you rekindled your friendship?"

"To some extent, but things were a lot different up here. I was still single when we started and Pudge was married. We both moonlighted to make extra money and spent long hours at work. We were on different tracks: Pudge wanted to do general cardiology and heart failure, and I was interested in arrhythmias. We didn't see each other too much, but we had fun when we did. You know what they say about old friendships."

"Then what?" Dick asked, anxious to get to the meat of the story.

"I left Boston and Pudge got a job at MGH. He set up their heart failure and surgical liaison services, and did very well for himself. He was ascending quickly on the academic ladder, a tough proposition in the Harvard system, and was being groomed to take over as department chief one day. And then Sebby Bergstrom happened."

"The media put out a million difference versions of that story," Dick snorted. "What's yours?"

"First of all, you need to know that I was involved in the Bergstrom case as an expert, so I was privy to a lot of the inside information."

"How so?" Dorothy asked.

"This happened before you and I got together. I was asked to help in the defense of Peter Friedberg. He was the electrophysiologist in the Bergstrom case. We got him out of the case in no time. Peter had recommended a defibrillator, which in retrospect was the right call, so they really had no case against him."

"Back up," Dick interrupted. "What's a defibrillator, and why did Friedberg recommend it?"

"I'm getting to that. Remember that Bergstrom went down on the ice during a hockey game. The game was broadcast throughout New England and also in the New York viewing area, so it got a lot of attention. Sebby was taken to a small hospital near the Garden where the Bruins' team physicians worked. They had little cardiology expertise there, mostly orthopedics, and after a day they discharged him home, telling him to rest. Sebby's father wanted more answers and found his way to MGH's cardiology program. He asked Pudge to take over the case, and Pudge agreed.

"The question everyone asked was, why did Sebby go down and did it have anything to do with his heart? The Bruins were frantic to find out, and decided, on their own, to call in a bunch of Boston experts to give them an opinion. So the father went to Pudge, and the Bruins went to consultant docs they called in."

"The so-called 'Dream Team'?" Dick cut in. "I remember that. Did the Bruins have Sebby's permission to convene those consultants?"

"Yes, as far as I know. Sebby's father, Karl, was living in the States and working for the Bruins to be with his son, so he was involved in everything, of course. He was frantic to get answers. I actually think he encouraged the Bruins to call in the troops. Also, he was naïve about the American media. When they got a hold of him, they extracted quotes and sound bites they used to rile up the public even more. By the time Sebby was evaluated at MGH, things were at a fever pitch."

"What was Mario's opinion?"

"Pudge wondered if Sebby's heart was the cause of the blackout, did a bunch of tests, and called in a million consultants. Peter Friedberg was one of them. Pudge asked him to find out if Sebby's heart went out of rhythm transiently. Peter did an electrical test and concluded that the spell had been caused by a dangerous arrhythmia from the bottom of Sebby's heart. That's when Peter told Pudge that Sebby needed an implant to shock his heart if it went out of rhythm again. And fortunately for Peter, he documented that opinion in Sebby's chart."

"This is the internal paddle idea?" Dick asked again.

"Exactly. It's highly effective, and Peter's recommendation was based on finding electrical issues on the tests he did, plus some other cardiac findings."

"What did the Dream Team have to say about that?"

"Most of them shared Peter's opinion."

"So if the experts said Sebby needed a defibrillator, why didn't he get one?"

"Well, Sebby wanted to play. And Karl loved his son. And the kicker is that Pudge was under immense pressure from the fans and even the Bruins. If he went with the experts' recommendations, Sebby's career would have been over. At that time, no one would have allowed Sebby to play hockey with a defibrillator in his chest. The Bruins would have had to pay out several million for the remainder of his guaranteed contract, and Sebby would have been finished at the tender age of twenty-one."

"What happened?"

"Peter went out of town for a weekend to attend a conference, but told Pudge he'd implant the device as soon as he came back. While he was away, Pudge did a tilt-table test."

"What the hell's that?" Dick asked, becoming frustrated with complicated medical issues.

"Pudge thought all along that Sebby had just fainted on the ice, and that his heart never *had* gone out of rhythm. Pudge was a highly experienced cardiologist and did a careful history and examination himself before he came to that conclusion."

"What do you mean by 'just fainted'?"

"That his blood pressure dropped because he hadn't used enough fluid or for some other reason. Sebby hadn't been feeling well the few days before this happened. He probably had the flu, so Pudge was not convinced it was an arrhythmic event and that a defibrillator was necessary."

"Fainting is common, right?"

"Very common, and usually benign and treatable with a lot of extra fluid intake and medications. People let themselves get dehydrated all the time."

"So he did the tilt-table test to prove his theory?"

"Exactly. And to Pudge's credit, it was clearly positive. When he put Sebby upright with his legs still on the table, his blood pressure crashed, his heart rate went down, and he passed out, just like he did at the game."

"Wow. That must have been a surprise," Dorothy

chimed in.

"Not to Pudge. As I said, all along he thought it was a faint, so the tilt-table test just confirmed his opinion. He was happy to throw the result in the Dream Team's face, too. He wasn't pleased with their interference. He had consistently maintained that it wasn't appropriate for anyone to give an opinion without talking to the patient, which none of the experts had, except for Peter of course."

"Then what?"

"Pudge told Sebby and his father that Sebby could be treated with medications, starting with a beta-blocker, and after a period of recuperation and practice, he could play in games again. The team called a news conference, and Pudge told the world that Sebby was fine and would be back on the ice soon. If you watch the tape of that news conference, you can see Peter Friedberg standing behind Pudge looking like he's going to vomit. He wasn't happy, and neither was the Dream Team. Several of them were quoted in the paper saying Dr. Angelucci was incompetent, and that Sebby was getting the wrong treatment.

"All of that didn't matter. Pudge was convinced that the Dream Team was just jealous of the positive publicity he and MGH were getting for having found a correctable problem. Pudge discharged Sebby and told him that after a brief period to make sure the medicine was agreeing with him, he could start practicing. The practices went fine, and Sebby started playing in games again. He had no medication problems, and generally felt great. Until that game in Washington. He went down again, but this time didn't get up. The team trainer started resuscitation but it took forever to get all of his pads off and start proper CPR. Pudge had told the team to keep an external defibrillator on their bench and always have someone there who could take it out and use it, but by the time they did that, it didn't do his brain a whole lot of good. They eventually got him back to Boston, where his final days played out. And that was the end of poor Sebby."

"I remember that his death caused a media shit storm."

"A continuation of the same storm is more like it. The media stayed nuts for the story. Reporters, expert commentators, fans… everybody weighed in. The story was a feature on Sports Center for weeks, and every paper in the country had it on the front page. The most prominent doctors on the Dream Team were interviewed in various places, all saying Pudge was an idiot for letting Sebby back on the ice and for not implanting a device."

"And then there was legal fallout," Dorothy surmised.

"Thad Robinson found his way to the family, and Karl hired him. Robinson unfurled his trademark offense, including legal actions and media manipulation. The Bruins tried to do damage control. They paid out the remainder of Sebby's contract, but Robinson smelled a big payday and advised Karl to go to court anyway. He knew he could get more than a measly $12 million if they sued everybody, and that's exactly what they did. The doctors, the hospitals, and anybody who had contact with Sebby were roped in."

"But Mario was the prime target?" Dick asked.

"Yeah. He wasn't the deepest pocket, but he was the cornerstone of the case. If his judgment was deemed appropriate, the entire case would fall apart, and Robinson knew it. So he worked very hard to prove that Pudge was careless and irresponsible."

"But it couldn't have gone directly to trial. Doesn't Massachusetts have a mandatory review panel for medical malpractice cases?" Dorothy observed.

"Yes, and that's exactly where the case went. The panel ruled that Pudge hadn't been negligent, which is the medical standard, as you know. But the ruling was non-binding."

"And the case went to trial."

"Not before a number of the other defendants extricated themselves, including Peter Friedberg. That one was easy, thank goodness for me. I would've hated to testify."

"Because you were essentially going to say that Peter was right and Mario was wrong?"

"Precisely. Peter was a friend from my training days, too, and I wanted to help him, but I sure didn't want to hurt Pudge. My attorney was pretty sure Robinson would have manipulated me to point a finger at Pudge."

"What happened at Pudge's trial?" Dick asked.

"Which one? There were two. The first one went on for three weeks and resulted in a hung jury. When some of the jurists talked afterwards, it was clear that the majority favored the plaintiff, but not enough to get a verdict."

"So they re-tried the case?"

"Yes, and it just prolonged Pudge's ordeal. This time it was a month with a five-day jury deliberation before they came back with a verdict that cleared him."

"He must have been relieved."

"He was at first. But he ruminated about the case endlessly and things started falling apart. His relationship with Deb and his kids was strained, and he started drinking a little too much."

"How did it go with the public?"

"Everybody in Boston wanted to lynch the poor son-of-a-bitch. Either they hated him for letting the lovable Sebby die, or they hated him because the team crumbled without their star goaltender. Whatever their reasons, he was the most reviled character since the Boston Strangler. He was getting death threats, for Christ's sake, and needed police protection for months after the trials."

"He must have been miserable."

"Actually, everyone who knew him was amazed by how well he held up, at least in public. Except for depositions and trials, he took relatively little time away from work. Only about a month, as I remember. And then he went right back to a full schedule. People thought he was a robot."

"Until…" Dorothy prodded.

"Until his car went off a cliff."

"Pretty grisly. Couldn't he have found some other way to off himself?" Dick asked.

Dorothy shot him a dirty look and tried to ignore the callous question. "Deb and his family must have been devastated," she offered.

"That's putting it mildly. Deb wanted to jump off the cliff herself and join him. Then she realized she had to stay strong for the kids. But she never really recovered."

"I didn't know you were in touch with her," Dorothy said.

"Whcn you and I first got together, I tried to talk to you about it, but every time I did, I would just get overwhelmed. I finally gave up and decided to help her on my own. I called her once in a while, and snuck in a visit whenever I came up here on business. That's why I came to this conference, but I never got the chance to see her—too many policemen asking me irrelevant questions."

"Philip, don't you think the police had a good rationale to question you?"

"I guess so, but they don't have any hard evidence."

"You were seen near the attack on a person who ran over your best friend from college," Dick interjected.

"Don't you agree that's enough 'evidence' to make you a person of interest, which is what you are right now?"

"I was out for an early run that morning. I explained that to the police. I couldn't sleep, so I just got up, put on my sneakers and hit the bricks. The only people I saw were homeless people and a few crazy joggers like me. And some lonely guy standing at the end of the bridge."

"Did you tell the police about the person you saw?"

"Yes, of course. I didn't really get a good look at his face, though."

"If you came across the bridge at the time you say, how come you didn't see Thad Robinson?"

"I have no idea. I must have gone by just before he crossed the bridge."

Silence while their food was delivered, and Dick and Dorothy assessed Philip's response. The look on Dick's face betrayed his skepticism.

"So where do we go from here?" Philip asked eagerly.

"I don't know Philip," Dick answered, struggling with his mouth full after his first bite of his monstrous sandwich. "I need to think about all of this stuff. One thing for sure, this guy Lentz isn't going to give up easily, nor is Robinson. So if we're going to get you clear, we'll need a plausible alternative theory about the crime. And that's going to require some effort."

"Are you serious? We have to try to solve this crime for the police?"

"We at least have to come up with a reasonable theory, Philip," Dorothy explained.

"So, we're going to be here for…"

"We'll be here for a while, Philip," Dorothy finished.

"Maybe for a significant while," Dick hastened to emphasize to a crestfallen Philip.

Chapter 13

After they paid the check, Dick and Dorothy suggested to Philip that he return to his conference while they began their investigation. "I'd really like to help you two get to the bottom of this," Philip protested.

Dick was his usual nurturing self. "Look, Philip, you might be a good doctor, but you don't know jack about our business. So I strongly suggest you get out of the way and let us do a little work on our own."

Dorothy tried a gentler approach. "My dad and I have been doing this for a long time, Philip, and we can work faster by ourselves. So if you want to get out of Boston soon, go back to your conference. We'll meet for dinner and fill you in then."

After Philip departed petulantly, Dorothy turned to her father. "I just tried to convince him we know what we're doing, but I don't have a clue what to do next."

"No worries, little girl. I made some other phone calls before I drove up to your place yesterday."

"To whom, Dad?"

"I know a couple PIs up here. I figured the Bergstrom case and the Robinson attack were so big that one of my contacts had to know something."

"And did they?"

"Sure did. I got some good stuff from a guy I trained in Philly who moved up here a few years ago."

"Do I know this person?"

"You do. He had the hots for you before he left town."

"Not helpful, Dad." Almost every single guy who worked for Dick Deaver was sweet on Dorothy. None of the overtures had turned serious, mainly because each of them knew that Dick would castrate anyone who made a serious approach.

"Remember Mike Benedict?"

"Vaguely."

"Young guy. Early thirties."

"Pretty good-looking but straight as an arrow?" Dorothy said.

"I guess you could say that. Smart kid who tried to make it in the food service business but was unhappy, so he took some criminology courses at St. Joe's and got a gofer job with me."

"That's the same way you started out, Dad," Dorothy recalled.

"Which is probably why I took him in without much experience. And he turned out to be a good worker."

"So why'd he move up here?"

"To *cherchez la femme*. A massage therapist, if you can believe that. I don't think it worked out, but he stayed with his Boston firm after she left him for a weightlifter."

"Wonderful. And what does he know about the Bergstrom case and Robinson?"

"When the shit hit the fan, the Bruins hired his firm. They wanted to get as much dirt as possible on all the combatants so they could plan their strategy."

"So he's got deep background on Robinson?"

"Don't know about that, but he said he'd meet us."

"Why?"

"He's grateful to me for helping him get started. I'm not sure how much he knows. Maybe he'll only be able to point us in the right direction. We'll have to see."

"When can we meet with him?"

Dick looked at his watch. "In about thirty minutes. He's going to meet us at our hotel."

"You really did do your homework, Dad."

"I can't afford to be up here long, my dear, so I figure the faster we get an angle on Robinson, the quicker we come up with alternate explanations."

"And solve the crime?"

"That's not our job. All we have to do is give Detective Lentz a few other 'persons of interest' to chew on so he extends the investigation, and then we can get Philip the hell out of Dodge."

Mike Benedict was waiting for them in the lobby of the Ritz. Dorothy recognized him on sight. Medium build, dark hair and features, conservatively dressed, pocket hanky, friendly smile. To Dorothy, he looked more like a mid-level executive than a PI, but maybe that was because her father and most of the people in his firm looked a little unconventional.

"Mikey, how ya doin'?" Dick said as he prepared to wrap Benedict in a Deaver man hug.

"Real good, boss," Mike gasped, using the little air still remaining in his chest cavity.

"Mike, you remember my daughter Dorothy, don't you?"

"Sure do. Hi, Ms. Deaver. Great to see you again."

There it was, Dorothy thought. That twinkle in the eye she saw in so many men. Obviously checking her out. Who was it that said men spend ninety percent of their time thinking about food, sports and…

"Dorothy, are you there?" she heard her father ask.

"Sorry, Dad. Just lost in thought for a moment. Hi, Mike, how've you been?"

"Just great, Ms. Deaver. It took a while, but I'm finally settled in up here."

"Mike, please call me Dorothy."

"Sorry. Old habit. Anyhow, I like Boston. It's a little lonely living up here by myself, but I've met some nice people. Nothing serious yet."

And there it was again. The next thing a single man needed to convey: *I'm available*. Time to change the subject.

"We really appreciate your willingness to talk with us about the Bergstrom case."

"I'm happy to share what I know. Most of it's in the public domain at this point, so I won't be divulging any privileged information."

"Nor would we want you to, Mike," Dick interjected, trying to sound sincere. "Why don't we grab a table in the coffee shop?"

After they were seated and each ordered a cup, Dick filled Mike in on why they were in Boston, and the reason for their interest in the Robinson case. Mike listened carefully, asking a few clarifying questions. Dorothy chimed in on occasion, letting her father frame the problem in a way Mike would best understand. Each was careful not to identify "the person of interest," nor Dorothy's romantic relationship with him. Just a friend of the family who needed a little of their professional expertise and assistance.

To Dorothy's surprise, Mike didn't seem at all suspicious of any of their manufactured cover story. He simply took it all in and replied matter of factly. "I've asked around a little, and from what I heard, people looking at the case think this wasn't a robbery or random attack. Somebody wanted to hurt that SOB badly."

"Do you think it was a botched murder attempt, or was the attacker really focusing on the guy's spinal cord?"

"Dick, that's a real tough one to answer. I'm far from being a medical expert, but I hear almost every physician who has had a chance to review this case is convinced it was a deliberate pithing."

"Pithing?"

"You know, Dad," Dorothy interjected. "Like they do to frogs? Sever the cord and paralyze the animal?"

"Right. Not an easy thing to do in a human, I guess," Dick said.

"But not that hard, from what I've been told," Mike replied. "You need a sharp knife, a strong thrust, and a bit of luck. And, I guess, you need to know the anatomy a little, and that if you push too hard, you'll hit the aorta and kill the person. But that wouldn't seem like too bad an outcome in this situation. Either way, you get caught, you're looking at attempted murder."

"Exactly. Which is why we're anxious to get our friend off thc hook."

"Which means you're trying to spotlight other people who may have had it in for the notorious Thaddeus Robinson."

"Yes," Dorothy replied. "And we know that the Bruins hired you when Bergstrom died..."

"So," Dick cut in, "I figured you must know something about the man who went after the team and the doctors who took care of Sebby."

"Which I do, and so here we are. What can I tell you? Understand though, this conversation is off the record."

"I understand. Now, for starters, what do you know about Robinson?"

"You got a couple of days? The guy is nasty as they come. He's smart as hell, has a great business mind, and works like a maniac."

"Doesn't sound nasty so far."

"And he has very few scruples."

"Oh. In other words, a perfect lawyer."

"A perfect scumbag lawyer. It was hard to find anyone who'd say he was incompetent, but nobody said they'd want to have a beer with him, either."

"So he's not going to win Mr. Congeniality. But that doesn't usually get you a knife in the back."

"I agree. But, as I recall, there were quite a few people who had a reason to hate the guy and maybe want to hurt him."

"Starting with his ex-wife?"

"So you know about the pre-nup controversy."

"Yeah, that came up on our standard search. A lot of legal back and forth. Do you have more?"

"Not really. Effie's lawyers made a giant stink about the document, claiming she had never signed it or even seen it, and that Robinson had manufactured it somehow."

"It cost her plenty."

"In the tens of millions, most likely," Mike agreed peeking over the tip of his coffee mug.

"Ever meet her?"

"No reason to. I was just doing background on the subject. The fact that he had a pissed-off ex didn't strike me as unusual or helpful to the Bruins. I don't know if she was angry enough to hire somebody to stick the guy, but the police must have at least considered it."

"What else ya got?"

"We discovered that he has the gambling bug."

"High roller?"

"Would you have expected less? Generally, he was

able to keep it in check, but every once in a while he went nuts and blew a large wad in a very short period of time."

"Vegas or Atlantic City?"

"Vegas, mostly. He got comped regularly out there and took advantage of it."

"How much are we talking?"

"Six figures in a night, never seven as far as I could tell. But enough to deplete his reserves and then some. That's when it got interesting," Mike smirked.

"Loan sharks?" Dorothy asked.

"Yep, and some other interesting characters, apparently."

"Got names?"

"I do, and will give them to you, but please make absolutely sure nobody knows where you got them. I don't want to have anything to do with those guys."

Dick nodded his agreement. "What about Robinson's colleagues? I'm guessing someone like him hasn't exactly treated them well."

"Treated them all like crumbs. He's apparently an equal opportunity prick."

"Any of 'em stand out?"

"The worst was Stu Slavinsky, one of the office drones. Robinson beat up on the guy regularly, and then nailed the poor schlump's wife, just to put a little icing on the cake."

"He screwed an employee's wife?" Dorothy blurted, not believing what she had heard.

"And everybody in the office knew, including Stu."

"Who was powerless to do anything."

"Not if he wanted to keep his job. Besides, his wife Laura didn't seem to mind, so Stu was on his own. And I gather he isn't what you'd call a strong personality."

"Does Stu have a medical background?" Dorothy

wanted to know.

"As a matter of fact, he was a doctor for a couple of years before changing his mind and going to law school."

"So he might have some idea of the anatomy of the spinal column."

"If that's your main criterion for picking out a suspect, you're in big trouble."

"Why?" Dorothy asked innocently.

"Robinson sued and screwed dozens of doctors here in Boston. And he was very much a general practitioner. He sued docs in all specialties, although he was particularly fond of nailing orthopedic surgeons, cardiologists, and heart surgeons."

"All with a pretty good knowledge of anatomy."

"Afraid so. We reviewed the cases pretty thoroughly to see if he had any particular pattern. I'd say that deep pockets was the common thread. Doctors and healthcare systems without big policies or a lot of reserve funds were let out of cases pretty damn fast no matter how obviously negligent. High-profile docs and big health systems were taken to the mat."

"I assume you have a list we can look at?"

"Again, off the record. Giving you that stuff violates a bunch of ethical codes."

"But you owe me."

"That I do," Mike nodded.

Dorothy wondered what that meant, but decided to stay out.

Mike drained the last of his coffee, put his cup down and looked Dick in the eye. "But the granddaddy of all the screw jobs had to be the Angelucci case. Robinson went after that guy with a vengeance."

"Why do you think he was so aggressive with Angelucci?" Dorothy asked.

"Bergstrom's father Karl may have had something to do with that. Sebby was Karl's pride and joy. After Sebby died, something happened to Karl. I don't know… he wanted somebody to pay for it or something. Maybe he had a guilty conscience for letting his kid go out and play again. And with Robinson at his side, the two of them kind of reinforced each other, each wanting Angelucci's hide, if for somewhat different reasons. So they didn't blink when the arbitration panel ruled in Angelucci's favor. Or when the first trial ended in a hung jury. They just kept coming."

"Robinson going after a deep pocket?"

"Sort of. Partners Healthcare is the system that MGH is part of. They're self-insured and have millions. But the Bruins had paid off Sebby's remaining salary to get out of the case, and a few other defendants had settled, so Karl had banked millions. Maybe he didn't think justice had been served? Or maybe Robinson felt he hadn't gotten a sweet enough taste yet. Who knows?"

"And you couldn't figure out why they never let up?"

"Never did, and neither could anyone else. Even the people at the office were surprised, although a few of them told me that every once in a while, Robinson would get zeroed in on somebody and wouldn't or couldn't give up, long past the time it'd be reasonable to stop. I guess he just hated Angelucci, plus which, it wouldn't have been hard to convince Karl to continue to take him down."

"What was Robinson's reaction when Angelucci killed himself?"

"The asshole said it proved what a jerk Angelucci was, leaving his wife with kids to raise with no doctor's salary and no life insurance. He showed no empathy whatsoever. Didn't even try to fake some."

"It looks like we have our work cut out for us,"

Dorothy mused.

Mike nodded. "It'll be one of those cases where you have an infinite number of people who were at least mildly interested in hurting the vic, but not very many with the juice or the skill. All I can do is wish you luck."

Mike stood to leave. "Later this afternoon, I'll give you a list of names of some of the people Robinson went after. I'll leave it at the front desk in a sealed envelope, and I'll try to give you an idea of who might be worth chasing down. As you'll see, some of the cases were pretty sad, but none worse than the Bergstrom fiasco."

Dick stood to shake Mike's hand. "We really appreciate your help, Mikey."

Mike looked at Dorothy. "It might be a tedious process for you guys, so if you want to escape for a drink or dinner with me, let me know."

Dorothy smiled politely, trying to hide her reaction. "We'll see how it goes," she said.

"No way, pal," she hissed when Mike was out of earshot.

"Give the guy a break. He doesn't know you're living with somebody."

"And I wasn't about to tell him the person I'm living with is the one we're up here trying to extricate."

"Where do you want to start, little girl?" Dick said, getting back to business.

"I say we talk to Slavinsky."

"Pretty obvious starting point, right? He knows anatomy, and his boss was boffing his wife. Call him and see if he has some time later this afternoon. Tell him we're making a list of the top cuckolds for *Boston Magazine* and he might be on the cover."

"Dad, that's not a good attitude going in."

"I know. We'll go easy on the guy. He's been through enough."

Chapter 14

Dorothy had a hunch that even on a Saturday afternoon in springtime, Stu Slavinsky might be in his office at the Robinson law firm. Not a lot of reason to be home with his adulterous wife, she figured, even if they were still together. So it was no surprise when she called the firm from her room at the Ritz and Stu picked up. She introduced herself as a private detective from Philadelphia investigating the attack on Thaddeus Robinson.

"Why is a dick from Philly up here working that case?" Stu asked.

"Our client is a suspect, and we're trying to get some background on Robinson. We were told you've been an employee at Robinson's firm for some time."

"I'm sure that's not all you've heard about me and good ol' Thad. Plenty of other people have worked at the firm a lot longer than me. And yet you called me. Why?"

"I'll be straight with you, Mr. Slavinsky," Dorothy said. "We're talking to people who might've had a reason to hurt Mr. Robinson."

Dorothy knew she had to soften the message or risk

spooking him. "You're not high on our list by any means, but we think you could give us some perspective on his nefarious behavior."

"'Nefarious' is an interesting adjective, Ms. Deaver. But why should I bother talking to you?"

"If we've identified you as a person of interest, the police won't be far behind. If you're innocent, and I'm pretty sure you are, anything we learn will likely be in your favor."

Stu paused, weighing the pros and cons of continuing. "I guess a little chat can't hurt anything, and maybe it will help you find the person who actually attacked Thad."

"I work with my father. Could he and I meet with you this afternoon?"

"Yes, but not in the office. We're across the street from Boston Commons. Meet me in front of our building at 3 P.M. It's a decent day outside. Maybe we can find a bench and watch the Swan Boats."

Stu was standing in front of his office as Dick and Dorothy pulled up. Dick had no trouble identifying him—his downtrodden appearance was consistent with Mike Benedict's characterization of him. "Looks like Rick Moranis, that little guy in *Honey, I Shrunk the Kids*," he observed.

Dorothy shot him an angry glance. "Don't start that crap, Dad. As you said, this guy has been ground down enough. The last thing we want is for him to clam up because he thinks we don't respect him."

But Dorothy had to admit her father had nailed it. Stu didn't exactly project a winning appearance. He was short, slight of build, with slicked-down brown hair, oversized horn-rimmed glasses, and an overbite just bad enough to call attention. His short-sleeved plaid shirt—

"business casual" for a Saturday in the office, apparently—completed the picture.

"Mr. Slavinsky?" Dorothy proffered as she approached, hand extended.

"Hi, Ms. Deaver. And you can call me Stu if I can call you Dorothy."

Dorothy nodded. "Sure."

"And this is your father?"

"Yes, I'm Dick Deaver. Thanks for making time to talk to us, Stu."

"No problem. I apologize for being a little difficult on the phone and for meeting out of the office. Other staffers are working today, and I didn't want to have to explain who you are."

"Perfectly understandable. Besides, it's too nice to be inside on a Saturday like today."

It was in fact a beautiful afternoon, the Friday nor'easter having cleared out the humidity. A warm sun brought out Bostonians as well as tourists. Stu led them to a small picnic table off the walking path around the pond. Dick and Dorothy sat opposite Stu so they could face him while they spoke. Dorothy asked Stu if he wanted anything to drink. Stu declined and Dorothy got right to the interview.

Leaning forward on her elbows, she said, "Stu, we want to be respectful of your time, so I'll come directly to the point. It seems that Thad Robinson was attacked by someone who wanted to hurt him in a way that was worse than killing him, a way that would basically torture him for the rest of his days. So we're looking for someone with a strong motive."

"And you think that's me?"

"As I said on the phone, you're not high on our list."

"For one thing, the person who did this was able to overpower Robinson from behind. No offense, but you look a little small for that," Dick added.

"None taken," Stu replied. He seemed chagrined.

"But let's be honest," Dorothy resumed, shooting a frown at her father. "A lot of people know about Thad and your wife. We can understand that would have angered you."

"That's an understatement." His mood was not improving.

"I'm sure. See, what we want is your perspective on Thad's behavior. And we want to know if there are a lot of people at the firm who, like you, were taken advantage of."

Stu looked down at his folded hands, trying to decide how much to divulge. When he looked up, he had tears in his eyes. "Let me start by saying I've fantasized about sticking a knife in that bastard's back. When I heard that somebody actually did it, I was a little jealous of the experience. But it wasn't me."

"I believe you," Dorothy said, empathetically. "But there may be others who won't. As I said on the phone, finding the attacker may be as good for you as for our client."

"And I accept that premise," Stu nodded.

"So maybe you can tell us a little about your background and your relationship with Thad?"

"The irony is that I started out wanting to become a doctor, not to sue them."

"What happened?"

"I got into Penn Med after only three undergraduate years at Yale, and took a residency in orthopedics. About two years into that training, I decided I didn't want to take care of patients, so I quit and applied to law school."

"That was a big change."

"I realized I just didn't like people very much, so

there was no point in learning how to set their fractures and replace their hips. I got into Temple Law and was surprised by how much I enjoyed it."

"And malpractice law must have seemed like a natural for you."

"Everybody I knew assumed that's what I would end up doing. So I never really gave it much thought. The only question was which side I'd pick. I always wanted to be the good guy. I loved how Perry Mason used to help people in trouble, so I was inclined to the defense. But I did a clerkship with Thad's firm and realized there was a lot more money on that side of the bar and I could still help people who had been harmed."

"Did Thad recruit you directly?"

"Not really. He let some of his junior people do most of the work, but he makes the final decision about hiring at all levels. I met with him a couple times. I guess he thought I would fit in. He made me a reasonable offer, and that was that."

"When did Laura come into the picture?" Dorothy asked quietly.

"The day after I arrived. She's a paralegal and was assigned to a few of my cases. She didn't waste any time, um, getting acquainted."

"Stu, I don't want to make you uncomfortable."

"Don't worry about it. We split up a few weeks ago, and I'm glad to be rid of her. So you can ask me anything you like. Maybe how she came on to me?"

"Tell us everything you're comfortable with telling us and that you think is important to the case," Dick encouraged.

"If you ever see Laura, you'll understand a little about how I got steamrolled. She's not a classic beauty, but she knows how to show off what she's got. What I didn't realize is that she's a gold digger. They tell me that from the minute she arrived at the firm, her goal was to snag a lawyer, preferably one with a lot of money or at least a bright future. Until I came along, the only people who paid attention to her were the old married guys who promised her the moon while they were screwing her but had no intention of leaving their wives."

"And a physician/lawyer must have been a particular attraction," Dick concluded.

"Especially a single guy like me, who never had a woman give him a second look. I was prime meat. And I can't say it was unpleasant. The sex was outrageous, if a little rough, and I enjoyed having an attractive woman on my arm. I stupidly proposed after dating her for only a month. She picked the engagement ring. The rock was huge, but she was happy, and that was all I cared about."

"Did you have a prenuptial agreement?" Dick asked.

"Oh, yes. I was an idiot in love and so it was lopsided in her favor, of course."

"How long did the marital bliss last?"

"A few months, and then things began to unravel. Laura became aloof and started to stay out late, coming up with a variety of excuses. None of them made much sense, but she didn't seem to care what I thought. I suspected she was fooling around, but I didn't want to be sure because then I'd have to do something about it. The sex was still good, and I craved her company, so I put up with a lot of crap."

"Where did Thad come in?"

"I noticed that Laura was being assigned to more of his cases. She was spending lots of time in his office with the door closed, and when I saw her after those appointments, her clothes were a little mussed, or her makeup smudged. And that damn smirk on her face. She never told me the truth, but she didn't have to. It was clear that Thad was having sex with her in his office, and wherever else they had opportunity."

"What was in it for her?"

"A promotion to head paralegal and a nice raise. She tried to convince me she earned it, but I knew she had gotten it the old-fashioned way."

"Did you confront her?"

"Only once did I work up the nerve to ask her directly if she was doing it with Thad. She threw her head back, laughed like a maniac, and told me I was a crazy person. Her behavior was so affected that I knew right away she was lying."

"What'd you do about it?"

"I went to Thad and told him I knew he was having an affair with my wife."

"And his reaction?"

"He just stared at me and told me to get out of his office."

"He didn't deny it?"

"Nope. Just glowered at me as if I were the problem."

"When did this all happen?" Dorothy cut in.

"About two months ago, I would say. I went home that evening and told Laura to pack up and get out. She laughed in my face again, and told me I should examine our prenuptial agreement before I went any further. I didn't have to. I knew I was screwed, but I didn't care. I just wanted her out of my face."

"And did she leave?"

"Yeah, but she took her sweet time. I guess she was looking around for somebody to shack up with. I came home one night a few weeks later and discovered that she had left and taken almost everything of value with her."

"You saw her after that, I suppose. At work, I mean."

"Every freakin' day. She sneered at me whenever I

saw her, or if she was talking to her buddies, she whispered things and they'd all laugh. It was awful."

"Was? Isn't she still with the firm?"

"That behavior stopped after Thad was attacked. She's been staying out of my way entirely."

"Does she suspect you attacked Thad?"

"Who knows? Maybe she's worried she could be next. In any case, I haven't gone out of my way to deny it. I kinda like having her keep her distance and her mouth shut."

"*Did* you attack Thad Robinson, Stu?" Dick asked.

"No way. I admire the skill of whoever did it since they apparently managed to ruin his life without killing him, at least that's what I've heard. But it wasn't me."

"Can you prove that?"

"I was out with some college buddies that night. We had dinner and then went to Fenway for a Red Sox game. They shut out the Yankees. I kept my ticket stub."

"But Thad was attacked in the early morning. Unless it was a scoreless tie and went thirty innings, the Red Sox story won't work, I'm afraid," Dick noted. Dorothy didn't appreciate her father's sarcasm.

"So you think I'd go out with my friends, enjoy a ball game, and then get up in the middle of the night and stab Thad Robinson? Well, the fact is I wasn't at home that night. We stopped off at a couple of bars after the game, and I had too many beers so I stayed at my friend's apartment near the Fenway. On the sofa."

"But not in the same room?"

"I'm not that kinda guy, Dick."

"Sorry, Stu. Wasn't suggesting anything. But theoretically, you could have gone out, stabbed Robinson, and gotten back to your friend's place before he woke up. Right?"

"How would I have known where to find him? I

skipped the party he threw to celebrate a big win, and, as I understand it, he left with someone. I couldn't have known where he went. And even if I did, it would have been a little tricky since I didn't have my car and I don't usually carry a knife around. Plus my friend didn't give me a key to get back into the apartment building. But other than all that, I guess it's not absolutely impossible."

"So that brings us to the $64,000 question, Stu," Dorothy said. "If you didn't do it, who do you think did?"

"If you've been getting familiar with the situation, you know there are dozens of people who detest Thad Robinson, including a lot of docs with the skill to rip his spinal cord to shreds with the precision of a diamond cutter. I don't have time to go back and sort through all his cases to look for suspects, but somebody should."

"Do you know anything about the Mario Angelucci case?"

"I wasn't involved, but I know about it. Who doesn't? I followed the story in the papers even before I joined the firm, and I heard the associates discussing the case several times."

"Thad went after Angelucci pretty hard, it seems. Does that case stand out in your mind as particularly egregious?"

"I guess so. The thing that made that case terrible was all the publicity. Angelucci was dragged through the mud, and Thad made sure the media got plenty of ammunition. He did everything he could to keep the story in the *Globe* and in the national news, while Angelucci twisted in the wind."

"And do you think Angelucci's suicide was the direct result of Thad's harassment?"

"It must have had a lot to do with it. I'm sure there

were other factors, but that man suffered horribly. It was a long fall from grace."

"Stu, is there anything else we didn't ask you that might help us?"

"Thad has an ex-wife, and there were always rumors about his gambling debts. So you can add to that an angry group of personal-injury defendants, and not just the doctors he went after. I honestly don't know who he pissed off enough to inspire a vicious attack. Like I said, as much as I loathed the guy, I couldn't bring myself to do that. So you have your work cut out for you."

"Yeah, I see. Okay. Well, thanks for meeting with us, Stu. We've taken enough of your time. And we know this wasn't an easy conversation," Dorothy said.

"No, but things are getting better. I'm getting used to life without Laura."

"Must be a tough place to work these days."

"For lots of reasons. Many of us are getting worried about our jobs. No one knows if and when Thad will be back, and without him, there isn't much of a firm."

Dick and Dorothy said goodbye to Stu and rose to leave. Stu remained at the table, sitting on the bench, gazing out at the Swan Boats, lost in thought.

"Poor guy," Dorothy observed as they walked away.

"Poor us," Dick observed. "It looks like it's going to take a lot longer to sort through the candidates than I thought."

"I say we make like Willie Sutton, and go for the money next," Dorothy suggested.

"The former Mrs. Thaddeus Robinson?" Dick asked.

"The very same," Dorothy said as they walked briskly across the sun-kissed walkways of Boston Commons.

Chapter 15

Dick and Dorothy decided to drive out to Effie Robinson's house unannounced. She was living now in Hanson, southeast of Boston, outside the beltway. They'd be getting there around dinnertime. Mike Benedict had told them Effie didn't have much of a social life, so they figured they had a good chance of catching her alone. Maybe, if they were lucky, she would have already had a cocktail and would be extra ready to provide some juicy information about Thad.

"I don't know what to expect," Dorothy said during the ride. "Hopefully she isn't so bitter and depressed that she won't speak to us at all."

"I was thinking the same thing," Dick said.

Coming into town, Dick remarked, "Look at this place. I can't believe a vital woman would choose to live out here after being in the middle of the city for so long."

Hanson was a sleepy rural town that high-speed trains and interstate highways transformed into a bedroom community for Boston. Couples gravitated to the simple environment with affordable housing, good schools and shopping, never expecting much of a night life or exciting entertainment. Strip malls featured the usual stores and outlets, with an occasional ice cream stand and sports bar. Residents drove everywhere, which had the effect of isolating the habitants and their kids from each other. In other words, it was Middle America at its best.

Effie Robinson lived in a cottage on the edge of the small downtown area. It sat on about an acre of land, back from the road a couple hundred feet. There was no landscaping to speak of, only a scruffy lawn with plenty of crabgrass, and a paved driveway with so many potholes that it gave the impression of a recent mortar attack. Several window shutters were missing, and the black paint on the front shingles was peeling in too many places.

A late-model Chevy Impala sat under the roof of a carport complete with rotting supports and droopy roof. Dick and Dorothy drove up the driveway, each grimacing in anticipation of meeting an unhappy and unkempt person living in a dump in the middle of nowhere.

The doorbell was unscrewed and disconnected, its guts hanging freely. Their sharp knock on the door was answered promptly. They were amazed to see an attractive, smiling, and pleasant woman who greeted them cheerfully. "Hello, can I help you?"

"Ms. Robinson?" Dorothy asked, taken aback.

"I suppose so," Effie answered. "I don't go by that name much anymore, though."

"Sorry, Ms…."

"Pew. Effie Pew. And you are?"

"My name is Dorothy Deaver, and this is my father Dick. We're private investigators from Philadelphia and we were wondering if you have a few moments to talk with us about your husband, I mean ex-husband, Thad Robinson."

"What kind of questions, Ms. Deaver?"

"We're trying to determine who may have attacked him…"

"Someone attacked Thad? What are you talking about?" Effie asked.

"You didn't hear? Maybe we should start from the beginning. May we come in?"

"By all means."

Effie stepped aside to let Dorothy and Dick into the house, and then escorted them to the living room. The interior of the house, in sharp contrast to the exterior, was spotless, well appointed, and conservatively decorated. Effie sensed their surprise. "The difference between the outside and the inside is startling, isn't it?" she said.

"I admit I was struck by the contrast," Dorothy replied, trying to be diplomatic.

"I'm renting this place and the landlord does a lousy job of maintaining the property. I can't do much myself on the outside, but I've worked hard to get the inside respectable. I painted a number of the rooms myself."

"You've done a terrific job," Dorothy said admiring the decorations. The furniture was inexpensive but clean and well kept.

"Thanks. I have a man friend who has been terribly helpful. He owns a furniture store here in town and doesn't mind helping with some of the work. He just isn't healthy enough to do the heavy work outside."

Dick and Dorothy sat on the sofa, Effie across from them on a Queen Victoria chair. Dorothy finally had a chance to size up Effie, and what she saw was surprising and impressive. Effie had clearly been a beauty in her day, and had kept herself in good physical condition. Her hair was graying, and she was making no attempt to color it, nor did she need to. Her clear complexion and bright blue eyes made her look young enough to be attractive, in a Cialis commercial kind of way. She dressed conservatively but thoughtfully, all in all a far cry from the unkempt, howling recluse Dick and Dorothy had feared they might meet.

"So, about Thad. Let me start from the beginning," Dick said, and proceeded to recap what had happened to Thad, and then drew Dick and Dorothy to Boston. He stopped intermittently to answer Effie's questions, politely but succinctly, avoiding anything remotely accusatory. At the end of his recitation, Effie lowered her head and sniffled enough to make her sorrow seem genuine.

"I'm so sorry to hear about this. I don't keep up with the news like I used to. But nobody, not even Thad, deserves to be savagely attacked and disabled."

"We're inclined to agree with you."

Suddenly Effie looked up, shocked by her own revelation. "Surely you aren't here because you think I had something to do with this."

"Let's be frank, Ms. Pew. Thad did you wrong, and many people would assume you'd seek revenge."

"That's ridiculous. I'd never do something like that. First of all, I'm not physically capable of attacking anyone, and I certainly don't have the means to have hired someone to do it for me."

"We agree, but it might be a good idea for you to give us your perspective on Thad, and what happened between you. The police are likely to follow us here, at some point, so you might want to have the facts straight in your mind."

"I don't want to be rude, but explain to me again: why are you investigating this case?"

Dorothy took the lead on this answer. "The police have questioned my significant other, a physician named Philip Sarkis, about this case. I won't get into the details, but we're convinced Philip had nothing to do with the attack, and thought that a little fact finding might help him out."

"So you want to throw the blame on somebody else, like me," Effie reflected, without any apparent scorn.

"I have to admit that we did wonder, but after meeting you, your involvement appears to be very unlikely."

Effie visibly relaxed. "I'm relieved to hear that. Thad treated me shamefully, but as you can see, I've landed on my feet."

"What do you do with your time, Ms. Pew?

"I have a clerical job at the local library that keeps me busy during the week."

"You must have had a difficult time adjusting to life out here," Dick said, probing as diplomatically as possible.

Effie didn't miss his intent. "You mean I must have been royally ticked off about being banished from Boston's high society, Mr. Deaver?"

"Something like that," Dick answered, with a barely discernible blush.

"Thad made me miserable for many reasons and for many years, but I had inertia. I should have left him, but couldn't summon up the energy until he pushed."

"And things are better for you here, Ms. Pew?" Dorothy asked, attempting to smooth over her father's ill-disguised accusation.

"Most definitely. I like my new life, my new friends. I even took in a couple of stray cats to keep me company."

"How did you meet Thad?" Dorothy asked, trying to keep the conversation moving to areas she cared about.

"At a fraternity party in Philadelphia. I was an undergraduate at Bryn Mawr and Thad was in law school at Penn."

"Are you from Philly originally?"

"Doesn't my maiden name give me away?"

"You're related to the Pew family?"

"The poor side, I'm afraid. The only perk was a college scholarship for any of the poor cousins who managed to get accepted. That's how I was able to afford Bryn Mawr."

"You and Thad hit it off right away?"

"I suppose you can say that. We went through the usual infatuation, but after the wedding the newlywed glow didn't last long. Thad was driven and worked hard. Once we got started, you could say we had a comfortable existence together. We were good business partners. I always managed to save money, so we could have a nice house and car. Thad was a spender, and the more he made, the more he burned."

"Did you get along?"

"We were good friends to each other and parents to our children for a long time—until Thad started wandering. You'll see, as you learn more about him, that Thad is an inveterate womanizer. He kept it under control when our children were young, but once they were out of the house, the man was entirely obsessed."

"And so your relationship deteriorated?"

"Yes, but slowly. I was determined not to be the one who ran off. It was Thad who finally decided to break up."

"We understand that there was a heated dispute over a prenuptial agreement?"

"I can tell you with complete honesty that there never *was* a prenuptial agreement," Effie declared indignantly. "There was no reason for one. When we were married, Thad had nothing but debt, and neither of us ever thought we'd be rich. We worked hard to pay off his student loans. I had jobs even when I had babies at home.

I never shied away from hard work, Ms. Deaver."

"So you're saying the prenuptial agreement he produced was a fake?"

"A fabrication, for sure. But one of the most skillful forgeries of all time. We had multiple experts examine it. Many had their reservations, but none could prove it was phony. The irony is that if Thad had just told me he wanted to leave me, my demands would have been modest. The forged pre-nup was so lopsided that my attorneys insisted that we contest it, which we did, unsuccessfully."

"How did your children react?"

"Angrily. By the time all of that happened, they already hated their father. He treated them poorly, and obviously didn't care about their lives. The three of us have been close, so the way he was treating me during the divorce, and even before, didn't make them particularly happy."

"Might they have the means to go after Thad?" Dick asked.

It took a few seconds for Effie to register the meaning of the question. "My goodness, Mr. Deaver, are you suggesting that they could have arranged the attack on Thad?"

"From what you say, they sound pretty mad."

"You have to know them to realize how outlandish that suggestion is. They're so ineffectual when it comes to relationships. It's such a shame to see. Thad just wore them down. Planning an attack on their father would have been impossible."

"What about your man friend? Does he know about Thad?"

"Henry? Oh my. He's an even more unlikely suspect than my children. I've deliberately kept most of Thad's evilness from him. It serves no purpose in our relationship. And that bad back of his keeps him from doing much heavy work around the house would certainly keep him from jumping somebody."

"If not you or your children or your friend, Ms. Pew, then who else might be suspects?"

"I have no idea. Thad excluded me from his business affairs, but I do know that he managed to galvanize the entire medical community in Boston by suing so many of its most famous physicians. Let's just say there are many people who wouldn't mind seeing harm come to him."

"So we've heard. Anybody specific come to mind?" Dick asked, trying to hide his impatience.

Effie paused again, judging the propriety of her next response.

"Mr. Deaver, Thad manipulates people for a living, and he carries it over to his private life. Or vice versa. At any rate, he's a user, a taker. Thad and people like him make lots of friends, or people who would appear to be friends, but many of them become enemies when they realize they're only being used, and maybe even abused."

"Thad is also shrewd," Effie continued. "He knows how far he can push people before they'll strike back. People like Thad don't let themselves get hurt very often—emotionally or physically."

"Do you have examples?"

"During our marriage, I watched him mistreat people all the time. He did it with my family, our neighbors, people who worked on our house. He bullies someone until they want to scream, but then he backs off and assuages them and plays the good guy. I think he gets a kick out of seeing how far he can push someone. He's always pushing the envelope."

"But Thad miscalculated with at least one person?"

"That's an easy explanation for what happened. But I'm not so sure. I think it's more likely that the attacker was somebody he didn't see coming. Someone who was furious with him but never confronted him until the rage boiled over. That would be my guess, at least, without having a lot of time to think about it."

Silence filled the room as Dick and Dorothy thought about what Effie said, realizing that she could be describing someone they knew well. Someone with a mean streak, his own idea of justice, and the willingness and means to make a villain pay the price.

After several long moments of anxious contemplation, Dorothy said, "Effie, you have been most kind. We really appreciate your insights."

"Where do you go from here?"

"I'm not sure. We have more people to talk to, but at this point, we don't have a clear suspect," Dorothy said, wondering if she believed it herself.

"I'd be happy to help you again if you have any more questions, off the record, of course, and after I have a chance to think about all this."

"We may take you up on that offer. And be assured that whatever you tell us, we'll keep it under our hat," Dick said as they made their way to the door. They said their goodbyes and walked back to their car.

Dorothy was eager to hear her father's take on their talk with Effie. "What did you think, Dad?" she asked as they climbed into their car and were out of earshot.

"She was honest with us. I suspect Robinson's shabby behavior is why she's glad to have him be part of her past."

"Yeah. It seems a lot of people got roped into his bullshit and had a hard time escaping."

"Until Robinson used them up and threw them away."

"I'm exhausted, Dad. What about you?"

"Yeah, this stuff is tiring. I think we need to call it a day."

"How about if I call Philip? I'll have him move his stuff over to the Ritz and stay with me. We can all have dinner at the hotel, plan tomorrow's interviews, then get to bed at a reasonable hour."

"I'm for that. We have Angelucci's wife and some of Robinson's, uh, 'bankers' to talk to for sure."

"Dad, do you think Philip did this?" Dorothy finally asked.

Dick had just clicked his seatbelt and paused before he started the car, looking over at Dorothy and holding her gaze. "I don't want to believe it, and I didn't until Effie profiled the person she thought might have had the nerve to attack her ex. I know the guy has a temper, and I can see how he would have gotten angry with Robinson, but was it enough to make him plan and then pull off that kind of attack?"

"The Deb Angelucci interview should be helpful."

"Unquestionably the most important interview from our perspective."

They sat silently for the most of the drive back to Boston, each trying to determine whether they really wanted to discover the true identity of Robinson's assailant.

Chapter 16

The next morning, Dorothy awoke early. The shades were pulled so the room was dark despite the impending dawn. Philip was well over to his side of the bed, snoring softly, enjoying a good night's sleep for the first time in a long time. Dinner the night before had been anything but relaxing. Philip was obsessed with the Robinson case, and every attempt Dick made to steer the conversation away from it was met with resistance. Tired from a long day, Dick had managed not to lose his temper, but Dorothy knew it had been a struggle for her father to maintain his composure.

Dorothy slipped out of the covers, put on her robe, and wandered out into the small living room that was part of the junior suite her father had reserved for her. She closed the double doors behind her softly. She wanted time at the computer, with no interruptions from Philip.

It was Sunday, and Dorothy was worried that Deb Angelucci might not be available or amenable to an interview. She didn't want to waste the day. Perhaps a little poking around in Thad Robinson's life would produce some other informants and subjects of interest.

Dorothy had spent several summers in her father's private investigator business, doing odd jobs and helping his associates with their tasks. Having an inquisitive nature, she asked questions endlessly, and being the boss's daughter, few refused to answer. In time, she acquired investigative skills that gave her an edge in her legal career. Many of those skills were not entirely legal, but Dorothy had learned how to be careful and to cover her tracks. Most importantly, she knew when to back off and when to take no for an answer. Consequently, she had a successful track record of extracting privileged information without getting caught. Even her father had no idea of her agility with databases. Thank goodness, Dorothy thought. He'd have a fit if he knew.

"I don't want to talk to any current employees," Dorothy reminded herself as she flipped open her laptop. "Let's see if any people have been released from his firm recently." After only a small amount of effort, Dorothy was able to infiltrate the Robinson's firm personnel files and find the names of several employees who had been let go or quit within the past six months. Most were temporary employees, but a few had been with the firm for some time. Heather Chesterton was an accountant recently discharged after five years of employment. Her dismissal had been abrupt and occurred only a few days before Robinson was attacked. Dorothy copied down Heather's contact information, along with the names of a few other employees who had been let go. Not enough motivation to knife Robinson, but they might be willing to shovel some dirt on their former employer.

It was going on 8 A.M. and Philip was still asleep. Dorothy needed some stress reduction. She closed her computer, stole into the bathroom, changed quietly into workout gear and sneakers, and spent the next hour in the hotel's exercise facility before meeting her father downstairs for breakfast.

"I called Deb Angelucci's house. No answer, so I left a message," Dick said.

"Maybe she's at church, Dad," Dorothy suggested. "She has a lot to pray for."

"Maybe, but now we're going to waste a lot of time waiting for her to call me back."

"Not necessarily. I got the names of some people who worked at Robinson's office and were recently let go."

"Really? How'd you do that?"

"Don't ask, Dad. Let's just say that those summer jobs I had at your firm paid off."

"I've warned you about hacking into business computers, Dorothy. It's very dangerous."

"I know how to be careful, Dad. And I've never come close to getting caught."

"One mistake and you could lose everything, you know."

"Are we going to argue, or are we going to make our plans for the day?" Dorothy asked.

"All right. Who do you want to call?"

"The best prospect is Heather Chesterton, an accountant who worked closely with Robinson. I'll go out to the lobby where I can get some privacy and call her."

Dorothy, still in her shorts and tank top, got a lot of unwanted attention as she rose from her seat and left the breakfast room. She had her head down, trying to ignore the stares, when she ran head-first into Philip.

"Where have you been?"

"What does it look like, Philip?"

"Don't you answer your phone?"

"I had my head phones on when I was exercising. I guess I didn't hear it ring."

"Where are you off to now?"

"Have to make a phone call. My father's eating at a table by the windows. Why don't you go in and get some coffee? I'll be back in a minute."

Philip wasn't happy, but decided not to argue. He joined Dick, who was monosyllabic when asked about the case, Dorothy, or anything else. Fortunately for both of them, Dorothy returned in just a few minutes.

"We're in luck. Heather's at home this morning and said she wouldn't mind talking to us."

"Who's Heather?" Philip asked.

"An accountant at Robinson's law practice. Or rather, a former accountant. I want her perspective on Robinson and whatever she might know about him."

"And you're going to meet her now?"

"Yes, Philip," Dick cut in. "And you're not invited."

"What the hell am I supposed to do all day while you two do your Dick Tracy act?"

"Chill, Philip," Dorothy suggested. "Take this as an opportunity to rest. Go to the pool, read a book."

"Sure, just pretend everything is dandy and I'm on vacation. Is that what you're saying?"

"I know you're anxious. But at this point, I don't think you need to worry. The police seem to have backed off, maybe because they know they've got nothing solid on you. We came up here to help, so let us do our job."

"See, if we throw enough alternatives at the police, they'll have to lose interest in you and start looking elsewhere," Dick added.

Philip didn't like the idea but agreed to stay around the hotel, at least for the morning, while Dorothy and her father had their chat with Heather.

Dorothy went back to the room for a quick shower and change. Dick had his car brought to the front of the Ritz. Dorothy got in and immediately pulled out her cell phone. "Time to talk to Will Lentz."

"Yeah, probably a good idea to see where he is with the case."

"I also want to know if he talked to this Heather person, and what he might already know about her."

"It's Sunday. I doubt he'll be working."

"I have his cell number. I think he gave it to me hoping for a date," Dorothy said, winking.

Before her father had a chance to react, Will answered.

"Hi, Dorothy," he greeted her, sounding like he was just waking up.

"Caller ID, huh?"

"It's handy for us cops sometimes."

"I hope I'm not disturbing you."

"No, just getting my day started. Glad you called. You were on my list of people to talk to today. What have you guys been up to?"

"Just seeing the sights and having a fun weekend in Boston," Dorothy answered, not trying to hide the sarcasm.

"I bet. Have you learned anything interesting about your boyfriend's case?"

"I haven't thought about it as 'his case,' Will. But we have spoken with a person at the Robinson law firm."

"And your conclusions?"

"Pretty much what you were thinking. There were several people with strong motives, but not many with the will or the means."

"Yep. So, what are your plans for today?"

"That's why I'm calling. Have you had a chance to talk to any of Robinson's employees yourself?"

"Only one I interviewed was his personal secretary, Michelle Mash. She provided some background, but not a whole lot else. Why do you ask?"

"We have others who might be of interest, but I didn't want to talk to them if you already cleared them."

"Like Stu Slavinsky?"

"He's the one we talked to yesterday. You know about him?"

"Michelle told me about his wife Laura. We haven't interviewed him yet, but he's on the list. What was your take?"

"Low likelihood, I think, purely from a physical point of view. And I don't think he has enough money to have hired somebody to do it for him. Plus he sort of has an alibi."

"Anything else you care to share?" Will asked, anticipating a turndown.

"Not yet. My father and I have other people we want to talk to, but it's very preliminary. Let's keep in touch."

"Always happy to keep a beautiful woman on my speed dial list."

"Goodbye, Will," Dorothy said before she rang off, not wanting to give Will any more time than necessary. Mimicking Will's voice, she said, "Always happy to keep a beautiful woman on my speed dial list." Then to her father, "The guy gives me the creeps, Dad."

"Just a lech, kid. A garden-variety lech. But if it makes him spill info to us that he shouldn't, let's use it."

"Easy for you to say," Dorothy sighed.

Dick and Dorothy discussed their interview with Heather Chesterton as they made the short drive to Jamaica Plain and Heather's home. Dick's GPS brought them to Pond Street, a few blocks from the center of town. Jamaica Plain had a reputation as a solid middle-class neighborhood with modest homes, lots of kids, and young parents doing their best to raise their families. On this bright Sunday morning, the path around the pond was crowded with bikers and runners, several towing or pushing kids, all trying to extend their life with a little workout, enjoying the sunshine and the return of pleasant spring weather.

"How come most of the people who exercise are already in shape?" Dick mused.

"Because slobs like you don't get it and never will," Dorothy teased.

Dick grunted, not wanting to re-open their standing argument about his refusal to diet and lose weight. Life was short, he rationalized, so why spend what's left doing things you don't like.

Heather's brick-and-frame home was neat and well maintained. Two Toyotas were parked in the driveway amid a collection of bicycles, skateboards, rollerblades, and wagons. As Dick and Dorothy approached the front door, they could hear pandemonium from within. Kids arguing, a parent scolding, dogs barking, all at the same time. When Dorothy realized that the doorbell hadn't been heard, she knocked hard on the door. Inside, a man yelled, "Honey, they're here!" The door was opened by a middle-aged man wearing a t-shirt and gym shorts, and sporting a three-day stubble and a smile.

"You must be the Deavers. Heather is expecting you. I'm her husband, Perry."

"Nice to meet you, Perry. I'm Dorothy, and this is my father Dick."

"Come on in. Heather's just getting out of the shower. Would you like some coffee?"

"No. thank you," Dorothy answered, "we just had breakfast."

"Well, have a seat. Heather said you have questions about Thad Robinson?"

"Yes. We understand she used to work with him."

"Man, the guy got stabbed last week. Incredible."

"Do you know much about that?"

"Just what we read in the papers. Robbery? Maybe even attempted murder?"

"That's what we've heard, too. We're trying to get an idea of who may have done it."

"The paper said the police have questioned some people but don't have any suspects."

"Hard to know if it was random, or if it was someone after him personally. There seem to be a lot of people who didn't like him. But we're not sure if any of them would have gone after him with a knife. Do you happen to know Mr. Robinson yourself?"

"I met him at a few office parties. Heather's the one you need to talk to, though. She handled his books for the last five years. She'll have a unique perspective, I'm sure."

The ruckus from kitchen reached a higher decibel level, and Perry excused himself to investigate. From their spot on the sofa, Dick and Dorothy had a look around the Chesterton living room. Cluttered but clean, looking like any house with several kids and working parents.

Heather appeared a minute or two later. She bounded down the stairs into the living room, full of energy and with a pleasant smile. Her hair was still wet, but that did nothing to diminish her Germanic healthy look. Certainly not the depressed, out-of-work accountant the Deavers were expecting. Dick and Dorothy rose to greet her.

"Hi, Mrs. Chesterton," Dorothy said. "Thanks for seeing us. I'm Dorothy Deaver and this is my father, Dick Deaver."

"Good morning," Dick added.

"Hello, and welcome to our hectic home. 'Heather' is fine, by the way. Sit, please. How can I help you?"

Dick and Dorothy sat as Heather settled herself into a second-hand air chair across from them. Dorothy said, "I must admit: I didn't expect such a cheerful person."

"Why not?" Heather asked innocently.

"Didn't the Robinson firm let you go recently?"

"Oh no. I quit."

"I'm sorry. It's just that I saw your employment was terminated rather abruptly so I assumed you were let go."

"Where did you see that? That wouldn't be public information."

"I had limited access to employment records," Dorothy replied.

"Okay, let's back up a second. Why are you looking into this? You didn't explain when you called. Did Thad hire you?"

"As a matter of fact, he did," Dick answered. He then decided to take a risk. "And you can call him and confirm that if you like."

"No, I really don't want to talk to him, so I'll take your word. I assume you're working with that goon of his, Luke Benjamin. How's Thad doing, by the way?"

"He's still in bad shape," Dick said, making a mental note to ask Dorothy about Benjamin. "He wants to get answers faster than the police are coming up with them, so he thought it would help if some other people investigated the case, before the trail goes cold. I'm sure you know that crimes aren't solved at all if they aren't solved quickly."

"Yes, that's true. I'll try to help if I can."

"So," Dorothy continued, "you weren't let go, you resigned."

"Yes, I quit."

"Forgive my misunderstanding, Heather. Again, given that your employment was terminated abruptly without a forwarding address, I assumed you were cashiered."

"I suppose I might have been eventually. The firm always seemed to be in turmoil with lots of people coming and going. I just decided I had enough of the nonsense. When an accountant quits a firm, they are usually shown the door pretty quickly so they don't have access to privileged information. Pretty standard operating procedure."

"You weren't happy in your job?"

"No, but I wouldn't say I was completely unhappy. Thad and I did work well together when things didn't go off track."

"You mean flirting and such," Dick interrupted.

"Exactly. He came on to me shortly after I was hired. I told him I wasn't interested, and Perry made sure he understood what would happen if he didn't leave me alone that way. I know he's fired women who told him to get lost, but he liked my work and kept me around."

"What did he like so much about your work?" Dorothy asked.

"Let's just say I was willing to be flexible."

"With the firm's funds?"

"Well, more precisely, with certain of the firm's funds. He never dipped into accounts designated for salaries. That would have jeopardized people's income, and I wouldn't have let that happen. But he dipped into the cash reserves several times. I didn't see why he couldn't as long as he made payroll, which he always did. And after all, the firm is all his."

"The money he took from reserves… what did he use it for?"

"Gambling, I think. Thad loved to bet on things."

"Anything in particular?"

"The horses, mostly, and sports, too. In his wastecan,

I used to see the daily racing form from Suffolk Downs, and the paper's sports section folded open to the page with the point spreads."

"Did his gambling ever get him into a jam?"

"There were times when I thought he'd gotten himself in deep, but then he'd suddenly show up with a lot of money to replace what he'd taken out of the reserves. Sometimes it was in cash, and he'd ask me to deposit it at the bank. Fortunately, our bank was just up the street. But it still worried me to be carrying a few hundred thousand dollars around in a briefcase."

"A few hundred thousand? Where did that much come from?" Dorothy asked.

"He was pretty silent about that."

"Loan sharks, maybe?" Dick asked.

"Could be."

"And do you happen to have any names?"

"Wait a minute, Dick. I don't work for Thad any more, but I'm not sure I'm comfortable giving you this level of detail about his finances."

"I understand, Heather. All we want is a name or two. We're just trying to identify people who maybe wanted to hurt Thad, and a frustrated money lender could qualify."

Heather thought for a moment, then continued. "I guess it can't hurt to say I overheard Thad talking to a guy named Whitey Feinstein once or twice."

"I gather he's a known money source in Boston?"

"There are all kind of rumors about him. He has partnerships in casinos in New England, and he's vying for a license in Massachusetts. People say he runs drug and prostitution operations, but I don't know much about that."

"So you think Thad borrowed money from him?" Dorothy asked, for clarification.

"Possibly, and if he did, it had to have been in substantial amounts, like I said."

"Yes, sounds like it. Is there anything else you can tell us that might help us find out who attacked Thad?"

"Probably Thad's most disgruntled employee right now is a guy named Stu Slavinsky. And Thad's got an angry ex-wife from a messy divorce. Maybe you know about those situations, already."

"Yes, we've heard."

"But I have to say, despite all his faults, Thad did work hard and really tried to be fair to his employees. He paid decent wages and provided a great benefit package. I couldn't fault him for any of his business practices." Heather shrugged, having no more to add.

"Thanks again for seeing us on a Sunday morning, Heather," Dorothy said. "This has been very helpful. Now we should get out of here and let you enjoy this beautiful day."

"Happy to help. I hope you can help the police find who attacked Thad. If you give me your number, I'll call if anything else occurs to me."

"That's very nice of you, Heather. What are your personal plans now, if I may ask?"

"I've enjoyed being home with the kids. Perry makes a nice salary, so I think I'm going to stay home and be a mom for a while. As you can see, that'll be a big job around here. And it'll cut the nanny costs out of our budget."

"I'm jealous," Dorothy said, knowing that a conventional home with kids was probably not going to happen to her for a long time, if ever.

Dick sensed her unease and rose from the sofa. "Well, goodbye, Heather, and thanks again."

Dick and Dorothy walked to the car in silence, not exchanging thoughts until they were buckled up and moving away.

"Who's Luke Benjamin?" Dick asked.

"I saw his name on the employee list this morning. Looks like a private investigator who works for Robinson."

"I bet he's doing some snooping around too."

"I'm sure. We have to be careful to steer clear of him."

"And what about Whitey Feinstein? Think I've heard of him," Dick said. "Should I pay him a visit?"

"Are you sure you need to do that, Dad? He sounds borderline dangerous at best. Do you want me to go with you?" Dorothy asked.

"What, my little girl is going to protect me?" Dick laughed. "You think your old man's never been around tough guys? No, you spend some time with your boyfriend this afternoon. I'll phone around and see if I can have a conversation with this character."

"Okay, but stay in touch. Remember, Deb Angelucci will be calling you back. We hope."

"Right. Geez, what a weekend. Not what I was planning a few days ago."

They fell silent, each aware that they were bcing sucked into yet another situation they didn't enjoy, courtesy of one Philip Sarkis.

Chapter 17

Dick pulled up to the entrance of the Ritz and asked to have his car valet-parked.

"Now go spend some time with your boyfriend," Dick told Dorothy again, as they entered the ornate lobby. The hotel was a former bank building, and had many of the vestiges of the halcyon days of finance in the United States, when big money was exchanged in relative secrecy, fortunes were made and lost, and bankers had more money than they could count. The stunning artwork was set off by exquisite furnishings that most of the clientele took for granted.

"I'm not particularly interested in leisure activity, Dad," Dorothy replied as they walked to the elevators.

"What are you going to do, get on your computer and do more snooping?"

"Precisely."

Dick's face reddened. "Didn't we just have this conversation?"

"Don't have a stroke, Dad. This'll be on the up and up. I want to work off the list Mike Benedict gave us and review Robinson's recent malpractice suits to see if there are any others that could have ticked someone off enough to want to do him bodily harm."

Dick calmed down a little. "Okay. That's information in the public domain, so you're safe there. Actually, it's a good idea. We have to do that eventually, so you might as well get started."

"I assume you'll try to see this 'Whitey' guy this afternoon?"

"Feinstein, yeah. But I'll need a scam. He's not going to answer questions from a PI from Pennsylvania just for the fun of it."

"Which of your fascinating identities will you use, Dad?"

"No access to fake IDs up here. Guess I'll have to be myself. Sort of." He winked at Dorothy.

"Just be careful. I have a feeling he's not the kind of guy who can take a joke."

Dorothy gave her father a peck on the cheek and got into an elevator. Dick headed to the business center to use one of the house computers. He wanted to learn a little about Feinstein before cold-calling him. What he discovered surprised him.

Whitey was not just some two-bit loan shark. He was a local celebrity. There were loads of stories about his legitimate casino interests but almost nothing to suggest, let alone prove, criminal behavior. Whitey had been in Boston longer than Fenway Park, it seemed, and had achieved comparable stature. He prominently supported local charities and gave generously to his synagogue. Everyone, even politicians, wanted to get their picture taken with Whitey at some function or other. And he looked good in the pictures: gray hair cut short, well-tailored conservative dress, medium tan, white teeth, and a welcoming smile. The media loved him and described him as a leading citizen and all-around good guy, and even glamorized his gambling connections.

Smooth as silk, Dick thought, and probably a tough nut to crack. He won't be very forthcoming unless there is something in it for him.

After combing through the material he'd found, Dick decided to work the gambling angle. Like other states, Massachusetts was tired of watching its citizens cart their spending money off to New Jersey and Nevada. In-state casinos were being planned, with perhaps dozens likely to be in place before the end of the decade. Whitey was in the thick of it, vying for licenses and greasing the palms of every politician who had a voice in the decisions. Media coverage was extensive; a casino license would mean millions. With so much at stake, the license applicants needed no hint of past improprieties.

If Dick could make Whitey believe that the state's Gaming Commission knew about loans to Thad Robinson and that it could constitute an ethical breach, he might be able to discover whether there was a problem with repayment big enough to make Whitey arrange an attack. It was worth a try, but he would need good fake documents going in.

Dick called his favorite gofer, Al Kenworthy, at home. "Al, can you do me a favor? I'm in Boston and I need a letter from the Massachusetts Gaming Commission to a guy named Whitey Feinstein, telling him they've authorized me to ask him some questions about his private loan practices."

"Do you want to use your real name?"

"Yeah, I'm going to have to, because if he asks for identification, I'll have to show him my driver's license. Hopefully the letter will be enough or I'll have to explain why I live in Pennsylvania. But I'm going to drop in unannounced, so he shouldn't have time to check me out on the Internet."

"When do you want the letter?"

"Within an hour?"

"Huh? It's Sunday, boss."

"I know, and it's a pain in the ass. But this is for Dorothy, and I know she'd be appreciative."

The magic words. Al had been chasing Dorothy for years, ever since she worked in the office as a college student, and Al had been an intern. "Enough to have lunch with me?"

As much as he hated to dangle his daughter before a charter member of the lonely hearts club, Dick knew he needed to give Al some extra motivation for this Sunday request. "She's always been fond of you and your work, Al. I'm sure she'd consider it." Dick did not believe it; hopefully Al would.

"That'd be a treat. I can be in the office in fifteen minutes. The Gaming Commission letterhead should be no problem. Email me the text you want, and I'll slap it on the letterhead and email the letter back to you as an attachment. Do you have a way to print it out?"

"I'm at the Ritz; they've got a good busincss center, so no problem. And while you're at it, can you get me a home address for Whitey Feinstein. I want to pop in on him unexpected like."

"Sure, boss. I have to use his address in the letter anyway."

"Oh, right. I really appreciate all of this, Al. And I'm sorry to disturb your day."

"No problem, boss. It's my job. Say hi to Dorothy for me. When are you guys coming back?"

"Hard to say, Al, hard to say. I'll be in touch."

Dick hung up, then got back on the computer to clack out the letter content and email it to Kenworthy. Satisfied, he went to the concierge lounge, found a copy of the Sunday *Globe*, and settled down with a cappuccino while he waited for Al to get back to him.

The paper happened to have a story about casino development. As they had in Pennsylvania, would-be profiteers were coming out of the woodwork, jockeying for position to snag a license that was a ticket to riches. The story focused on potential locations for new casinos, including such garden spots as Springfield, Everett, and Suffolk Downs. In each case, Whitey's name figured prominently. He seemed to be using every connection he had, including the media, to pitch his case for a license. He really wants it, Dick thought; I'll be able to play him like a fiddle.

As expected, Al came through with a beautifully fashioned letter, which included Whitey's home address. Dick printed it, went back to his room, and put on a rep tie and blue blazer. "Does this make me look the part?" he muttered to himself, standing in front of the mirror. "Close enough for fake government work," he laughed as he left his room.

Sunday afternoon traffic was light, and the drive west was pleasant. Whitey Feinstein lived on a fashionable street in Natick, one of Boston's nicest bedroom communities. His large Tudor sat well back from the street, fronted by an impeccably landscaped yard. Dick parked a few doors away. He didn't want to explain how a mid-level state bureaucrat saved enough money to drive a 500 series BMW.

The door was answered by an elderly, distinguished African American wearing a suit and bowtie. Smiling, he said, "Good afternoon, sir, how might I help you?"

"Good afternoon. My name is Richard Deaver. I'd like to see Mr. Feinstein."

"And I am Gerard. May I ask what this in reference to?"

"I've been sent by the Massachusetts Gaming Commission to ask a few questions about some loans he tendered."

"May I see some identification, please?" Gerard said. This may not be so easy, Dick thought.

"I don't have my badge with me, but I have a letter of introduction from the Commission stating my business, and authorizing my visit to Mr. Feinstein."

"The letter may be sufficient. Thank you."

Dick handed Gerard the letter. Gerard gave it a cursory glance, and said, "If you wait here, I'll take it to Mr. Feinstein. Thank you."

The door closed, and Dick waited on the step, hoping that Feinstein wouldn't take time to verify the credentials or ask for ID. After only a minute or two, Gerard reappeared. "Do come in. Mr. Feinstein will see you in the library."

Gerard led the way. The interior was impressive, starting with the high-ceilinged lobby decorated with stained glass and marble floors. Gerard escorted Dick down a hallway featuring Impressionist paintings, to the wood-paneled library complete with shelved volumes of rare books displayed tastefully on all sides of the room. Feinstein was sitting behind a large antique partner's desk littered with papers, files, and envelopes. He was dressed in khakis and a black sport shirt. He stood and greeted Dick with a broad smile.

"Mr. Deaver, a pleasure to meet you. But what business is so important that you must work on a beautiful Sunday afternoon?"

Dick was taken aback by Feinstein's unexpectedly pleasant manner. "Thank you for seeing me, sir. Uh, the Gaming Commission has just a few questions about some, uh, loans you've made?" he stammered.

"And this couldn't wait till tomorrow."

"Well, we're on a tight schedule, sir. As you know, the Commission is trying to get the licensing decisions made soon, and that means weekend work is required."

"Okay, we'll try to make this fast, for your sake. Now, you say you have questions about loans. Does the Commission think I've done something that would jeopardize my license applications? Because if that's the case, I know my attorney wouldn't want me to talk without his being present."

Dick could see that Feinstein's congenial mood was beginning to evaporate. "No, sir, I wouldn't say that, Mr. Feinstein. It's just a couple of questions that you should be able to address without much of a problem. It would certainly speed up the process for us."

"Okay. Ask and I'll decide whether to answer."

Feinstein led Dick to a seating area in the room. Dick sank into a sofa. Feinstein sat across from him in a rocking chair, crossed his legs, and sat back. "May we offer you a beverage, Mr. Deaver?"

"No, thank you. I don't want to take much of your time. My questions have to do with Mr. Thaddeus Robinson. You know him, I assume?"

"I do. He's a friend."

"You know, then, that he was attacked on the Harvard Bridge last week and is hospitalized at MGH?"

"Yes, it's in the news."

"Have you been to see him, or spoken to him recently?"

"Not since the incident. Now what about the loans, Mr. Deaver?"

"Sorry, sir. During the police investigation of the crime, it came to light that Mr. Robinson is, shall we say, a heavy gambler."

"I've heard that as well. What does that have to do with me?"

"In attempting to identify individuals who might have had a reason to harm Mr. Robinson, the police detectives determined that he incurred some heavy debts that even threatened the integrity of his law practice."

"I ask again: What does that have to do with me?"

"Did you lend money to Mr. Robinson, sir?"

"Would that be a crime, Mr. Deaver?"

"By no means, Mr. Feinstein. However, the Gaming Commission believes that individuals who lend money to gamblers who get in over their head may not be the best people to oversee a gaming operation for which the state is partially responsible. So, with respect… did you lend money to Mr. Robinson?"

"First of all…"

"Before you answer, Mr. Feinstein, please be aware that lying to me or not answering and requesting an attorney may be worse than simply coming clean. The Commission isn't terribly concerned about this problem. They just want to tick off the box on your application that says you haven't facilitated reckless gambling behavior. If you obfuscate in any way, that will raise a red flag and your license application will be, um, detrimentally affected."

Feinstein paused, wheels turning, considering his alternatives. Finally, after several moments of reflection, "Yes, Mr. Deaver, I did lend money to Mr. Robinson. Never more than six figures, with fair interest, and for short-term use."

"How did you meet Mr. Robinson?'

"At social events around town, and we became friends."

"And after he got to know you, he asked for money?"

"He asked to borrow some for short periods. He said

he had cash flow issues."

"And you believed him?"

"I had no reason not to."

"What did he use the money for?"

"He said it was to make payroll at his firm."

"Did you know about his gambling?"

"I'd be lying if I said I didn't know he bet heavily, on lots of things. But I swear I didn't knowingly lend him money to support his habit. He was a friend, and he asked me for the loans as a favor. I felt obliged to help."

"Did he repay you on time?"

"Never missed a due date."

"How much does he owe you currently? And please don't tell me what you think I want to hear."

"He owes me nothing right now. He repaid his latest loan about two weeks ago, with interest."

"Do you happen to know if Mr. Robinson was in the habit of borrowing money from other people?"

"You mean loan sharks?"

"Anyone."

"I don't think so, but Thad could answer that better than I can."

"So as far as you know, Mr. Robinson borrowed money from you, and you alone, because you were his friend?"

"Yes. To the best of my knowledge."

"And he repaid everything he owed you."

"Yes, and with interest. But never anything more than I could have made by investing it."

"And you never considered the money you gave him to be an inducement to participate in compulsive or reckless gambling?"

"No, I never did."

"Then I believe that's all, Mr. Feinstein. I see no problem here. You may receive an affidavit to execute that basically restates what we just talked about. You'll want to review it with your attorney. However, if the Commission is satisfied, even that may not be necessary. I'll recommend they continue to process your applications without impediment. Thank you for your cooperation."

Feinstein finally smiled again. "Thank *you*, Mr. Deaver. You've been honest and helpful, and I appreciate it. My license applications are very important to me and my partners."

"I understand," Dick said, rising from the sofa, preparing to leave.

"Do you have a card, Mr. Deaver?"

Dick opened his wallet and feigned surprise. "Darn it," he lamented with his most serious frown. "I forgot to put the new cards in my wallet. Let me write down my cell number, in case you need to reach me."

Dick scribbled a Boston area code followed by a random number on the back of one of Whitey's cards, grabbed his briefcase, thanked Feinstein again and made his way out, grateful that his cover had not been blown.

Once in his car, Dick called Dorothy. "Forget our pal Whitey."

"What happened, Dad?"

"It went well. Turns out he did lend money to Robinson, but there was no outstanding debt at the time of the attack. And Whitey was fairly sure Robinson had no other lenders."

"So that's a dead end."

"Seems that way. We better move on. "

"Has Deb Angelucci called you back?"

"No. Maybe you should try." Dick gave Dorothy the number.

"Thanks, Dad, I will. But I also want you and me to look over a few of Robinson's malpractice cases."

"Find something interesting?'

"I think so, but I want your opinion before we start interviewing people. When you get back here, call me and I'll come to your room with my laptop. Philip's got a ballgame on, and I don't want him interfering anyway."

"On my way. If we don't spend too much time looking at the malpractice cases you found, maybe we can still see a few more people today."

"Right. The sooner we can produce alternative theories of the crime, the sooner we can establish Philip's innocence."

Innocence? Dick thought. That's quite an assumption, isn't it, little girl?

Chapter 18

Arriving at the Ritz, Dick left his car with the valet again, and headed for the elevators. People-watching in a hotel lobby was always one of his favorite pastimes, and the Ritz offered ample opportunity. There seemed to be a lot of elderly guests who were deeply interested in how they looked, and were willing to pay serious money to have the best clothes, the most fashionable hair styles, and the least obvious cosmetic surgery. And then there were the youngsters, spoiled by parental indulgence, wearing intentionally torn jeans, inhabiting their smartphone worlds, withdrawn and non-communicative, pouting over a perceived slight delivered via Instagram, WhatsApp, or some other online service that was hot at the moment. Dick remembered when it had not been like this. There was a time when people actually talked to each other. Hotel lobbies had been a good place to meet people. Those days were gone.

Fortunately, his annoyance was short-lived because the elevator arrived quickly. "I'm here," he announced to Dorothy on his cell phone as he made his way to his room. "Remember, it's Room 1245."

"Great, Dad. I'll be there in a minute."

Dorothy arrived, sat at Dick's desk, hooked up her laptop, and began. "I found about a dozen personal injury cases that Robinson worked on in the last year. The Bergstrom case, by far, got the most notoriety. I excluded most of the others, generally because they were nuisance cases or no one was particularly angry about the verdict."

"That's sounds sensical," Dick agreed.

"There were two cases that didn't get much publicity, but had a lot of collateral damage."

"To the defendants?"

"Or their families. I had to go through the cases pretty carefully to find the evidence. I cross-referenced the cases with court records and found these two where the defendants not only lost their case, but had a personal loss shortly afterward."

"Isn't it common for defendants in a personal injury case to have mental problems?"

"Yes, so I wasn't surprised, but as you'll see, these cases were pretty extreme."

"Were they both medical malpractice cases?"

"One was. The other was a product liability case."

"Are the people local?"

"Yes. One in Chestnut Hill, the other in Brighton."

"Maybe if we're fast, we can see both of them yet today."

"Especially since I haven't had much luck getting to Mrs. Angelucci."

"Should we call first or just get on our horse?" Dick asked, knowing which he'd prefer.

"I say let's just go. I've got the addresses."

"That's my girl. Now tell your boyfriend we'll catch up with him later."

"Yeah, he'll love that idea. Meet you in the lobby."

They headed to Brighton first. It was closer, and if their target wasn't home, they could easily double back after their journey out to Chestnut Hill for the other interview.

"So who are we visiting here?" Dick asked, as they turned onto Polstead Street. "A doctor? This doesn't look like a neighborhood a doctor would live in."

"How about a doctor's estranged husband?"

"Uh-oh, I betcha I know where this is going."

They pulled up in front of a house on a hill. It was a nice enough neighborhood, with economy cars parked on the street in front of modest but well-kept homes. A warm breeze reminded them of summer's approach.

"Before we go in, let me give you a capsule summary," Dorothy suggested.

"Okay, shoot."

"Robinson was the attorney in a malpractice suit against a family doctor named Rebecca Shames. She worked in a primary care practice nearby in Brookline. She lost the case, left the practice, then left her husband. She just fell off the grid."

"You mean you can't figure out what happened to her."

"Right. I can't find her in or out of Boston. Her medical license lapsed, there's no mention of her in the local papers, and she isn't listed in any of the medical societies. I called her old practice and got the weekend answering service. The person I talked to never heard of her."

"So what do we have to go on?"

"Only that this is her last known address, and the husband is still here. The guy's name is Jeremiah. Jeremiah Shames. So now we'll go see."

Dick and Dorothy walked to the front door. Bikes and toys were carefully arranged on the porch, and they could hear a television in the living room. Peeking in, they saw two men of about the same age, forty-something, sitting on the sofa with two children, a boy and girl, about nine or ten. All seemed engrossed in the program, smiling and laughing intermittently. It was a peaceful sight and, for a moment, Dorothy thought about walking away. She was yanked back to reality by her impatient father.

"Let's get on with this, little girl. I want to do the other visit before it gets too late."

"Okay, Dad." Dorothy rang the doorbell and watched one of the men take a kid off his lap, and walk to the door."

"Can I help you?" he said.

Dorothy sized him up. Dark features, well groomed, and fit. "Mr. Shames?"

"Yes?"

"My name is Dorothy Deaver and this is my father, Dick. I hope we're not interrupting you."

"Well, yes you are. But what do you want? We're not interested in buying something or signing anything," Shames said.

"No, nothing like that, Mr. Shames. And we are sorry to interrupt. We're private investigators looking into the attack on Mr. Thaddeus Robinson last week and wanted to ask you a few questions."

Shames frowned and said, "I'd prefer not to talk about that asshole, excuse the language."

"Sometimes no other word will do," Dick replied. "But it isn't Robinson we want to talk about. It's your wife."

"She doesn't live here anymore."

"Yes, we know. We're trying to figure out what became of her," Dick replied.

"May we come in?" Dorothy asked.

"Would you mind if we sat out here on the porch?"

"Not at all."

"It's just that I don't want to upset the kids again. They've been through so much."

"That's why we're here. We want to find out what happened."

Shames walked them over to a wicker sofa. He sat on a rocking chair and pulled his cardigan sweater over his chest as he sat down.

"You say you're private investigators? What do you want with me?"

"We're interviewing anybody who may have had a motive to attack Mr. Robinson," Dick said.

"The police can't do that?"

"Well, yes, they can, and they are, but it's been nearly a week and they don't have anything solid yet. We've been asked to help out." Dick hoped that Shames wouldn't ask more questions.

"Okay. Where do you want to start?"

"Tell us about the malpractice case."

"It was horrible. I'm not a doctor, so I can't give you a lot of detail."

"That's okay. Just what you know."

"Becky was a great doctor, you know? She really cared about her patients and spent a lot of extra time with them on the phone and in the office. I used to be a sales rep for a medical device company, but when we had kids, I quit to be home with them. Becky didn't miss a beat in her practice; in fact she worked harder than any doctor I know. I'm telling you this so you can understand what happened to her."

"Anything you think is important," Dorothy said.

"Becky was especially careful with medications and lab tests. She always talked about making sure her patients were getting the right meds and were being monitored carefully. That's what made what happened to her even more bizarre."

"The case involved warfarin, correct?"

"Yes, it was an African American woman who was getting it because she had some kind of heart rhythm problem."

"Atrial fibrillation?"

"Yes, I think so. That sounds familiar. Anyhow, the woman needed a tooth pulled and the oral surgeon called Becky to ask if he could tell the patient to stop the blood thinner."

"And Becky agreed?" Dorothy said.

"With the usual warnings about the risks of stopping warfarin."

"Like what?" Dick cut in.

"Stroke is the main thing," Shames answered. "The problem is that Becky was busy and didn't document the warnings in the patient's chart. The patient had the procedure, went back on warfarin a few days later, but had a big stroke before the warfarin kicked back in."

"Did she die?" Dick asked.

"No, worse. She lost all mental function. Now she's in a nursing home, basically a vegetable."

Dorothy winced. She hated that dehumanizing term that had become popular parlance for mentally gone. "And the family sued?"

"At first, they were fine. Becky met with her kids several times, and they seemed to understand what happened. Becky told them she warned the oral surgeon and also their mother about the risks. They were okay with that until some damn nephew from out of town started telling the kids they were missing a big chance to get money to help take care of their mother.

"The children didn't do anything for several months. Then about two weeks before the statute of limitations would have run out, Becky got the summons. The kid who had power of attorney saw one of Robinson's commercials on TV, called the 800 number, and got the ball rolling just in time."

"Becky must have been devastated."

"That's putting it mildly. She couldn't believe the family was going after her and not the oral surgeon. Her malpractice insurance company got her an attorney who pretty much mailed it in. She didn't give a crap about Becky, and just turned the crank, made her money, and then, after about seven years, turned around and recommended that Becky settle the case."

"Seven years?" Dick asked incredulously.

"It just went on forever."

"And Becky refused, correct?"

"Yes, she insisted on the case going to trial. And Robinson took Becky to the cleaners."

"Big verdict?"

"To the limits of Becky's policy, thank goodness, or we wouldn't be sitting on this porch. But it didn't matter, really."

"Why not?"

"Because Becky was ruined by the experience. Professionally and personally. She couldn't function at work. She became a purely defensive doctor, ordering every conceivable test, double- and triple-checking everything, documenting way more than she needed to. She got so obsessed with the process that she couldn't make any decisions. She was anxious and angry all the time, and rode her staff hard. She couldn't keep any help in the office, and her partners started looking for other jobs."

"This went on for a long time?"

"About a year, and then she disappeared. One day I came home from a movie with the kids, and most of her clothes and other things were gone. She left a note, said she couldn't take it anymore, but didn't say where she was headed."

"You must have been frantic."

"I tried to keep it together for the kids, but yes, I was a wreck. I reported her to the police as a missing person, and they put out an alert. They found her a week later on a back road in North Carolina. She'd been driving around pretty aimlessly, sleeping in her car, but with a plan to go to her parents, who lived near there.

"The police took her to her parents' home and they called me. I went down the next day, and it was pretty obvious that her mind was blown. She couldn't speak coherently, was unable to take of herself, and claimed that people were talking about her."

"A psychotic break?" Dorothy asked.

"That's what the psychiatrists called it. They recommended hospitalization immediately, to start anti-psychotic meds."

"Did they work?"

"A little. She wanted to stay down there with her folks, and bounced in and out of the hospital several times over the next few months. At the moment, she's in the hospital again."

Dick made a mental note to confirm that Becky was in the hospital at the time of the attack and in no shape to have had anything to do with it.

"So you're no longer together?"

"We were barely together before she left. We weren't getting along well, hardly talking and not sleeping together. She was pretty impossible."

"You must have been angry about the whole situation," Dick suggested.

"Not really. Just incredibly sad."

"I hesitate to ask, but where were you last Wednesday

morning?"

Shames stopped to think for a minute. "Right here, with the kids, as usual."

"Anyone else with you?"

Shames leaned forward, elbows on knees and hesitated. "There's another reason why Becky was having a tough time of it before she left."

"Does it have anything to do with the man on your sofa in there with your kids?" Dorothy asked.

Shames looked up, relieved. "I don't know how you came up with that one, but yes, Bern and I are a couple."

"And your wife found out during the malpractice litigation?"

"No, I never would have saddled her with another problem. But afterward, when she was so dysfunctional, I started leaning on Bern more and more. Becky may have been disturbed, but she isn't an idiot. She eventually figured it out, and confronted me."

"And you confessed."

"What choice did I have? I was tired of living a lie. But I know that this had to be part of the reason she became unglued, and why she left." Shames buried his face in his hands. "And it makes me feel so guilty."

Dorothy paused. Then, "And Bern was here with you and the kids last week?"

"Yes."

"The whole week."

"Yes, he stays over a lot."

"And he'd be willing to testify to that if necessary?"

"We'd hate to be outed that way, but yes, Bern would speak up if it would get me off the hook for attacking Robinson. Which I didn't."

Dick gave Dorothy the high sign. It was time to wrap up. "Mr. Shames, thank you for your time. We hope we didn't upset you too much. As we said, we're just interviewing anybody who may have wanted to hurt Mr. Robinson."

"You're going to be busy. I'm sure that's a lot of people."

"Fortunately, it looks like you'd be able to prove that you and your wife didn't," Dorothy said.

"She's still my wife, after all, and I do care about her. I just don't know how to help her. I only hope she recovers and can get back to some kind of life. The kids miss her."

Dick and Dorothy rose to leave. Dorothy couldn't resist walking to the seated Shames and placing a hand on his shoulder. "I hope the same thing, Mr. Shames, for you as well as your wife."

Dick and Dorothy walked to the car. "Do you have the energy for another encounter before we call it a day?" Dick asked across the roof of the car.

"We might as well. Can't get much worse," Dorothy replied, hoping she was right.

Chapter 19

The drive from Brighton to Chestnut Hill took about ten minutes. Dick and Dorothy used the time to review what they had just heard, independently reaching the conclusion that Becky and Jeremiah Shames were hardly in a position to have harmed Thad Robinson, or to pay someone to do so.

"What a wretched situation," Dick said. "Why the hell couldn't they have resolved that malpractice case and let Becky get on with her life?"

"That's what terrorizes doctors who get trapped in them. The cases go on forever, and just make people miserable. Someone calculated that the average doctor spends eleven percent of his or her professional career with an unresolved malpractice case hanging over their head. Most times the defense wins or the case settles, but in the meantime, there's an awful lot of hand-wringing that goes on."

"It must affect the way doctors practice, don't you think?"

"No question. Did you hear what he said about his wife, checking and rechecking everything she did? Ordered lots of tests and I'm sure prescribing therapies that weren't needed? It's what doctors do to keep from getting sued again. The irony is, it doesn't work."

"What do you mean?"

"There's a lousy correlation between poor care and lawsuits. Doctors get sued for a lot of reasons, but many times their worst decisions aren't acted on or even detected by patients."

"So the system just plain sucks."

"That's what Philip has been saying all along, and I have to admit he has a point. Patients don't get compensated fairly, and physicians get put through the wringer. Usually the docs manage to move on. And sometimes they lose it."

"And sometimes they turn into amateur sleuths and nearly get their loved ones jailed or killed."

Dorothy chose not to respond. Dick was referring to two previous cases where Philip stubbornly refused to let go, and the consequences for Dorothy. It was time to change the subject.

"The person we're about to visit is named Dean Baptiste."

"Is he a doctor?"

"Trained that way. He went to a small Catholic college in Pennsylvania and was the first person from that school to go to Harvard Medical School. He went back to Philadelphia to do his training as a cardiologist, and then took a job with a prestigious practice on the Main Line."

"So Philip maybe knows this guy?"

"I haven't asked him but I'd be surprised if he didn't."

"What's he doing in Boston?"

"Hang on, I'm getting there. The guy was in practice for about four years, enjoying himself, building a nice reputation in interventional cardiology, when he decided to quit."

"Quit? Why?"

"I don't know, Dad. It's one of the things I want to ask him. He left medicine and went to work for industry. He started at Merck, transferred to AstraZeneca, and then became a VP at Johnson and Johnson, where he was a rising star. Then he made another career change; he left J&J and started his own biotech firm up here."

"Why here?"

"The 128 corridor is the place to be these days in biotech, sort of like Silicon Valley was twenty years ago. Lots of brainy people finishing their training at places like Harvard and MIT, a nice place to live and raise a family, and local government incentives to start new businesses."

"So what was Dean's idea?"

"When he was with the big pharma companies, Dean got interested in new ways to reduce cholesterol."

"You mean better than statins? I thought they were the miracle drugs."

"They're excellent, but ten to twenty percent of people can't take them because of side effects like muscle cramps, and not everybody gets their bad cholesterol down low enough."

"And they don't raise good cholesterol very much, right?"

"Very good, Dad. You've been reading."

"You've been reading, too, sounds like," Dick said.

"I told you I was going to search the web while you were seeing Feinstein," Dorothy replied. "Anyway, Dean supervised a search for new agents that could lower bad cholesterol dramatically and raise good cholesterol. The initial studies weren't terribly successful. Big pharma has little patience for developing drugs that don't have a big market potential, so they abandoned the program. But they knew that they had a few good candidates that might be used to treat highly selected patients."

"Like who?"

"There's a rare disease called familial hypercholesterolemia that affects children and young adults. It's devastating. Young people have such high cholesterol levels that they get heart attacks and strokes and disfiguring lipid deposits that make their shortened lives truly miserable. Nothing works well to treat them. J&J had a few drugs that looked like they could work for some of those patients. Dean's idea was to start a company to develop one of them for a niche indication."

"So what wouldn't work for a large company might be perfect for a small one."

"Precisely, and there's plenty of precedent for that idea."

"Did it work out?"

"Spectacularly. Dean surrounded himself with the smartest lipid people he could find, and together they attracted enough venture capital to purchase the compounds and then do a series of trials that got their lead candidate, Beschol, on the market."

"Wow. Quite an accomplishment."

"You bet, and they completed the trials in record time. It didn't go unnoticed. Dean was touted as the Steve Jobs of the drug world. Creative, decisive, charismatic. And then Thad Robinson happened."

"Oh shit."

"Oh shit is right. Beschol had been studied in hundreds of patients before it was approved by the FDA. Usually, cholesterol drugs are studied in thousands to test their safety, but remember, this was a drug being used for a relatively uncommon disease. There was no way to test Beschol in that many patients, so the FDA allowed it on the market with a promise from the company that it would monitor carefully for problems."

"Had there been any problems in their clinical trials?"

"Liver enzymes went up in a few people, but the same was true for the comparison patients who had not been given the drug, so the FDA didn't flag it."

"But it became a problem later?"

"Apparently. A couple of people died of liver failure, the cases were reported in the literature, and Robinson jumped all over it."

Dorothy's tale was interrupted. "We're here," her father said, as they pulled up in front of an impressive stone and brick home with a for-sale sign on the lawn.

"Dad, maybe it's best if we get the rest of the story from the horse's mouth."

"I agree, if he's home and willing to talk."

"Let's find out," Dorothy said, opening her door and climbing out.

They walked to the front door of the mini-mansion, noting the recent landscaping and fresh paint on the trim. "Yep, getting ready to sell," Dick observed. Dorothy nodded. A glance inside revealed moving boxes, bare walls, and newspapers thrown about.

The doorbell was answered by a pretty woman, in her forties, dressed in jeans and a sweatshirt, a little out of breath. "Hi, can I help you?"

"My name is Dorothy Deaver and this is my father, Dick. We're investigating an assault on an attorney named Thaddeus Robinson and would like to ask Dean Baptiste a few questions. Is he home?"

"Dean didn't attack anyone. Why should he speak with you?"

"Excuse me, are you Mrs. Baptiste?"

"Soon. I'm Dean's fiancée, Jackie Hopewell."

"Ms. Hopewell, Dr. Baptiste isn't a suspect. We just want some background information about his product liability case. It'll help our investigation."

Just then, a short, portly man with a receding hairline and friendly face came from around the open door and hugged Jackie from behind as he addressed Dorothy. "I'm always glad to be helpful, Ms. Deaver. I heard you announce yourself, and why you're here. I know about the attack and figured someone would be by to ask me some questions. So, sure, let's chat for a few minutes. But as you can see, we're in the middle of packing, so we can't give you a whole lot of time."

"And we won't take much, I promise," Dick added.

"The dining room hasn't been packed up yet. How about if we sit there? Can I offer you a beverage?" Jackie asked as they walked in and seated themselves.

"No thanks, Dorothy answered. "We're fine. First, you should know that we represent Dr. Philip Sarkis, who's been a person of interest in the Robinson case."

"Philip!" Dean exclaimed. "Are you serious?"

"You know him?"

"I've known him for years. We worked in neighboring hospitals when we were just out of training, and I used him a few times as a consultant."

"Can I ask why you left your practice in Philly?"

"Got sued in a malpractice case, and it just wiped me out. So I decided to get out of clinical medicine."

Dorothy glanced at Dick, whose eyebrows went up in acknowledgment of what they had just been wondering about in the car.

"Why is Philip involved in the case?" Dean asked. "He's a person of interest? That doesn't sound good."

"It's a long story. The police have questioned him, even though there is little reason to believe he did anything wrong. We're doing some background work to understand the case better, talking to people who have had run-ins with Mr. Robinson."

"Dorothy… can I call you Dorothy?"

"Sure."

"Thanks. And I'm Dean. If you two are friends of Philip's, then you're friends of mine. Anyway, Dorothy, you can certainly say I've had a run-in with that clown. In fact, it might even be fair to say he ruined me and my company."

"That's why we're here, Dean. We want to hear more about his tactics, and your experience with him and his firm," Dick said.

"My case was a little complicated. Do you know about Beschol and its history?"

"Yes," Dorothy said. "I read up on it and gave my father some background on our way over here."

"So you know that the development program was extraordinary. In fact, Philip came in and helped us a few times. He agreed it was exemplary. We did everything by the book, including frequent conversations with the FDA about development milestones and safety events. The drug went to the endocrine/metabolism advisory committee, and they did a thorough job scrutinizing our data. They concluded that the drug was safe and effective, and could be marketed for a small, well-defined group of patients. We agreed on a careful post-marketing surveillance plan, and instituted it shortly after the drug was released. Everything looked to be shipshape."

"But there was a liver problem?"

"Yes and no. In the trials, there were a few patients whose liver enzymes went up. Those patients were also on other drugs like statins that could have been responsible, and there was a similar signal in the placebo arm. That's the comparison group; they weren't given Beschol. What made the data particularly hard to interpret is that patients with severe lipid disorders had a background incidence of hepatic abnormalities. In other words, as a group, they already had some liver issues. In any case, we were very careful. We brought in liver experts, had them go through everything, and presented their findings to the FDA, and they climbed all over it, too. They even got their own world-class consultant, Mel Junior, to look at the data. Everybody agreed there was no clear problem with the drug, but that it needed to be watched after the drug was approved."

"And some things happened after the drug was on the market?"

"Yes, one person died of liver failure and another required a transplant. Both cases were picked up by our surveillance system and reported promptly to the FDA, just as they should have been."

"What'd the FDA say?"

"They reviewed the cases carefully and agreed with us that the likelihood of liver failure being caused by the drug was low, given the circumstances and timing. Hell, one of the patients had been off the drug for a month before she got sick. Anyway, the FDA didn't ask us to do more than send out a Dear Doctor letter, letting practitioners know about the issue and asking them to be vigilant."

"That's pretty standard procedure in cases like this, no?" Dorothy asked.

"Absolutely," Dean answered, sitting forward now in his chair, getting excited.

"But that didn't deter Thad Robinson. He jumped on the case faster than the hundred other sharks who wanted to establish a class action. He started advertising for patients, and before we knew it, he had a whole bunch of people who'd been treated with the drug who were willing to say their livers had been harmed. A lot of those people had been treated off-label. They didn't have the real disease, but their doctors had given them the drug to lower their cholesterol when statins didn't work or caused side effects."

"Did Robinson have proof that these patients were actually harmed?"

"I have no idea. But who needs proof? All you need to establish a class action is a lot of 'victims' and that was the easy part for Robinson."

"Then what?"

"My lawyers and I went to him and pleaded our case. I begged him to back off and give us some time to investigate the cases and deal with the FDA. He laughed and said he was going to do the right thing for his clients."

"He did the right thing for himself," Jackie said, rubbing her hand along the edge of the table and looking off into the empty living room.

"Robinson did the predictable thing," Dean went on. "He went to the media and told the story of hundreds if not thousands of poor souls, frantic about their risk of having a heart attack or stroke, being preyed upon by a ruthless drug company that was only interested in profits and making money. They interviewed the family of the patient who died and the liver transplant patient, who all said they had no idea the drug could cause a liver problem. Of course, we had put that information in the product label, just as the FDA told us, but the *Times* reporter didn't bother to mention that. We even made it onto *60 Minutes* in their story about the evils of the drug industry. We were the example of the fledgling drug company trying to cash in. They called us a one-hit wonder. I went from being a guru to a villain in about three months. Quite a rollercoaster ride."

Dean paused, took a big breath, exhaled audibly, and sat back. Dick and Dorothy remained silent, anticipating a continued outpouring. "We had already started negotiations with some of the big pharma companies to help us with marketing, and to begin trials in a more mainstream patient population," Dean went on. "The negative publicity sent them running for the hills, and they never came back. We couldn't *give* the drug away, let alone sell it. Insurance companies wouldn't pay for it, hospitals refused to put it on their formularies, and the whole enterprise just fell apart."

"And so did his company," Jackie added, sadly.

"I'm afraid we really were a one-trick pony, at that point. Without Beschol, we were pretty much dead in the water. We had other projects, but our venture capitalists didn't want to talk to us after taking a bath on their original investment."

"The company went bankrupt," Jackie added. "It was awful."

"And just to make it a little worse, I had sunk almost all of my savings into the company. In retrospect, it was an idiotic thing to do, but I think we just got caught up in the moment. We had momentum, and it looked like a clear path to success."

"Is that why you're moving?" Dorothy asked.

"Afraid so. We can't afford this place, or even its upkeep, and I have to get a job."

"Where are you headed?"

"We're getting married next week and moving to an apartment in North Jersey, the land of drug companies. I have a few leads there, so I should be able to get something soon. It won't be much, but it'll pay the rent."

"And I'm going to work as a site monitor for a research company down there," Jackie added. "I've worked in that space for several years. That's actually how we met after Dean's wife died. Dean's kids are old enough to take care of themselves after school, and I'm kind of looking forward to helping out with the finances."

Dorothy noticed that Jackie's facial expression was not nearly as positive as her words, but chose to move on.

"I hate to do this, but can you tell me where you both were last week?"

"You mean when Robinson was attacked? Do you really think I had something to do with it?"

"We're talking to people who were harmed by Robinson and may have had a motive."

"Easy. We were in Jersey lining up an apartment."

"I assume you have a motel or hotel receipt."

"We do, if you want to see it."

"At some point, maybe," Dorothy answered, trying to soothe ruffled feathers.

"I've been in the drug business a long time, Ms. Deaver," Dean said. "I've seen some amazing things. Thaddeus Robinson is a son-of-a-bitch, no question. He single-handedly deprived thousands of patients of a treatment that would have extended their lives, and he did it for his own personal gain. But this kind of thing happens more than you might think in drug development. I guess you could say it's business as usual. And if I went around knifing every scoundrel who got in my way, I'd never be able to get the blood off my hands. So no, it wasn't me who knifed Robinson, and I wouldn't have wished it on him, either."

"Wouldn't have wished it on him? That's remarkable, given what you went through."

"Well, it just doesn't pay to be bitter. You have to move on in life, you know? That's what Jackie and I are trying to do."

Dick and Dorothy rose and prepared to leave. "Thanks for all of your help, and sorry again to interrupt you on a Sunday," Dick said.

"Tell Philip I said hello. I hope you're able to clear him," Dean replied. "He was a wonderful consultant in the old days, and a big help to the drug industry."

"I have a feeling that we'll be able to get our job done soon, Dr. Baptiste. Good luck in your new life."

Dick and Dorothy made their way to their car, each processing this latest batch of information. "I'm exhausted," Dorothy said as she strapped herself into the passenger seat. "Let's get back, have some dinner with Philip, make plans for tomorrow, and hit the sack."

"Good idea. Deb Angelucci is who I really want to talk to. I think that's where the money is. But I also want to look into the Bergstrom situation, too."

"I should spend time with Philip, Dad. I'm worried about his psyche."

"That sounds familiar. Okay, here's the plan. We'll call Deb Angelucci tomorrow morning. If we can see her early, we will. Otherwise, why don't you plan some time with your boyfriend, and I'll go over to Mass General and talk to some of the people who took care of Sebby Bergstrom to see what they think about his case."

"That should work. I'll call Deb first thing and we'll go from there."

The ride back to the Ritz was short. Traffic was light on Storrow Drive, and on the surface streets of Boston. Neither spoke as they mulled over what they had discovered this day, each aware that nothing they had heard or seen so far was enough to allow them to present the police with an alternative theory of the crime, and certainly nothing that made Philip appear less likely to have taken a sharp knife and mutilated Mr. Thaddeus Robinson.

Chapter 20

After a restless night, Dorothy awoke early the next morning. She lay in bed for a few minutes, gathering her senses. Philip had stayed up late reading medical journals, and woke her up when he had finally come to bed. She hazily remembered his inquiry about the possibility of sex and her sharply negative reply. How could the idiot have sex on his mind? And then he was all over the bed, his snoring and burping punctuated by the occasional fart. A freakin' one-man band, she thought. Real happy I found this guy.

But in fact she was glad to have found Philip, despite his quirks and faults. He loved her dearly and treated her well. If he could just stop becoming a person of interest in police investigations of violent crimes, she could put up with his nuttiness. Had he finally gotten himself embroiled in a case that would take him down? Despite his laid-back persona, Will Lentz was a person who played for keeps, and he had Philip firmly in his sights.

Which is why Dorothy and her father decided to abandon their plan of finding other suspects, a plan that was not yielding results, and look further into the Angelucci case. The most important connection that Philip had to Thad Robinson was through Pudge. Now it was time to assess whether that link was strong enough to make it plausible that Philip was the one who planted a knife in Robinson's back.

After a few minutes of useless rumination, Dorothy climbed out of bed, used the toilet, and went straight to the in-room Keurig, where she brewed the strongest cupboard selection she could find. Sipping the coffee, she went onto the balcony to make the phone call to Deb Angelucci that would key the rest of her day. This time the call was answered after just two rings.

"Mrs. Angelucci, my name is Dorothy Deaver. My father Dick and I are investigating the Thaddeus Robinson attack that occurred last week."

"Yes, I got your father's phone message and didn't have time to call back. Two detectives already talked to me about the case. Did Robinson die?"

"No. He's expected to recover, but with severe damage to his spinal cord."

"And you want to talk to me because of what happened to Pudge, I mean, Mario? I don't know anything about the attack on Robinson. And I wasn't in Boston when it happened."

"I understand. What we'd like to talk to you about is the relationship between your husband and Philip Sarkis."

"The detectives wanted to know the same thing. Is Philip under arrest?"

"No, but they regard him as a person of interest. We can talk more when we meet. If you have time, my father and I would like to come to your home today."

"I guess that's okay. Especially if it will help Philip. He was a good friend of Pudge's for years."

"It will help, I promise. When's a good time?"

"I have to work this afternoon. How about this

evening, say about five o'clock?"

"That's perfect."

"Do you know how to get here?"

"Yes, we have your address. We'll see you then. Thank you, Mrs. Angelucci."

Dorothy rang off and sent a text to her father. He would be free to talk to Sebby Bergstrom's father and roam around the General all day if he wanted to, and she could have some time with Philip. Maybe it would be pleasant, she thought. Then she shook her head. It was torture to deal with Philip in the midst of a yet another criminal matter in which he was implicated. She could conjure up no reason why this day would be any different.

Dorothy spent the next hour going through emails, waiting for Philip to wake up. One of the messages was from Will, entitled "new development." Dorothy froze, afraid to hear more bad news about Philip's involvement. It turned out to be routine: "The police dragged the Charles near the bridge and couldn't find a knife. They did find Robinson's engraved watch. It was diamond encrusted. Seems strange that a robber wouldn't have kept it for the jewels, don't you think?" The message ended with an invitation to a lunch for further discussion, which Dorothy quickly declined, while conceding that the watch find made random theft less likely as a motive.

Philip finally emerged from the bedroom, in a foul mood. "I have a hard time sleeping in hotel rooms," he groused, yawning and scratching random body parts. "When do you think we're going to get out of here?" he asked.

"Dad and I have a few more people to talk to, and then we're going to ask Lentz to put up or shut up. We're keeping you in Boston as a courtesy but there are limits."

"Why the hell should we be nice to Lentz? He's just focused on me and not taking any other suspects seriously."

"Person of interest, Philip," Dorothy corrected. "It's important that you not think of or refer to yourself as a *suspect*."

"Whatever. Last night you said there are a lot of people who might have had a reason to stab Robinson. What about that cuckold Slavinsky?"

"Lentz knows about him, and all of the other possibilities. None of them are plausible. They all have a decent alibi, or they lacked the wherewithal to attack Robinson or pay someone to do it."

"So Slavinsky couldn't pay some two-bit hoodlum?"

"Based on what we know, this wasn't an amateur performance. Whoever did it was shrewd and calculating, and also knew something about anatomy."

"Give me a break. People have spinal cord injuries from knife wounds all the time. This could have just been a botched murder attempt during a random robbery, for all we know."

Dorothy paused while she decided whether to share Will's information about the found watch. She decided against it. The more Philip knew, the more he'd want to be involved. Dorothy changed the subject.

"My father's busy this morning, so why don't you and I grab a little breakfast and then take in a museum? I picked up some brochures in the lobby, and the Isabella Stuart Gardner Museum looks wonderful. It's open on Mondays, so let's go."

Philip glowered at Dorothy. "Is that really a good use of our time?"

Dorothy was not to be put off. "Look at yourself,

Philip. You're a wreck. You haven't slept well, you aren't exercising or eating right, and you're driving us crazy. Some you-and-me time would do us both good."

Philip dropped into an armchair, looked out the window at a beautiful morning, pursed his lips and relented. "Okay, I guess a little tourist time with the most beautiful woman in the world wouldn't kill me."

"Good. Now hit the shower, put on something comfortable, and let's get out of here and have some fun."

While Philip showered, Dorothy shot a text message to her father, confirming she would keep Philip occupied. "Where are you, Dad?" she finished.

A few seconds later, the reply: "Just getting to the Copley Square Marriott to meet Karl Bergstrom."

Dorothy sighed as she put her phone aside and prepared to dress, "Now that's a conversation I'd love to have on tape," she said to herself.

Earlier, Dick had called Will Lentz, ostensibly to provide an update on their investigation, but also to get some information. Maybe Will would be willing to swap. Will didn't answer so Dick left a voicemail. Dick's phone rang a few seconds later. It was Will. "Sorry, I was shaving and couldn't get to the phone. Have you talked to Dorothy this morning?"

"Not yet."

Will told Dick about the watch find, hoping for a reaction. Dick knew better than to blurt out a response until he had time to process the information. He went on with his own agenda.

"Thanks for the information, Will. Dorothy and I will discuss it. But the reason I called is that I'd like to talk to Karl Bergstrom, and wondered if you could help me do that somehow."

"Maybe, Dick. What do I get in return? Probably not

lunch with your daughter."

"Can we talk business and not fuck around, Detective?"

"Sorry, Dick. Just trying to lighten things up."

"I don't need comedy, Will. I need to know how to get hold of Karl."

"I figured you'd want to talk to him at some point. If I tell you where he is, do you have something for me?"

"I'll tell you that we've interviewed a bunch of people who might have had a motive to go after Robinson. But we haven't come up with any high probabilities yet."

"That's potentially useful. Have some details?"

Dick reviewed the work he and Dorothy had done over the weekend, including their assessments of the people they had interviewed. Will took notes and thanked Dick.

"Okay, Dick, you're in luck. Karl is in town, staying at the Marriott on Copley Square for a few days. He's registered under an assumed name. Ivarsson. Olav Ivarsson, something like that. Wants to avoid the media."

"Thanks."

"Let me know what you learn. The conversations I've had with him haven't yielded much."

"Sure, I'll be happy to share."

"And say hello to that pretty daughter of yours for me," Will added as his line went dead.

Dick called Karl in his hotel room while he waited for his car at the Ritz. After Dick introduced himself and briefly explained his interest in the Robinson case, Karl agreed to meet. Karl said he was in Boston only for a day or two to work on Sebby's estate, but he was willing to talk to anyone if it might lead to more information about his son's death.

They met at the Marriott's registration desk, Dick

having described himself and what he was wearing. It was a good thing he had. The lobby was a flurry of activity. A computer tech convention was in town, attracting nerds from the world over, most of whom seemed to be convening in the Marriott lobby. Fortunately, the opening session, previewing the latest smartphone technology, was about to begin, and the geeks were flocking in the direction of the massive convention center.

Karl approached Dick and stuck out his hand. Given Sebby's goaltender bulk, Dick was surprised to see a somewhat diminutive man, well-dressed, with a neatly trimmed goatee, gray hair, and bright blue eyes. Dick shook hands and introduced himself. "Mr. Bergstrom, let me first tell you how sorry I am about your son. I know you must be devastated."

"I am, Mr. Deaver. Thank you for your kind words."

"And I must say, your English is excellent," Dick observed.

"It's commonly taught in our schools. That's where Sebby learned it as well. And each of us had careers that gave us many opportunities to use it."

"It looks like the place is emptying out," Dick observed. "May I suggest we find a table and have a little breakfast while we chat?"

"That would be pleasant, thank you again."

The hotel restaurant had tables near the lobby and a well-stocked buffet, which Dick and Karl visited. After they made their selections and found a table, Dick got down to business.

"I think I need to give you a fuller explanation of why I wanted to speak with you. It's really only for background. My daughter's live-in boyfriend, a physician named Philip Sarkis, was a close friend of Mario Angelucci years ago. They trained together and kept up their friendship, even though they worked in different cities. I myself didn't know about Mario until recently. Philip happened to be up here at a medical conference last week when Thad Robinson was attacked. I assume you know about that."

"Yes, the police informed me."

"Anyhow, the police detectives on the case think Philip may have had something to do with the assault."

"Revenge for what Thad did to Angelucci?"

"Exactly."

"Is there any other reason why the police think this Philip person was involved?"

"There might be. Let's say that a combination of circumstances have them looking at Philip. We're trying to learn everything we can about the Angelucci case. We might uncover a reason for the police to look elsewhere."

"And would I be one of those places to look?"

"I'm sorry, Mr. Bergstrom. I didn't mean to give that impression." Dick paused, then continued. "What can you tell me about Thad Robinson?"

"To be honest, Mr. Deaver, I do not like him as a person. He's a disrespectful human being. I didn't like the way he interacted with people, even me, a client."

"But you stayed with him through two trials."

"Because of his abilities as an attorney. He was a powerful advocate for my deceased son. So I decided to tolerate his less attractive characteristics."

"But he lost the case. That must have been a terrible disappointment for you."

"Yes, it was. But it wasn't about the money."

Karl could see Dick's skeptical reaction.

"No, really. Money was not the object," Karl insisted. "The Bruins paid out the remainder of Sebby's contract, and my business success in Sweden has already made me financially comfortable, anyway. What I wanted was justice for my son, for the world to see, and for Dr. Angelucci to see, that wrong had been done, and that a price must be paid. So that a lesson could be learned."

"The lesson being?"

"In business, bad decisions have consequences, and fortunes can be lost. In medicine, bad decisions have consequences, and lives can be lost. Fortunes can be made back again; lives cannot. I lost the most precious person in my life because Dr. Angelucci clearly made a bad decision. I could not realize it at the time, but too late I saw that letting Sebby back on the ice without protection was the wrong decision. Maybe he wanted to be the big hero by clearing the star player to return to the team, I don't know. But it was a bad decision and now my son is dead."

"But didn't you ask Dr. Angelucci to take care of your son?"

"I did. He was a world expert on cardiomyopathy, and that's what Sebby apparently had. That's what makes the result even worse. Instead of staying in the mainstream of thought, Dr. Angelucci looked for a problem that was more easily addressed so he could save Sebby's career, when he should have been thinking of his life. I think he lost his way, and to my eternal regret, I went along with it for Sebby's sake. He was desperate to get back out on the ice."

"You must have been surprised by the verdict."

"I was and I wasn't. I knew that defendants usually prevail in malpractice cases, and Dr. Angelucci had outstanding attorneys and medical experts who raised enough doubt in the minds of the jurors. It didn't matter that we had testimony from some of the most prominent doctors in Boston and the world who stated that my son should have received a defibrillator."

"That would have ended his career."

"Most likely, although this very year, professional organizations have changed their minds and have not strictly recommended against active competition for high-level athletes with defibrillators. So who knows where an implant would have led us?"

"Had you been in contact with Thad Robinson after the trials?"

"Once in a while we would talk. We considered an appeal, but he wasn't optimistic. There was no legal basis for such a thing, and the odds of winning were low. He and I had already spent a great deal of time and money on the case, and we ultimately decided to forego any further legal action."

"And why are you in Boston."

"I come back to settle some estate issues for Sebby from time to time."

"Were you here last weekend, when Thad was attacked?"

"No, I was in Sweden with my family."

"Is there anything else you can tell me about the Angelucci case that could be helpful to Dr. Sarkis?"

"Help Dr. Sarkis, Mr. Deaver? Help a friend of Dr. Angelucci? For all I know, he gave Dr. Angelucci advice that contributed to my son's death. I'm afraid you're asking too much."

Dick lowered his head. Karl was right: there was no reason to expect sympathy for Philip's plight, even though Philip had agreed with a defibrillator implant. On the other hand, Dick was now fairly confident that Karl had no axe to grind against Robinson. Another potential attacker to strike from the shrinking list. But breakfast had not been a total waste; Karl's perspective on the Angelucci case was useful.

When they finished coffee, Dick thanked Karl and offered his condolences once again.

"It's hard to describe how much hurt is caused when someone like my Sebby is taken away. And it has nothing to do with his earning potential. I'd be just as devastated if my son had been a trash collector."

"I've never lost a child, so I can't imagine your pain, Mr. Bergstrom."

And the object of my game, Dick thought as he walked away from Karl and out of the hotel lobby, is never to suffer a similar tragedy myself.

Chapter 21

Dick called Dorothy from his car to update her and to see if Philip had any new revelations. Dorothy was seated in the Ritz lobby waiting for Philip to finish up with a few patient calls that his office had forwarded. She was grateful not to have the nosy Philip within earshot.

"How'd it go with Bergstrom?"

"Good, I think. He's a sincere person. And he's not pissed at Robinson. He thinks Robinson's a jerk, but he's satisfied that the case was handled skillfully. He's still angry with Angelucci, which is understandable. He thinks the doc got his head turned around and did the popular thing, or the easy thing or something, and made a decision that cost Sebby his life. But he's not blaming Robinson."

"So Karl can be dismissed as a suspect?"

"Yeah, and if you saw him, you'd agree that he'd have a hard time doing the deed himself. Just a little squirt of a guy. Plus, he said he was in Sweden when it happened."

"I guess we can confirm that if we need to. Are you

headed to the General?"

"Yeah. I did a little homework after we got back last night. I don't think I need to see more than one person."

"Let me guess: Peter Friedberg."

"Spot on, little girl. He knows the Angelucci case better than anyone, and can give me the Dream Team perspective, too."

"Will you be able to get in to see him?"

"I called his office just now. His secretary said he's got patients today, but his eleven o'clock cancelled. He told her he could see me then."

"That was good of him. This afternoon we can catch up before we go see Deb Angelucci."

"And maybe I can squeeze a nap in there somewhere. You're running your ol' man pretty darn hard."

"Wait a minute, you're the one who wants to hurry up and get out of Boston."

Dick chuckled. "Just trying to make you feel guilty. Old habit. What's up with Philip?"

"Nothing much. I convinced him to take in a museum with me today."

"Good idea. I'll be in touch after I finish with Friedberg."

They rang off and Dick maneuvered his way back down Storrow Drive to the hallowed campus of MGH. What began in the eighteenth century as a small infirmary for Boston's indigent population had morphed into a mega-medical center. MGH was a colossus that kept devouring its surrounding neighborhood with new buildings and wings, purchased from an enormous endowment fed by grateful patient donors, eager to have their names attached to any structure, room, or light fixture in the storied institution.

Navigating the medical complex was no mean feat.

Signage was fair, but the distance between parking and offices was immense. Dick hurried along the corridors, following color-coded footprints to the Eisenberg Cardiovascular Pavilion. I wonder who Eisenberg was, or is, Dick thought. And what heart disease brought him here and made him so grateful? Or was he a she? Dorothy would be happy that he entertained that possibility.

His musing was interrupted by his arrival at a large elevator bank that would take him up to the cardiac clinic where Friedberg was spending his morning. Dick stepped out on the fifth floor and was immediately impressed with the light and airy atrium, large reception desk, and a smiling receptionist who welcomed him warmly.

"Hello. My name is Cassandra. How may I direct you, sir?"

"I'm here to see Dr. Peter Friedberg."

"And your name?" asked Cassandra, scrolling her computer screen.

"Dick Deaver."

Cassandra frowned. "I'm sorry, Mr. Deaver, but I don't see your name on his appointment list. Are you a new patient?"

"I'm not a patient, Cassandra. I'm here on business. His secretary knows about me, so he should be expecting me."

"Oh, in that case, please take a seat, Mr. Deaver, and I'll let Dr. Friedberg know you're here."

Dick looked at his watch. Five to eleven. Let's see if the good doctor is punctual, Dick wondered, or if he's like most doctors and takes his sweet time getting around to me.

At 11:02, Dick took note of a distinguished-looking physician who stopped at the reception desk. Out of habit, he inventoried the doctor's appearance: middle age with a mustache; wearing a polka dot bow tie, dark blue shirt, and khakis. And, of course, a long, starched white coat. After a brief exchange with Cassandra, he walked over to Dick who rose in greeting, and shook hands. "You must be Dr. Friedberg," Dick said.

"I am, in fact, and you're Mr. Deaver?"

"Please call me Dick, and thanks so much for meeting with me."

Friedberg led Dick through a maze of examination rooms to an office with a large desk and adjacent seating area. "We use this space for family conferences and extended consultations. We should be comfortable and undisturbed here."

"Thanks, Doctor," Dick said, taking a seat in an armchair across from Friedberg.

"I'll warn you that I only have about twenty-five minutes until my next patient, and I don't like to be tardy."

"I understand. It's refreshing to see a punctual physician, actually. It was nice of you to make this time for me."

"To be frank, I didn't intend to make any time at all for you. I hate to have interruptions on days devoted to patient care. But my secretary said something about Dr. Sarkis."

"You know him well?"

"Philip and I were fellows together at the Brigham back in the day. How do you know him?"

"He's my daughter's boyfriend. Well, more than boyfriend. They live together."

"Small world." Friedberg paused, waiting for Dick to continue.

"And Mario Angelucci was in the same group?"

"That's right. In fact, it was Pudge who introduced us. They knew each other from college, in Philadelphia.

I was from New York, Columbia to be exact. Boston was a new place for all of us. We hit it off and hung out together."

"Have you stayed friends with Philip?"

"We see each other at meetings, but we don't socialize any more. We both got busy with our jobs and families, and I don't get down to Pennsylvania very often."

"What about Dr. Angelucci? You remained friends with him, I imagine."

"Yes, but I didn't see him as much as I did when we were fellows. My wife and I went out to dinner with Pudge and his wife occasionally and saw them at hospital functions. And, of course, we worked together on cases sometimes. Pudge was interested in heart failure and cardiomyopathy, and those patients frequently have heart rhythm problems, which is where I come in."

"Uh huh."

"Mr. Deaver, you seem to be leading up to something. In the interest of time, let's get to it."

"Yes, sir. Sorry. I'll get to the point. Philip was here in Boston last week…"

"At the Heart Rhythm meetings. Yes, I was there, too."

"Right, I should have known that. The meeting was at the convention center, but he was staying in Cambridge. Does that strike you as strange?"

"Not really. Many people stay at hotels and B&Bs remote from the meeting. It gets a little hectic at the main meeting hotels."

"His place was near the Harvard Bridge. An attorney named Thaddeus Robinson was attacked there."

"I saw that in the *Globe*."

"You remember Mr. Robinson, of course."

"Yes, he was the attorney for Sebastian Bergstrom's family."

"Right. The police have questioned Philip in connection with that assault."

"My lord, he isn't a suspect, is he?"

"Not officially. They're calling him a person of interest. I'm trying to get information that could help the police investigation somehow, and also Philip. But I have to start with this: Do you think he could have done it?"

"Of course not. Philip is a gentleman. He would never do such a thing."

"Not even if he was furiously angry about a wrongdoing?"

"You mean Robinson's aggressive prosecution of the case against Pudge?"

"And Dr. Angelucci's subsequent suicide."

"Pudge's suicide was tragic, no question. But laying it at Robinson's feet is disingenuous. Pudge had psychological problems that many of us discounted over the years. He was a very serious and moody person. The Bergstrom case obviously was the tipping point."

"What was your take on the case, Doctor?"

Friedberg smiled. "I hope you aren't expecting an expert opinion. I'm anything but a psychiatrist. And I'm not unbiased. I still think of Philip as a friend."

"I mean did Dr. Angelucci make a mistake letting Bergstrom back on the ice?"

"He made a difficult judgment that in retrospect was incorrect. Sebby Bergstrom was one of the most complicated patients MGH has ever seen. And I don't think any medical case ever got so much public scrutiny. At the time, Sebby was the best and most loved athlete in Boston. He was on his way to heights achieved by Carl Yastrzemski and Larry Bird. The Bruins hadn't made a run at the Stanley Cup in years, but with Sebby in goal his rookie year, they made it to the semis. A hot goaltender can take you that far, and farther. Which is where they were headed the next year..."

"Until Bergstrom passed out."

"When Sebby passed out in that game at the Garden, the town went nuts. The *Globe* carried the story with a banner front page headline, and the coverage never stopped. The Bruins over-reacted, brought on the Dream Team, and the initial frenzy was capped off with his admission to the General."

"That Karl Bergstrom had insisted upon."

"And the Bruins didn't dispute. Karl had heard of Pudge and wanted his expertise."

"And yours."

"I was an afterthought. Yes, Pudge did solicit my opinion and consulted me formally. I was flattered, and fought against being swept up in the media maelstrom. It's hard to think straight when your name is in the paper every day and reporters are waiting outside the hospital to yell questions at you every time you walk to your car."

"But you did keep your head screwed on tight, didn't you?"

"I think so. I must tell you that the medical stuff was very complicated. And the stakes were high. Losing consciousness during exertion is a very worrisome symptom, and if you don't get it right…"

"Bad things can happen." Dick interrupted.

"And they did. I spent a lot of time on that case. I called a lot of people to get opinions. I even called Philip during the case to see what he tought."

"You did? I didn't realize that."

"He knew about the case; Pudge had already contacted him for the same reason."

"And he agreed with the idea of an implantable defibrillator?"

"We were all of a similar mind. Even Pudge, at that point. Our tests indicated that Sebby's heart was not normal. His walls were thick. Athletes generally have thick-walled hearts, but when we did nuclear resonance imaging, we established that Sebby's heart was scarred."

"Scarred? From what?"

"The most common cause is an infection, like a virus. We asked Sebby about drugs, because cocaine can damage the heart like that, but he denied using them and had never tested positive. We couldn't identify the cause. We then did some electrical testing, and in the laboratory we observed some very abnormal responses to electrical stimulation. When I added it all up, I had to recommend a device to shock Sebby's heart back to normal if he had any more arrhythmias."

"And you did."

"Yes, and I documented that in Sebby's chart."

"What happened next?"

"I went out of town on a Friday to a conference in San Francisco. Before I left, I told Pudge I planned to put the defibrillator in on Monday, when I got back. I had spoken with Sebby and his father, and everyone was in agreement."

"Including the Dream Team?"

"For sure. They unanimously agreed, and so did Philip."

"You called him again?"

"No, I saw him in Frisco at the conference. We had a drink, and talked about what kind of device to implant. I remember being very nervous about the procedure. I had done hundreds, but never in such a high-profile person."

"But the implant never happened. Why not?"

"While I was away, Pudge decided to do a tilt-table test. It's a test to diagnose a common reason to pass out. One of the possibilities for Sebby's loss of consciousness was a simple faint. Most of us didn't believe it because people don't usually faint in the midst of heavy athletic activity. But Pudge was being his normally compulsive self and wanted to check all possibilities. As luck would have it, the test was positive."

"What does that mean?"

"When Pudge put Sebby upright on the tilt table with his legs immobilized, his blood pressure and heart rate both plummeted and he lost consciousness. Pudge put the table down, and when Sebby woke up, he said that the symptoms during the test were identical to what he had experienced on the ice. Pudge was ecstatic. In his mind, the results meant that Sebby didn't have a malignant condition, he could be treated with medications, and he could resume hockey.

"By the time I got back from San Francisco, Pudge had called a news conference to announce the findings and his recommendations. He wanted me there even though I was in disagreement, and had pleaded with him not to go out on that limb. I asked him to take his time, to consider all the alternatives, and maybe do a few more tests."

"He didn't listen?"

"He was in an absolute frenzy. I'd never seen Pudge like that. It was as if he'd taken a stimulant drug. He had pressure of speech, he kept laughing and telling weird jokes and giving everybody high fives. I couldn't understand why he was choosing to rely on the tilt-table test. It gives so many false positives."

"You mean people can have a positive test even though it wasn't a faint that they'd had earlier?"

"Right. Anyhow, Pudge discharged Sebby on a beta-blocker and saw him in the office the following week. Sebby felt okay so Pudge gave him permission to rejoin the team. Everything seemed fine until Sebby collapsed at that playoff game in Washington. It was all downhill after that."

"And Mario's reaction?"

"'Devastated' would be an understatement. The man was useless. The department chief told him to go home and stay there indefinitely. He locked himself away for several days before he finally returned to work. The media camped out on his front lawn, badgering anyone who came anywhere near the place. The police even started sending patrols around, when the death threats started. MGH and the Bruins made it clear that it was Pudge's decision to release Sebby, but the fans climbed all over the team officials, too, furious that their hero had been struck down. It took months for the furor to settle, only to be re-ignited by the trials."

"So Pudge was wrong to do what he did?"

"Obviously I disagreed with him, but like I said, cases like this are judgment calls, and Pudge made his best conclusion. Unfortunately, it turned out wrong. With everything that was happening, I don't believe he was thinking clearly. I think he got swept up in the moment."

"So you don't fault Thad Robinson for Pudge's death."

"No. Pudge must have had a screw loose to kill himself like that. Robinson did have a reason to litigate what in the end was a bad decision. I hate the kind of lawyer he is, the way he does things, but he shouldn't be blamed for Pudge's death. That would be irrational."

Irrational, Dick thought. Who do I know that fits that description?

"You were sued in the case, as well?" Dick continued.

"Yes, as was everybody who had gotten anywhere near Sebby. Robinson wasn't taking any chances on having an empty chair at the trial."

"You mean, someone at fault who wasn't included in the lawsuit."

"Exactly. But that note I put in Sebby's chart recommending a device helped my attorney get me out of the case quickly. That, and a strong and cogent opinion from Philip, who was still at the top of his game then."

"Didn't that effectively pit Philip against Mario?"

"Not really. Pudge was still able to argue that he had enough reason to let Sebby play again. And Philip knew he would never testify in court if it came to that. So helping me didn't necessarily hurt Pudge. At least that was how Philip saw it."

"Doctor, I've taken enough of your time. You've been most helpful, and I truly appreciate your willingness to speak with me."

"I don't know how much I helped Philip."

"Anything we can learn about the case is helpful. I'll give him your regards."

"Please do."

Peter led Dick out to the atrium. After finding his car, Dick took out his phone and texted Dorothy. "Cross Friedberg off list. Lots of info but no reason to go after Robinson. Fill you in at hotel."

Neither Dick nor Dorothy doubted that the stage was set for their most important interview, with Deb Angelucci. Only a few missing pieces were left to try to fill in what was becoming a very scary puzzle. They were definitely running out of suspects… except for Philip.

Chapter 22

Dick arrived at the Ritz just as Philip and Dorothy were returning from the museum. They decided on lunch at a bistro a few doors down from the Ritz. They took a corner table near a window where they could people-watch. They scanned the menus and ordered, all without much conversation. Philip had not emerged from his foul mood, insisting on leaving the museum after only a few minutes. Dorothy was exasperated. Dick just wanted some time to debrief with his daughter before heading out for the Angelucci interview.

"So what are your plans for the afternoon, Philip?" Dick asked, hoping for something definitive.

"I have to get on some stupid teleconference with a company that's developing a new antibiotic."

"It has a cardiac safety problem?" Dorothy asked, trying to stimulate a normal conversation.

"Doesn't every drug?" Philip cracked.

"I do seem to hear about heart problems with drugs all the time," Dick said. "Must keep you busy."

"It used to," Philip replied. "Now I just get the jobs nobody else wants." Since his fall from grace after the Hamlin case, Philip's consultant opportunities had diminished substantially, with corresponding effects on his ego and wallet.

Conversation remained strained throughout lunch. Philip picked at his chicken Caesar wrap and Dorothy her spinach salad, while Dick wolfed down a super-sized BLT, fries, and slaw. "Not many things knock me off of my appetite," Dick had been heard to say during his most difficult cases. And a sulking Sarkis was no exception.

Service was tardy during the lunch hour rush. Philip was impatient, so Dorothy gave him an out. "Philip, why don't you go ahead and start your call? Dad and I'll wait for the check and will do a few things before we go off to our next meeting."

"Wanna get rid of me, right?"

"No, you're welcome to stay. But I can see you're restless."

"Might as well. I have to read some stuff before I get on the call, so I guess I'll see you later?"

"We should be back around dinnertime. How about if we hit a steak place for dinner?" Dorothy suggested Grill 23 in Back Bay, Philip's favorite.

"Sounds fine."

Philip moped off. When he was out of earshot, Dick shook his head and said, "It's hard being around that boy when he's like this."

"He's under a lot of pressure, Dad. Being a person of interest can't be much fun."

"I know. And we're here trying to help him out. But he doesn't seem to appreciate that very much. Screw it; let's just get down to business."

Dick summarized his meetings with Bergstrom and Friedberg, being careful to convey Peter's strong feelings about the medical aspects of the case, and Angelucci's tainted approach. "He made it very clear that

Mario was super-excited about finding an alternative explanation for Bergstrom's blackout."

"The savior of the Bruins."

"If he had been right and the Bruins had won the Cup, his name would have gone down in Boston sports history."

"I think it did anyway, but not the way he might have envisioned."

They went on to plan their interview with Deb Angelucci. "I don't want to upset her, but we really need to get details about what happened, and where Philip fit in," Dorothy said.

"I agree. The key question is how strongly Philip felt about Pudge, and if he could possibly have been motivated to go after Robinson."

"Or did Deb arrange it herself? She obviously had a motive."

"Well, little girl, I'm going to use the fitness center, swim a few laps, then take a nap before we go out there."

"Sounds good, Dad. I have to get some real work done, so I need a couple hours of Internet time. Philip will be yakking on the phone, so I think I'll go to the business center."

"I'll have the car brought up and meet you at the hotel entrance around four?"

"See you then." And with that, they went their separate ways, each feeling surprisingly anxious about their next interview.

The afternoon passed swiftly. In what seemed like a very short time to each, Dick and Dorothy were on their way to Newton. Deb and her two children lived in the house she had purchased with Pudge soon after he had completed his fellowship. It was modest, by any account, far less imposing than the homes of many of his

MGH colleagues. But Pudge and Deb were conservative souls who decided to live without much debt and to stash money away for their kids' education. The house was paid off, taxes and upkeep light, and so Deb, despite the loss of Mario's income, was able to keep the place and not move.

Dick and Dorothy pulled up outside Deb's home a few minutes before five. "Pretty nice digs, but hardly that of a famous Boston cardiologist," Dick observed.

"Some people prefer to live modestly, Dad."

As they sat there, Deb arrived, driving a late-model Jeep Cherokee. She pulled into the driveway, got out of her car, and spotted Dick and Dorothy. She waved hello and pointed toward the front door.

Dick and Dorothy hurried up the walk. "Hello, Mrs. Angelucci. I'm Dorothy and this is my father, Dick Deaver. We spoke on the phone earlier today?" Dorothy said as she extended a hand in greeting.

"Welcome," Deb answered cordially. "Come on in."

The Angelucci home was pretty much as Dorothy had imagined it. Neat, well maintained, and tastefully decorated. Lots of family photos, including several of Pudge with his children that didn't seem to revive Deb's grief enough for her to put them away. She led them to the living room and offered them a seat on the sofa and a beverage, which they declined. They wanted to get to the business at hand.

"We'll try to be brief, Mrs. Angelucci. May we call you Deb?"

"Yes, of course. I'm so happy to meet you both. Philip spoke of you often and fondly."

Dick and Dorothy exchanged glances. He did?

"Philip sends his regrets, Deb," Dorothy lied. "He's attending to some post-conference business."

"I understand. He was just here last week, and we had

a chance to catch up."

"Yes, for the heart conference," Dorothy said, realizing Philip had lied to her at Hymie's when he said he hadn't seen Deb.

Dorothy pushed on. "Deb, I think our visit will be most successful if we put all of our cards on the table. As I said when we talked on the phone this morning, Philip is a person of interest in the Robinson attack. My father and I came up to see if we could learn something that would make Philip, uh, less interesting to the police. We've talked with various people, and one of the most important things we learned was from Philip himself."

"What was that?" Deb asked.

"This is a little embarrassing, maybe, but it was only a few days ago that I learned Philip has been in touch with you, and you're the real reason he came for the heart conference."

"Yes, well. He has his ways, does he not? Philip's been an old and dear friend of ours for years. Granted he and Pudge didn't see a lot of each other the last few years before Pudge died, but I know they spoke on the phone frequently, especially when Pudge was dealing with the Bergstrom case and the lawsuits."

"And their relationship goes back to college days, I understand?"

"They were roomies before they went off to different medical schools."

"And when did you meet Philip?"

"Also in college. I went to Rosemont, a small school on the Main Line. I met Pudge at a mixer at one of the boathouses in Philly. Pudge was there with Philip. The three of us hit it off and we hung out together a lot. Pudge and I liked having Philip around, and he was pretty good at figuring out when he needed to disappear, if you know what I mean."

"Did you know Philip's first wife, Nancy?"

"Yes. I met her shortly after he did, when he and Pudge were at the Brigham for their fellowship. Pudge was best man at their wedding, in fact. We also saw them when Pudge and I visited Philly, after Philip started his first faculty job. I can't say I exactly clicked with her. We had somewhat different personalities and expectations."

"From what Philip has told me in the past, I gather her desires were somewhat, shall we say, lofty?"

"That's a good way to put it. She wanted a great house and expensive things and so on. You can see that was never our priority."

"So you didn't see much of them."

"Not the two of them together, no. Pudge and I had dinner with Philip a few times, at conferences, for example. And then Philip had that terrible malpractice case of his own, and we lost contact with him for a few years. Ironically, just as Philip was recovering with you in his life, Pudge's life took a turn for the worse, with the Bergstrom matter."

"I'm sure they commiserated quite a bit?"

"Well, you would know that, wouldn't you?"

"It's odd, but whenever I'd ask Philip for details, he seemed evasive."

"That's like Philip, isn't it? Never reveals more than he wants to. Anyway, Philip tried to be supportive, using his experience to help Pudge feel a little better about his chances. I'm not sure how well that worked."

"What is your perspective on the Bergstrom case?"

"I'm not a medical person by any stretch, so most of what I know came through Pudge. I saw how he agonized about what to recommend for Sebby. He called just about every big name in his field, and consulted the right people at MGH. In the end, he went with his own best judgment. And for that, he was sued."

"I'm sure you don't believe the lawsuit was justified."

Deb paused. "I can understand that Sebby's family was angry. Pudge reached out to them several times to apologize, but the father refused. Once the lawyers got involved, the case took on a life of its own."

Dick interrupted. "One thing I don't understand. Pudge and his legal team won in the end. Why do you think your husband was so depressed?"

"The case sucked the life out of him, and he knew it'd be a major stumbling block in his career no matter what the verdict. But he had stopped drinking heavily and seemed less depressed long before the crash, which is why we originally thought it was an accident. Until, of course, the investigation concluded."

"You mean the insurance company inquiry."

"Yes. Pudge had a large life insurance policy for us. If his death had been natural, we'd have gotten $2 million. But they said his death was a suicide, so we got nothing."

"How did they conclude that?"

"Pudge was driving on a lonely road, coming back from a dinner program for referring docs up on the north shore. The weather was good, and there wasn't much traffic. An unmarked police car saw him parked on the other side of the road. He was squatting next to the car, looking at the front tires. The cop had to drive about half a mile until he could find a place to cross the median and turn around to come back and help. By that time, Pudge's car had gone down a steep incline, broken through the guard rail, and went airborne down into a deep ravine.

"When they examined the car, it was so damaged that they couldn't even tell how many times it had flipped and rolled. But they couldn't find any evidence of tampering. The inquest concluded that Pudge had deliberately driven off that cliff and killed himself."

"He didn't leave a note?" Dick asked.

"On his desk at work the next day, they found a printed message that said, 'Forgive me.' It wasn't signed."

"His death must have been a terrible shock," Dorothy said.

"I'll never get over it, and I don't think the kids will, either," Deb replied, tears filling her eyes. She reached for a tissue box. "But we have to move on, don't we?"

Dorothy rushed to change the subject. "Where are you working now?"

"I'm a purchasing agent at Nordstrom's. Pudge and I managed to save some money, so the kids and I can get by on my salary."

"And your children?"

"They're okay. Mario junior's in ninth grade and wants to be a doctor. I'm not sure we can afford that. Janis is in fifth grade. They both help out around the house. They're good kids."

"I hate to ask, Deb, but can you tell me about the conversation you had with the two detectives about the Robinson attack?"

"Lentz and Socks, their names were. There wasn't much to talk about."

"Did they ask if you had an alibi for the time of the attack?"

"Do you seriously think I could have been the attacker?"

"Police like to check off their little tick boxes," Dick noted.

"No, they didn't ask, but I was in New York overnight at an auction in the garment district. The kids were here with a sitter. And if you want to see my bank account, it'll be pretty obvious that I couldn't have paid anyone to do it. And besides, I don't hate Thad Robinson or Sebby's family. You have to move on."

"You said you and Philip had a chance to catch up last week?" Dorothy asked.

"I think I saw him before the assault on Robinson. We talked a lot about Pudge, who is still very much on Philip's mind."

"How so?"

"I think he still blames himself for not being more forceful with Pudge, and insisting that he recommend a defibrillator for Sebby. He also didn't have nice things to say about Robinson. He was pretty angry about all of it."

Dick and Dorothy again exchanged glances. Testimony to that effect would weigh heavily with a jury if Philip were ever prosecuted.

"Deb, is there anything else about Philip and Pudge's relationship that might shed light on the Robinson situation?"

Deb hesitated, eyes darting back and forth between Dick and Dorothy. "No," she finally answered. "I don't believe so."

"Then we'll let you get dinner started. I'm sure your kids are hungry. Please call us if we can be of any help, or if you think of anything we should know."

"I certainly will," Deb said, escorting Dick and Dorothy to the door. As they walked down the few steps to the walkway, Deb called out. "Dick, could I have a word with you in private?"

Dick and Dorothy turned, startled. "But of course," Dick said, and followed Deb back into the house.

"Dick, I didn't want to risk upsetting Dorothy, but there is one more thing you should know. I hesitate to admit it, but it may explain some of Philip's behavior."

"I'm all ears. And it'll stay between the two of us."

"When Philip was a fellow with Pudge in Boston, and Philip hadn't met Nancy yet, Pudge and I went through a rough patch and separated for a few months. Philip was very helpful to both of us. He gave me a shoulder to cry on, and I was grateful.

"When Pudge and I got back together, we still weren't sure if things were going to work out. One evening, when Pudge was out of town, I had Philip over for dinner. Philip was hopeful that Pudge and I would be able to continue in our marriage, but he told me I had to follow my heart. Pudge and I were childless at that point, and Philip said that if Pudge and I couldn't make a go of it, it was better to go our separate ways before kids were part of the equation.

"We both had a little too much wine, I was feeling lonely and unwanted, and… Well, one thing led to another."

"I see." Dick didn't need it spelled out for him.

"Yes," Deb blushed. "The affair only went on for a few weeks. We finally came to our senses and were completely embarrassed and ashamed. We swore secrecy, and never told anyone. Pudge and I were able to patch things up but I… I…"

"You became pregnant?"

"Yes," Deb gushed, relieved that Dick had said it, not her. "Philip and I being together in that way turned out to be the wake-up call I needed. I went back to Pudge, but I've never known if Mario junior is Philip's or Pudge's. They both have the same Mediterranean coloring and features. Philip has always wondered, too, but we resolved never to find out who the real father is."

"Wow, that's a blockbluster," Dick exclaimed, trying in vain to assess the significance of this new information.

"I'm sorry to lay this just on you, Dick. But I didn't want to upset or embarrass Dorothy. You see, Philip's anger about Mario's suicide is partly because he knows Mario won't be around to support my children, one of whom may be his own son."

"Giving Philip even more of a motive to seek revenge against the man he perceived as the cause of Pudge's suicide."

"I suppose so. I can't believe Philip actually did it. I certainly wouldn't tell this to anyone else, but since you're trying to help Philip, it's best for you to know the entire story."

Dick paused, lost in thought. "I'm glad you told me, and that Dorothy has been spared this information, at least for the time being. You know she's going to find out eventually, whether I tell her or not."

"I understand, Dick. I just didn't want to be there when she heard the news."

"I'm going to have to process this a bit, Deb. As I said, it's our secret for as long as you wish, but I may want to ask you some more questions later. Would that be okay?"

"Certainly."

Dick walked out to the car, where Dorothy was waiting. "What was that all about, Dad?"

"Little girl, give me a while to work through it. And then we may have to have a father-daughter chat."

Chapter 23

Philip was beside himself. His conference call with the pharma company had not gone well at all. The advice he had previously given them was not heeded, and the company's meeting with the FDA had been unpleasant, to say the least. The agency remained concerned that the antibiotic the company was developing prolonged the heart's QT interval, and they worried it could cause a lethal rhythm in susceptible patients. The company was having a difficult time identifying exactly how much the drug prolonged that critical measurement, since that, in turn, would indicate how many patients the drug might harm. Philip had outlined a research protocol the company needed to follow to answer the question, but the company thought the study Philip proposed was too expensive. They did a different study instead, its results were inadequate, and now they were faced with the prospect of non-approval by the FDA. And if the FDA rejected their application, regulators in other parts of the world would follow suit.

Ordinarily, non-approval of an individual drug was not a disaster; other, approved drugs could take its place.

However, the early data on this particular antibiotic suggested it would work well against some especially resistant bacteria, in particular a strain of Staphylococcus that literally ate flesh and could not be killed by conventional antibiotics. Everyone in the academic community, including the FDA, recognized its importance, so the regulators were anxious for the company to do the right thing and clear the air on the safety issue.

Philip's message to the company's leadership was deliberately harsh. They had to allocate resources to get the data the FDA required. No, there was no other way, and yes, Philip would be happy to review a protocol synopsis and help organize things. "Just get off your butts and do it," were his final words as he rung off.

He looked around the hotel room. What the fuck am I doing here? he thought. And even worse, he was alone again. Dorothy and her father were off on another interview, and he was firmly excluded. What the hell were they up to? Sure, they had come to Boston to help, but he thought he would be privy to the information they were gathering. Instead all he got was the occasional reassurance that everything would be all right. Really? Then how come I'm still stuck in this stupid hotel, away from the comforts of my home and my dogs, inconveniencing my staff and jeopardizing my patients? And why is Lentz trying to make a case against me? It's time to go home, damn it.

Philip paced around the room, working himself into a frenzy of frustration. Fortunately, he had enough clarity to realize he would go insane unless he escaped, and for Philip, that meant exercise. He looked out the window. There was still enough light. I need a long run, he thought. He quickly changed into running shorts, a t-shirt, and jogging shoes, and hurried out to the elevator, stretching and running in place while waiting for the lift.

The door opened to reveal several well-dressed Asian tourists. Their chattering ceased as he entered. What the fuck are you looking at? Philip almost muttered. He imagined their disdain, but didn't give a rat's ass about what they thought of him.

Philip was the first off the elevator, pushing past the startled Asians. As he jogged through the hotel lobby, the doorman saw him coming and quickly opened the door. Philip glided through, turned to say thank you, and ran headlong into a very large man standing by a black limousine. Philip bounced off him like a tennis ball off a backboard, and nearly fell. The gray-haired hulk grabbed Philip by the arm to stabilize him. Philip regained his senses. "I'm so sorry," he muttered.

"No worries," came the reply. Philip realized he was looking almost straight up at the man whose pockmarked face was twisted into a smile. "Are you all right?"

"Fine, and sorry again," Philip replied as he backpedaled and began his run down Boylston Street. He looked back over his shoulder; the large man had disappeared.

Philip's run took him over some of the surface streets of downtown Boston. His goal was to get down to the Charles, cross over to Cambridge, and head west along the river. It was turning into a beautiful evening, the air clear and crisp. Traffic along the drives was heavy, rush hour in full swing. Philip enjoyed marking his progress, looking at cars that were proceeding along the route much more slowly than he. The frustration of living in a large city, Philip thought. Something he no longer had to spend time worrying about.

His mind starting wandering, as it usually did during a run. Yeah, traffic was no longer an issue in his life, but neither was a true academic career. That had been taken away from him by Bonnie Romano and Hugh Hamlin. He was now doomed to be a two-bit, outpatient cardiologist in rural Pennsylvania. Granted, he still went to conferences and wrote a few journal articles, but most of his writing was penny-ante stuff, like case reports published in free medical journals, commonly known as "throwaways," read by few, and referenced by none.

Keep running, Philip, he thought. He knew that as the endorphins kicked in, his mind would turn to positive thoughts. He had much to be thankful for, after all. He was living with a beautiful person, who understood and took good care of him. He still got to see his kids, and they enjoyed their visits. Nancy had been difficult during the divorce, but once the financial arrangements were in place, she had calmed down and cooperated with Philip to raise their children. And he had his doggies, Mitten, Buffy and Meeko, and they gave him pleasure every day. Every day, he was home, that is. And home is now where he wanted to be. That wonderful refuge in the mountains where life proceeded at a comfortable pace, and where there was always time for diversion.

On he ran, losing track of time and even place, until he found himself in a dodgy part of Cambridge, way past the MIT and Harvard campuses and their nice neighborhoods. He also realized that he was beyond parched. His salty lunch was exacerbating his running thirst. He spied a corner convenience store and jogged over, happy that he remembered to squirrel away a few bucks in his running shorts. He went to the cold-drink case and found a Gatorade that he started gulping while waiting in line to pay. He was clearly out of place, again. Most of the patrons were locals who ran only when chased. The store clerks were an Indian man and woman who were clearly intrigued by their scantily clothed visitor. Philip ignored their stares, eager to pay and find his way back to the Ritz.

Philip finished his refreshment as he left the store, threw the bottle into a trash bin, and started running back along the path on which he'd come. His mind was now on the time. He had left the hotel about an hour ago and it was already 6:15 P.M. He worried not only about impending nightfall, but Dorothy and Dick planned to meet him for dinner. Of course he hadn't brought his phone on the run and pay phones were a thing of the past. How many times had Dorothy admonished him about keeping his cell phone with him? Now he would need a faster pace to get back so she wouldn't worry about him.

His thoughts were interrupted by a loud noise, almost like a peal of thunder. He stumbled and fell to the ground, just as he heard a second explosion, followed by a screech of tires and a roaring engine nearby. Philip rolled over, sat up, and felt liquid running down his leg. His first thought was that he had fallen into a puddle, but when he saw the liquid's color, and the pain started, he realized, with much disbelief, that he had been shot.

He cried out, "Can someone help me, please?" The store clerks and a few customers were peering out the window, afraid to venture out. "Please," Philip beseeched, clutching his thigh, "I've been shot."

No movement in the quiet evening. Philip realized he had to get back to the store and out of harm's way on his own. He took off his shirt and used it to put pressure on the wound. Half walking, half crawling, trying to stem the bleeding from his leg, Philip made his way along the sidewalk. The store people opened the door and helped him in. They huddled around him, looking at his leg, not knowing what to do.

"I'm a doctor. I need bandages; do you have any?" Philip kept holding his shirt to his thigh.

The Indian man hurried away, down aisle five, where he got some medical supplies and brought them back to Philip. The lady clerk asked Philip if he needed anything else. "Can you please call 911?"

"I've already done that. I'm sure the police will be here very soon."

As if on cue, Philip heard sirens in the distance. The cavalry was on the way. Their impending arrival gave Philip the courage to lift the cotton gauze he had placed on the wound. He was relieved to see that the bullet had entered and exited in the fleshy part of his leg, missing bone and arteries.

Philip was also comforted to hear the police cars pull up. Two very young-looking Cambridge policemen ran in. One had her gun drawn and quickly surveyed the scene before reholstering her weapon. The young man went directly to Philip, still tending to his leg.

"An ambulance is on the way, sir. How bad is it?"

"The wound is pretty superficial. I think I'm okay."

"Okay, good. Well, not good, but… I'm Officer Feeney, and that's Officer Stubbs over there. Can you tell me your name and what happened?"

Philip explained that he was out for a run, stopped to purchase a drink, and was heading back to his hotel when he was shot.

"Did you see anyone with a gun?"

"No. There were two shots, I think, and then I heard a car speed off. I assume that's who shot me, but I didn't see much."

Feeney asked Philip a few more questions, including the name of someone to contact at his hotel.

"Okay, we'll secure the area and get some crime scene investigators out here."

"People," Office Stubbs addressed the few customers and clerks, "we'll want to get your names and ask you a few questions before you leave the store."

As predicted, the ambulance arrived quickly. The paramedics documented that Philip's vital signs were excellent and that wound control was good. Philip was wrapped in a blanket, placed on a stretcher, and loaded into the ambulance for the short ride to Bunker Hill Hospital, the nearest medical center, quite experienced at dealing with the "knife and gun club" victims in its neighborhood.

Just before the ambulance doors closed, Officer Feeney came over to check on Philip. "Dr. Sarkis, I called the Ritz and left a message for Dorothy Deaver. The hotel is trying to reach her on the cell number she gave them. And I've been notified that Detective Wilson Lentz will meet you at the hospital. He'll be in charge of the investigation."

What a coincidence, Philip thought, as he saw the ambulance doors close.

Philip was admitted to the Emergency Department at Bunker Hill Hospital, and attended to by Dr. Ira Gomberg, a free-spirit, former hippie who gloried in his work in a ghetto hospital. Adorned with ponytail, earring, and African dashiki, Ira liked to joke with his patients, sometimes when humor was not entirely appropriate. He persisted, however, reasoning that humor was a great healer. So what if one of his bad jokes had gotten him ejected from the Tufts residency program? He landed on his feet at Auburn Hills, and was having fun on staff at Bunker Hill after all.

"So, what have we here? Somebody trying to make Swiss cheese out of a good Jewish boy?"

"I'm not Jewish," Philip replied testily.

"Wow, are we sure? Nurse, pull back his covers and

let's see if this young man has been serviced by a mohel."

Philip glared at Gomberg. "Just kidding. A little joke to lighten the day."

"Can you please just take care of the wound and get me the hell out of here?"

"Certainly, Mr. Sarkis," Gomberg said. Squinting at Philip's information on the computer screen next to the stretcher, he added, "Says here you're a physician, so it's Dr. Sarkis?"

The general information that Philip had provided to a clerk was now in the electronic record that Gomberg was perusing. "You were coming out of convenience store when this happened?"

"That's right."

"Shot once in the left leg."

"I heard two shots, actually. The other one must have gone over my head when I fell."

"And you didn't see anybody?" Ira asked as he pulled back the sheets to examine the wound that had been temporarily dressed by the admitting nurse.

"No."

"Probably one of those random shootings that happen around here. It's like walking around in a shooting gallery, except instead of clay ducks, we have people."

Gomberg looked at the wound carefully. "You're a lucky man, Dr. Sarkis. May I call you Philip?"

"Whatever," Philip answered.

"It's basically superficial. It looks like it went in and out of the muscle and soft tissue in the back of your leg. We'll get an X-ray to be sure. But most likely, all we have to do is clean it up, dress it, get you on an antibiotic, give you a tetanus shot, and you should be good to go."

"Thanks."

"We'll give you a follow-up appointment in our surgery clinic in a few days, too."

"Hopefully I'll be home by then."

Gomberg checked the computer screen again. "They have doctors in the Poconos, yes?" Gomberg joked.

"A few, and they know how to treat gunshot wounds."

"Hunters shoot hunters all the time, I'm sure. Just ask Dick Cheney!"

No response from Philip. Gomberg decided he wasn't going to cheer Philip up, so he quietly went about dressing the wound. As he finished, Dorothy and Dick were escorted into the cubicle by an ER attendant. Dorothy rushed to the stretcher and hugged Philip, tears filling her eyes.

"Are you all right?" Dick asked, looking over Dorothy's shoulder.

"Yes, Dr. Gomberg here has taken very good care of me," Philip answered, disentangling himself from Dorothy. "The wound isn't serious and will heal up fine."

"Hi, Mrs. Sarkis," Gomberg said. "I'm Ira Gomberg. I am sending your husband for an X-ray. If it's okay, we will give him an antibiotic to take for a week and something for the pain. He'll be uncomfortable for a few days. Obviously, no heavy activity, and he may need crutches to get around for a while. We can give you a pair, if you like."

Dorothy nodded, neither she nor Philip feeling the need to correct Gomberg about their marital status.

"What on earth happened to you?" Dorothy gushed as soon as Gomberg left them.

Philip's answer was interrupted by the arrival of Will Lentz. "I was going to ask the same question, Dr. Sarkis," he said as he pushed the drapes aside. "Maybe you could answer for all of us?"

"Happy to, Detective, because there's almost nothing to tell. I was out for a run…"

"Anybody following you?"

"Not that I saw, but I wasn't paying attention. I ran further than I intended and ended up in a borderline neighborhood…"

"And went into a convenience store," Will interrupted again.

"Yeah, to get a drink. I was walking out, had just finished the Gatorade and was starting to run again, when I heard a noise and fell. Then there was a second shot."

"That obviously missed you," Dick chimed in.

"Right. Then I heard a car speeding away. I made it back to the store, they called the police, and here I am."

"Did you get a look at the car?"

"Not really. I glanced in the direction of the sounds and may have seen a moving car. It looked like a big sedan, dark color, blue or black, but I'm not sure."

"Can you think of anyone here who might have wanted to harm you?"

"Come on, Lieutenant. Are you saying *you* can't think of anyone?"

Will looked at his feet. "We have to consider all possibilities."

"All right, try this one: Thaddeus Robinson paid somebody to shoot me."

"Okay, I concede that's a possibility."

"A pretty damn good one, Lieutenant."

"Dr. Sarkis, you were in a dangerous neighborhood. It's a place where people do get shot. Could have been a gang initiation rite, or maybe they don't like the store owners and wanted to shoot up the place. So, if I had to put my money on the table, that would be my bet. But we're doing a careful crime scene over at the store. My partner is supervising the neighborhood canvas and the ballistics search."

"That's good, Detective," Dorothy replied. She was sitting on the side of the bed holding Philip's hand and trying to keep back the tears. "Because we're frightened."

"I understand, Dorothy, believe me, and we'll work hard on this. I may have some more questions for you later, Dr. Sarkis, and I'll let you know if we learn anything from the witnesses. I suggest you stay in your hotel while we sort this out."

After Will departed, Philip went to X-ray. Shortly after his return, Gomberg came by to tell Dorothy and Philip that he had been correct, and there was no major damage to bone. An ER nurse then came in, gave Philip his initial antibiotic dose, and started discharge procedures. Philip changed into clothes Dorothy had brought and was able to limp to Dick's car without crutches. After a stop to fill prescriptions, they arrived back at the Ritz. Dick waited in the lobby while Dorothy took Philip back to their room. He desperately wanted a shower but had to be satisfied with a sponge bath, assisted by Dorothy. He was greatly relieved when he could finally lay down.

"Hungry, Philip?" Dorothy asked once he was settled.

"No. My appetite is shot right now. Ha, I made a pun."

"How about a couple of the Percocets?" Dorothy said, holding out pills and a glassful of water.

"Yeah. I just want to lie here a little." Philip took the pills, and before Dorothy turned out the light and closed the door, he was sound asleep.

Dorothy joined her father in the lobby. "Is he okay?" Dick asked.

"Tired and frightened, mainly. Which isn't surprising. He's been through a lot lately."

"You too, little girl, you too. And I'm afraid things aren't going to get any easier."

"What do you mean, Dad?"

"Let's find a nice quiet place to grab a bite to eat and figure out where we are with everything."

"Where to?" Dorothy asked.

"Doesn't matter. After all of this, I doubt that either of us will taste much of whatever we order."

Chapter 24

Sergeant Michael Aloysius Sweeney was a veteran of the Boston PD. He liked to tell his family and friends that, in his twenty-eight years at the intake desk, he had seen it all. From drunken politicians to naked rabbis to professional athletes in drag. Every permutation of humanity had, at one time or another, passed in front of his desk at the A-1 precinct in downtown Boston. He had long ago given up being surprised. Sweeney's response to most situations was predictable: glower, hiss, and then utter a comment or command, fully expecting it to be heeded and fully prepared to make someone face the consequences if it wasn't. But not many failed to cooperate with him. With a beefy, red complexion, a network of broken blood vessels adorning his bulbous nose, and small, often bloodshot eyes, Sweeney's countenance clearly advertised that he was in no mood for games. His features, of course, also belied his eagerness to hoist a few with his mates after eight hours of regarding the dregs of humanity from his desk, strategically positioned high enough off the floor for people to look up if they wanted to talk to him.

Sweeney was on his perch Tuesday morning when a suggestively dressed young woman approached carrying a package about the size of a shoe box. She had already drawn the attention of most of the male officers who were circulating in the precinct, and she was enjoying the notice. She walked slowly, swaying ever so gently, slightly bent at the waist to give her cleavage added exposure. It was her perfume that alerted Sweeney to her arrival. He looked up from his paperwork.

"And what may I be helping you with, ma'am?" he asked, delighted with his lofty vantage point, as he always was when talking to well-endowed females.

"Sergeant… Sweeney?" she said, squinting to see his nameplate. "I have a package for you."

"Do you now, lass?" Sweeney said, doing his best Irish brogue. "And who might you be?"

She hesitated before saying, "My name is… Sally."

Sweeney raised a well-practiced eyebrow. "Is that right?" he asked. He was beginning to enjoy the interchange but knew he had to maintain concentration.

"And might you have a last name you care to share?"

"Ah… Jones?"

Sweeney was now on full alert. People with fake names walking into police stations with packages needed to be taken seriously, and the department had strict policy about such situations. "Tell you what, Ms. Jones. I'm going to ask one of Boston's finest to escort you to a room so we can ask a few questions and take that package off your hands. Is that okay with you?"

Sally hesitated. "I just wanted to drop it off, like the man asked." The look from Sweeney quickly convinced her that his question was rhetorical and she had no choice.

"Of course, Sergeant," Sally said. "I have nothing to hide."

Sweeney smirked at Sally's double entendre. Judging from her wardrobe choices, the only things she did have to hide were things you'd have to pay for. "We promise not to keep you long, Ms. Jones. Haggerty, get over here. You too, Lopez."

Sweeney ducked down behind his desk and whispered instructions to Haggerty and Lopez. Lopez led Sally to a room near the intake desk. Haggerty, looking nervous, took the package to a room at the end of the corridor, as far away from anyone else as possible. He then stationed himself at what he hoped was a safe distance and kept guard on the corridor. Sweeney called his lieutenant. He was close to retirement and he didn't need anything to get in the way of a smooth departure.

"LT, we have a hooker who brought in a package that some guy asked her to give us. I'm calling the bomb unit."

"Great. Just what I need this early in the morning."

"I'll keep you posted, Lieutenant," Sweeney said, "unless you hear a big boom."

The bomb unit was on precinct property, in an adjacent building that had been a garage in the old days. After 9/11 and the Boston Marathon bombing, the city realized it needed to have facilities to deal with suspected terrorists. Specifically, it needed a secure place to dismantle bombs or suspicious packages, where an explosion would do little or no damage. They maintained a site outside the city for major threats, but the garage near the A-1 was good enough for the untended backpack found on the street that now worried everyone but was rarely the real deal. The bomb crew was expected to be able to investigate as well as deal with small-time threats, too. When things were quiet, they spent a good part of their day killing time, or tinkering with devices as they stood by waiting for calls like Sweeney's.

"This is Sergeant Sweeney at the A-1 intake desk. Who am I speaking with?"

"Jimmy Flynn, Sergeant" the answer came back. "What can I do for you?"

"A hooker supposedly named Sally Jones came in with a package she was told to deliver to us. Size of a shoebox, maybe. We put her in one room and the package in another. Need you guys here ASAP."

"Where'd she get it, Sergeant?"

"Jesus, I don't know! Some john or something. Get over here and you can ask the questions!"

"On our way, Sergeant."

"Hurry the fuck up. I want that package out of my building pronto."

Jimmy put the phone down and looked across at his partner, Gabe Williams. "We got us a hooker and maybe a itty-bitty bomb next door at A-1 headquarters. So get off your black ass, my man."

"Yes, massah. I be comin', I be comin'. And can I get you a mint julep to sip on the way over?"

For laughs and to amuse, Jimmy and Gabe played their racial differences with each other and for their colleagues in the bomb unit. In reality, they were fast friends, each fairly sure that one would lie on a bomb to save the other's life. In their private moments, they did have to wonder sometimes how an Irish kid from Southie and a black guy from Roxbury had formed this friendship. It was a crazy, mixed-up world for sure.

They decided not to go full tilt on their protective outfits. They did wear protective goggles and padded overalls that would limit the damage from shrapnel. Walking into the station, they were immediately met by Haggerty, who directed them down the corridor leading to the room with the package. They thanked him and said they'd be back to talk to the hooker, assuming the package didn't kill them. "Or at least my Negro friend here," Jimmy added. Once in the room, Jimmy gingerly picked up the package, as Gabe opened the nearby doors leading to a parking lot and the bomb unit's building just beyond. They walked the short distance and disappeared inside.

Jimmy had noted how light the package was, but nevertheless donned a helmet and more protective gear. He took the package into a metal-lined shed and placed it on a table while Gabe watched through a small reinforced window. Carefully, he cut open the box. He was relieved to see no wires, batteries, or a cell phone. Instead, there was a stuffed manila envelope. Carefully, again, he cut the envelope open and unraveled the packing, finding only a bloody knife in a plastic container with a scribbled note that said "Thaddeus Robinson."

"What the fuck," Jimmy muttered into the intercom.

"Damn," Gabe replied.

Jimmy held the plastic container to the window. "Gabe, does this name mean anything to you?"

"Nope."

"Me neither. Call Sweeney and ask him to run it."

Gabe walked over to the phone while Jimmy placed the knife and the note in separate bags. Gabe came back a minute later. "Sweeney's running it but he said he didn't have to because he knows Robinson is the guy who got knifed on Harvard Bridge last week."

"No shit. Now I remember. Do you think this is the weapon?"

"Good chance. Anyhow, Sweeney will confirm and then call the detectives on the case."

"Who's that?"

"Two of our faves: Lentz and Socks."

"Good. Let's go talk to our gal Sal while we're waiting for Will and Harry to get here.

"Sounds like a plan," Gabe agreed. "Better'n handling explosives."

"Right. But I'll bet that package's little surprise *will* blow up in somebody's face."

Jimmy and Gabe walked into the room where Sally and Officer Lopez had been having a little chat. Jimmy relieved Lopez, and he and Gabe had a seat.

"Ms. Jones, my name is Jimmy Flynn and this here is Gabe, don't call him Gabriel, Williams."

"Pleased to meet you boys," Sally answered, crossing her legs.

"Ms. Jones, first of all, may I call you Sally?"

"Sure, Officer. Can I call you Jimmy?"

Flynn ignored her question. "Now Sally, we need to know who gave you that parcel."

"I don't know his name."

"Okay. Then can you tell us how you met him?"

"Before I do, Officer, can you assure me I'm not going to be get pinched for prostitution?"

"Sally, I can't guarantee you won't get 'pinched' but we aren't going to bother you with any charges. Right, Gabe?"

Gabe nodded and put his foot up on the stool next to Sally.

"All right, then. I'll tell you exactly what happened. I was walking down Franklin Street…"

"In the old combat zone?" Jimmy interrupted.

"I don't like calling it that, but I guess that's right."

Jimmy smiled at her reluctance to use the common name for the area of Boston known for hookers, porn, and drugs. Even hookers clung to some shred of decorum, apparently.

"Sorry to interrupt, Sally. Please go on."

"Anyhow, I was minding my own business when this here car pulled up and a guy asked me if I wanted a job. I started to tell him I was off duty, so to speak, when he said he only wanted me to messenger a package."

"Is that exactly what he said?" Gabe chimed in.

"Pretty much."

"What'd he look like?"

"I couldn't see him real clearly. He had sunglasses on, even though it was dark, and a Red Sox cap."

"Distinguishing features, facial hair…"

"He may have had a beard, but I'm not sure. He had a pretty dark complexion but he wasn't no ni… Sorry, officer, he wasn't African American."

Gabe was stone-faced. "And the car?"

"Some economy number, maybe a Toyota. It was pretty small. I tend to notice stuff like back seat size."

"I'm sure you do, Sally," Jimmy replied.

"So then what happened?" Gabe asked.

"I told him I could deliver the package for him, but it would cost. He said fine, how much, and then he gave me the package and the money and the address of the precinct."

Jimmy, "Dare I ask how much?"

"A C note. I asked for it, and he didn't flinch."

"So you brought it here like he told you. You weren't surprised or worried about taking it to the police?"

"Why should I care? I ain't done nothin' wrong, least not today. And a hundred dollars without unzipping any clothes is a good thing, Officer."

"Okay, Sally. There are detectives on their way to talk to you some more. We'll send Officer Lopez back in here to keep you company until they get here. Is that okay?"

"Thank you, guys," Sally said with a seductive wink.

Chapter 25

Jimmy and Gabe parked themselves on stools in the hallway outside of the interrogation room, waiting for Will and Harry. They had placed the envelope and all of its contents into plastic bags, labeled them carefully as evidence, and sent them to the lab for analysis. They put a rush on it and hoped the detectives would get some usable information by the end of the day. They were anxious to lateral Sally and her story to someone with a chance of making sense of it. With no bomb around, their joh was done. Timc to move on to something more important, like lunch.

Harry and Will arrived about thirty minutes later. "Hey guys, I heard you got some information on our case," Will said.

"You bet, Will. Good golly Miss Sally Jones is waiting in Room 101 for your particular brand of expertise," Jimmy replied sarcastically. He had worked with Will on a few cases and knew he had a sense of humor. He wasn't so sure about Socks the Serious.

Jimmy summarized what he and Gabe had learned in their brief interview, including a sketchy description of the man who had given her the package.

"So, completely out of the blue, this guy stops her, gives her a package with a knife and Robinson's name, and tells her to bring it here?" Harry reiterated.

"You can't make this shit up, Detective," Gabe said, somewhat defensively.

"I don't doubt what you're saying. I just can't figure it out. Who would do that?" Harry wondered aloud.

"Beats us. Is there anyone you guys like for the attack?" Gabe asked.

"Yeah, our leading candidate is a guy named Sarkis. Not a strong suspect at this point, but a few things point in his direction. Do you think this Sally could ID him if we showed her some photos?"

"You can try. She said the guy was pretty covered up with sunglasses and a baseball cap."

"Yankees?" Will asked.

"Sox," Jimmy replied.

"Too bad. I'd rather nail a Yankees fan," Will said. "Okay, thanks guys. We'll take it from here."

Will gestured to Harry: time to get started. They walked into the room and dismissed Officer Lopez. Sally pouted and waved goodbye with a flutter of her fingers to her latest friend.

"Hi, Sally," Harry began. "Or perhaps we should start by having you give us your real name."

"And who are you?" Sally asked.

"Sergeant Detective Harry Socks. This is my partner, Lieutenant Detective Wilson Lentz." They flashed their badges.

"Well, Detectives, those other guys promised I wouldn't be hassled about… my occupation, if you know what I mean."

"Sally, or whatever you name is," Will cut in, "the last thing we care about is how you make a living. Just tell us your real name, let us ask you a few questions, and we'll cut you loose."

It didn't take long for Sally to reply. "Okay, my name is Molly Stevens. I grew up in New Hampshire. Manchester."

"Got some ID?"

She handed Will her driver's license. Harry took notes and handed it back to her.

"What are you doing in Boston?" Will continued.

"I came here to get a job in the entertainment industry."

"Looks like you succeeded. How long ago did you make your way to our fine city?"

"About two years."

"And you live where?"

"With my cousin. She has an apartment in the Seaport area."

"Okay, so you were walking along minding your own business, and this guy gave you a package."

"I told the other officers I was off duty. Are we going to go over all of that again?" Molly asked.

"No, but I want you to look at a photo for me and tell me if this is the guy."

Will handed her a photo of Philip he had taken off the Internet. She looked at it for several seconds. "The guy I saw had on a baseball hat and sunglasses."

"So you can't tell?"

"It could be this guy. Same complexion and beard, but I can't say for sure."

"Anything about his voice? An accent?"

"No, sounded pretty American to me."

"Did you happen to get a look at the license plate?"

"Massachusetts, I think. Don't remember the number."

"Okay, Molly. Thanks for trying to help us. If you remember anything or if anyone contacts you to ask if you delivered the package, call us right away. Here's our number."

Molly put the card in her purse and slung it over her shoulder, eager to make tracks. "Don't worry. I will, Detective."

"Stay in the area, Molly. We may have more questions for you."

"You'll know where to find me, Detective. A girl's gotta make a living."

Harry and Will retreated to their office, where they reviewed the case status with Captain Pokorney. All agreed there wasn't much to do until the lab reported its findings about the knife. They were shuffling papers around their desks, working on other cases, when Jie Chin, their favorite lab geek, surprised them shortly after lunch with a personal visit.

"Jie, how the fuck are you?" Will greeted him.

Jie smiled his lopsided grin. A recent immigrant, he was still refining his skills in English, particularly with regard to idioms. "How fucked are you, Will?"

Harry turned away, biting his cheek, trying not to laugh.

"I guess that depends on what you have to tell us."

"I have good informations for you, Will. Five fingerprint on knife, all same person. Blood, too. I got lucky with matches."

"Excellent, Jie. Tell us about the matches."

"Okay. First, blade good match to wound. Same pattern both places."

Will nodded while Harry jotted notes.

"And the blood? Was it from Thaddeus Robinson?"

"Yes. All blood is Robinson."

"What about the fingerprints?"

"Same with prints. One guy, Cassius Small. Found him in system."

"He's in jail?"

"Yes. Gang shooting in Southie. Little girl get hit. They arrest Small. Charge him with manslaughter."

"When did this happen?"

"Two night ago."

"You mean just this week?"

"Yes."

"So he wasn't in custody when Robinson was attacked?"

"Don't know, Will."

"Jie, thanks for your quick work."

"More to do, then I write report."

"Okay. Let us know if anything changes."

Jie smiled ear to ear as he backed away. "Can do. Fuck great to see you, Will," Jie said, obviously proud of his contribution to the case.

"Yes, Jie, you should always fuck great. Thanks again."

After Jie left, Harry and Will pondered the new information. Harry spoke first. "Are you shitting me? A banger from Southie by himself on thc Harvard Bridge? Decides to stick a guy?"

"I hear ya, Harry. Think he's being set up?"

"The only motive would be robbery. We never found Robinson's wallet, but the watch wound up in the river."

"Maybe he just dropped it?"

"Right. A banger scores a ten-grand Rolex and then, 'Oops, it slipped out of my hand!' Unlikely."

"We could sit here all day hypothesizing. Need to talk to the dude. And we don't have to strain our brain to find him."

Will and Harry were able to reach the detectives who

had arrested Cassius Small for the gang shooting. He was being held in a municipal lock-up for having fired a gun that killed a five-year old girl playing in the street with her friends. He had been processed and was awaiting a bail hearing later in the week.

They were also able to retrieve background information about Small: African American, Iraq War vet, part-time truck driver, mostly kept his nose clean. He had a couple of arrests in his youth for misdemeanors, but never anything involving a weapon. The shooting was distinctly out of character, and he had adamantly proclaimed his innocence at his arraignment. Nonetheless, he was charged, probably wouldn't make bail, and would likely do some hard time unless his wet-behind-the-ears public defender could mount a plausible defense.

Will asked the detectives on that case if he and Harry could interview Small, and were advised that Small would need the option of having his attorney present.

"Better call over there and see if he'll waive that right," Harry said to Will.

The message came back an hour later. Small was happy to be interviewed without his worthless attorney. He figured he had nothing to lose.

Will and Harry decided to split up for the afternoon. "Let me go have a talk with this guy," Will suggested. "Maybe you can get a warrant and search his residence?"

"Sure, Will, that's fine," Harry replied, not so sure it really was fine, but unwilling to get into an argument over who would get the more interesting task.

Boston's County Jail, located in the government area near Faneuil Hall, was a dump and a tribute to the graft and corruption that had plagued the city for years. Despite some of the highest property taxes in the country, the city's government struggled to fund essential services like schools, trash collection, fire-fighting, and city building maintenance. Not that Boston was unique. Virtually every city in the northeast had similar issues.

The good news was that the tide had begun to turn. The flight to the suburbs had been stemmed with the arrival of young professionals who wanted the excitement of city life and had the money to pay for it. And then there was the reverse migration of the empty nesters who no longer needed large houses and yearned for the convenience of urban living. Although new condos, restaurants, and shops abounded, the city government had not yet been able to fully capitalize on the new prosperity. *The Boston Globe* asked the obvious question: "Where are all the new property tax dollars going?" No one seemed to know, but the politicians and their cronies drove nicer cars and had bigger houses than ever.

Will parked in the visitor's lot and made his way to the lock-up, located in the basement. It was a depressing place, bearing a stark resemblance to medieval jails but for the fact that a toilet stood in the middle of a cell instead of a chamber pot. The hallways were dark, the walls stained, and the flooring worn. Will was escorted to an interview room, where he could talk to Small across a table under strict observation.

Small made his entrance, escorted by a guard who directed him to sit with his arms and hands in full view. Will was surprised by Small's appearance: he didn't look like a gang banger. No tattoos, close-cropped hair, clean shaven except for a well-trimmed mustache, and reasonably good looking, with clear and penetrating brown eyes.

"Good afternoon, Cassius. My name is Lieutenant Detective Wilson Lentz."

"The guards told me you were coming. What can I do for you?"

Another surprise. Small was fairly articulate and soft-spoken.

"I'll come to the point. A little over a week ago, an attorney named Thaddeus Robinson was stabbed on the Harvard Bridge. Your fingerprints were on the knife that was used in the attack."

"I don't know anything about that."

"Do you know Robinson?"

"Never heard of him."

"Where were you last Wednesday morning, about 5 A.M.?"

"Let's see. I would have been home, sleeping."

"Alone?"

"As usual."

"You aren't married."

"No. Divorced about three years ago."

"No children or others living with you?"

"No, I live alone. I get work driving a truck when I can, otherwise I exercise and hang out."

"So you have no idea how your prints got on the knife used to stab Robinson."

Small looked down at his folded hands. "That's correct, Detective."

"You didn't stab him and take his watch and wallet because you needed the money."

"How many times do I have to tell you? I wasn't anywhere near the place. I have no idea what you're talking about."

"Why are you being held, Cassius?"

"You know why. The cops say I shot some kid."

"Did you?"

"Absolutely not. I was walking along, minding my own business, when I heard a bunch of shots fired. I hit the ground, and next thing I know, a cop is standing over me telling me to stay down. He cuffed me, read me my rights, and brought me to this place."

"Unlucky guy, aren't you Cassius? First you get arrested for a shooting you didn't do, and then somebody with your fingerprints knifes an attorney."

"I've never had very good luck, Detective."

"In love or in war," Will joked, not expecting a reply.

"Especially not in war."

"I saw you served in Iraq."

"Unwillingly."

"Why? Did they restart the draft just for you?"

"Oh, I signed up, but not for Iraq. The recruiter sold me on medic training. Said I'd be assigned to an army hospital nowhere near any fighting, and maybe even stateside. But they assigned me to a combat patrol unit and I nearly bought it more times than I care to remember."

"Medic, huh? How come you didn't do something in healthcare when you got out?"

"I wanted to, but I needed more money than I could get as an orderly or nurse's assistant. My father got me a job driving truck, and it paid well for a few years. Things have dried up recently; now it's too late to go back."

"Cassius, I think you're a good guy. I really do. I'm willing to believe that you were just in the wrong place at the wrong time, and that you didn't shoot that little girl. The problem is that several people say they saw you do it and you're going to get burned. Judges get really pissed when a little kid takes a bullet. If you come clean on the Robinson attack, I can try to help you get a break on your sentence so you might have a prayer of seeing daylight before you die. But if you keep lying, you have a good chance of living the rest of your life in jail."

Cassius paused, pondering his options. "Sorry, Detective. I can't confess to something I have no idea about and didn't do."

The guard came over signaling that time was up.

"Okay, Cassius. I'll come back later this afternoon and maybe we can talk some more," Will suggested.

As he was led away, Cassius replied over his shoulder, "Great. That'll give you a chance to meet my new lawyer."

Will stopped at the visitors log book, then wasted little time getting to his car. He pulled out his cell phone and called Harry, who answered after two rings.

"He won't cop to the stabbing, even though he has no alibi and no job and could have used the money. I don't think he has a prayer."

"You got that right, especially with what I found at his apartment."

"Let's hear it."

"He lives in the projects in Southie, not too far from where the girl was shot. I talked to a few of his neighbors. He keeps to himself. They see him jogging a lot in the neighborhood. In fact, that's what he was doing the night of the shooting."

"What did you find, Harry?" Will asked, trying to keep the impatience out of his voice.

"The apartment was pretty clean. Not much out of place. We went through it thoroughly and came up with bupkis until we looked in his bathroom."

"And what did you find in the bathroom, Harry?" Will asked gritting his teeth.

"A box of rubber gloves."

"Christ, more rubber gloves? What the fuck?"

"Yep, and they were the same make as the empty package we found in Sarkis' room, the kind they use to do procedures in hospitals."

"That's a weird coincidence."

"To say the least."

"This guy does have a medical background. He was a medic in the service."

"So he knows something about anatomy."

"I guess so," Will answered and lapsed into silent thought. There was no reason to state the obvious: Cassius Small was suddenly becoming an interesting part of a progressively bizarre saga.

Chapter 26

Will and Harry returned to the precinct and sat at Will's desk for the next hour, making notes and trying to piece the case together before they went to Captain Pokorney. Having been focused on Sarkis for so long, neither one was happy about tagging Cassius Small as the perp, but they couldn't ignore the physical evidence.

As if reading Will's mind, Harry started in. "Will, if Small didn't do it, how did his prints get on the knife?"

"He would've had to handle it after the attack."

"Yeah, right. So how could he have done that while in lock-up? Has he had any visitors?"

"After I talked with him, I checked the logs," Will answered with a sigh. "Only his lawyers."

"Lawyers? He has more than one?"

"They appointed a PD. I know the guy a little. A fucking wet-behind-the-ears know-it-all who went in once but stayed for only a few minutes. Yesterday, a North End Italiano dude named Greco visited Cassius and was back to see him again this morning."

"Did Small call him?" Harry asked, his interest piqued.

"No record of it."

"So we don't know how Greco got to be Small's attorney. What do we know about this Greco guy?"

"He's not a regular around here, but he works other precincts pretty hard. A lot of people think he greases palms so the cops pass his name on to high-profile defendants. I guess Greco figured Small's case was going to get a lot of publicity, and the asshole wanted in."

"And Small let him. I wonder why?"

"Dunno. Greco would have to be cheap. Cassius isn't exactly rolling in dough."

"They do a search before lawyers get in to see their clients, right?"

"It's their policy. How much it's enforced, who knows?"

"Do they have a surveillance camera in the visitor area?"

"We can check but I doubt it. They supposedly have a guard in the room, but he's usually jerking off and not paying attention."

Will and Harry gathered up their notes and walked into the captain's office. Pokorney was sitting at his computer, squinting at the screen and cursing under his breath. "Got a minute, Cap?" Will asked.

"When will the goddamn drones who run this fucking department realize that we can't spend all our time filling out forms and then be expected to catch bad guys?"

Harry and Will shook their heads, pretending to commiserate. Actually, they were tired of dealing with bureaucratic nonsense themselves and didn't need the reminder. Besides, there was no answer to the captain's question, so why belabor it? Will was quick to push on.

"Cap, we need some advice. We had a development in the Robinson stabbing."

"I heard. New physical evidence?"

Will and Harry took turns explaining the crime lab report on the knife and Cassius Small's story.

"And you're sure this prostitute was just a messenger?"

"Pretty sure, Cap. We still have some checking to do, but so far it looks that way."

"Where did you leave it with Small?"

"We told him we'd be back this afternoon to talk to him again. He wants his lawyer there this time."

"Who is it? Anybody we know?"

"Some guido named Joe Greco from the North End."

"Okay. Let's see if Small has anything to add."

"We were also going to call Sarkis to see if he knows about Small."

"Why would he?"

"Who knows, Cap? I can't rule anything out. Sarkis' girlfriend and her father have been snooping around and they've gotten pretty fired up since Sarkis was plugged in the leg."

"I suggest you go hard with Cassius this afternoon. Physical evidence will trump whatever circumstantial stuff you have on Sarkis. If Small doesn't cop to the crime, you're back up shit creek, looking for a paddle."

Will and Harry nodded. "You got that right, Captain," Will said, shaking his head. "Sarkis just sticks in my craw. The guy had a good reason to attack Robinson and the logistics seemed perfect."

"We have to get over to talk to Robinson about the shooting at the convenience store, but I bet we will have a hard time hanging that on him," Harry added.

"Stick with the bridge attack for now and try to get that resolved," Pokorney said. "Unless he's a magician, there's no way Sarkis would've been able to put the knife in Small's hand, in which case he's going to walk."

"Yeah. It's all about Small, I guess. We'll keep you posted, Cap."

While Harry went off to do some paperwork, Will called Sarkis at his cell number. He was pleasantly surprised to hear a woman's voice.

"Hello, is this Dr. Sarkis' cell phone?"

"It is. Who's calling?"

"Dorothy, is that you? This is your favorite detective, Wilson Lentz."

"Hi, Will. What can I do for you?" Dorothy asked, trying to sound nonchalant. Her stomach was churning.

"I need to ask Dr. Sarkis a few questions. Is he around?"

"In the bathroom. Can I help you?"

"I guess so. We have some new evidence in the case that points to a person named Cassius Small. He's got a record. Would Dr. Sarkis happen to know anything about him?"

"I'll ask, but the name doesn't sound familiar."

"While you're at it, could you also ask him if he knows a young lady of the night who goes by the name of Sally Jones or Molly Stevens?"

"A prostitute? What's going on, Lieutenant?"

"Dorothy, I can't go into detail, but we have evidence that might help us solve this case and exonerate Dr. Sarkis. It's essential that he cooperate so we can clear him."

"I'll talk to him as soon as he's dry and dressed, and he'll call you back."

"Thanks, Dorothy," Will said. "And don't forget that my lunch invitation…" He stopped talking, realizing that Dorothy had already hung up.

Philip emerged from the bathroom a few minutes later, wearing a Ritz robe and drying his hair. He looked more calm and composed than he had in a long time.

"Did I hear my phone ring?"

"It was Will Lentz."

"Oh? What'd he want?" Philip asked with disdain.

"He wanted to know if you know someone named Cassius Small or a prostitute named Sally Jones or Molly Stevens."

Dorothy watched Philip's reaction carefully. He limped casually to the catering tray that had been brought up for lunch, poured himself a cup of coffee, and plopped down in an armchair, never saying a word.

"Philip, did you hear me? He wants to know if you know a hooker and a guy with a record."

Philip looked up, seemingly unfazed. "Never heard of 'em."

"That's all you have to say? Don't you want to know why Lentz is asking?"

"Yeah, sure I do."

"Really? You're acting like you're not terribly interested."

"What do you want me to say?"

"I don't know—something to make me believe you give a shit, maybe?"

"Of course I care."

Dorothy paused and took a deep breath. Philip the chameleon was doing another one of his transformations from wild fanatic to Mr. Cool, Calm, and Collected. She wasn't going to find out why—at least not now.

"Lentz said they have new evidence. It might implicate at least one of these people, and exonerate you. He wants your cooperation. I'll ask you again: do you know either of them?"

"No."

"Philip, if you hired a prostitute and this guy Small is her pimp, I'll be very hurt and disappointed, but I'll get over it. But if you're hiding something and Lentz finds out, he'll come after you even harder, until he nails you to the wall."

Philip didn't miss a beat. "I have never hired a prostitute, and I don't know either of those people."

Dorothy's intuition was that Philip was covering something up, but she also believed his assertion about never using women of the night. It wasn't his style, or at least she didn't want to think it was.

"Okay. Let me talk to my father to make sure he doesn't know anything about this, and then you can call Lentz back and tell him what you don't know."

"Happy to. And then, I guess we can start to pack."

"Huh? Why do you believe we can leave now?"

"If Lentz has an alternative theory of the crime, he can forget about me, and we won't have to bother with this anymore."

"What makes you think he has a good case against these people? Philip, is there something you aren't telling me?"

Philip didn't answer. He got up, and walked back to the bathroom. "I have to dry my hair and pack my suitcase."

Exasperated with Philip's ennui, Dorothy grabbed her room keys and stormed out, slamming the door behind her. Unless her father could shed light, she was going to be left with an uneasy feeling about Philip, one that she could by no means simply dismiss.

Philip's phone call to Will was brief and the news expected. No, Philip had nothing to do with Cassius or Sally, and had never heard of them. Will warned Philip that he was not yet in the clear, so he asked that he remain in Boston, at least for a few more hours, while the police pursued their new lead. "Yeah, sure," was Philip's reply. Curiously, Philip didn't ask the questions Will expected regarding the case developments and new evidence. Philip seemed more interested in getting off the phone.

Finished with his paperwork, Harry had gone for a mid-afternoon snack for himself and his partner. He came back with something for each of them that he had purchased off a truck parked in front of the precinct. Apples.

"What the fuck, Harry?"

"Will, you need to eat better or you're going to kill yourself."

"Are you my fucking mother?" Will snapped.

Harry laughed it off; they'd had such exchanges before. As they munched, Will called the holding area and asked for time with Cassius. He was put on hold while the clerk checked to make sure that Cassius agreed and that his lawyer could be present. After about ten minutes, the interview was arranged for four o'clock.

"The captain is right—we have to sweat him hard this time," Harry said.

"His lawyer'll get in the way."

"I expect so; Small has his rights."

"Every scumbag does, even Thaddeus Robinson," Will said.

"I wonder what it feels like to have so many people hate your guts."

"I dunno, Harry. But I think some people enjoy the idea of being reviled. And who knows, Thaddeus Robinson may be one of them."

Chapter 27

Will and Harry arrived at the jail building a few minutes before four, just as a black Lincoln Town Car pulled up to the curb. Out of the back seat stepped a dark-haired, middle aged, handsome man dressed in a blue serge suit, designer tie, and well-shined, black tasseled loafers. After issuing orders to the driver holding the door for him, he ascended the stairs to the main entrance, carrying a document bag and looking quite confident as he approached the security checkpoint. Will and Harry slowed up to watch him, each fairly certain that Joe Greco had arrived to represent Cassius Small during their second interrogation.

By the time they reached the interview room, Cassius was seated next to Greco, each poring over a document Greco had brought for Small's review. They spoke in whispers so as not to be heard by the staff, who they knew were eavesdropping on the other side of the two-way mirror. As soon as Will and Harry opened the door and entered, Greco closed the folder and placed the document in his briefcase before standing to greet them.

"Detectives, my name is Joe Greco and I represent Mr. Small."

"Hi, Mr. Greco," Will answered, shaking hands as he

took his seat. "I'm Lieutenant Detective Wilson Lentz and this is my partner Sergeant Detective Harry Socks. We've been working on the Thaddeus Robinson case for the last week. Our interrogation today will only be about that. We're not here to discuss the crime for which Mr. Small was originally arrested."

"Very good, Detective. I want to be clear that Mr. Small is eager to cooperate."

"We appreciate that. And we don't want to jeopardize his defense against the shooting charge, either. We actually only have one topic to discuss, and that's the presence of his fingerprints on the handle of a knife we believe was the weapon used to stab Mr. Robinson."

"That's a fair question, Detective. Mr. Small and I have discussed this at length, and I believe he wishes to make a statement."

Will and Harry didn't expect it to be this easy, and it took them a second or two to recover. "Well then, Counselor," Harry finally replied, "would you mind if we record the statement?"

"Certainly, Detective Socks. As long as I can review the transcript after it's prepared and before it's entered into evidence."

"Agreed, Mr. Greco, and we'll put that directly on the record."

Harry set up his recorder and began taping by saying the date, time, place, and circumstances of the meeting and its attendees, and making the appropriate disclaimers. He then introduced Cassius, who began straightaway, obviously rehearsed.

"My name is Cassius Small. I live on West Seventh Street in South Boston. I'm currently being held on a charge that I shot a person. During the course of my stay here, I've also been accused of attacking a person named Thaddeus Robinson with a knife.

"I'm innocent of the shooting charge for reasons that I'll bring forward at my upcoming hearings. However, I admit that I stabbed Thaddeus Robinson. I did it to steal his wallet and jewelry. I didn't intend to hurt him, but he kicked me in the groin and started to run away, so I lunged at him with my knife and stuck him in the back. I'm sorry for what happened. It was an accident."

Harry and Will looked at each other, dumbfounded by Cassius' brief and surprising statement. "So just to be clear, you're admitting to stabbing Mr. Robinson but you're telling us that you didn't intend to hurt him?" Will asked.

"I used the knife to show him I meant business. I never intended to stick him with it. It was an accident."

"Like the girl who accidentally fell on somebody's dick and got pregnant?"

"Detective, let's keep this professional," Greco said.

"You're right, Counselor, but you have to admit that Mr. Small's statement is disingenuous. Robbery with a deadly weapon is a serious crime, and making preposterous excuses about how the knife ended up in the victim's back… well, it's simply not credible."

"It's not up to you to determine what's credible, Detective. It's only important that you know Mr. Small admits to the crime and is heartily sorry."

"I have a few questions, if you don't mind," Harry said.

"Certainly, Detective Socks. Please proceed."

"Cassius, you have no record of armed robbery. Why did you decide to hold somebody up this time?"

"I needed the money."

"Like you never needed it before?"

"I was hungry. I never was that low before. I usually could scare something up, but this time I was stuck."

"Interesting choice of words," Will remarked, drawing an angry glare from Greco. "And so you waited for a stranger to walk across Harvard Bridge damn near dawn to get his watch and wallet?"

"Detective, my client doesn't have to explain why he did it."

"No, he doesn't. I'm just trying to understand the circumstances a little better."

"With all respect, go home and put on your thinking cap, Detective. We're not here to expand your intellectual horizons."

"Fair enough, Mr. Greco. But perhaps Mr. Small can tell me why Mr. Robinson's watch was found at the bottom of the river, and how the weapon got into the hands of the prostitute who delivered it to our precinct."

"Cassius, do you want to answer the Detective, please?"

"Sure. I dropped them."

"You dropped them?" Will asked incredulously. "Where?"

"On the bridge."

"Are you fucking kidding me? You dropped the weapon and the watch, but you held onto the wallet?"

"I was running away and didn't realize I lost some of the stuff until I was almost home."

"Which leads to my next question," Harry jumped in. "How did you get home? You don't own a car."

"Took a bus."

"So… you stabbed Robinson, ran off the Harvard Bridge, dropped most of what you had in your hands, and then stood at a bus stop and waited for a bus back to Southie?"

Cassius nodded.

"Do you think the bus driver will remember you?"

"I didn't talk to the driver. I just sat in the back."

"What happened to the wallet?"

"I took the money out and threw it in a trash can near where I live."

Will shook his head, making it obvious he wasn't buying the story. "Do you have any idea how the knife ended up in the hands of a prostitute?" he continued.

"No."

"She said that some guy in a car called her over and handed her a package that was later found to contain the knife. Any idea who he might have been?"

"No."

"And you expect us to buy all of this."

"Again, Detective, your expectations aren't relevant."

"But you'll forgive my incredulity, won't you, Mr. Greco?"

"Mr. Small is confessing, sir. End of story."

"Not really, Counselor. Lots of people confess to crimes they haven't done. Sometimes because they're mentally ill, sometimes because they're stupid, and sometimes because they have something to gain. Would you care to share the document you and Mr. Small were reviewing when we came into the room?"

"Attorney-client privilege. You should know that."

"What I'm getting at is, has Cassius been offered some kind of a deal in exchange for a confession?"

"That's absurd. By whom?"

"Monty fucking Hall! How the hell should I know? But when we talked to him earlier today, he denied the whole thing. And suddenly he's Mr. Forthright. You have to admit that his rapid change of heart is a bit suspicious."

Greco rose from his chair. "I believe we're finished here, Detective. I suggest you prepare a transcript of this interview. I'll review it, he'll sign it, and we'll get on with processing, the details of which are none of your business."

"And one more thing," Greco continued. "I recommend strongly against trying to impugn Mr. Small's story. My friends in your department will take a dim view of detectives wasting time challenging confessions freely given and clearly verifiable."

Greco left the room without shaking hands, immediately after which Small was escorted back to his cell. Will thought he detected a smirk on Cassius' face when he went by, but elected not to lock eyes with him.

"I guess that closes this case, Will," Harry said dejectedly after the door shut. "Unless we want to spend time chasing our tails and then get called on the carpet for it."

"Come on, Harry. You know as well as I do that this is bullshit. Somebody put a deal on the table for this guy, something he couldn't turn down."

"You don't know that, Will. You're guessing."

"An educated guess. But you're right. We could check on the bus thing, but I doubt the driver will remember him, and I don't think we'll find the empty wallet. I think we're finished with the case. Just have to dot the *i*'s and cross the *t*'s."

"Are you going to call Sarkis and let him know what happened?"

"I'll do better than that."

"You'll deliver the news in person? Oh wait… there's that woman."

"Might as well pull something good out of this mess, Harry."

Will phoned Dorothy and told her he had some important news about the case. If she were so inclined, he could meet her in the Ritz coffee shop in thirty minutes. What he didn't count on but should have expected was that Dorothy would bring Philip along. When Will arrived at the Ritz, the two of them were sipping a late-afternoon tea, looking like tourists.

"Damn," Will muttered to himself as he walked through the doorway. "Should have told her to come alone."

Will walked to their table and sat down. Philip barely acknowledged him, looking down at the table, subtly shifting in his chair. Dorothy, on the other hand, was sitting forward, intently focused. "Will, we can't wait to hear your news."

Will told them about the physical evidence that had led them to Cassius Small, followed by a brief summary of Small's confession. With each new piece of information, Dorothy became more relieved, and she finally broke into a wide smile.

"Am I getting this right, Will? This guy confessed to the crime, and there's physical evidence linking him to the weapon?"

"Yes, Dorothy. That's what I'm telling you."

"So Philip is completely in the clear."

"Unless Small's story falls through, which I doubt."

Dorothy was so thrilled by the news that she hadn't noticed Philip's reaction. As he had earlier in the day, he sat quietly, showing no emotion. He had taken out his Blackberry and was scrolling through emails, seemingly paying no attention to the conversation.

"Philip, are you okay?" Dorothy finally asked.

"Sure. I feel great."

"Are you registering what Detective Lentz just told us?"

"Yep, got it. Now we can go home and I go back to my thrilling job in the cardiology clinic. Real exciting." Lethargy seemed his mood of the moment.

Dorothy fumed, "You've been exonerated in a case of attempted murder. I'd have expected more of a positive reaction."

"Okay. I'm *positively* looking forward to getting out of this fucking place," Philip replied. "And in fact, I'm going to finish packing right now. So I'll leave you two here, if you don't mind. I'm sure you won't, Detective Lentz."

With that, Philip shuffled off, favoring his wounded leg a little. Dorothy bore holes in his back with her stare. "That man can be infuriating," she blurted, momentarily forgetting that Will was sitting right there, then reminding herself not to give Will any ammunition.

"Men can be like that sometime, at least that's what my ex-wife used to say."

Dorothy was embarrassed to have revealed negative feelings about the man who, until a few minutes ago, had been the prime target in a high-profile case of serious assault, and maybe even attempted murder. "Sorry, Detective. I don't always feel that way about the big lug."

"No worries, Dorothy. I understand. But if I may say so, his reaction *was* a bit strange. He didn't seem relieved, or even surprised."

Dorothy could only nod. Detective Lentz had just given voice to her worst fear.

Chapter 28

When Dorothy knocked on his hotel room door to brief him on the latest, Dick's reaction to the news about Cassius Small was a mixture of surprise and skepticism.

"Let me make sure I understand this, darlin'. The police had the weapon dumped in their lap complete with fingerprints, and that led them to a defendant in a recent shooting who denied the crime at first, and then happily copped to it after his second attorney arrived?"

"According to Lentz there was no shaking him but the story seemed to have a number of holes."

"Especially that crap about dropping the knife and the watch. One ends up in the river, and the other gets couriered to the police," Dick said, shaking his gray head.

"Lentz may do a little more background on Small, but unless he comes up with something extraordinary, they're going to pin the attack on him and move on."

"What was Philip's reaction?"

"He was pretty quiet. Like he didn't give a damn."

"That boyfriend of yours is one weird dude, my dear."

"You'll have a chance to tell him that yourself. We're all driving home together as soon as we get packed up."

"Now? It's suppertime!"

"He wants out of here as soon as possible. He's already returned his rental car."

"Boy's in a hurry. Well, I am, too, I guess. We've spent enough time on this little adventure."

"If he stays subdued, at least you won't have to put up with a lot of his yakking."

Dick grunted in grateful acknowledgment. He was happy to be getting out of Boston, but he wasn't sure that the trouble he and Dorothy had gone to had done anything to get Philip off the hook. That bothered him.

The ride home was uneventful. Early in the trip, Dick couldn't help himself, and made the mistake of asking Philip a few questions. Did you know this Cassius Small? No. Do you think he did it? Don't know. Do you think somebody put him up to it? How would I know? It took Dick longer than Dorothy would have guessed—all the way to the 128 beltway, in fact—to finally give up and leave Philip alone to brood in the back seat.

For the rest of the five-hour ride, Dorothy and Dick struggled to find things to talk about that would not interest Philip. Dick finally turned on the radio, looking for some sports. They were within New York City's broadcast range, and Dick found a station covering a Rangers-Bruins game, being played in Boston's TD Garden.

"Hey, great!" Dick said. "Playoff implications for both clubs in this one. This'll get us a good part of the way home."

Not a hockey fan herself, Dorothy was nevertheless happy to have some kind of noise in the car. Philip remained silent.

While they listened, the Rangers managed a breakaway, their center skating swiftly toward the Bruins goal, as Bruin defenders scrambled to get into position.

An adept stickhandler, the Rangers' center flicked the puck back and forth in front of him; then, near the goal, he unleashed a slap shot that beat the goalie on his glove-hand side.

"And the Rangers draw first blood!" the Rangers' play-by-plan man gleefully announced to the radio audience.

"And the Boston faithful are not happy about that," the color man added. "Just listen to them!"

"*I-I-I-I-C-E berg, I-I-I-I-C-E berg*," came that singsong chant from the Bruins fans. What had begun in Providence as a cheer for a promising young goalie and had followed him to Boston, where he achieved superstar status, was now a lament, as well as a rebuke not only to the beaten goalie, but to the entire Bruins organization.

"The fans got it right," the announcer replied. "Sebby would have stopped that one."

"I wonder where this Bruins team would be today if Sebby were still alive," the color man added.

"I wonder where the three of us would be today if Sebby hadn't died," Dick said. "Probably not making nice with Boston's finest." He glanced into the rearview mirror to see if it drew a reaction from Philip. There was none; Philip continued to gaze impassively out the window.

They arrived in the Poconos an hour or two after dark. Dick wasted little time getting the bags out of his car and skedaddling, spraying loose stones and practically laying rubber as he accelerated out of the circular driveway in front of Philip and Dorothy's lakeside home. He was gone before Philip opened the front door. Philip was practically knocked over by Mitten, Buffy, and Meeko, who seemed intent on showing their master and mistress how much they were missed. Their neighbor Dana came out behind them, laughing at the ridiculous reception Philip and Dorothy were afforded by their pups, complete with growling, play biting, licking, and jumping up on their hind legs.

As if by magic, Philip the chameleon's mood immediately improved. He got down on his knees, playing with the dogs, obviously overjoyed to be home and in their good company. Dorothy herself had to smile at the spectacle, relieved to see Philip happy and finally at peace. She had been right about their move to the Poconos years before. It *was* therapeutic, and it had been a positive thing for Philip and for their relationship.

Philip and Dorothy thanked Dana and paid her for her time and then started in on the business of unpacking and getting settled. The doggies followed them from room to room, begging for attention and treats. Philip himself was in a frenzy of activity, putting clothes in the laundry, going through the mail, adjusting thermostats, and straightening up every room as he whirled around the house. Dorothy urged him to leave it for the next day, but he said he wanted to be "at home" as soon as possible.

No matter how many times she had seen this abrupt change in Philip's demeanor, Dorothy couldn't understand it. Was there something about his brain chemistry that predisposed him to mood shifts? He had described this kind of behavior in his mother, seemingly oblivious to the possibility that he had inherited the trait. Or was it some inner workings of Philip's mind that caused his temper to swing from bad to good and back again in the snap of a finger, and sometimes without a hint of a cause? It mystified and troubled her.

Next Philip wanted a pizza, plausibly claiming that the candy bar he got when they had stopped for gas was not nearly enough. Dorothy was more tired than hungry, but she acquiesced. Philip called the local fast-food joint, Amadeos, and convinced the proprietor to deliver after closing time by promising a hefty tip. Thirty minutes later, they were seated, munching on an extra cheese and pepperoni pizza, washing it down with beer while the doggies begged pieces of crust, which Philip was happy to provide over Dorothy's objections.

Dorothy thought that Philip had over-ordered when he asked for an extra-large pie but his mania extended to his appetite. Philip consumed all but three pieces in record time, while they watched the late news on a local TV station. When he finished, Philip sat back, burped, and announced he was going to the bedroom to watch the end of the Flyers-Blues game, which had gone into overtime. She was relieved to have Philip out of the way.

Dorothy decided to leave the mess for the morning, but the doggies needed to do their business, so she let them out and killed time by looking through the mail. Philip had sorted through the pile that Dana had collected, segregating Dorothy's stuff from his own. She got through most of it quickly, retaining bills and notices that would require her attention and consigning the junk mail to the recycle pile. She was amazed at thc large accumulation of sale flyers, and then remembered that summer was approaching, an opportunity for local merchandisers to advertise lawn seed and fertilizer, garden supplies, pool equipment, and anything else that would guarantee an idyllic summer season.

Instead of instantly disposing of the flyers, Dorothy explored them a bit more carefully, searching for samples of outdoor furniture. The table on the back deck needed to be replaced. There was quite a selection at Lowe's and Walmart, but the most attractive selection seemed to be at the local garden store. Dorothy made a mental note to stop by on the way home from work the next day.

In the middle of the pile of circulars, Dorothy found a newspaper clipping from *The Boston Globe*. Her first thought was to push it to the trash, but as she did, her eye caught a photo and familiar name. Cassius Small was pictured on his way to his arraignment after being charged with the shooting of a little girl in the Southie section of Boston. Why on earth was this clipping in with the junk mail that Philip had gone through? As Dorothy scanned the article, her eye was drawn to the bottom of the page, where someone had written a phone number. Dorothy looked at the shape of the individual numbers and recognized Philip's scrawl. She gasped when she looked again at the number itself. Area code 215 with a Philadelphia exchange that looked eerily familiar.

Despite the late hour, Dorothy felt compelled to call, to check her suspicions. She rose from her chair and picked up the phone on the kitchen wall. After dialing the number she steeled herself, waiting for the connection. When she heard a familiar voice in an automated greeting at the other end, her heart sank. "No, Roe, you can't help me," Dorothy muttered into the phone before the greeting finished, realizing that Roe would never hear her. From the bedroom, a jubilant Philip shouted, "Good night and good hockey!" She assumed the Flyers had won the game. With much foreboding, she let the doggies in and went to bed.

It had been an eventful day for Thad Robinson, as well. Early in the day, he had been discharged from Mass General to his penthouse condo. His maid and housekeeper scurried through the apartment, arranging everything the way Thad wished, while he followed them and barked orders from his motorized wheelchair.

Jenny Browne, the home healthcare worker who had accompanied him from the hospital, surveyed the apartment in amazement. It was not only luxuriously appointed; it was enormous.

"I can understand why you didn't want to go to rehab, Mr. Robinson," she gushed as she walked through the living area.

"Damn right," Thad answered with enthusiasm. "We can easily do the rehab here. All you have to do is tell me what kind of equipment we need."

"The rehab staff will be here first thing tomorrow," Jenny answered. "They'll know what they need and can get it quickly. How much they bring in will depend on what you want to spend."

Thad didn't bother to reply. Money was not an issue, but he knew it didn't really matter. Nothing was going to get him back on his feet. The best he could hope for was to get his upper body strong enough to make the transfers from wheelchair to bed without assistance. He had regained some sphincter control, and his doctors thought he might be able to use a toilet soon. What a relief that would be. Having an audience and clean-up team every time he moved his bowels was humiliating.

Truth was that Thad wasn't sure if he even wanted to live this way for the rest of his life. The only thing that had kept him going since the attack was his desire to find out who had done it and to make sure the person paid the price. That idiot detective, Wilson Lentz, had stopped by the hospital a few times to ask silly questions but refused to give him any news about the investigation. Lentz had called this afternoon and had left a message about a Cambridge shooting that might be linked to Thad's case. He wanted to meet with Thad at his condo after he was settled.

Thad also had Luke Benjamin snooping around, and

he had mentioned that the police were chasing down a few leads, but the lumbering hulk had stopped keeping in touch. Not like him, Thad thought. He had recently tried a few times to call Luke from the hospital, but there was no answer at his apartment or on his cell.

By the time Thad had his dinner and bath, he was exhausted. He told the home healthcare worker and his staff he wanted to go to bed early. He watched a little television on the sixty-five-inch flat screen installed in his bedroom and dozed off. He awoke a short time later with a large hand clamped across his mouth. Thad stared up into Luke's pock-marked face.

"Sorry, boss. I don't want anybody to know I'm here."

As soon as Luke took away his hand, Thad whispered, "What the fuck, Luke?"

"I know you been trying to get ahold of me."

"Yeah, but I thought you'd answer your phone, not break into my house and scare the crap out of me."

"Sorry, boss. I didn't think you'd want anybody to know we've talked lately."

"Why not?"

"I fucked up and maybe got us both into trouble."

"Spill it, Luke. What's going on?"

"Last time we talked, you told me to do some digging. Remember how I told you the police were interested in this Dr. Sarkis guy, and they also wanted to talk to Angelucci's widow?"

"Yeah. And…"

"And you told me to see if there was some sort of connection between them?"

"Yeah?"

"Well, there is. The two docs were buddies. And Sarkis actually helped defend one of the other docs in the case when you and the Bergstrom family sued Angelucci."

"I remember that now. So the police thought Sarkis knifed me for revenge."

"It played pretty well, especially since Sarkis was staying in a bed and breakfast near where you got it. And he's not exactly your typical country doctor."

"Did the police arrest him?"

"They questioned him pretty heavy and were getting ready to bring him in. That's when I decided to intervene."

"What did you do?"

"Shot him. Meant to take him out, but he moved at the very last minute, and I got him in the leg."

"Are you totally out of your mind?"

"I was just trying to be helpful, boss. I knew how much you wanted to get the person who did this to you, so I wanted to give him to you as a present. I was going to do it and then disappear for a few weeks until things blew over, but I missed and I'm kinda glad I did."

"Why?"

"Somebody else copped to your attack."

"Who?"

"Black guy named Cassius Small." Benjamin provided some background on Small, including his arrest for the shooting in Southie.

"So it was just a two-bit robbery gone bad?"

"That's what it sounds like. They're charging him. I suspect Lentz will call you tomorrow to give you the official word. And I'm afraid he will also ask you what you know about Sarkis getting shot. So I wanted to give you a heads-up."

Thad didn't answer. He simply looked up at the ceiling, thinking. Was it that uncomplicated, after all? Just some hoodlum looking for an easy score? Did he have himself to blame for being incredibly stupid?

Luke continued, "I don't think the cops have anything to link me to the shooting, but I've been laying low up in New Hampshire. Staying at a motel just over the border, in Nashua. I plan to go to Canada for the summer. I have some friends up there who'll put me up for a while. If things are cool here in the fall, I'll come back. I wanted to fill you in before I left but not in public, just in case the cops are onto me. I didn't want to get you into any trouble, you know?"

Thad was grateful and sympathetic. Luke was at least trying to keep him out of harm's way. "Do you need any cash?"

"Nah. I saved up a lot when I was working regular, so I'm fine. I don't need a lot to live on, and my friends up there will give me room and board. I'm actually looking forward to it. It's like a vacation, if you know what I mean."

"Good."

"Want me to do anything about this cocksucker Small before I split?"

Robinson paused, once again lost in thought. Small had confessed and would be punished for both the shooting and the knifing. As much as he wanted revenge, Thad wasn't sure he hated Small enough to put himself at risk of prosecution, or to put Luke in jeopardy. Besides, Luke had just failed to take out an unsuspecting Sarkis who was by himself; taking out a prisoner with guards around was more than Luke could be expected to do cleanly.

"Leave it for now," Robinson finally answered. "Let's see what the criminal justice system does with him before we decide. You know the saying about revenge…"

"Yeah, it's a dish best served cold," Benjamin said, a rare smile appearing on his face. "Whatever you say, boss. I know you won't let it die."

"No, Luke. I won't be able to forget what that person did to me. But if this was just a robbery, I have to take some of the blame myself."

"Don't be too hard on yourself," Luke said. He patted Thad on the shoulder as they shook hands. "Well, I better be on my way. I'll let you know when I'm back in Boston, and we'll catch up."

"I'd escort you out, but as you can see…"

Luke smiled again. "No worries, boss. I'll ease my way out just like I eased my way in."

And he was gone, leaving Robinson wide awake with the rest of the night to ponder what had happened to him and, most importantly, what the future might hold. His bedroom was far removed from the door into his penthouse suite, so he didn't hear the thump in the hallway just after Benjamin departed, or the low-pitched scream in the elevator that the neighbors put down to hearty partiers.

Chapter 29

Dorothy lay awake most of the night, struggling with her long-running suspicion that Philip was a vigilante who dispensed his own particular brand of justice, possibly with the help of some friends in South Philly. She dreaded the phone call she knew she would make in the morning. Fortunately, Philip had a meeting at his office and departed earlier than usual. Dorothy feigned sleep until he was safely out the door. She put on the morning news, fed the dogs, made coffee, and tried to distract herself until 9 A.M., when the appliance store opened.

Roe answered the phone on the first ring, cheerfully announcing "Romano Appliances."

"Hi, Roe. I don't know if you remember me. My name is Dorothy Deaver. I visited Giancarlo and Vincente a couple of times a few years ago."

"Of course, Ms. Deaver. I remember you. How've you been?"

"Fine, thanks," Dorothy answered, wondering if all Mafiosi employed such friendly secretaries. It certainly was disarming. Sort of took your mind off the fact that they were sizing you up for a garrote necktie.

"I was wondering if I might be able to meet with the gentlemen later today about a personal matter."

"Hold on, and let me pull up their calendars on my screen."

So now they use a computer. So much easier to get the hits done on time.

"Uh, it looks like I can squeeze you in at 2 P.M. Does that work for you?"

"Sure," Dorothy answered. "I have to move a couple things around, but that gives me enough time to drive down there."

"Yes, I remember you live in the Poconos. Lovely area, although I must say I'm a beach person myself."

Dorothy suppressed the temptation to ask Roe how she felt about taking people out on fishing boats. She had obviously watched the *Godfather* movies too many times.

"It's nice up here, but a little lonely at times," Dorothy said. "I'll see you at two."

"If you can get here a few minutes early, we can proceed with our 'preparations' and have you ready to see the guys promptly."

"Yes, of course," Dorothy answered, dreading the near-strip search that had become such a fun part of her visits to the Romanos' establishment.

Dorothy decided to work from home, taking a few conference calls and trudging through a long list of emails, trying to distract herself. After walking the dogs around the block, Dorothy showered and dressed. She decided on a light sweater, nice jeans, and shooties in muted colors. Hair tied back, no jewelry except for a plain watch, trying to look as bland as possible. She checked the floor-length mirror on the bedroom door and liked how she looked. The years had been kind to her, though Philip had to be responsible for a few gray hairs and worry lines that she surveyed with dismay.

The drive south to Philadelphia was routine, although the eternal construction projects on the northeastern extension of the Pennsylvania Turnpike created cattle shoots that made Dorothy more nervous and on edge. In the city, traffic was light. Lunch rush was over, and most workers were back in their offices fighting to stay awake through their mid-afternoon lull. South Philly hadn't changed much since her last visit, still a mix of architecturally interesting homes, shops, restaurants, and churches, all contributing to a diverse and rich urban environment. She noticed more young people moving about, reflecting the influx of students and young professionals fueling an urban renaissance.

Dorothy found a parking space on South Broad, fed the meter, and walked to the Romanos' appliance store, its main display window now sporting a high-tech screen featuring the smiling faces of the Italian gentlemen she was about to interview.

Roe greeted her warmly and apologized profusely during the search she conducted with her customary efficiency. She offered Dorothy coffee or tea, the latter accepted for the sake of appearing cordial. Dorothy remembered that manners were everything to the gentlemen, no matter if they intended to open your chest and have a look around.

Roe escorted Dorothy to the well-appointed office that the brothers shared and invited her to take a seat on the sofa. Dorothy placed her teacup on the coffee table and surveyed the richly furnished office, fit for a bank president or captain of industry. The Romanos were clearly doing well in their appliance business, and whatever else occupied their time and attention.

After a long, anxious minute, Vincente and Giancarlo

entered, concluding a conversation about a matter that obviously held their interest. Dorothy caught only a few words about an overdue shipment, and a promise to track it down by end of business. She couldn't help but wonder what (or who) might be in the crates they were waiting for.

When they saw Dorothy, each brother broke into a warm smile, and hurried over to greet her.

"Ms. Deaver, it's so wonderful to see you again," Vincente gushed as he shook Dorothy's hand with both of his. "And I must say you are looking as radiant as ever."

"You're too kind, Mr. Romano. And I remember that we used first names the last time I visited?"

"Of course, Dorothy, that is my mistake. Giancarlo and I think of you and Dr. Sarkis, uh Philip, as family, so I'm sorry to have been overly formal."

Giancarlo came up behind Vincente and bowed stiffly as he took Dorothy's hand. "How are you Dorothy?"

"I'm well, Giancarlo. My, neither one of you has changed a bit."

And Dorothy was not exaggerating; neither man had aged an iota. "God has been good to us, Dorothy. Our parents lived long lives, so I suspect we have a genetic advantage."

And excellent bodyguards, Dorothy thought.

Vincente and Giancarlo arranged themselves in Queen Anne armchairs across from Dorothy. After a quick glance at their apparel, she realized with relief that her casual clothes selection had been sound. The brothers were attired in colorful cashmere sweaters and khakis with soft loafers, as if prepared for a leisurely stroll on a golf course.

"How can we help you today, Dorothy? Are you interested in some new appliances?" Vincente asked, smiling.

"As I recall, the last time I was here, we spent way too much time beating around the bush until we came to the real reason for my visit," Dorothy said, reciting the lines she had rehearsed in the car. "I know you're both very busy men, so I'll come to the point. I need to know what you know about the attack on Thaddeus Robinson in Boston about a week ago."

Uncharacteristically, Giancarlo spoke first, wanting to have her first question addressed just so. "Dorothy, can you tell me what led you to believe that we would know the details about a lawyer who was knifed in a city where we do not live?"

Dorothy was quick to reply. "Well, for starters, the fact that you know the victim's profession and the weapon used."

"Dorothy," Vincente said, taking over. "Giancarlo wasn't saying that we are unaware of the case. He just wanted to know why you came to us for information about it."

Dorothy saw no reason to be evasive. "I found your phone number at the bottom of a newspaper clipping that Philip had. The story was about Cassius Small, who confessed to the attack."

"Oh, my. That's unfortunate," Vincente said.

"Unfortunate because Philip had your number, or because I found the clipping? Or are you sorry about poor Thad?" Dorothy asked, having a hard time keeping the sarcasm out of her voice.

"All right, Dorothy. So you know of our involvement in the case. If you tell us specifically what you want to learn, we will tell you what we can. But understand: Roe has helped us determine that this conversation is not being recorded, and we will publicly deny anything we tell you. Also, if you divulge what we tell you to anyone, there will be repercussions."

Dorothy looked down at her hands, waiting for her pulse and respirations to slow down enough so she could speak with a steady voice.

"You have my word," she finally said.

"Excellent, Dorothy," Vincente replied sweetly. "Don't get me wrong. We trust you implicitly, and the last thing we want to do is make threats. It's just that this crazy world we live in makes us very paranoid."

"I understand. All I really need to know is what Philip had to do with it."

Vincente glanced at Giancarlo, who returned a knowing look. They've already orchestrated their response, Dorothy thought. No surprise.

"You may have guessed that there is a connection between us and Mario Angelucci," Vincente began.

Dorothy nodded her head. "It's what I surmised."

"Mario was the son of one of our good friends in New Jersey. Like many of us, Dominic wanted his son to have a good education, and he worked hard to put money aside. As it turned out, Mario was very bright and easily obtained scholarships that took him all the way through college and medical school."

"Dominic was so proud of that young man, as we were of John, my son the obstetrician," Giancarlo added.

Dorothy nodded, remembering that John's death at the hands of his wife Bonnie had unraveled the Hamlin case years before. The gentlemen had made sure that Bonnie and Hugh had paid the price.

Vincente continued. "So, naturally, we followed the Sebastian Bergstrom case in Boston quite closely, given Mario's involvement, and we were as distressed as everyone when Sebastian died and Mario was sued for wrongful death. We try to be tolerant of our legal system, Dorothy, but we became quite angry when we saw the heavy-handed tactics that Thaddeus Robinson chose to use against Mario."

"He was like a nephew to us. We did everything we could for him," Giancarlo interjected. "We even tried to persuade a few judges to rein Robinson in, but to no avail."

"I'm afraid our ability to influence judicial officials in Boston is not, shall we say, as strong as it is here in our hometown, Dorothy," Vincente observed with a hint of a smile, knowing this observation would stir memories of crooked judges with whom Dorothy had dealt in her past. "And besides, the Bergstrom case was very high profile, and any judge would have been taking a considerable risk to try to manipulate the outcome."

"So we were forced to watch from the sideline as Mario was assassinated by the Boston media. Small wonder that he sank into a deep depression..."

"...and committed suicide." Dorothy finished.

After a pregnant pause, Giancarlo asked, "Do you truly believe that, Dorothy?"

Dorothy stammered, "That he killed himself? Why wouldn't I?"

"Are you aware of the circumstances of Mario's death?"

"Yes. He drove his car off a cliff."

"Really, Dorothy? And have you seen a detailed report of the accident scene and the car itself?"

"No."

"And you can't, because the original report somehow disappeared. The insurance company conducted its own 'detailed investigation' and came to the conclusion—supported by the authorities, I might add—that Mario intentionally drove off the road. It was to their advantage to do so, of course, because they could then deny paying his widow because of the suicide clause in Mario's life insurance policy. However, when our attorneys attempted to obtain a copy of the accident report, they were told it was missing. That led us to talk to the people who actually inspected the car and the scene. The long and the short, there was ample evidence that Mario did not kill himself."

"So you suspected foul play?"

"Let's just say we were able to connect Sebastian's father, Karl, to some amateurish hoodlums from the south side of Boston. I believe they call it Southie up there."

"You think that Karl Bergstrom had Mario murdered?" Dorothy asked incredulously.

"An interview that friends of ours conducted with two of the hoodlums led us to that conclusion. And we think it is well supported."

"Did you 'interview' Karl, too?"

Vincente laughed, "Are you serious, Dorothy? How likely would it have been for him to be honest with us?"

"Then perhaps I'll speak with him."

Another pause before Giancarlo answered, looking down at his folded hands. "That might be a little difficult right now."

"Even if he's back in Sweden, it shouldn't be difficult to connect with him somehow."

"Harder than you would anticipate, Dorothy. Perhaps even impossible."

Before she could stop herself, Dorothy's hand went to her mouth. "Oh my God," she gasped.

Vincente rose from his chair, sat next to Dorothy on the sofa, and took her hand. "May I get you a glass of water, Dorothy?"

It took several seconds for her to answer. "I'm okay," she said, not sounding at all like she was. "Let me understand. You avenged Mario's death, and it had nothing to do with Robinson?"

"That's a good synopsis, Dorothy. Karl Bergstrom chose to take the law into his own hands, so we were forced to do the same."

"That's not to say that we were displeased to hear that Robinson had fallen victim to an assailant," Giancarlo interjected. "And we were gratified that he was not killed, but was instead permanently disabled. Perhaps his attacker knew what he was doing."

"The attack on Robinson reinforced our sadness over Mario's death, and the grief that his father still feels," Vincente continued. "And then, to make it worse, our friend Philip was being bothered by the police. Our fear was that he was in danger of arrest and prosecution."

"You believed him to be innocent?"

"It was our hope. In any case, it was a relatively simple matter to induce Mr. Small's help with our dilemma."

"How could you do that?"

"We may lack sufficient influence in Boston to intercede in a high-profile case, Dorothy, but finding a cooperative official to maneuver the sentencing of a small-timer like Mr. Small isn't that difficult."

"So Cassius agreed to take the fall…"

"In exchange for a lighter sentence on both counts, to be served concurrently."

"How did you manufacture the physical evidence?"

"We know some clever people, countrymen if you will, who had access to Mr. Small in jail, and to his apartment where we were able to plant rubber gloves that the police 'found.' That evidence also persuaded Cassius to be cooperative."

"Unfortunately, we didn't move fast enough, and an associate of Mr. Robinson, named Luke Benjamin, shot Philip," said Giancarlo, shaking his head. "We're not sure if Robinson ordered the hit or not but we doubt it.

Fortunately, Mr. Benjamin succeeded only in wounding his victim."

"And what of Benjamin? Do you plan to turn him into the police?"

Before she had the words out of her mouth, Dorothy realized how ridiculous her question was. Giancarlo and Vincente looked down at their laps again, not wanting to embarrass Dorothy for her naiveté.

"That situation has also been handled, Dorothy," Giancarlo said softly, head down, this time to hide what could have been a smirk.

Dorothy's head was now swirling. In the course of just a few minutes, she had become privy to the reach of the Romano tentacles, spreading out in many directions. To Karl Bergstrom, Cassius Small, Thad Robinson, and Luke Benjamin. And, closer to home, to Philip, her idiot boyfriend who couldn't, or wouldn't, understand just how dangerous these men were.

But in their minds, they were just seeking to set things right. To her own horror, Dorothy realized that she was beginning to understand their logic, almost accepting what they had done as ordinary. Was she losing her moral compass? Had the Romanos and Philip corrupted her to the point that she could understand why justice needed to be meted out by goons in black suits, black shirts, and white ties?

"Are you all right, Dorothy?" Vincente said, interrupting a prolonged silence. "You look pale," he said, massaging her hand, which he was still holding. His face bore a look of true concern for her.

"Yes, I'm sorry. I'm just trying to absorb a lot of information all at once."

"Disturbing information, to be sure," Vincente allowed. "But I'm also certain your mission today was not simply to discover what happened to strangers up in

Boston."

Dorothy looked directly into Vincente's eyes. This remarkable man knew so much more than Dorothy had imagined. He sensed she needed reassurance on one particular point, just as she had on the other two occasions she had visited the Romanos appliance store.

"Philip," she said, half sobbing.

"Your man has a remarkable ability to find trouble, doesn't he, Dorothy? He has a bad habit of being in the wrong place at the wrong time. I do admit we were quite distressed when he was questioned by the detectives."

"And we can understand why the police suspected Philip in the attack on Mr. Robinson. After all, there was a good deal of circumstantial evidence," Giancarlo added.

"Now remember, we already had friends of ours up there looking into the Bergstrom matter. Without going into details, I can tell you categorically that Philip was not the person who assaulted Mr. Robinson."

"Are you sure?" Dorothy asked, not certain herself if she should be challenging the answer she had longed for.

Vincente looked her in the eyes and, with his free hand, pushed back a strand of hair that had fallen onto her forehead, as her father had done so many times when she was a little girl. "Dorothy, we know how much you love Philip. And we care for you. The last thing we would ever want is for you to spend your life with a bad person, or someone you didn't trust, so I will tell you the truth.

"Philip was not in Boston to harm Mr. Robinson. But he did use that silly conference as a pretext for being in town. He was actually there as a friend of ours, to help us look into the Bergstrom matter. We needed some deep background, and to have someone available whom Deb Angelucci would talk to. She trusted Philip."

"Are you telling me that Philip helped you get Karl Bergstrom killed?"

"We can assure you that Philip was not involved in how we resolved the matter, nor did he even know what we might do with the information he kindly gathered for us," Giancarlo said, choosing his words carefully. "He merely obtained details from Deb that helped us understand the situation better."

"So you see," Vincente continued, "since we told Philip that Mario had not committed suicide, but had been murdered, Philip would have had much less reason to attack Mr. Robinson."

Giancarlo's turn. "We also made our own inquiries and accumulated sufficient evidence to establish Philip's innocence in our eyes. Yes, he abhors Mr. Robinson for treating his friend as he did, but we believe his animosity lessened when he realized that Mario did not take his own life in despair."

Dorothy sighed, tears of relief welling up in her eyes. "So you are telling me that Philip is innocent after all?"

"Unquestionably, Dorothy."

"Thank you so much for meeting with me and answering my questions. I can't tell you how relieved I am."

"As we have said many times, Dorothy, we regard you as a friend, and friends help each other. We want you and Philip to be happy, now that this unpleasant matter has been settled. Justice has been dispensed, and innocent people will not be implicated. Out of love for Mario and respect for his father, Deb Angelucci is now well provided for, monetarily, and she and her children can move on with their lives. No one can ask for more than that."

Dorothy rose from the sofa. "I won't keep you longer. Thank you again for everything. I promise that none of this will ever be spoken of again."

"I doubt that, Dorothy," Vincente said.

"Why?" Dorothy asked, now nonplussed.

"I suspect that you and Philip will be having a very long chat about all of this. And your father may need an explanation. All we ask is that the three of you keep everything to yourselves, and to your beautiful dogs, of course."

Dorothy smiled, as she made her way out. Yes, of course they know about our dogs, she thought. And yes, they know she will need to have a chat with Philip and her father. These men are very knowing, indeed. Which is precisely why they're oh so dangerous.

Chapter 30

Dorothy walked out of the store and onto Broad Street in a trance. It took her a few minutes to get her bearings and remember where she had parked her car. Turning to her left on the sidewalk, she ran into a young girl, chewing gum, head down, earplugs in place, typing on her smartphone. After colliding with Dorothy, the young lady bounced backward, recovered, and started walking forward again like a wind-up toy, oblivious to her surroundings, never taking her eyes off her screen. Dorothy looked at her in bewilderment, too surprised and distracted to comment or protest.

She finally got to her car, settled in, and began the long drive home. Once she was out of the city, she switched off the radio, anxious to talk to her father about what she had learned of the happenings in Boston, still processing the story she had just been told by the Italian gentlemen.

Dorothy punched in Dick's office number, hoping he was available. She needed to talk to him now, while it was all fresh in her mind. Dick's secretary picked up.

"Hi, Sadie, is my dad around?"

"He's on another call, but I think he's almost finished. Let me go into his office and see."

Dorothy waited, trying to decide if she needed to distill any of the information. She decided no, she would tell her father everything, even if it further compromised his already low opinion of Philip.

"I'll put you through now," Sadie said.

"Hi, sweetie," Dick started. "What's up?"

Dorothy told Dick about the newspaper clipping and phone number she had discovered the night before, and her decision to visit Vincente and Giancarlo.

"Dorothy, I really wish you had called me before you did that."

"Why, Dad? You don't know those guys, and I doubt they would have been very talkative with you there."

"Did I say I wanted to go with you? You need to stay away from those people, Dorothy. They're dangerous."

Silence for a minute. Dorothy grimaced, remembering her father's involvement in the Adolphus case. Maybe she should not have assumed he hadn't met them, and maybe his impressions of them didn't come from second-hand experience. But maybe now was not the time to open that can of worms.

"It might have been okay for you to have gone fact hunting," Dick conceded. "But it makes me nervous when you interact with them."

"There was no other way, Dad. And it turned out that what they had to tell me was pretty important. I'm sure I don't have to tell you this, but they were very clear that I not talk to anyone. Except you and Philip. I wonder why they made you an exception."

"Because I'm your father?" Dick said, sounding wounded. "And nobody knows better than me what happens when people start talking out of turn."

Dorothy plowed ahead, going on to tell her father that

Philip had been recruited to go to Boston to get background information from Deb Angelucci. The Romanos were distressed by the death of their friend's son, and had undertaken their own investigation, which led them to believe that Mario had not committed suicide and that Karl Bergstrom was in fact responsible for Mario's death. In the course of their inquiry, they decided to use Philip as a fact-finder.

"How plausible is that?" Dick asked. "Your boyfriend is a rank amateur. Why would those professionals have called him in?"

"Maybe they thought his relationship with Deb would get him somewhere they couldn't go otherwise?"

"And while their 'investigation' was going on, Thaddeus Robinson just happens to get himself knifed in the back."

"Yes."

"Someone, either by chance or by intent, managed to sever his spinal cord without killing him. And this occurs near where Philip happens to be camped out?" Dick asked, his voice dripping with sarcasm.

"Yes."

"And you believed thcm?"

"Dad, as they pointed out, Philip's motive for revenge against Robinson would have diminished as soon as he found out that Robinson hadn't driven Mario to suicide."

"Well, maybe so. But one hell of a coincidence, don't you think?"

"Absolutely. Because apparently Robinson believed that Philip was the attacker as well. They told me Robinson may have arranged for a guy named Luke Benjamin to kill Philip, but he botched the job."

"Let me guess: Luke Benjamin has disappeared."

Silence again, Dorothy not wanting or needing to fill in the blank with the obvious answer.

"So where does Cassius Small figure in?" Dick asked.

"That's where the story gets a little nuts."

"A *little* nuts, Dorothy? You mean that so far everything else makes perfect sense?"

Dorothy ignored that comment and described how Cassius was played as a pawn, agreeing to take the rap for the Robinson attack in exchange for sentencing considerations in the neighborhood shooting that the Romanos had managed to arrange.

"Falsifying physical evidence and getting it to the police was a real piece of work. I'm in awe."

"They didn't say how they pulled off that trick. They just said they know some clever people."

"I'll bet they do, I'll bet they do. So… Cassius takes the fall, the case gets closed, but we don't really know who attacked Robinson."

"I know. It's been bothering me too. Maybe it was that Slavinsky character, after all."

"There are lots of people it *could* have been, dear daughter, but you and I both know the most likely suspect."

"But why, Dad? If Philip knew that Mario hadn't killed himself, why would he have gone after Robinson?"

"Analyze it as if you were Philip. First of all, the guy's been pissed off at malpractice attorneys for a long time. For Karl Bergstrom to go to the trouble to kill Angelucci, however he did it, he had to have been whipped into a frenzy. Who was more likely to fan that fire than the attorney he hired to sue the doc. So even if Robinson wasn't directly responsible, Philip had to figure that he had a lot to do with Angelucci's death."

"I guess so. But I still don't understand why Philip's emotional attachment to Mario and his family would be so strong that he would do that."

Dick swallowed hard. He wasn't about to drop another bomb on Dorothy. The paternity question was her idiot boyfriend's problem. He simply said, "He's your boyfriend, my lass. If you can't explain his behavior, then neither can I."

"I have to talk to him, and he has to tell me the truth for a change."

Still, Dick felt the need to protect his daughter. "Sometimes the truth hurts too much, Dorothy; sometimes honesty isn't the best policy. If you dig deep enough, you might discover something you won't be able to put aside. Love doesn't always conquer all."

After a pause Dorothy said, "I understand, Dad. I'm almost home. I'll let you know how it goes."

She disconnected after her lie: she still had a long way to drive on the turnpike, but she needed the time to screw up her courage and to rehearse her unpleasant conversation with Philip. And despite her father's not so subtle hints and metaphors, Philip had a lot to explain.

Dorothy pulled into the driveway, relieved to see Philip's car in the open garage bay. She parked in the driveway and opened the front door. The house was empty and quiet. She walked through their living area and peered out at the back of the property, which ended at their beautiful lake. The trees had not fully leafed out, so she could see their dock, sitting atop the glistening water. There stood Philip, in jeans and an old rugby shirt, contentedly tossing treats into the water as Mitten, Buffy, and Meeko swam from side to side scarfing them up, looking for more.

It was a moment of perfection for Dorothy, and a scene that had, more than once, convinced her that she didn't need to interrogate Philip about the Hamlin or the Adolphus cases. That it didn't matter if he had somehow arranged to have people drowned in a river or incinerated in their business building. They were bad people, as Philip and Dorothy had established, and they got what they deserved, so why ruin a relationship over it?

But this time, it felt different. Philip's supposed motive was not as clear to her. It seems he should have been less invested in this case, and yet he may have physically attacked someone, cruelly maiming him for life. Further, he had gathered information that would enable the Romanos to carry out a murder. And all this while on a business trip taken under false pretenses. And then there was the outright lie he had told her about not seeing Deb Angelucci while he was up there; past white lies of his had never involved other women. It was all very disturbing.

Dorothy changed into a pair of sweatpants and a hoodie. She mixed two vodka tonics, gathered up some chips and salsa, and carried their "docktail" tray down the stone path. The dogs saw her first, dashed out of water, and made a beeline for her. She was able to dissuade them from jumping on her with their wet paws. Philip ran to greet her and took the tray. He already had cushions on the rocking chairs, and end tables in position. They settled in while the dogs, exhausted after a long play session, circled and found that perfect spot to lie down at their feet.

Philip was in a good mood. He talked about his return to work, and cheerfully reviewed all of the things that had happened there during his absence. Dorothy didn't know whether to be happy to see him in good humor, or sad that she was eventually going to ruin this idyllic moment. She had demurred so many times in the past that she began to think maybe she should do so again. *No*, she thought; she needed more this time. Philip would just have to deal with it.

Dorothy silently rehearsed her interrogation as they looked out over the lake. When windless, as it was this evening, the lake was glass-like, mirroring the trees and houses on the opposite shore. Their club's pool, across the way, lay dormant, quite in contrast to the madhouse it would become in a few weeks when the summer season officially got under way. Philip and Dorothy liked to see the place busy in the summer. It was good for the real estate values, but they didn't appreciate the screeching kids and the megaphone used to announce every event that occurred around the pool.

In the end, Dorothy decided to let Philip have a few moments of peace. He had been through an ordeal in Boston as well, although Dorothy was now convinced that most of it had been of his own doing. So they sat and rocked, sipping their drinks, bending over now and again to pet the hounds, pretending that their lives were as placid as the lake.

Coming in after sunset, neither had the energy to make an elaborate dinner. After some hemming and hawing, Dorothy decided on a salad and Philip a sandwich, each hastily constructed on the kitchen counter, consumed in minutes while they watched a *Seinfeld* rerun. The dogs greedily chewed their Greenie treats, and all adjourned to the bedroom after the few dishes were placed in the dishwasher, and ice water prepared for the bedside table.

After they had brushed their teeth and gotten under the covers, Philip reached for the remote, assuming that Dorothy would read one of the many murder mysteries that populated her bedside table. The dogs arranged themselves at the bottom of the bed, ready for a good night's sleep. Dorothy realized that if she didn't say something now, as tranquil a scene as it was, she might never again have the courage.

"Philip, why did you bring back a copy of the *Globe* article about Cassius Small?"

"I did?"

Dorothy expected his usual vacuous response.

"You know you did. I found it in the pile of mail last night."

Dorothy could immediately tell that Philip had been looking for it. His expression said, "*That's* where I left it?" His words were, "I read the *Globe* while I was up there. Maybe part of a page got torn off."

"That one page, by pure coincidence."

"I was interested in the story, so I guess I decided to keep it."

"And write a phone number at the bottom of the page."

That one stopped Philip. He paused, trying unsuccessfully to look nonchalant.

"A number?" he finally said.

"A familiar number: 215 area code and a Philly exchange."

"Really? I have no idea…"

"Save it, Philip. I spent part of my day in South Philadelphia today, visiting the Italian gentlemen you've obviously become so fond of."

Head down, Philip asked, "And what did they have to tell you?"

"You know what they told me. How they recruited you to talk to Deb Angelucci about what happened to Mario, and to gather information about the accident investigation."

"Okay."

"Okay? That's all you have to say?"

"I'm not going to deny it. They asked and I went."

"Did you think about letting me know first?"

"I thought about it, but I knew you and your dad

would have been opposed to it. I wanted to spare you the anxiety."

"Nice job with that, Philip, wouldn't you say?"

"It sure didn't turn out the way I expected. How was I supposed to know that somebody was going to attack Thad Robinson while I was in Boston?"

"Philip, for the sake of my sanity, I'm going to assume you weren't the person who did that."

"Good assumption, because it's pretty clear that Cassius Small did it."

"Fuck you, Philip, for your inane stupidity. Or is it just arrogance?"

"What do you mean?"

"Cassius Small is a two-bit hoodlum; that's what Vincente called him. He said they induced him to take the fall. Because they were concerned that their dear friend Philip was about to get arrested. Our Mafia colleagues appear to have taken a real shine to you!"

"Well, if Small is so innocent, why would he have confessed, and where did the physical evidence come from?"

"Don't insult my intelligence. I think you know full well what happened, Philip. And tell me this: why would you feel so strongly about the Angelucci case that you would attack Robinson…"

"That wasn't me!"

"…and even contribute to the murder of Karl Bergstrom. Explain all this!"

Philip jumped out of bed and began to pace back and forth, like a caged lion.

"Look, I don't know what you're talking about," Philip said.

"You know *exactly* what I'm talking about, Philip. The Romanos didn't call you, did they?"

Philip's pacing picked up speed despite his limp.

"Philip, stop your stomping around and answer the fucking question."

"What are you talking about?" Philip said, as if the needle were stuck.

"Philip, focus. Explain why *you* called the Romano brothers."

Philip stopped pacing and walked deliberately to Dorothy's side of the bed. In an instant, his expression and entire manner had changed from agitated to calm. Regardless of how many times she had witnessed this transformation, Dorothy never failed to be awed. But this time Dorothy was also frightened, for a second, envisioning Philip striking her… or worse. His mouth curled into a demonic smile, which did nothing to reassure her.

After what seemed to Dorothy to be hours, in an almost mechanical voice Philip said, "All right, Dorothy, I'll explain what happened. I should have told you the truth long ago. I believe it will help you understand why I did what I did."

"I'm listening, Philip." So were the dogs, who chose this moment to sit up, ears perked, and heads cocked.

Philip sat on the bed next to Dorothy, who scooched over to make room.

"Back in college, Pudge and I went to a mixer on Boathouse Row. That's where he met Deb, and I did, too. The two of them became an item, but I hung out with them a lot."

"I know. I got that much from Deb."

This gave Philip pause. "You've talked to Deb? When was that? Just now in Boston?"

"That's right."

"And you didn't tell me?"

"Like you, I wanted to spare my mate the aggravation," Dorothy said curtly. "Keep talking."

Dorothy could see Philip's wheels turning.

"Well, like I told you in Boston, she and Pudge got married and I lost touch with them during medical school. But when Pudge and I wound up at the Brigham together, the three of us were back together."

"I have a feeling that there's more to tell."

"Right. Pudge and Deb were married, and I wasn't yet. They sort of adopted me, had me over to dinner pretty frequently. We'd go out on the town like the three amigos. Once in a while Deb would fix me up with one of her single friends, but I didn't pay much attention to them because…"

"Because you were paying attention to Deb."

"You have an uncanny ability to guess what I'm going to say next."

"I know you well, Philip."

"Then you can understand how difficult it has been to tell you the truth."

"That you still love Deb."

"No, I actually don't love her anymore. I longed for her for years, but when you came along, my desire for her, and for anybody else, melted away."

"Nice try, Philip, but so far all we have is a lovesick puppy having fantasies about a friend's wife. That makes you like a million other men in the world. There's got to be more."

"Let me go on. Deb and Pudge separated for a while during the first year of our fellowship but got back together and things seemed to be going better. A few weeks later, Pudge was at a meeting. Deb called me and asked me if I wanted to get together for dinner. It wasn't the first time we had dined together when Pudge was away, and every time before, there was never any indication she was interested in me. Nevertheless, I jumped at the chance to see her. She suggested that we have dinner at their house, so I brought a nice bottle of wine and flowers.

"As soon as Deb opened the door, I knew I was in trouble. She was a vision. She was dressed in a highly revealing little black dress, her hair was down to her shoulders, and she was wearing Obsession. Sound familiar?"

"Oh my God, that's the perfume and outfit I wore..."

"The night of my seduction at Le Bec Fin."

"You make it sound like that was my fault."

"Okay. You're right. It takes two to tango."

"And the outcome of your little dance number with Deb was the same?" Dorothy asked, not really wanting to know the answer.

"More or less. Deb was loaded for bear. She had the lights down, soft music on the CD player, Prosecco well chilled, and a wonderful dinner."

"You were toast."

"I don't know how we got all the way to washing the dishes. I brushed up against her while putting one of the pots away, she spun around, and the next thing you know, we were ripping each other's clothes off. Should I spare you further details?"

"This is your life, Philip Sarkis, so get it all out of your system."

"We had intercourse a few times. Pudge called around midnight. Deb was out of breath when she picked up the phone reflexively, and had to lie about why she was panting. She gave such a stupid excuse that I had to put my head under the pillow so he wouldn't hear me laughing in the background. I finally left her house around dawn, utterly spent but ecstatic."

"And that was the end of it?" Dorothy asked hopefully.

"No, we had another two or three nights together over

the next several weeks, and we had to work very hard to find opportunities. We even rented a seedy hotel room in Brighton one afternoon. But we finally snapped to our senses and realized that the affair was not going to go anywhere. Deb stopped showing interest, and around that time I met Nancy."

"What a wonderful love story."

"If only that was all. You see, shortly after that, Deb discovered she was pregnant."

Dorothy nodded, at first failing to understand, and then gasped, "My word!"

Philip nodded. "A paternity issue, to be sure."

"So you're not sure if Deb's first child is yours."

"Correct."

"And Pudge had no idea?"

"None, as far as we know. According to Deb, they had been trying to get pregnant for a while, but they weren't intimate often. Fortunately, they were having sex often enough to make her pregnancy at least plausible."

"Do you think she got pregnant on purpose?"

"I have a suspicion that her abrupt change in attitude toward me that night may have been because she suspected that their fertility problem was Pudge's and not hers."

"Interesting way to test a theory."

"I'm sure there was more to it than that. But if she did manipulate me, it was very clever. Pudge and I both have a big nose, brown eyes and hair, and a dark complexion. Who would know the difference?"

"So do you think that their first kid is yours?"

"I can only guess. Mario junior looks a lot like me, but I'm sure I'm reading into it. Anyhow, when Pudge was sued and then committed suicide, I was doubly angry. My son lost his father, and I was determined to make whoever was responsible pay for it."

"Philip the vigilante. We've seen that before."

"Vigilante, street justice… call it what you like. I call it accountability."

Dorothy felt tears coming. Philip continued.

"So you were right, after having it gnaw at me for, what—it's been a few years since Pudge's death?—I called the Romanos and asked them to investigate."

"I knew it. They led me to believe that they enlisted you, but I didn't know if I could buy that. I wanted to, God knows."

"They're kind men, Dorothy."

"Sure they are."

"And as it turned out, Pudge's death had been eating at them, too, because of ties between his family and theirs. So the cardiology conference served as a convenient cover for me to go up there and poke around, and they sent some people up there at the same time."

"A wonderful partnership, you and the Romanos."

Philip ignored that. "What I really wanted was for Robinson to pay a price somehow, I admit it. But with the information I got from Deb, coupled with stuff their guys obtained, we were all surprised to learn that Pudge's death was murder arranged by Karl Bergstrom. So that changed things."

"At least you didn't go to Sweden to hold him accountable."

"I'm not sure Karl even made it out of Boston last week, actually."

Now Dorothy wondered what role Philip may have played in *that*.

"And Robinson getting attacked while I was in town? It wasn't any fun being a suspect, but now that it's over, I must say I'm pleased with how it all worked out."

Dorothy was feeling spent intellectually and emotionally. She could muster only one more question. "After all this, are you happy with yourself, Philip?"

Philip considered the question. "Happy? No, I wouldn't say that. I'm still very sad about Pudge. I lost a great friend."

"Who you cuckolded."

"I was manipulated."

"No, Philip, you manipulated your cock into Deb Angelucci, a married woman."

"As you manipulated my cock into you when I was married to Nancy," Philip shot back without thinking.

"I'm sorry," he muttered. "That was mean."

Before Dorothy had a chance to protest, Philip rose from the bed, bent over and kissed Dorothy on the head. "I love you with all my heart, Dorothy Deaver. I did what I had to do, and I feel good about it. With your permission, I'd like to see Deb and the boys once in a while. Not because I still have any feelings for Deb, you understand. It'd be a way to stay close to Pudge."

"Look, Philip, I'm in psychic overload right now, and certainly in no mood to discuss your new family ties."

"I understand."

"And, under the circumstances, would you mind sleeping in the guest room? I've got to be alone tonight."

Philip nodded. He walked to his side of the bed, grabbed his glass of now lukewarm water, petted the dogs, and shuffled out of the room without a word. Ever faithful to Philip, Meeko, the baby pup, rousted herself and followed him. Dorothy's bedside light clicked off just as he closed the door.

Dorothy never got any real sleep that night. She dozed a few times but was quickly awakened by easily interpretable dreams that symbolized, in various ways, her relationship with Philip, where they had started and where they now found themselves. She spoke softly to

Mitten and Buffy, who kept the vigil with her, listening to her sighs, feeling her distress, and, as they always did, trying to make things better by cuddling close.

By six o'clock, the sun had begun to rise over the eastern half of the lake, illuminating the thick clouds that had gathered overnight, creating a rich tapestry of colors that reflected through the trees that were coming back to life after a long winter's rest. A new day would start soon, and it would be left to Dorothy, once again, to decide whether she would choose to share any more mountain dawns or season changes with Dr. Philip Sarkis.

Peter R. Kowey

Dr. Peter Kowey is a cardiologist and an internationally respected expert in heart rhythm disorders. After college at St. Joseph's University in Philadelphia, he attended medical school at the University of Pennsylvania and trained in cardiology at the Peter Bent Brigham Hospital and the Harvard School of Public Health in Boston. For the past 33 years, he has developed a large referral practice and has directed the cardiology program at Main Line Health System in Philadelphia. He is also a Professor of Medicine and Clinical Pharmacology at Jefferson Medical College and holds the William Wikoff Smith Chair in Cardiovascular Research at the Lankenau Institute for Medical Research.

Dr. Kowey's research has led to the development of new cardiac drugs and devices. He has authored hundreds of scientific papers and textbooks and has taught and mentored scores of medical students, fellows, residents and physicians in practice. His most recent venture has been fiction writing. His first two novels, *Lethal Rhythm* and *Deadly Rhythm*, were published in 2010 and 2012.

Dr. Kowey and his wife Dorothy have three successful daughters and two sons-in-law, all attorneys, and six grandchildren. Their permanent residence is in Bryn Mawr, Pennsylvania, but they spend time throughout the year with their three Portuguese water dogs at their Pocono Mountain lake house.

PETER R KOWEY MD